THE CLOCKWORK SKY

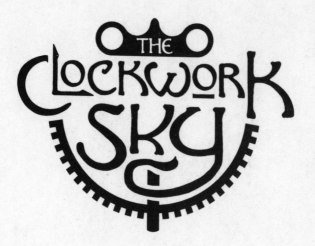

THE CLOCKWORK SKY

VOLUME ONE

Story and Art by
MADELEINE ROSCA

Lettered by
TOM ORZECHOWSKI

TOR®

A TOM DOHERTY ASSOCIATES BOOK
NEW YORK

This is a work of fiction. All of the characters, organizations, and events portrayed in this graphic novel are either products of the author's imagination or are used fictitiously.

THE CLOCKWORK SKY, VOLUME ONE

Lettered by Tom Orzechowski

A Tor Book
Published by Tom Doherty Associates, LLC
175 Fifth Avenue
New York, NY 10010

www.tor-forge.com

Tor® is a registered trademark of Tom Doherty Associates, LLC.

ISBN 978-0-7653-2916-5

First Edition: September 2012

Printed in the United States of America

0 9 8 7 6 5 4 3 2 1

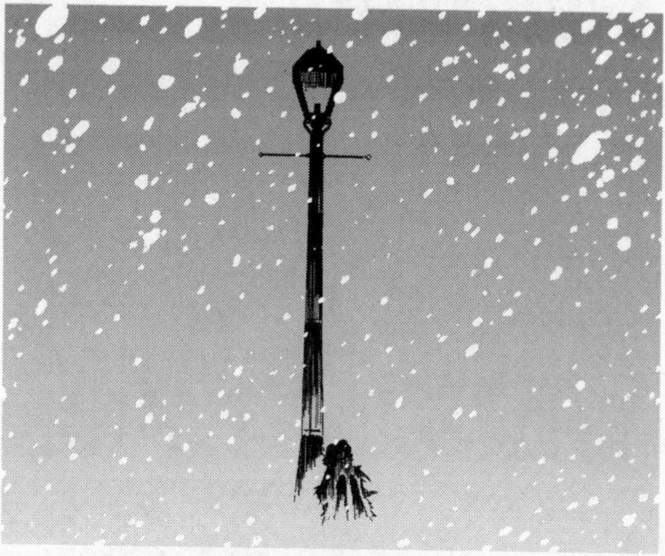

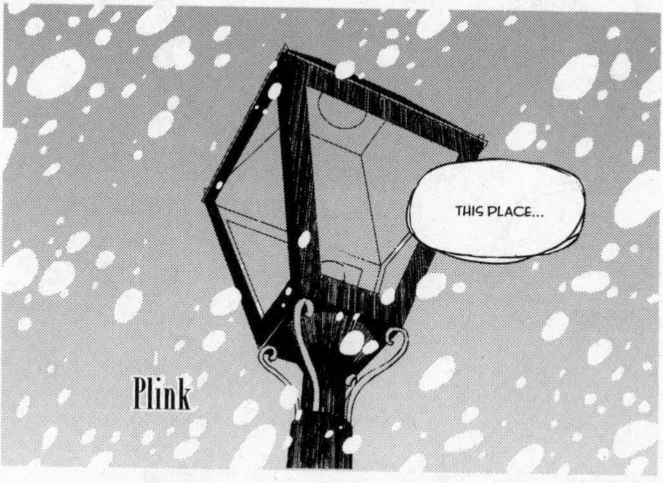
THIS PLACE...
Plink

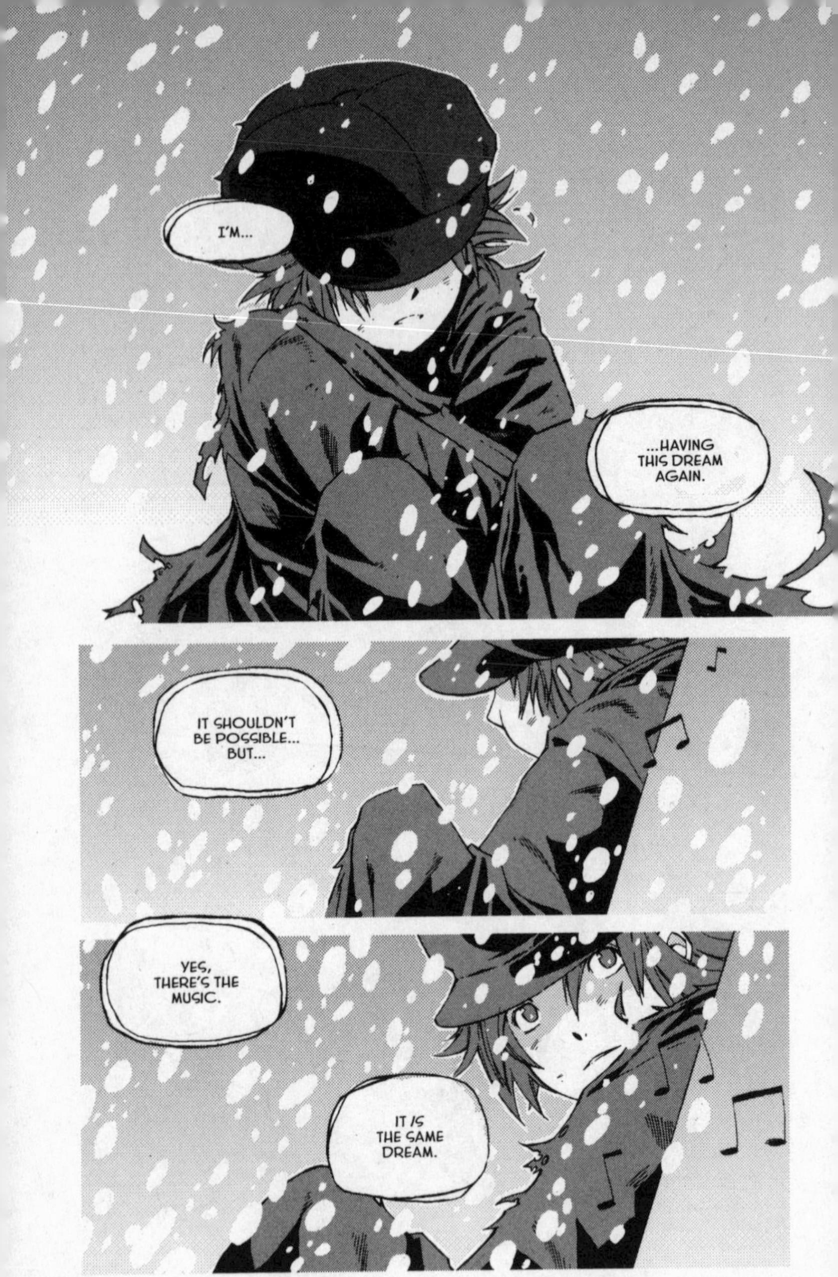
I'M...
...HAVING THIS DREAM AGAIN.
IT SHOULDN'T BE POSSIBLE... BUT...
YES, THERE'S THE MUSIC.
IT IS THE SAME DREAM.

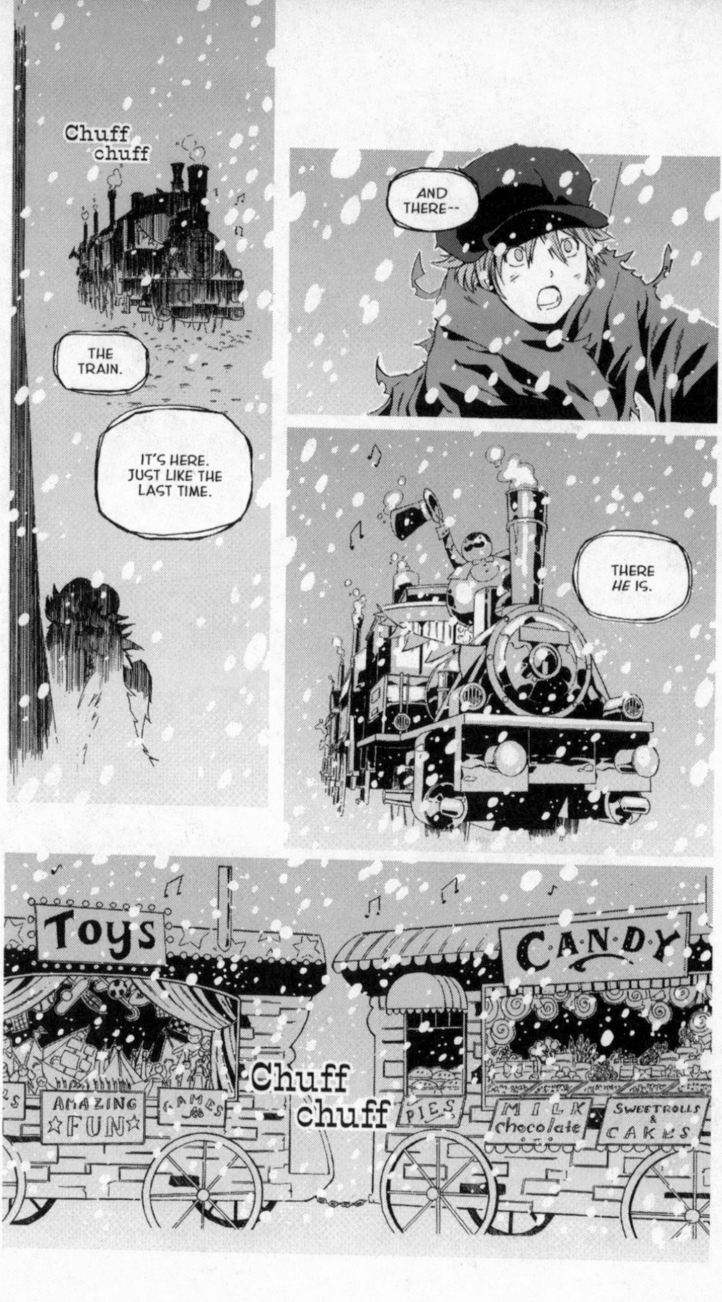
Chuff chuff
THE TRAIN.
IT'S HERE. JUST LIKE THE LAST TIME.
AND THERE--
THERE *HE* IS.
Toys
CANDY
AMAZING FUN
GAMES
Chuff chuff
PIES
MILK chocolate
SWEETROLLS & CAKES

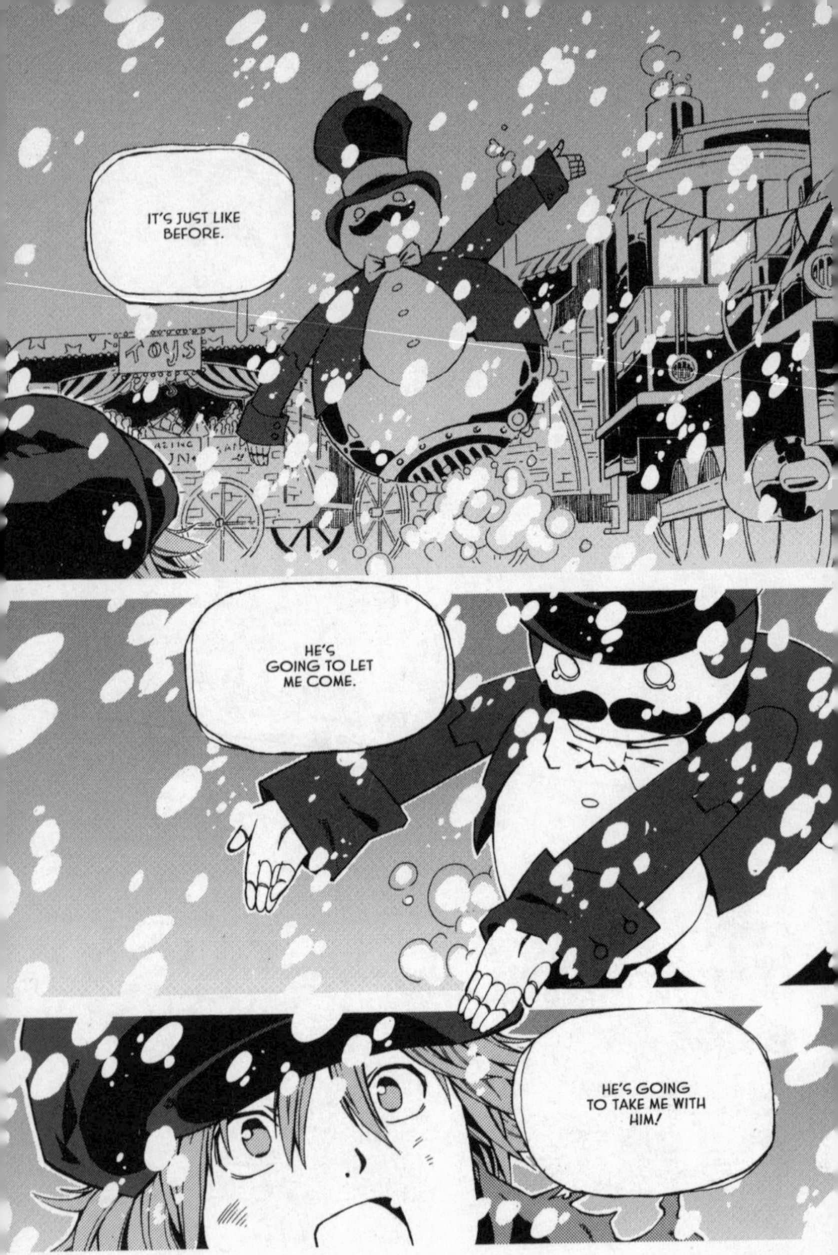
IT'S JUST LIKE BEFORE.
TOYS
HE'S GOING TO LET ME COME.
HE'S GOING TO TAKE ME WITH HIM!

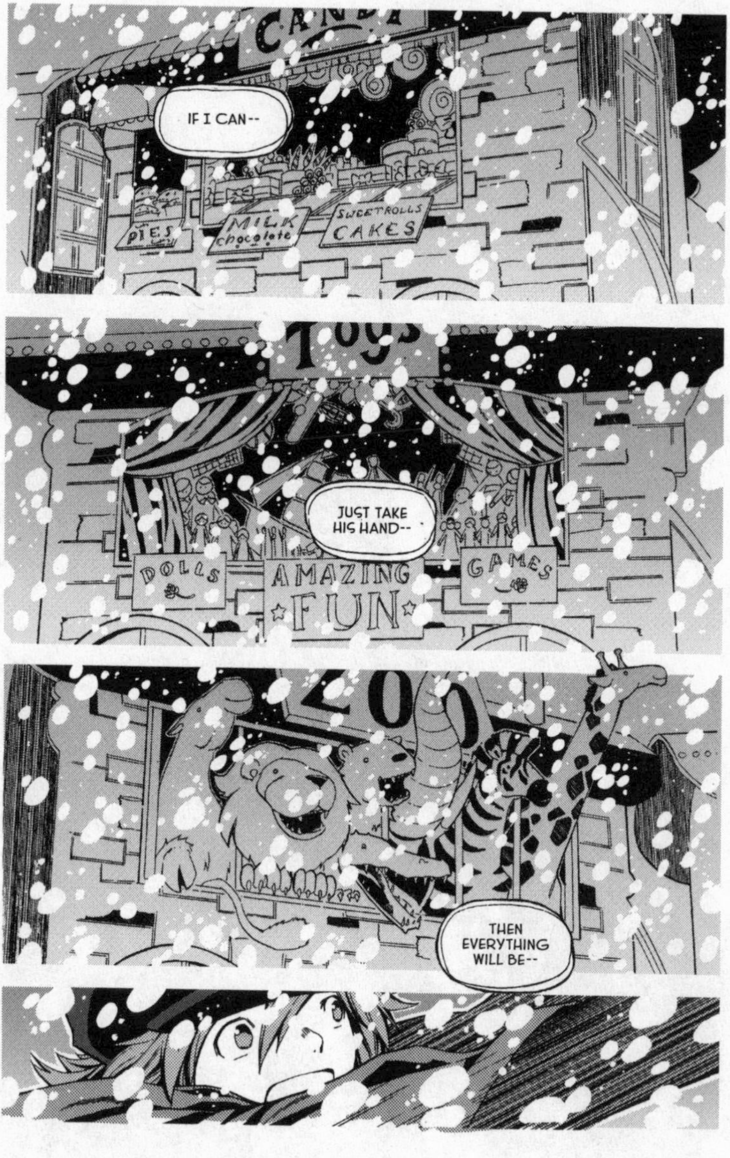
IF I CAN--
PIES
MILK chocolate
SWEETROLLS CAKES
JUST TAKE HIS HAND--
DOLLS
AMAZING FUN
GAMES
THEN EVERYTHING WILL BE--

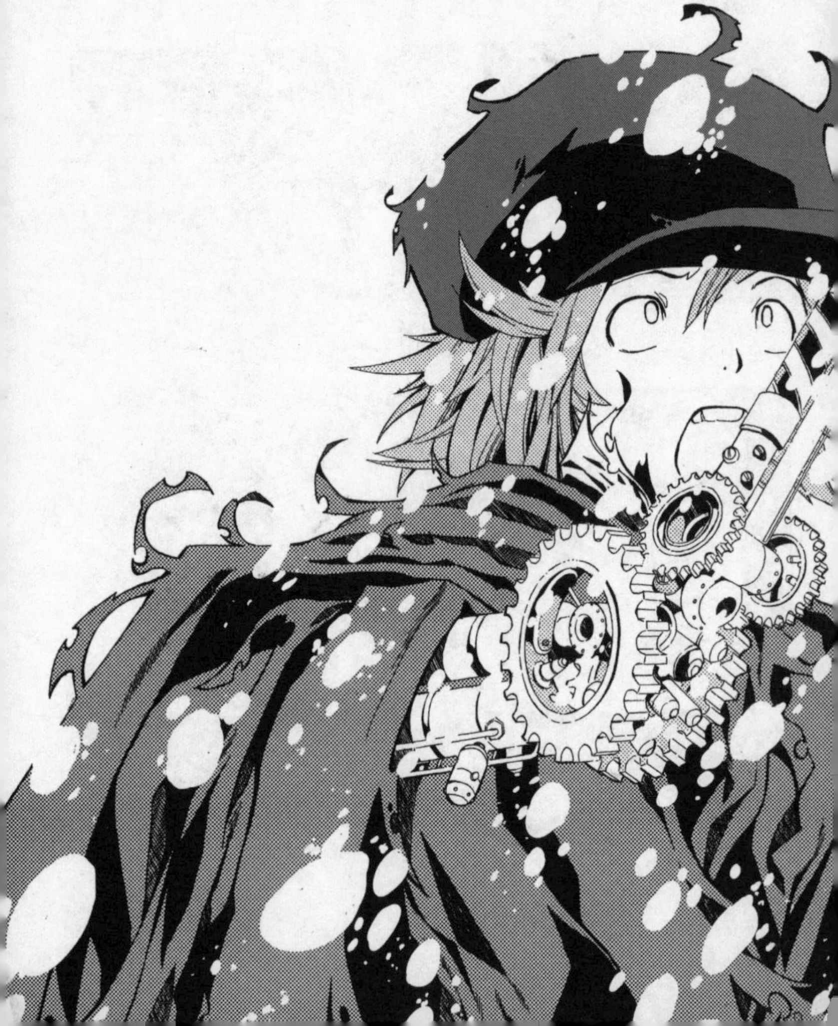

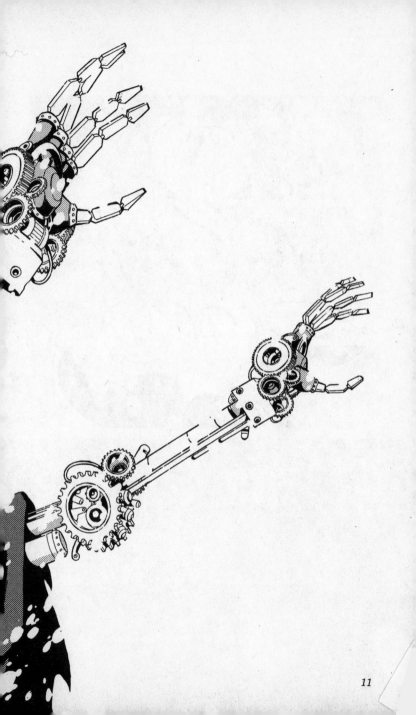

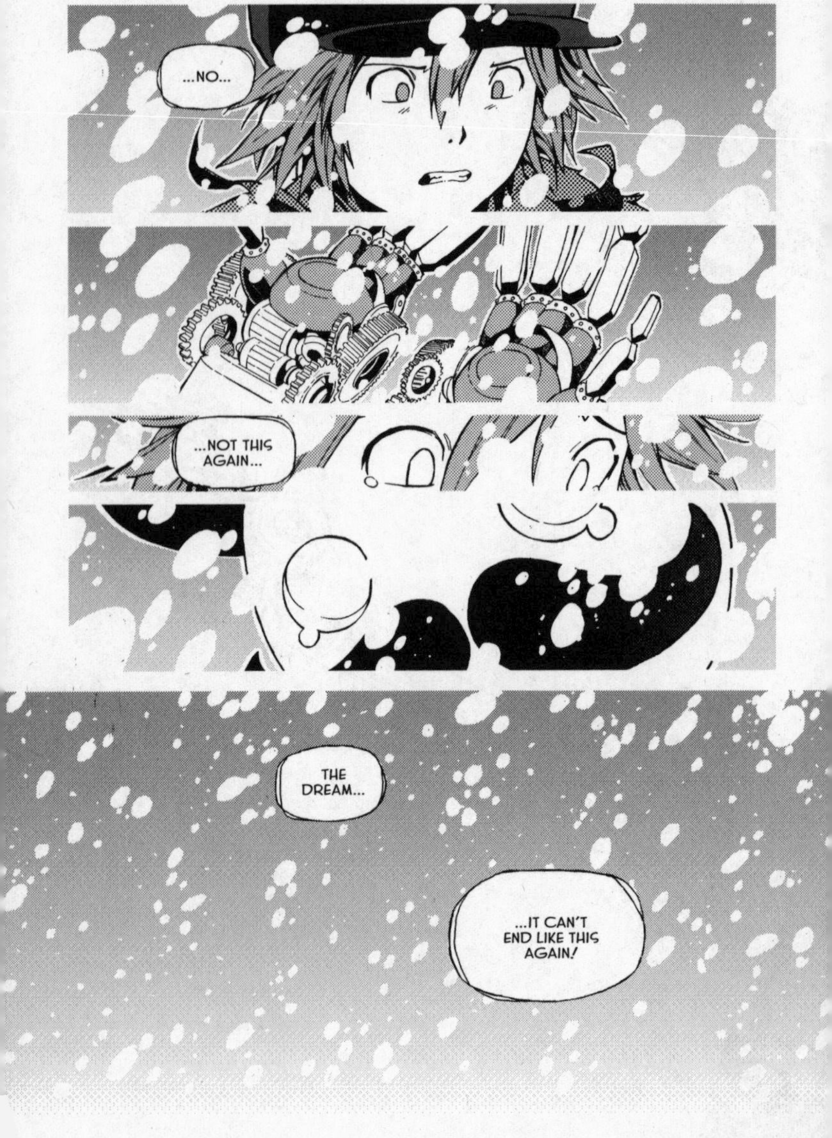
...NO...
...NOT THIS AGAIN...
THE DREAM...
...IT CAN'T END LIKE THIS AGAIN!

CHAPTER 1

The Ember Corporation presents :

"Hurrah for Ember!"

An "Educational Cinematoscope"
for the younger generation of British citizenry.

copyright 1895

In the 1880s, the city of London was most certainly down in the dumps. Crime was high, paupers wandered wherever they pleased, and respectable folk were forced to rely on the labour of blue-collar ruffians!

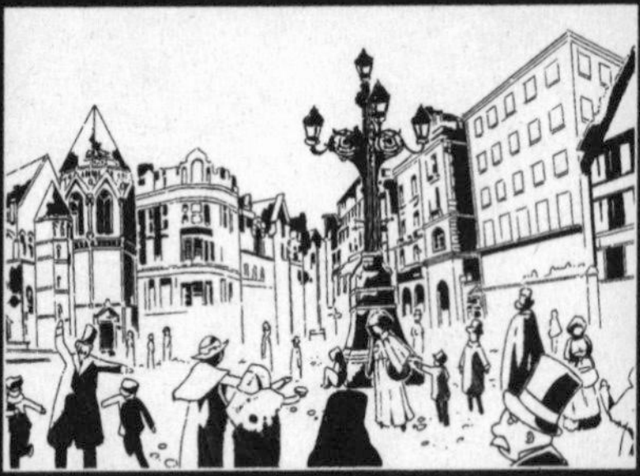

If a gentleman wanted to staff his household adequately, he was forced to employ scoundrels and ne'er-do-wells from the slums. Disgusting! How could London's elite avoid rubbing shoulders with this riffraff?

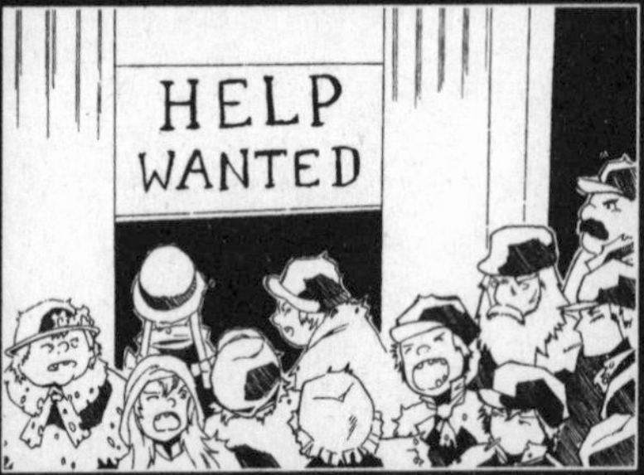
HELP
WANTED

But one bright inventor saw a better way...with the advances of STEAM POWER, he began to build a workforce of automatons and clankbots worthy of serving London!

With his raw ingenuity and his fortuitous family connections, this man was able to create the Ember Robotics Factory and mass-produce London's first steam-driven workforce!

Now, armed with these wonderful machines, the elite of London do not have to rely on a grubby human workforce that cries for demands such as food and sleep. It's full steam ahead for London's factories!

MISS SALLY!

It's all down to this man, boys and girls. The Ember Corporation's brilliant founder and current chairman

— Mr. Erasmus Croach!

MISS SALLY PEPPERS!

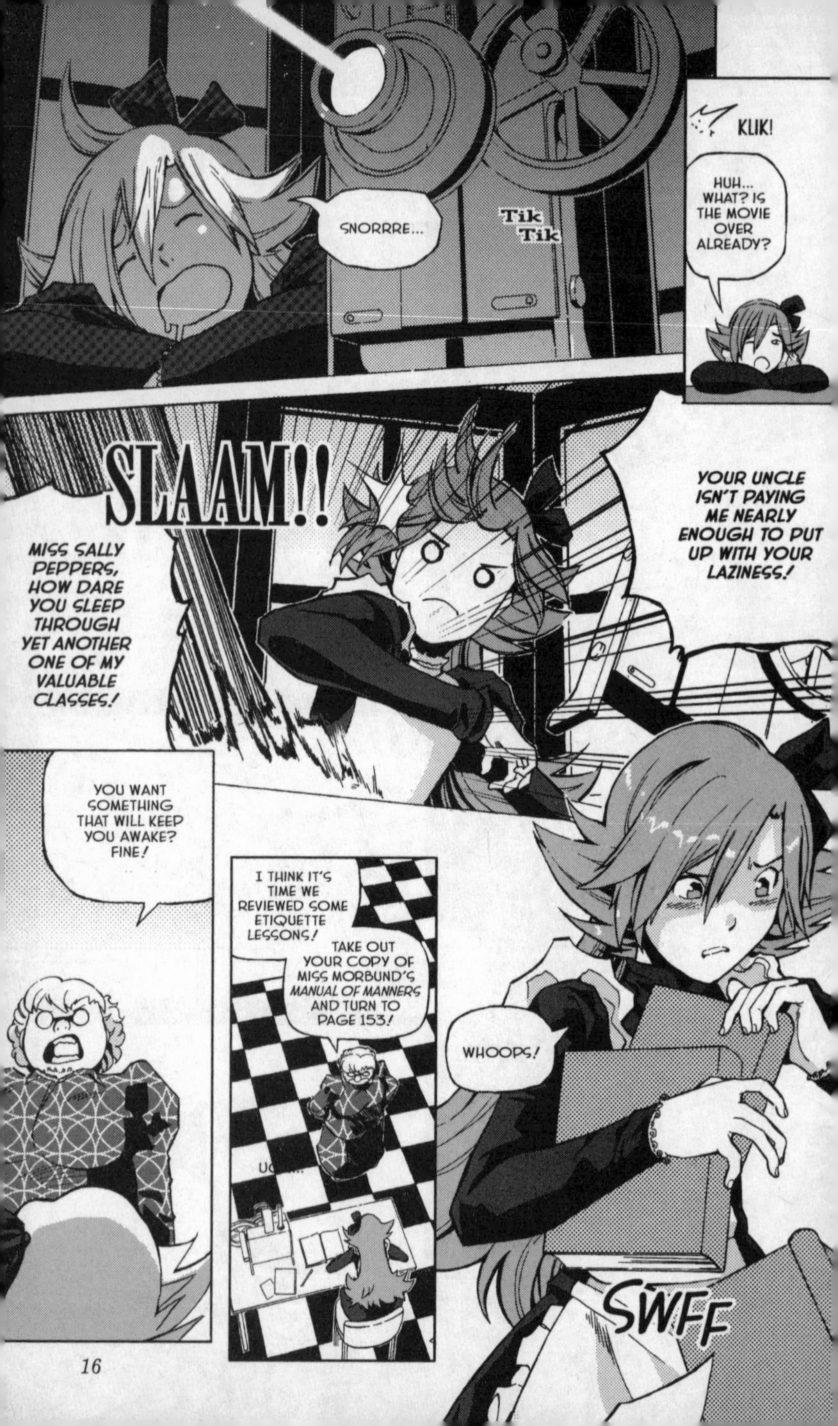
SNORRRE...
Tik Tik
KLIK!
HUH... WHAT? IS THE MOVIE OVER ALREADY?
SLAAM!!
MISS SALLY PEPPERS, HOW DARE YOU SLEEP THROUGH YET ANOTHER ONE OF MY VALUABLE CLASSES!
YOUR UNCLE ISN'T PAYING ME NEARLY ENOUGH TO PUT UP WITH YOUR LAZINESS!
YOU WANT SOMETHING THAT WILL KEEP YOU AWAKE? FINE!
I THINK IT'S TIME WE REVIEWED SOME ETIQUETTE LESSONS!
TAKE OUT YOUR COPY OF MISS MORBUND'S *MANUAL OF MANNERS* AND TURN TO PAGE 153!
WHOOPS!
SWFF

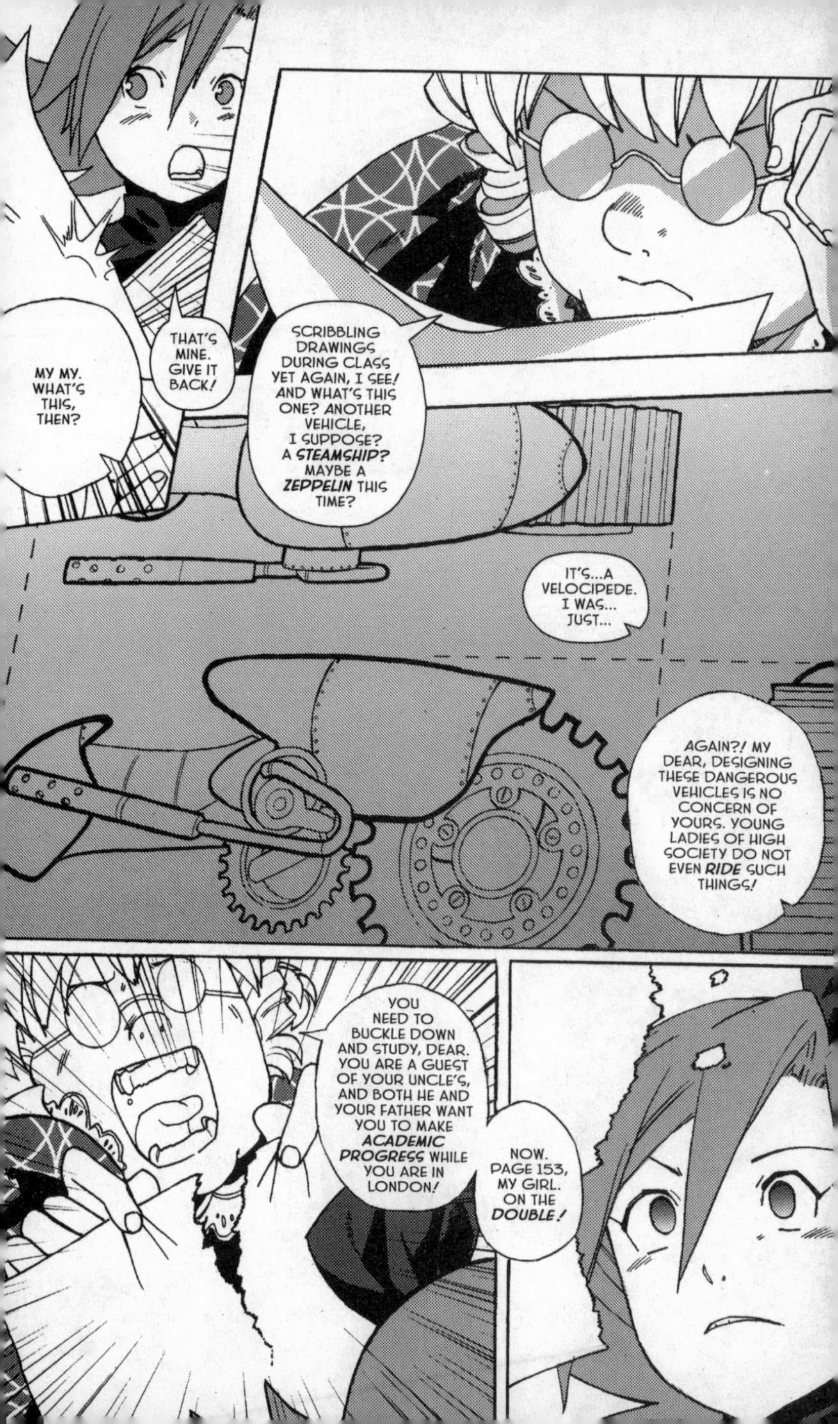
MY MY. WHAT'S THIS, THEN?
THAT'S MINE. GIVE IT BACK!
SCRIBBLING DRAWINGS DURING CLASS YET AGAIN, I SEE! AND WHAT'S THIS ONE? ANOTHER VEHICLE, I SUPPOSE? A **STEAMSHIP?** MAYBE A **ZEPPELIN** THIS TIME?
IT'S...A VELOCIPEDE. I WAS... JUST...
AGAIN?! MY DEAR, DESIGNING THESE DANGEROUS VEHICLES IS NO CONCERN OF YOURS. YOUNG LADIES OF HIGH SOCIETY DO NOT EVEN **RIDE** SUCH THINGS!
YOU NEED TO BUCKLE DOWN AND STUDY, DEAR. YOU ARE A GUEST OF YOUR UNCLE'S, AND BOTH HE AND YOUR FATHER WANT YOU TO MAKE **ACADEMIC PROGRESS** WHILE YOU ARE IN LONDON!
NOW. PAGE 153, MY GIRL. ON THE **DOUBLE!**

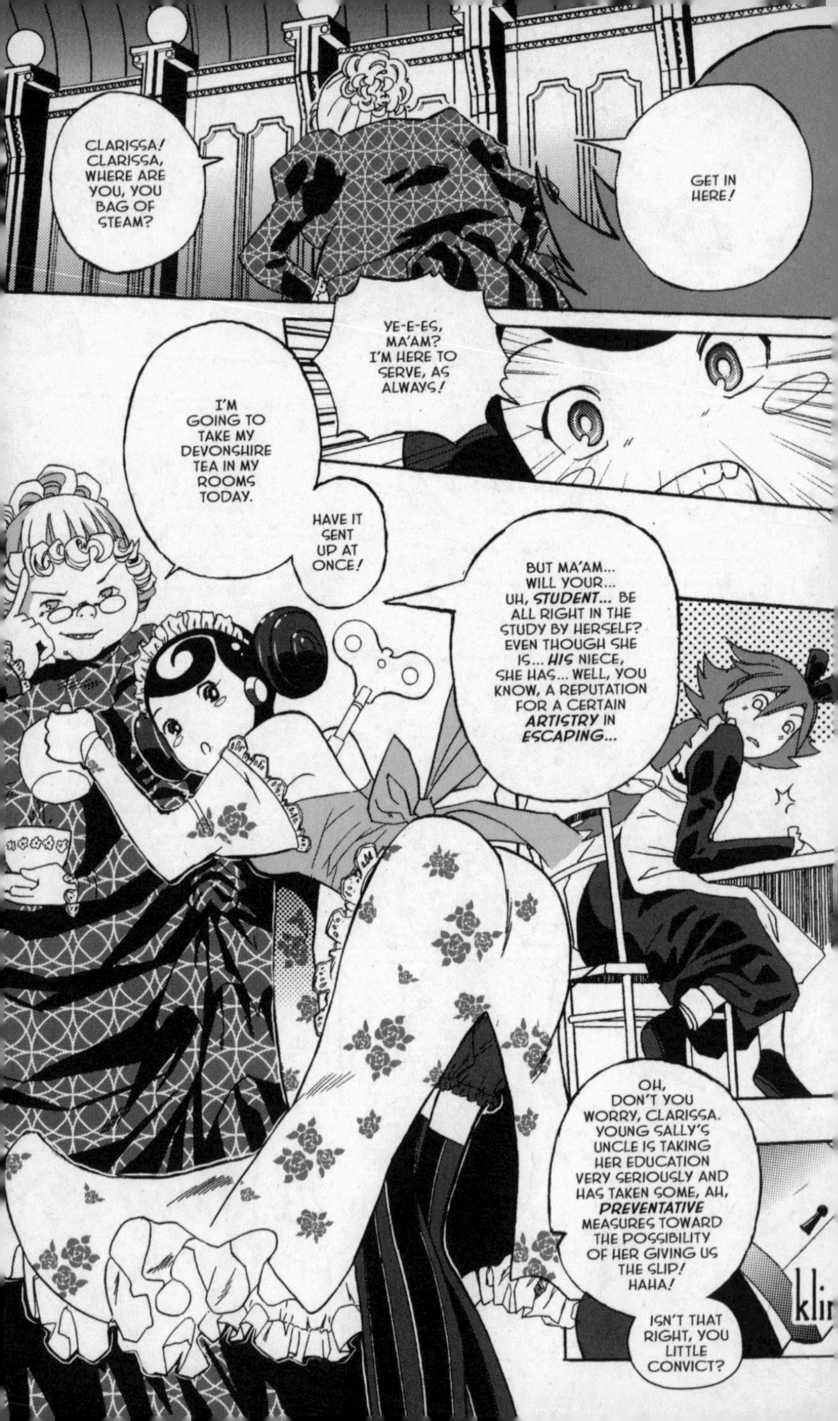

CLARISSA! CLARISSA, WHERE ARE YOU, YOU BAG OF STEAM?
GET IN HERE!
YE-E-ES, MA'AM? I'M HERE TO SERVE, AS ALWAYS!
I'M GOING TO TAKE MY DEVONSHIRE TEA IN MY ROOMS TODAY.
HAVE IT SENT UP AT ONCE!
BUT MA'AM... WILL YOUR... UH, *STUDENT*... BE ALL RIGHT IN THE STUDY BY HERSELF? EVEN THOUGH SHE IS... *HIS* NIECE, SHE HAS... WELL, YOU KNOW, A REPUTATION FOR A CERTAIN *ARTISTRY* IN *ESCAPING*...
OH, DON'T YOU WORRY, CLARISSA. YOUNG SALLY'S UNCLE IS TAKING HER EDUCATION VERY SERIOUSLY AND HAS TAKEN SOME, AH, *PREVENTATIVE* MEASURES TOWARD THE POSSIBILITY OF HER GIVING US THE SLIP! HAHA!
ISN'T THAT RIGHT, YOU LITTLE CONVICT?

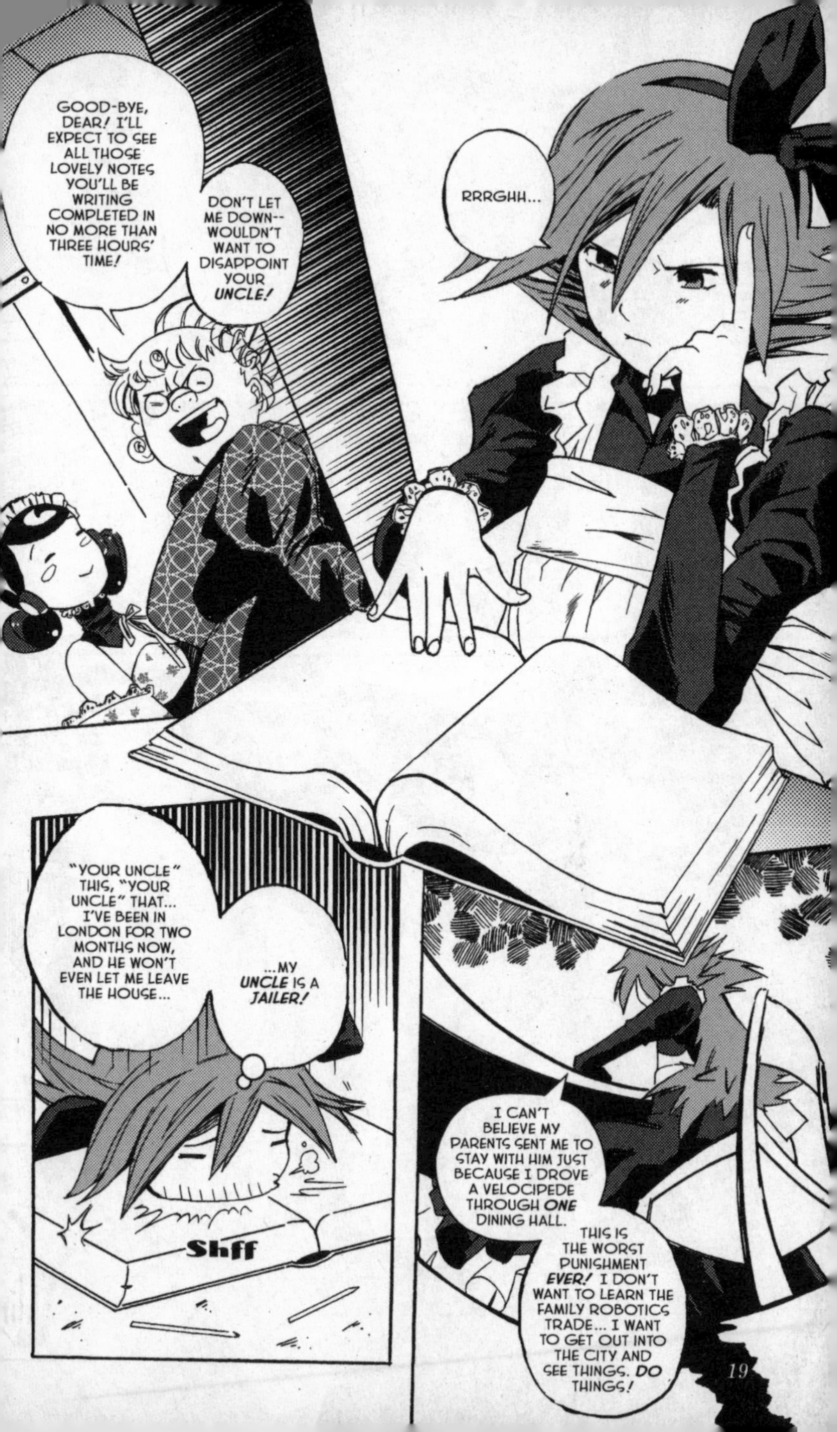
GOOD-BYE, DEAR! I'LL EXPECT TO SEE ALL THOSE LOVELY NOTES YOU'LL BE WRITING COMPLETED IN NO MORE THAN THREE HOURS' TIME!
DON'T LET ME DOWN--WOULDN'T WANT TO DISAPPOINT YOUR *UNCLE!*
RRRGHH...
"YOUR UNCLE" THIS, "YOUR UNCLE" THAT... I'VE BEEN IN LONDON FOR TWO MONTHS NOW, AND HE WON'T EVEN LET ME LEAVE THE HOUSE...
...MY *UNCLE* IS A *JAILER!*
Shff
I CAN'T BELIEVE MY PARENTS SENT ME TO STAY WITH HIM JUST BECAUSE I DROVE A VELOCIPEDE THROUGH *ONE* DINING HALL.
THIS IS THE WORST PUNISHMENT *EVER!* I DON'T WANT TO LEARN THE FAMILY ROBOTICS TRADE... I WANT TO GET OUT INTO THE CITY AND SEE THINGS. *DO* THINGS!

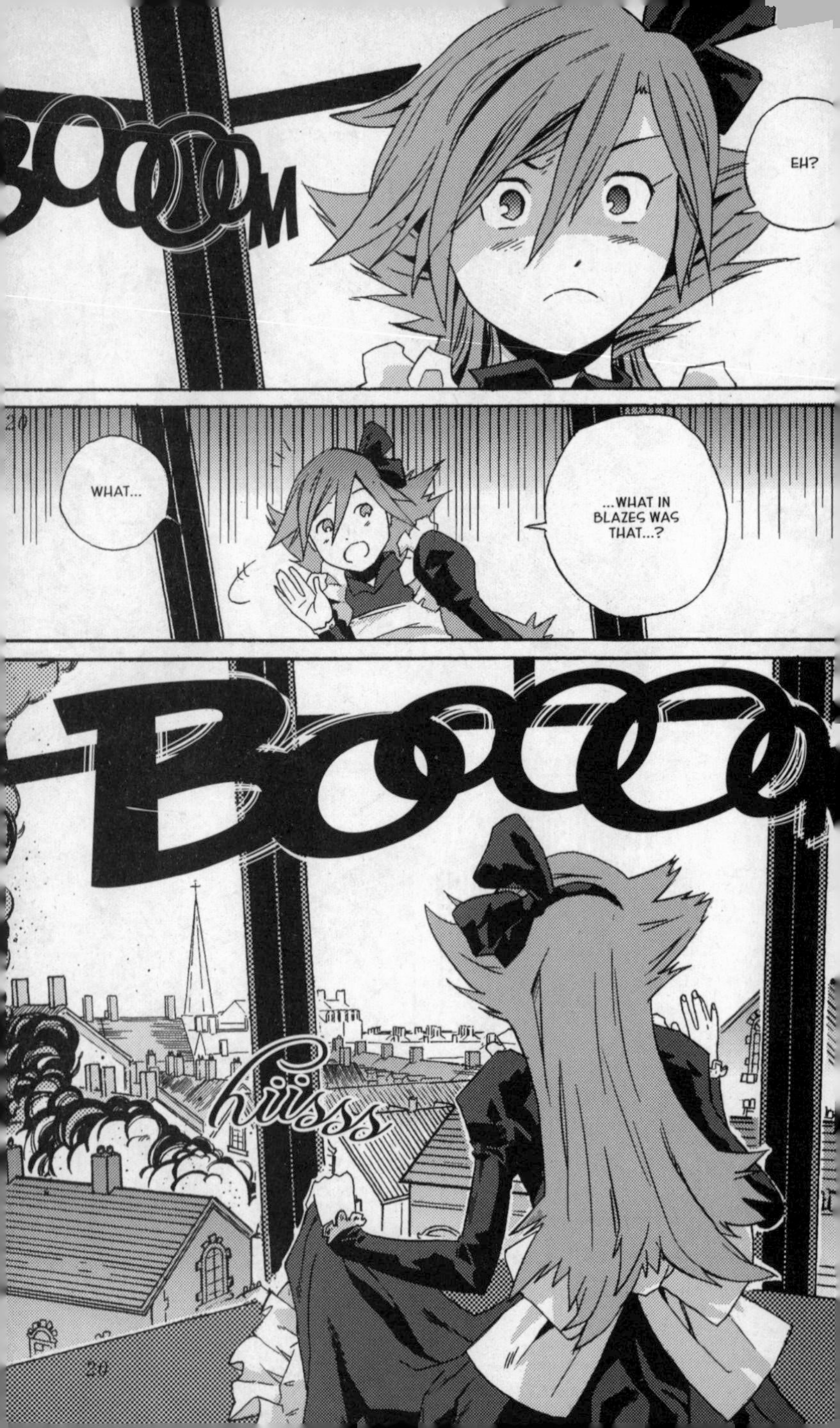
OOOOM
EH?
WHAT...
...WHAT IN BLAZES WAS THAT...?
BOOOO
hiisss

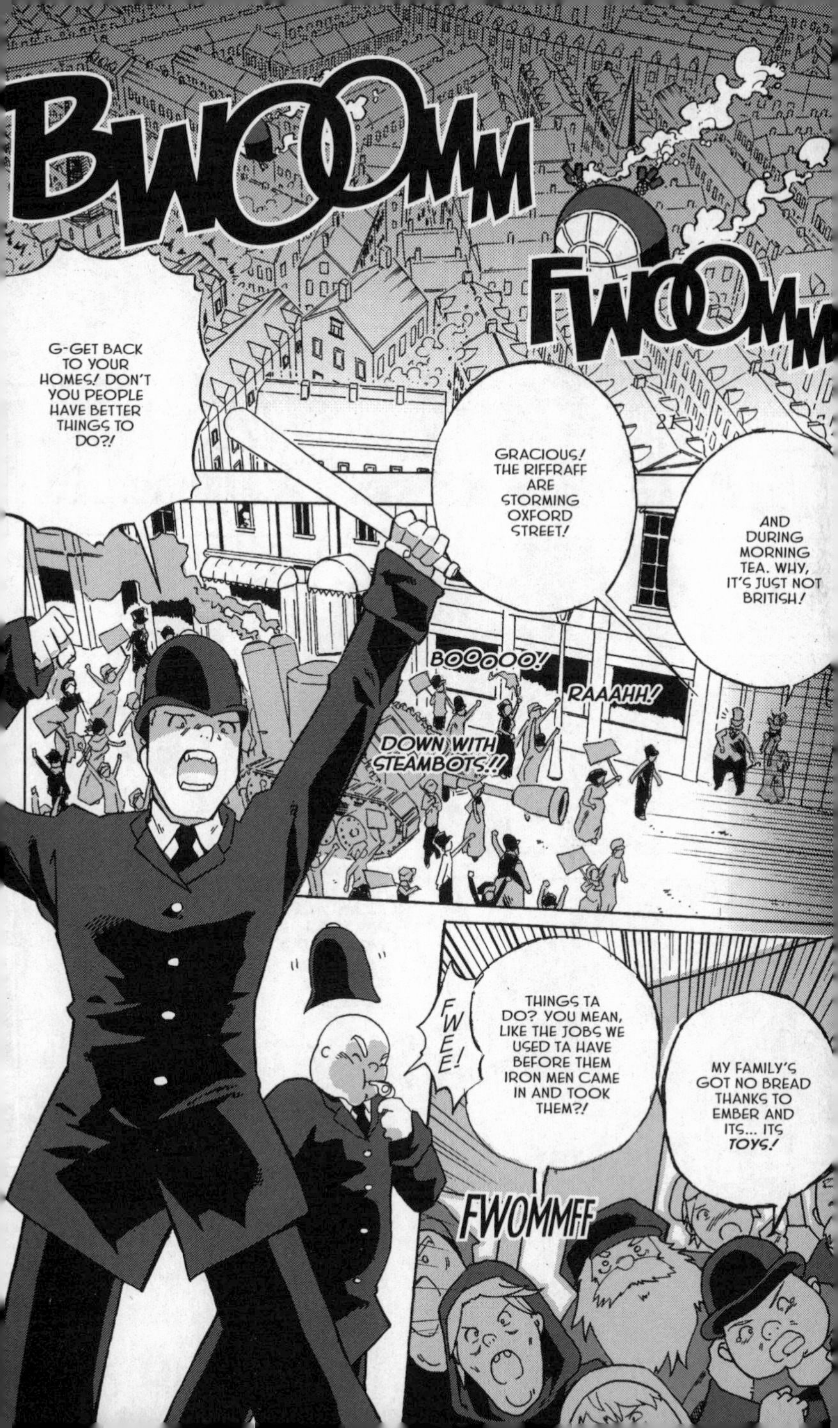
BWOOMM
FWOOMM
G-GET BACK TO YOUR HOMES! DON'T YOU PEOPLE HAVE BETTER THINGS TO DO?!
GRACIOUS! THE RIFFRAFF ARE STORMING OXFORD STREET!
AND DURING MORNING TEA. WHY, IT'S JUST NOT BRITISH!
BOOOOOO!
RAAAHH!
DOWN WITH STEAMBOTS!!
FWEE!
THINGS TA DO? YOU MEAN, LIKE THE JOBS WE USED TA HAVE BEFORE THEM IRON MEN CAME IN AND TOOK THEM?!
MY FAMILY'S GOT NO BREAD THANKS TO EMBER AND ITS... ITS *TOYS!*
FWOMMFF

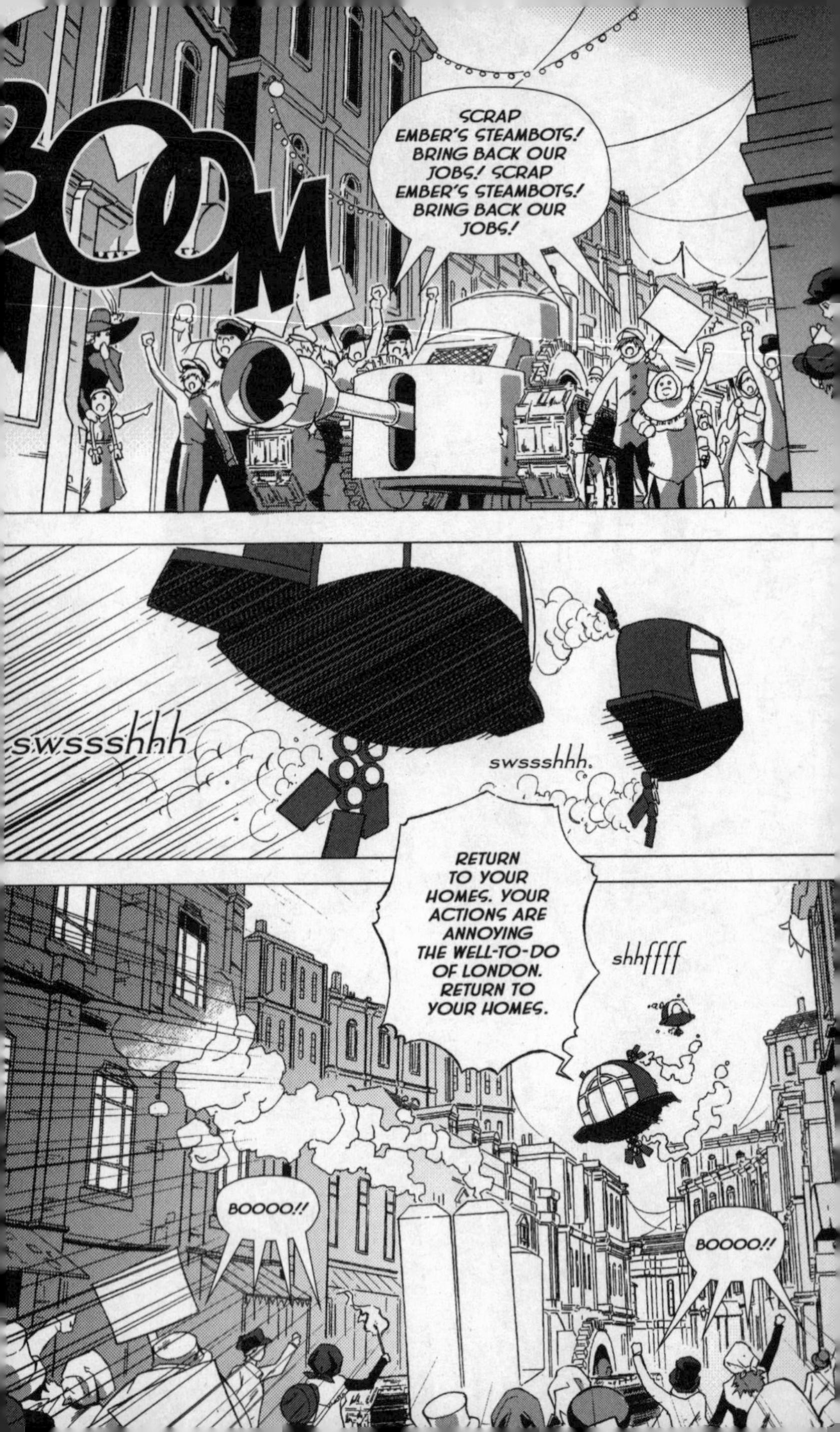
BOOM
SCRAP EMBER'S STEAMBOTS! BRING BACK OUR JOBS! SCRAP EMBER'S STEAMBOTS! BRING BACK OUR JOBS!
swssshhh
swssshhh.
RETURN TO YOUR HOMES. YOUR ACTIONS ARE ANNOYING THE WELL-TO-DO OF LONDON. RETURN TO YOUR HOMES.
shhffff
BOOOO!!
BOOOO!!

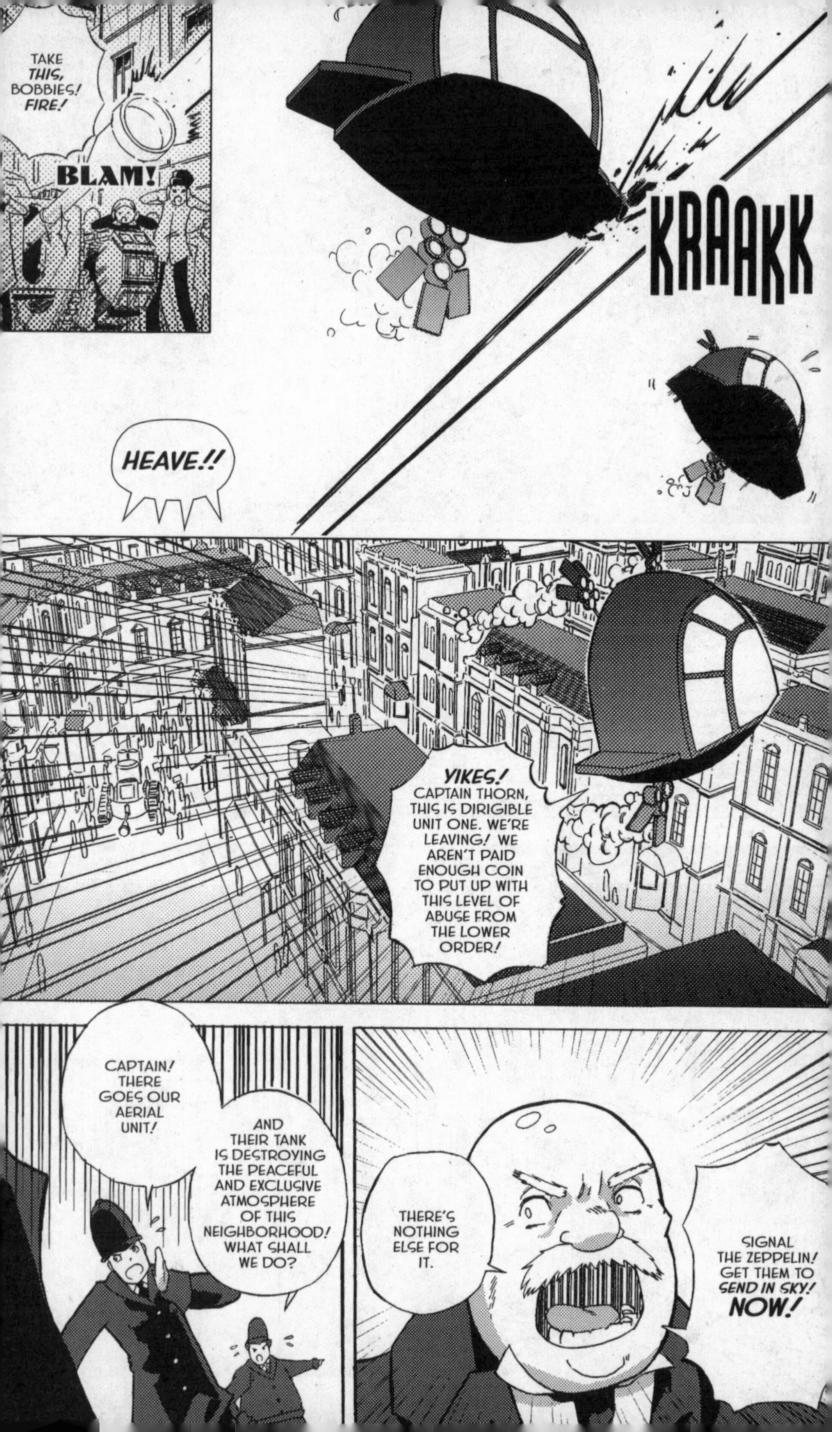
TAKE THIS, BOBBIES! FIRE!
BLAM!
KRAAKK
HEAVE.!!
YIKES! CAPTAIN THORN, THIS IS DIRIGIBLE UNIT ONE. WE'RE LEAVING! WE AREN'T PAID ENOUGH COIN TO PUT UP WITH THIS LEVEL OF ABUSE FROM THE LOWER ORDER!
CAPTAIN! THERE GOES OUR AERIAL UNIT!
AND THEIR TANK IS DESTROYING THE PEACEFUL AND EXCLUSIVE ATMOSPHERE OF THIS NEIGHBORHOOD! WHAT SHALL WE DO?
THERE'S NOTHING ELSE FOR IT.
SIGNAL THE ZEPPELIN! GET THEM TO SEND IN SKY! NOW!

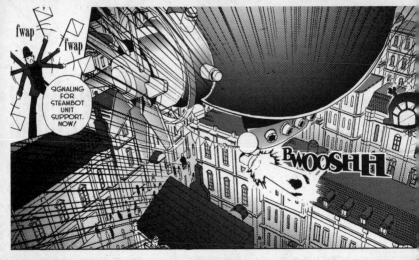

fwap
fwap

SIGNALING FOR STEAMBOT UNIT SUPPORT. NOW!

BWOOSHH

FWOOOOM

Shhhaaa

Plink Plink

KREEEAK

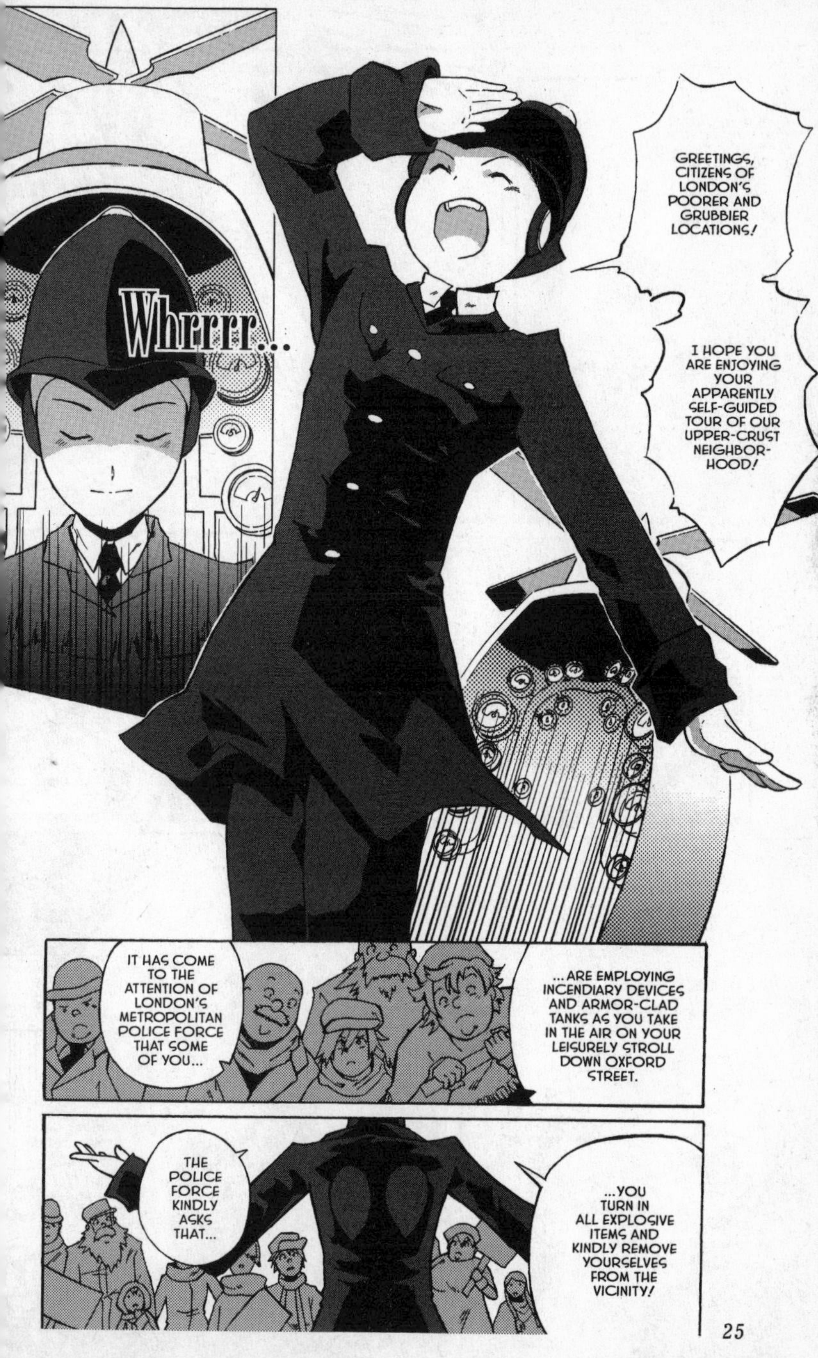
Whrrrr...
GREETINGS, CITIZENS OF LONDON'S POORER AND GRUBBIER LOCATIONS!
I HOPE YOU ARE ENJOYING YOUR APPARENTLY SELF-GUIDED TOUR OF OUR UPPER-CRUST NEIGHBOR-HOOD!
IT HAS COME TO THE ATTENTION OF LONDON'S METROPOLITAN POLICE FORCE THAT SOME OF YOU...
...ARE EMPLOYING INCENDIARY DEVICES AND ARMOR-CLAD TANKS AS YOU TAKE IN THE AIR ON YOUR LEISURELY STROLL DOWN OXFORD STREET.
THE POLICE FORCE KINDLY ASKS THAT...
...YOU TURN IN ALL EXPLOSIVE ITEMS AND KINDLY REMOVE YOURSELVES FROM THE VICINITY!

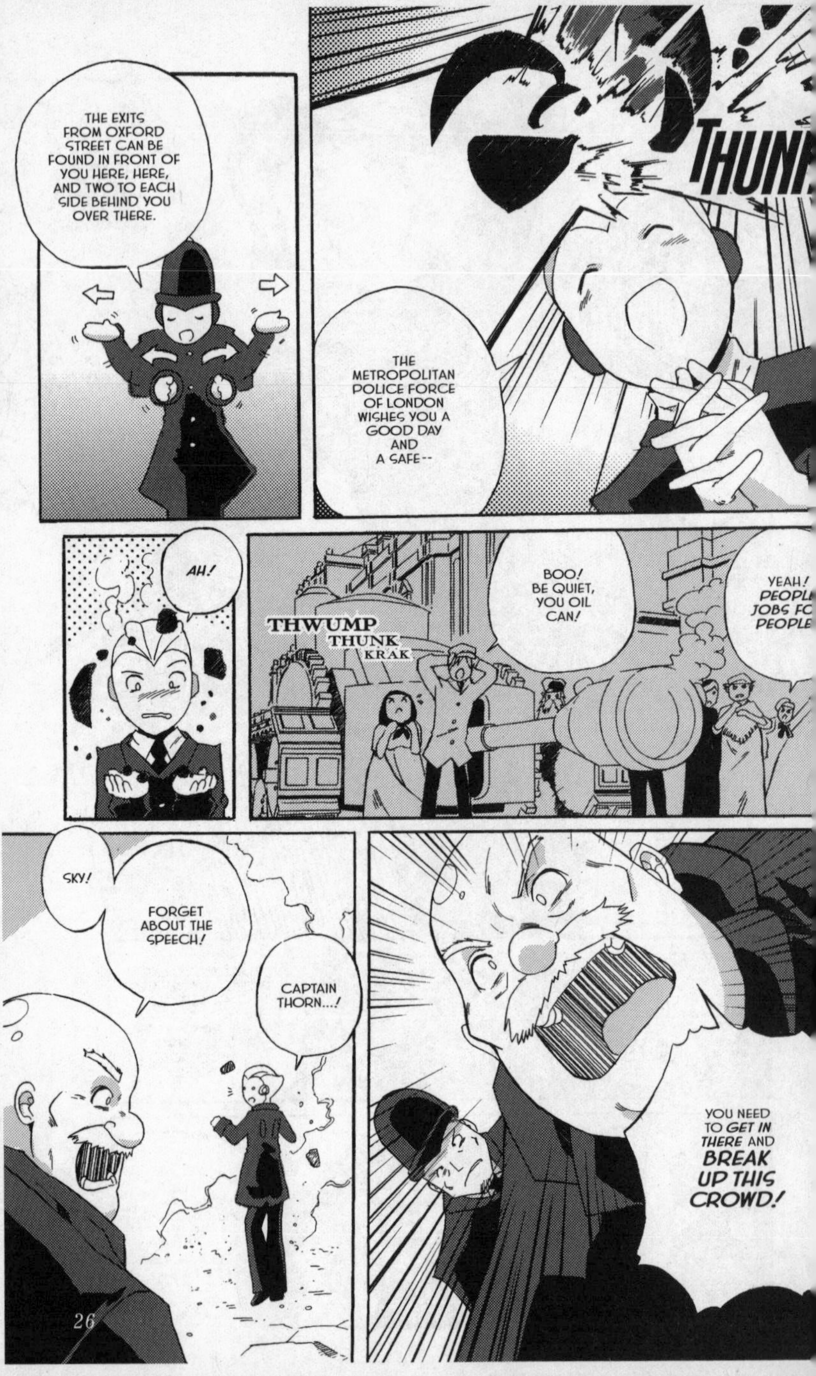
THE EXITS FROM OXFORD STREET CAN BE FOUND IN FRONT OF YOU HERE, HERE, AND TWO TO EACH SIDE BEHIND YOU OVER THERE.
THE METROPOLITAN POLICE FORCE OF LONDON WISHES YOU A GOOD DAY AND A SAFE--
THUN
AH!
THWUMP
THUNK
KRAK
BOO! BE QUIET, YOU OIL CAN!
YEAH! PEOPL JOBS FO PEOPLE
SKY!
FORGET ABOUT THE SPEECH!
CAPTAIN THORN...!
YOU NEED TO GET IN THERE AND BREAK UP THIS CROWD!

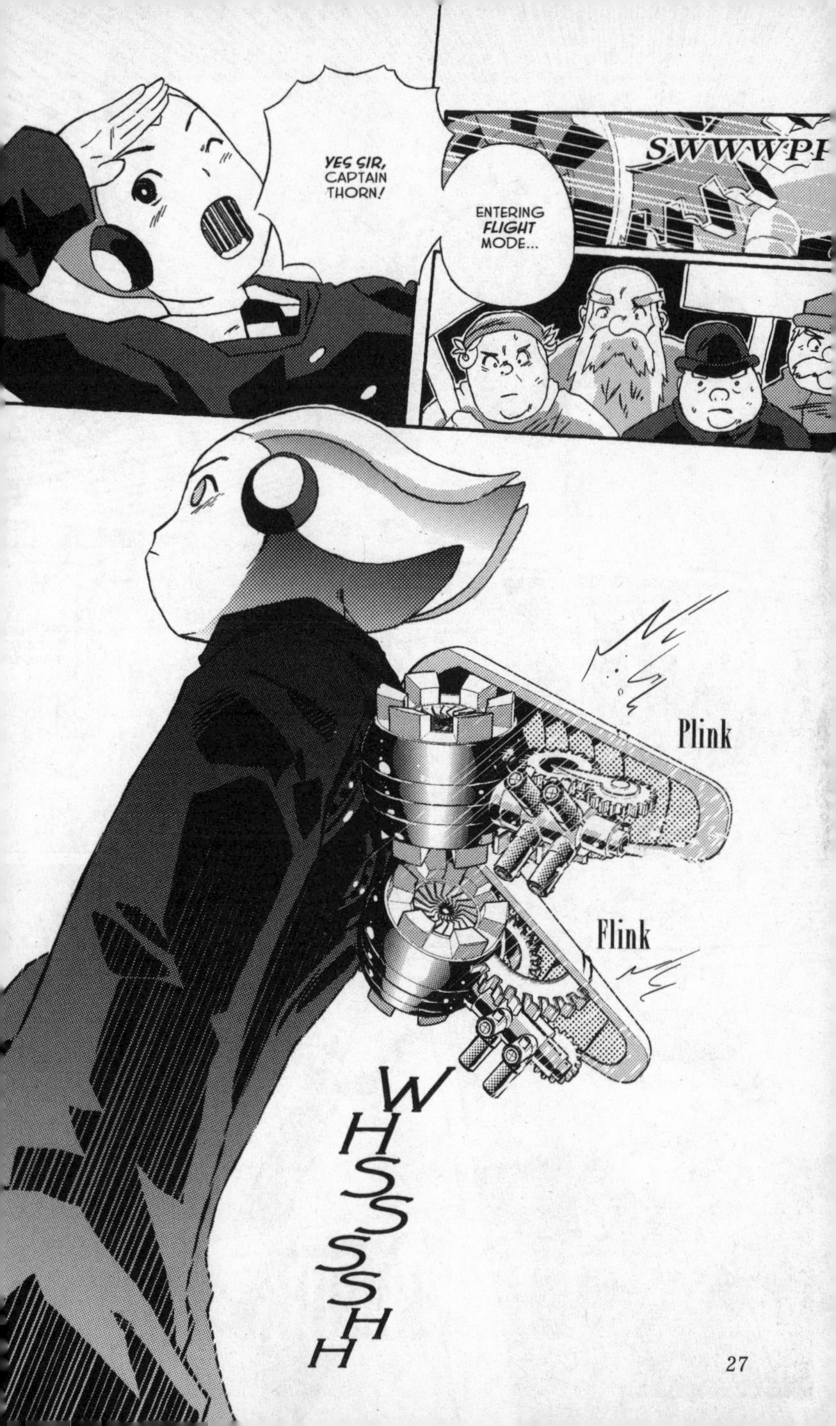
YES SIR, CAPTAIN THORN!
ENTERING FLIGHT MODE...
SWWWPF
Plink
Flink
WHSSSSHH

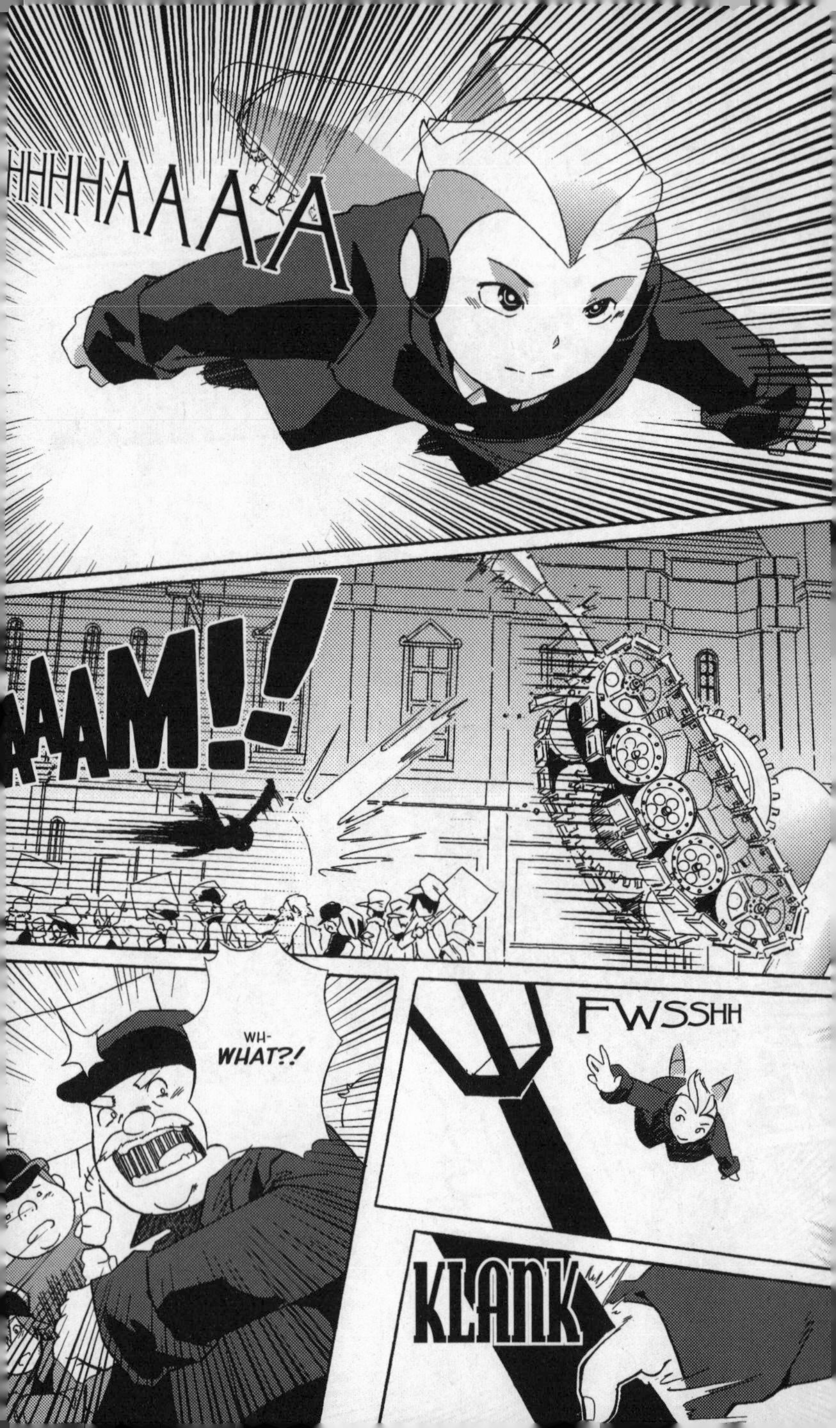
HHHHAAAAA
AAAM!!
WH-
WHAT?!
FWSSHH
KLANK

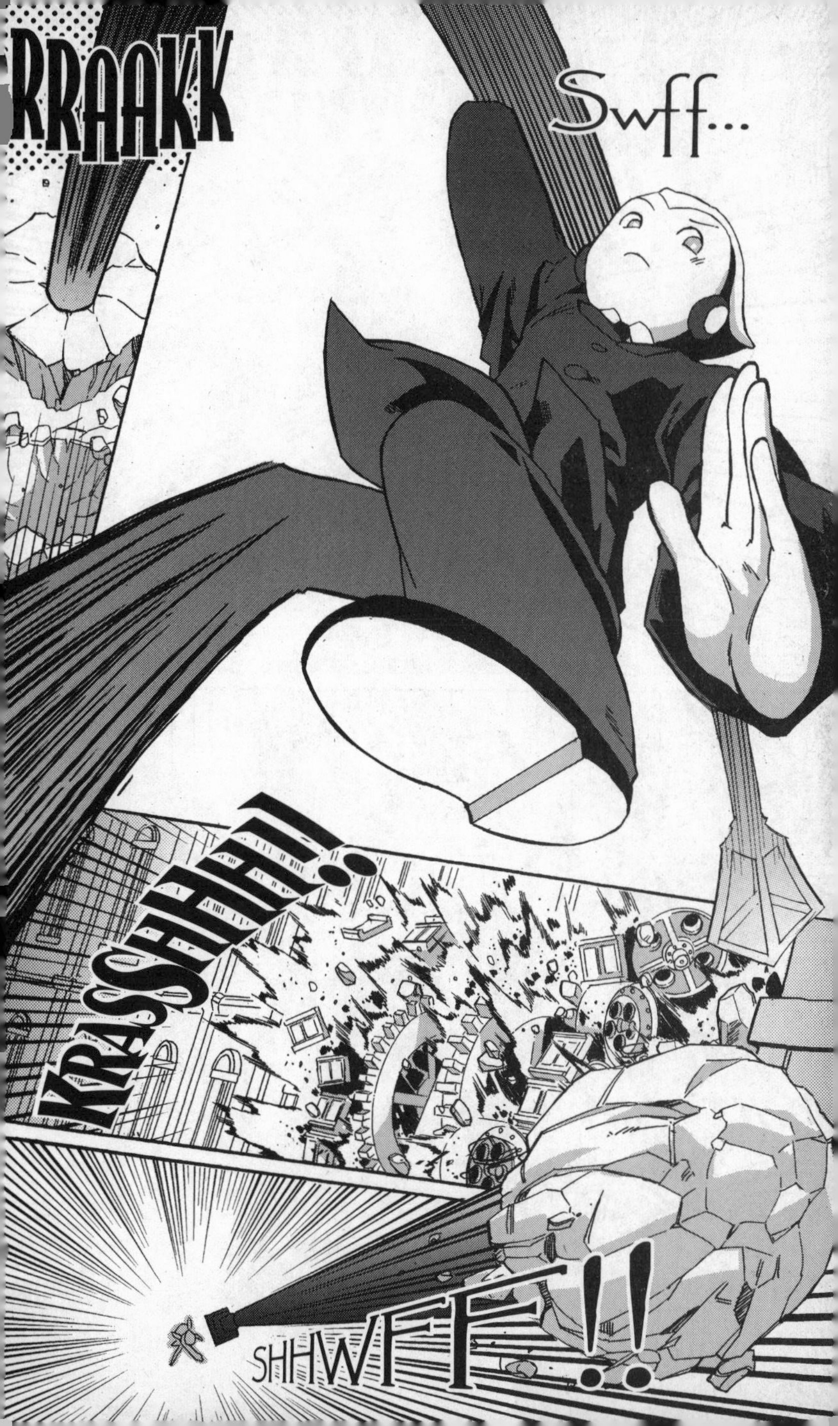

RRAAKK
Swff...
KRASSHHH!!
SHHWFF!!

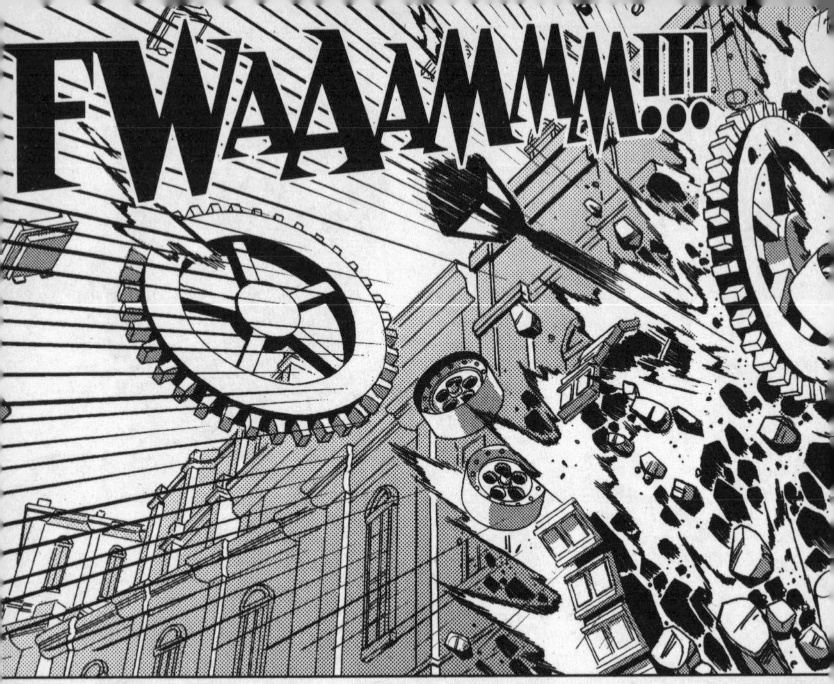
FWAAAMMMM!!!...

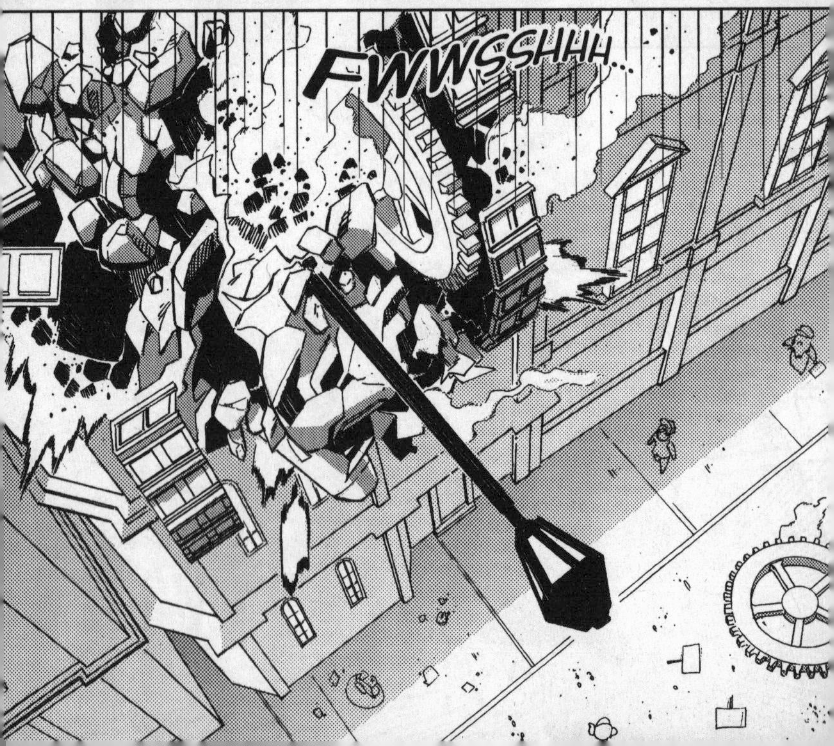
FWWSSHHH...

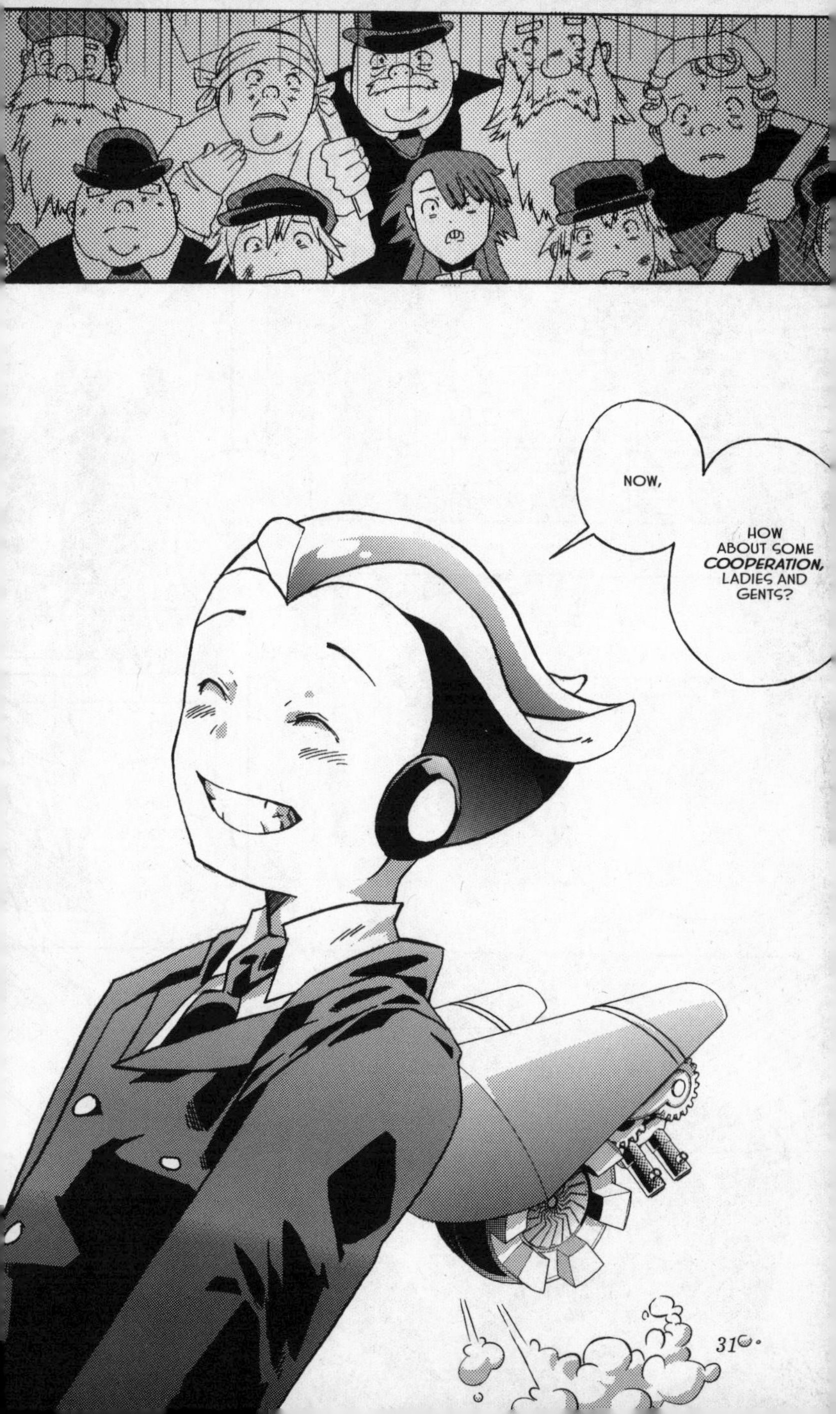
NOW,
HOW ABOUT SOME **COOPERATION,** LADIES AND GENTS?

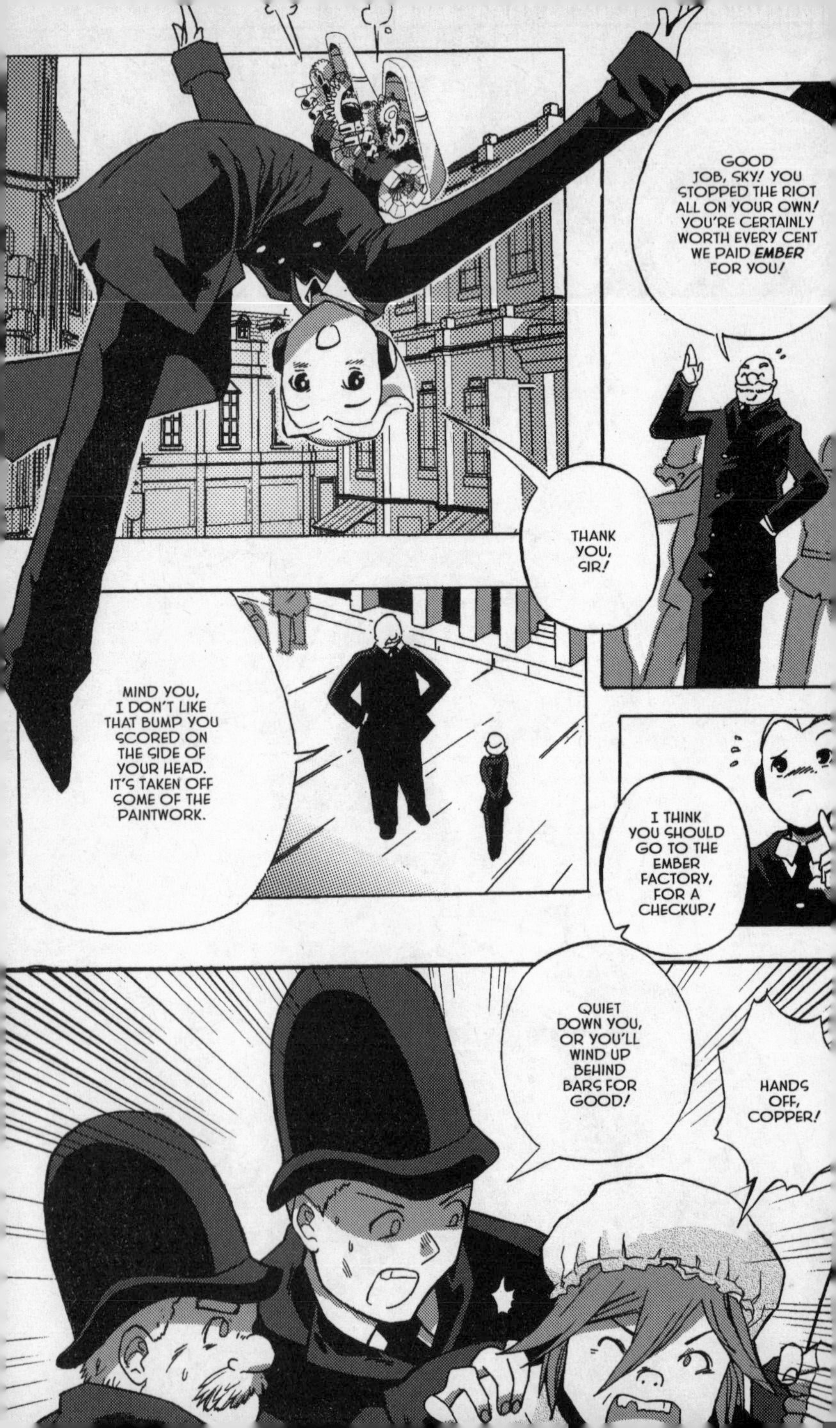
GOOD JOB, SKY! YOU STOPPED THE RIOT ALL ON YOUR OWN! YOU'RE CERTAINLY WORTH EVERY CENT WE PAID *EMBER* FOR YOU!
THANK YOU, SIR!
MIND YOU, I DON'T LIKE THAT BUMP YOU SCORED ON THE SIDE OF YOUR HEAD. IT'S TAKEN OFF SOME OF THE PAINTWORK.
I THINK YOU SHOULD GO TO THE EMBER FACTORY, FOR A CHECKUP!
QUIET DOWN YOU, OR YOU'LL WIND UP BEHIND BARS FOR GOOD!
HANDS OFF, COPPER!

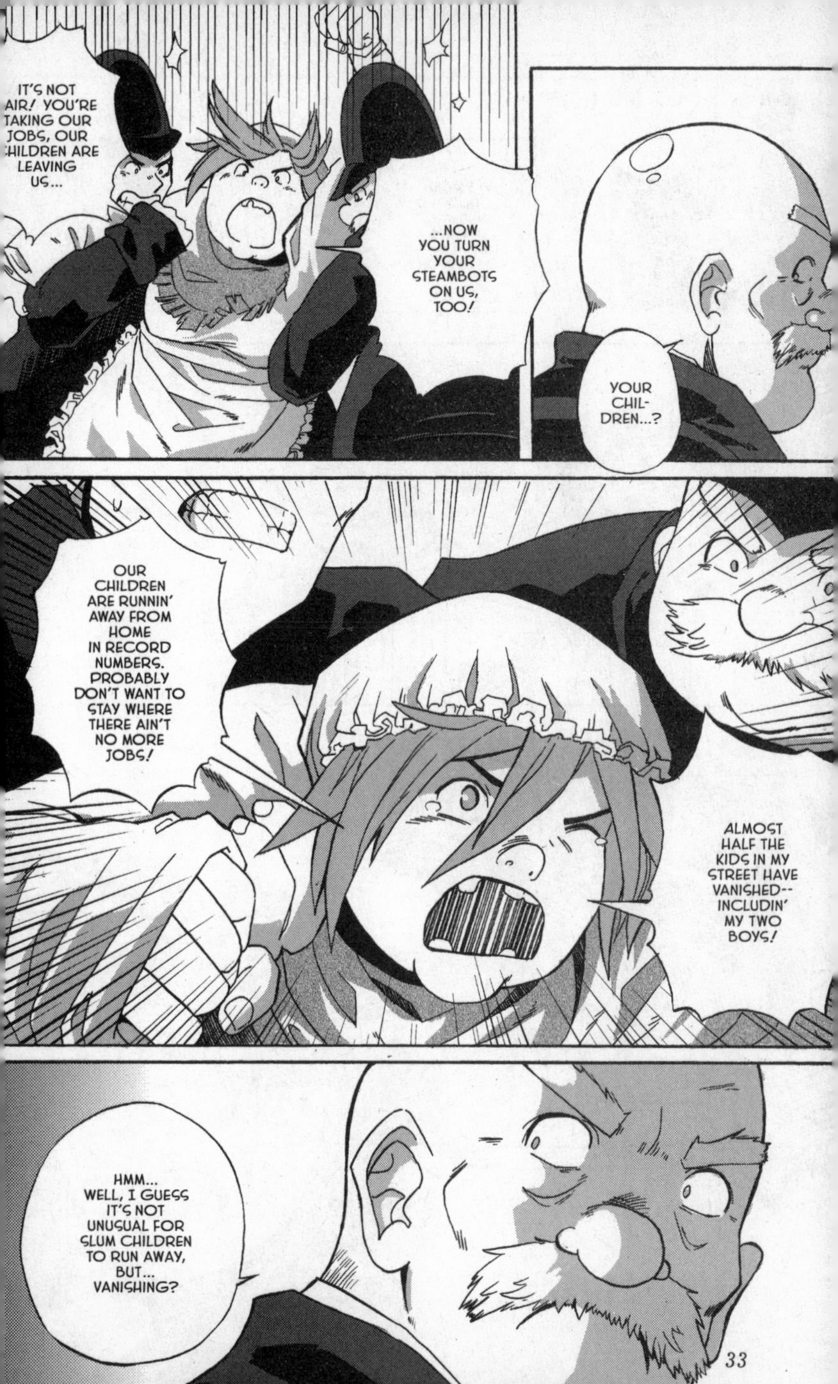

IT'S NOT AIR! YOU'RE TAKING OUR JOBS, OUR CHILDREN ARE LEAVING US...
...NOW YOU TURN YOUR STEAMBOTS ON US, TOO!
YOUR CHIL-DREN...?
OUR CHILDREN ARE RUNNIN' AWAY FROM HOME IN RECORD NUMBERS. PROBABLY DON'T WANT TO STAY WHERE THERE AIN'T NO MORE JOBS!
ALMOST HALF THE KIDS IN MY STREET HAVE VANISHED--INCLUDIN' MY TWO BOYS!
HMM... WELL, I GUESS IT'S NOT UNUSUAL FOR SLUM CHILDREN TO RUN AWAY, BUT... VANISHING?

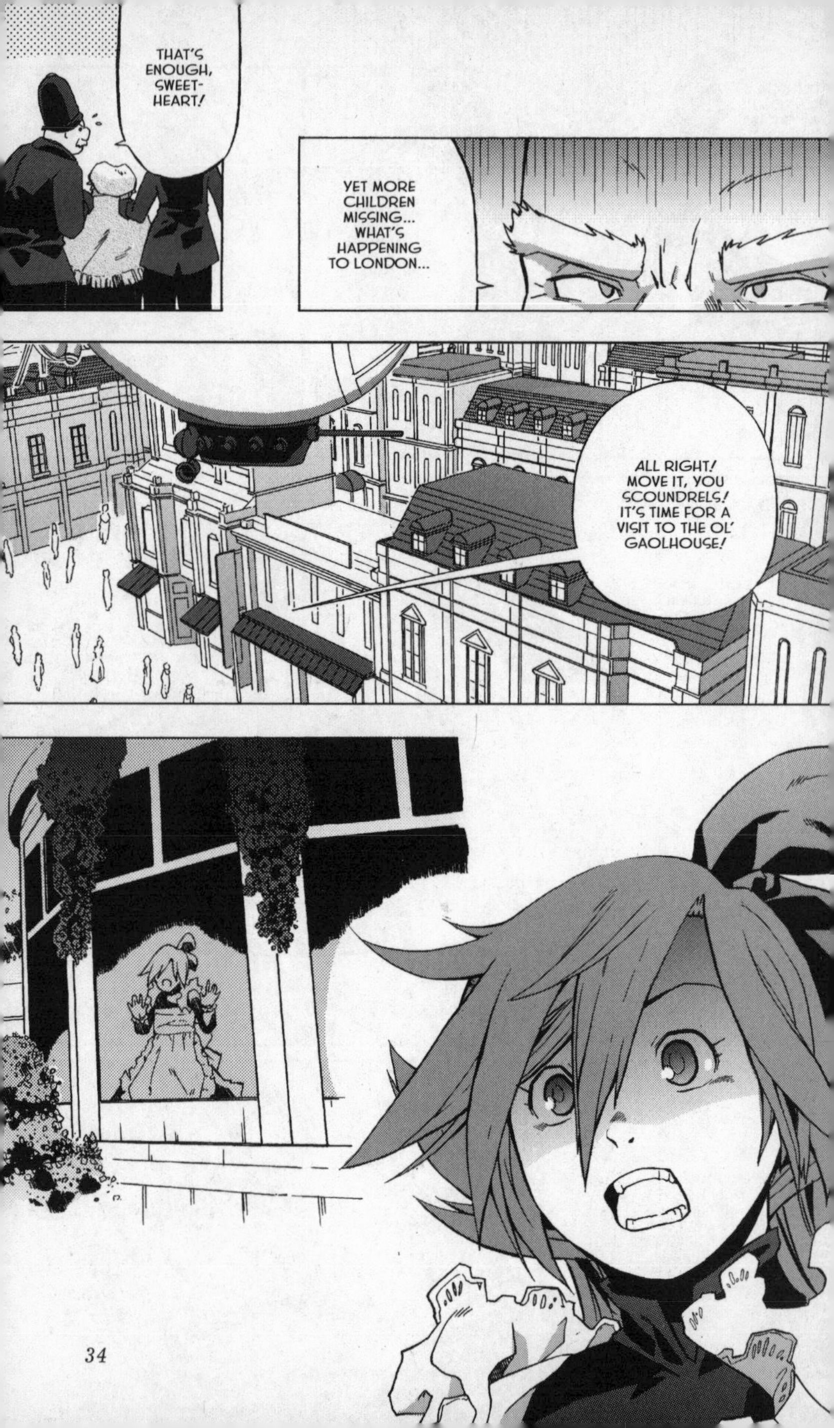
THAT'S ENOUGH, SWEET-HEART!
YET MORE CHILDREN MISSING... WHAT'S HAPPENING TO LONDON...
ALL RIGHT! MOVE IT, YOU SCOUNDRELS! IT'S TIME FOR A VISIT TO THE OL' GAOLHOUSE!

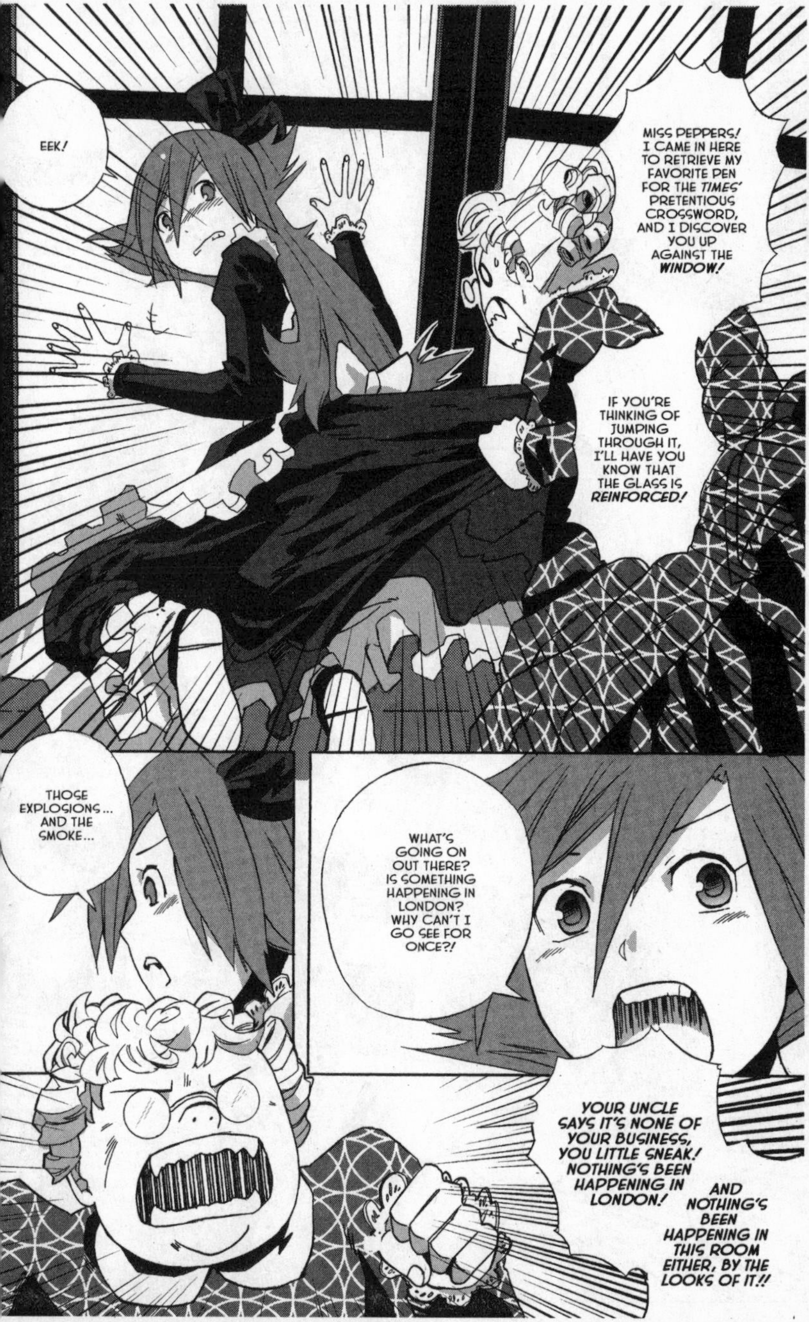
EEK!
MISS PEPPERS! I CAME IN HERE TO RETRIEVE MY FAVORITE PEN FOR THE *TIMES'* PRETENTIOUS CROSSWORD, AND I DISCOVER YOU UP AGAINST THE ***WINDOW!***
IF YOU'RE THINKING OF JUMPING THROUGH IT, I'LL HAVE YOU KNOW THAT THE GLASS IS ***REINFORCED!***
THOSE EXPLOSIONS... AND THE SMOKE...
WHAT'S GOING ON OUT THERE? IS SOMETHING HAPPENING IN LONDON? WHY CAN'T I GO SEE FOR ONCE?!
YOUR UNCLE SAYS IT'S NONE OF YOUR BUSINESS, YOU LITTLE SNEAK! NOTHING'S BEEN HAPPENING IN LONDON!
AND NOTHING'S BEEN HAPPENING IN THIS ROOM EITHER, BY THE LOOKS OF IT!!

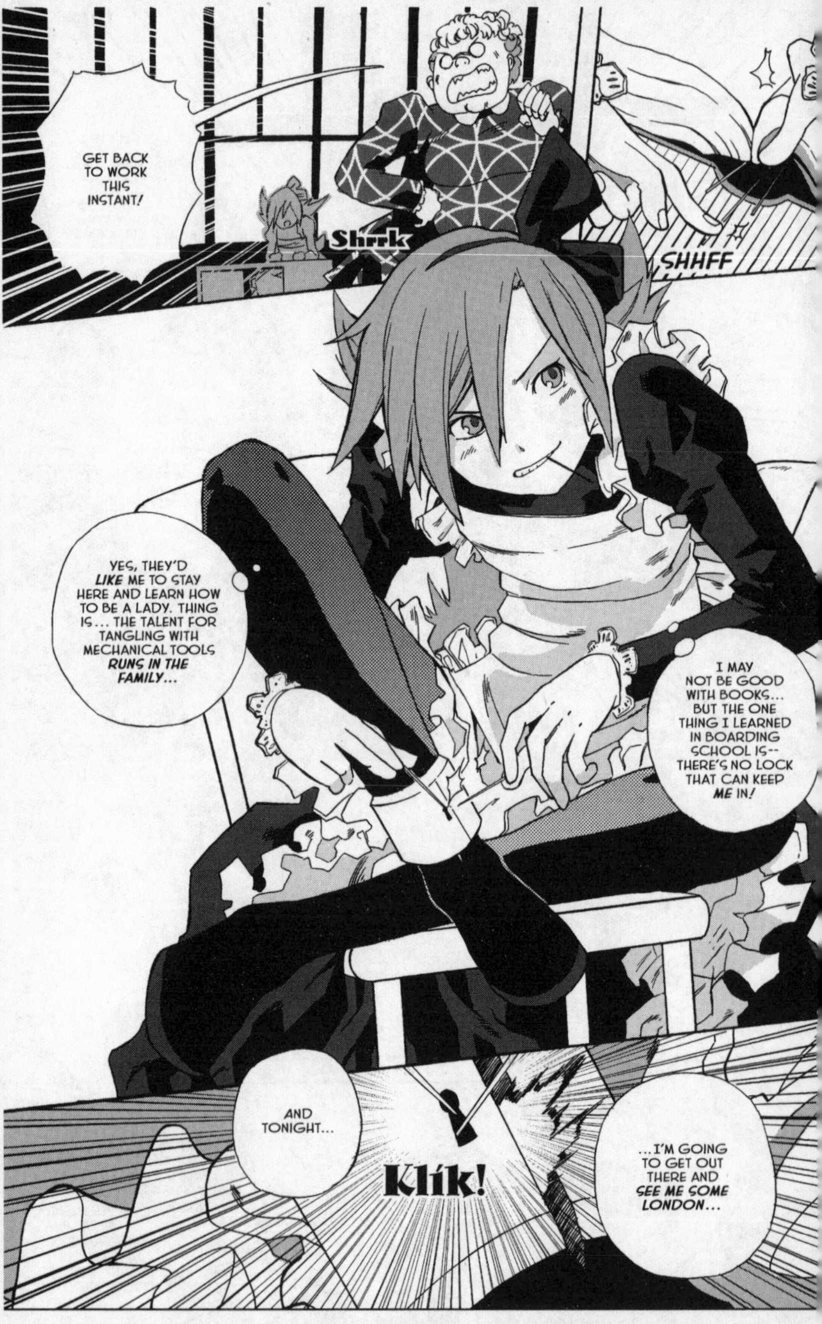
GET BACK TO WORK THIS INSTANT!
Shrrk
SHHFF
YES, THEY'D *LIKE* ME TO STAY HERE AND LEARN HOW TO BE A LADY. THING IS... THE TALENT FOR TANGLING WITH MECHANICAL TOOLS ***RUNS IN THE FAMILY...***
I MAY NOT BE GOOD WITH BOOKS... BUT THE ONE THING I LEARNED IN BOARDING SCHOOL IS-- THERE'S NO LOCK THAT CAN KEEP ***ME*** IN!
AND TONIGHT...
Klik!
...I'M GOING TO GET OUT THERE AND ***SEE ME SOME LONDON...***

CHAPTER 2

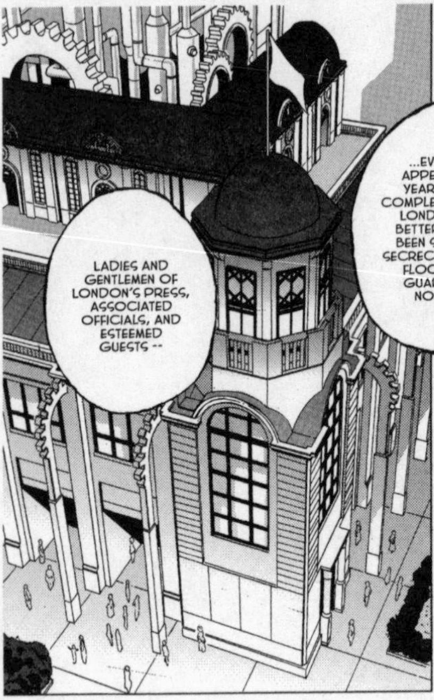
LADIES AND GENTLEMEN OF LONDON'S PRESS, ASSOCIATED OFFICIALS, AND ESTEEMED GUESTS --
...EVER SINCE IT APPEARED THREE YEARS AGO AND COMPLETELY CHANGED LONDON FOR THE BETTER, EMBER HAS BEEN SHROUDED IN SECRECY; ITS FACTORY FLOORS TIGHTLY GUARDED. WELL, NO LONGER!

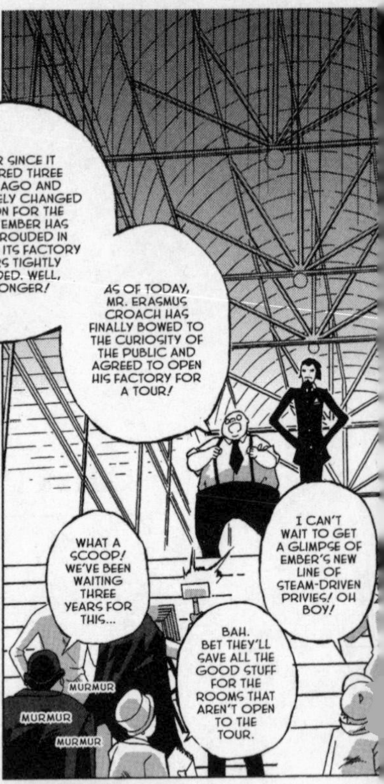
AS OF TODAY, MR. ERASMUS CROACH HAS FINALLY BOWED TO THE CURIOSITY OF THE PUBLIC AND AGREED TO OPEN HIS FACTORY FOR A TOUR!
WHAT A SCOOP! WE'VE BEEN WAITING THREE YEARS FOR THIS...
I CAN'T WAIT TO GET A GLIMPSE OF EMBER'S NEW LINE OF STEAM-DRIVEN PRIVIES! OH BOY!
MURMUR
MURMUR
MURMUR
BAH. BET THEY'LL SAVE ALL THE GOOD STUFF FOR THE ROOMS THAT AREN'T OPEN TO THE TOUR.

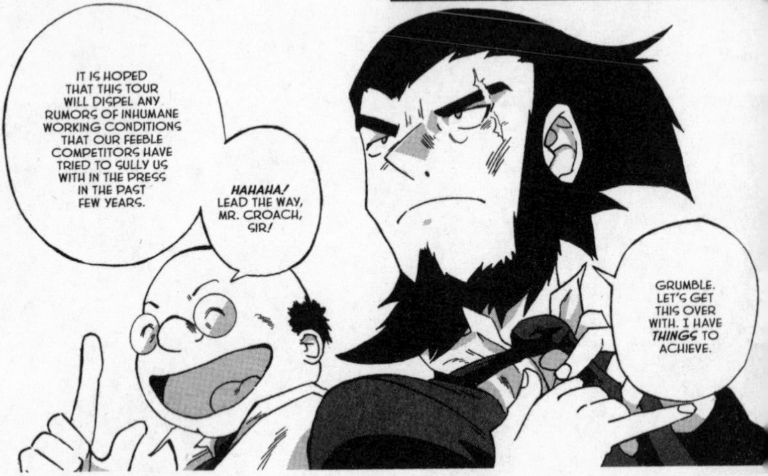
IT IS HOPED THAT THIS TOUR WILL DISPEL ANY RUMORS OF INHUMANE WORKING CONDITIONS THAT OUR FEEBLE COMPETITORS HAVE TRIED TO SULLY US WITH IN THE PRESS IN THE PAST FEW YEARS.
HAHAHA! LEAD THE WAY, MR. CROACH, SIR!
GRUMBLE. LET'S GET THIS OVER WITH. I HAVE *THINGS* TO ACHIEVE.

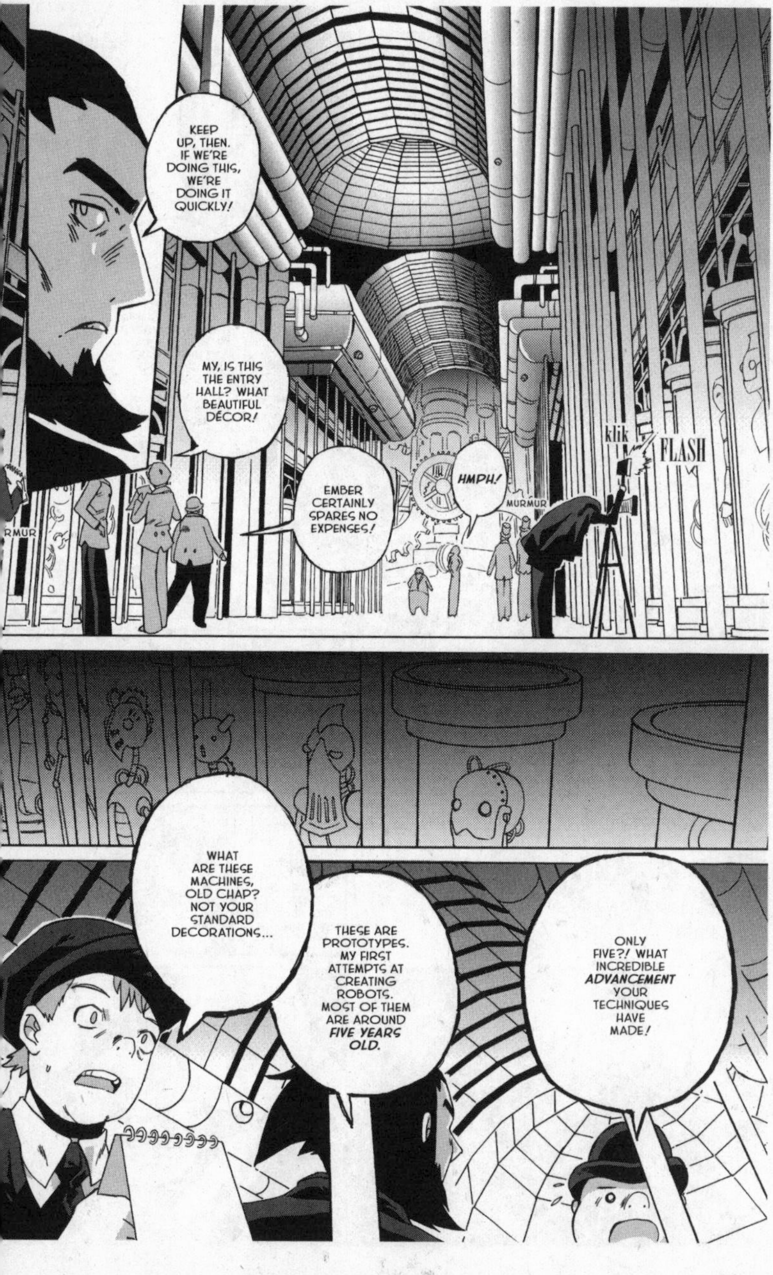
KEEP UP, THEN. IF WE'RE DOING THIS, WE'RE DOING IT QUICKLY!
MY, IS THIS THE ENTRY HALL? WHAT BEAUTIFUL DÉCOR!
MURMUR
EMBER CERTAINLY SPARES NO EXPENSES!
HMPH!
MURMUR
klik
FLASH
WHAT ARE THESE MACHINES, OLD CHAP? NOT YOUR STANDARD DECORATIONS...
THESE ARE PROTOTYPES. MY FIRST ATTEMPTS AT CREATING ROBOTS. MOST OF THEM ARE AROUND *FIVE YEARS OLD.*
ONLY FIVE?! WHAT INCREDIBLE *ADVANCEMENT* YOUR TECHNIQUES HAVE MADE!

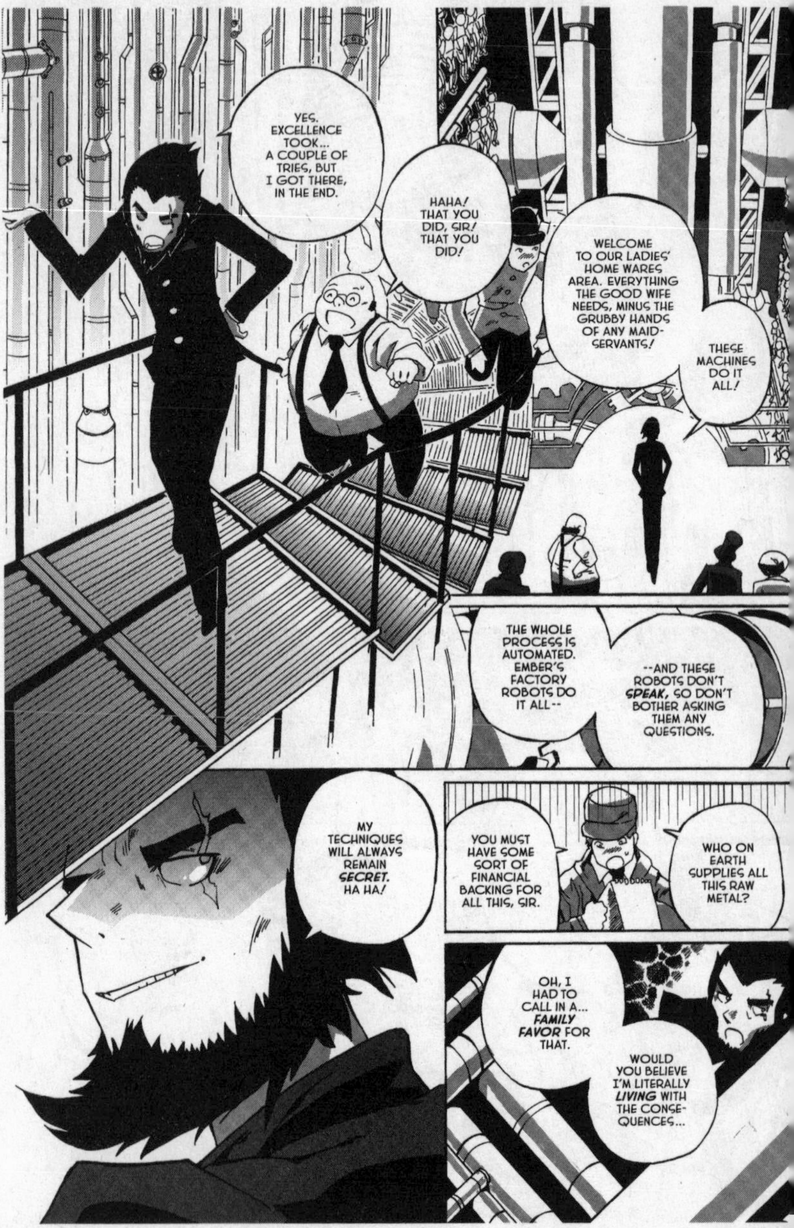
YES. EXCELLENCE TOOK... A COUPLE OF TRIES, BUT I GOT THERE, IN THE END.
HAHA! THAT YOU DID, SIR! THAT YOU DID!
WELCOME TO OUR LADIES' HOME WARES AREA. EVERYTHING THE GOOD WIFE NEEDS, MINUS THE GRUBBY HANDS OF ANY MAID-SERVANTS!
THESE MACHINES DO IT ALL!
THE WHOLE PROCESS IS AUTOMATED. EMBER'S FACTORY ROBOTS DO IT ALL--
--AND THESE ROBOTS DON'T *SPEAK*, SO DON'T BOTHER ASKING THEM ANY QUESTIONS.
MY TECHNIQUES WILL ALWAYS REMAIN *SECRET*. HA HA!
YOU MUST HAVE SOME SORT OF FINANCIAL BACKING FOR ALL THIS, SIR.
WHO ON EARTH SUPPLIES ALL THIS RAW METAL?
OH, I HAD TO CALL IN A... *FAMILY FAVOR* FOR THAT.
WOULD YOU BELIEVE I'M LITERALLY *LIVING* WITH THE CONSE-QUENCES...

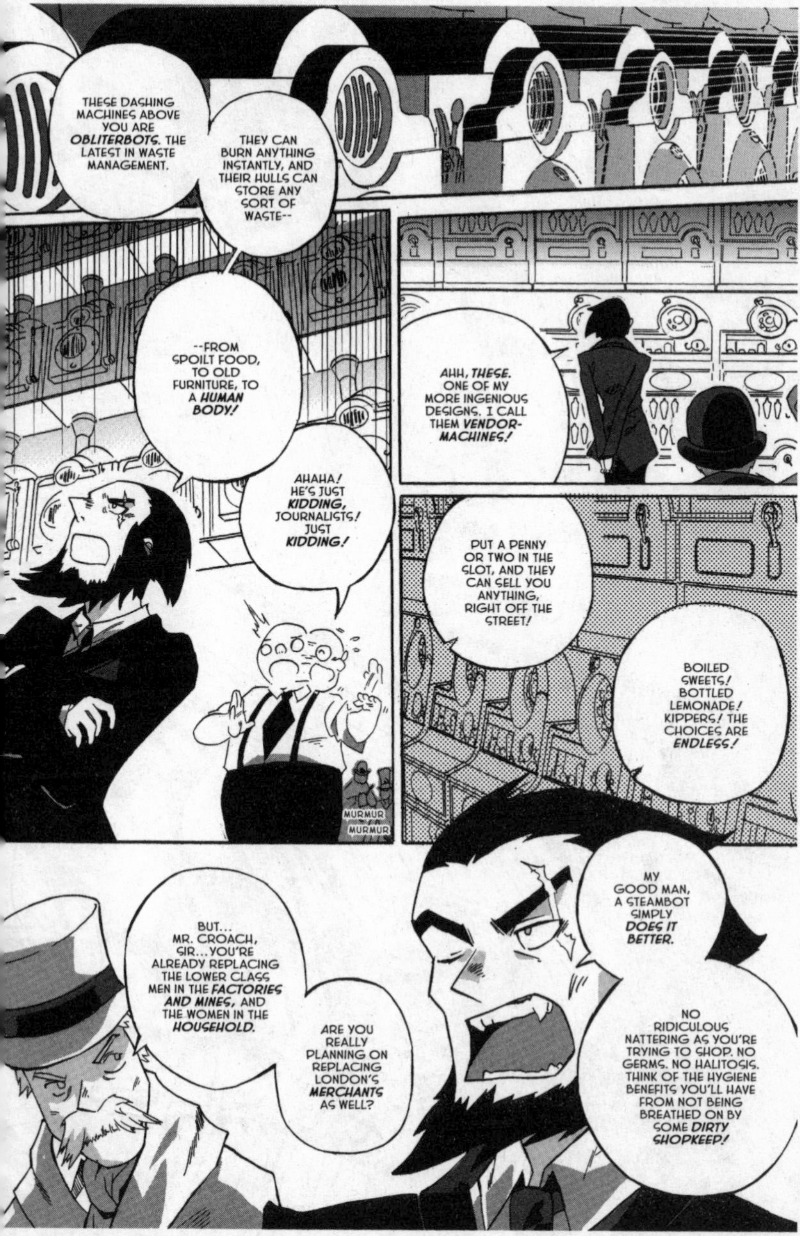
THESE DASHING MACHINES ABOVE YOU ARE OBLITERBOTS. THE LATEST IN WASTE MANAGEMENT.
THEY CAN BURN ANYTHING INSTANTLY, AND THEIR HULLS CAN STORE ANY SORT OF WASTE--
--FROM SPOILT FOOD, TO OLD FURNITURE, TO A HUMAN BODY!
AHAHA! HE'S JUST KIDDING, JOURNALISTS! JUST KIDDING!
MURMUR MURMUR
AHH, THESE. ONE OF MY MORE INGENIOUS DESIGNS. I CALL THEM VENDOR-MACHINES!
PUT A PENNY OR TWO IN THE SLOT, AND THEY CAN SELL YOU ANYTHING, RIGHT OFF THE STREET!
BOILED SWEETS! BOTTLED LEMONADE! KIPPERS! THE CHOICES ARE ENDLESS!
BUT... MR. CROACH, SIR... YOU'RE ALREADY REPLACING THE LOWER CLASS MEN IN THE FACTORIES AND MINES, AND THE WOMEN IN THE HOUSEHOLD.
ARE YOU REALLY PLANNING ON REPLACING LONDON'S MERCHANTS AS WELL?
MY GOOD MAN, A STEAMBOT SIMPLY DOES IT BETTER.
NO RIDICULOUS NATTERING AS YOU'RE TRYING TO SHOP. NO GERMS. NO HALITOSIS. THINK OF THE HYGIENE BENEFITS YOU'LL HAVE FROM NOT BEING BREATHED ON BY SOME DIRTY SHOPKEEP!

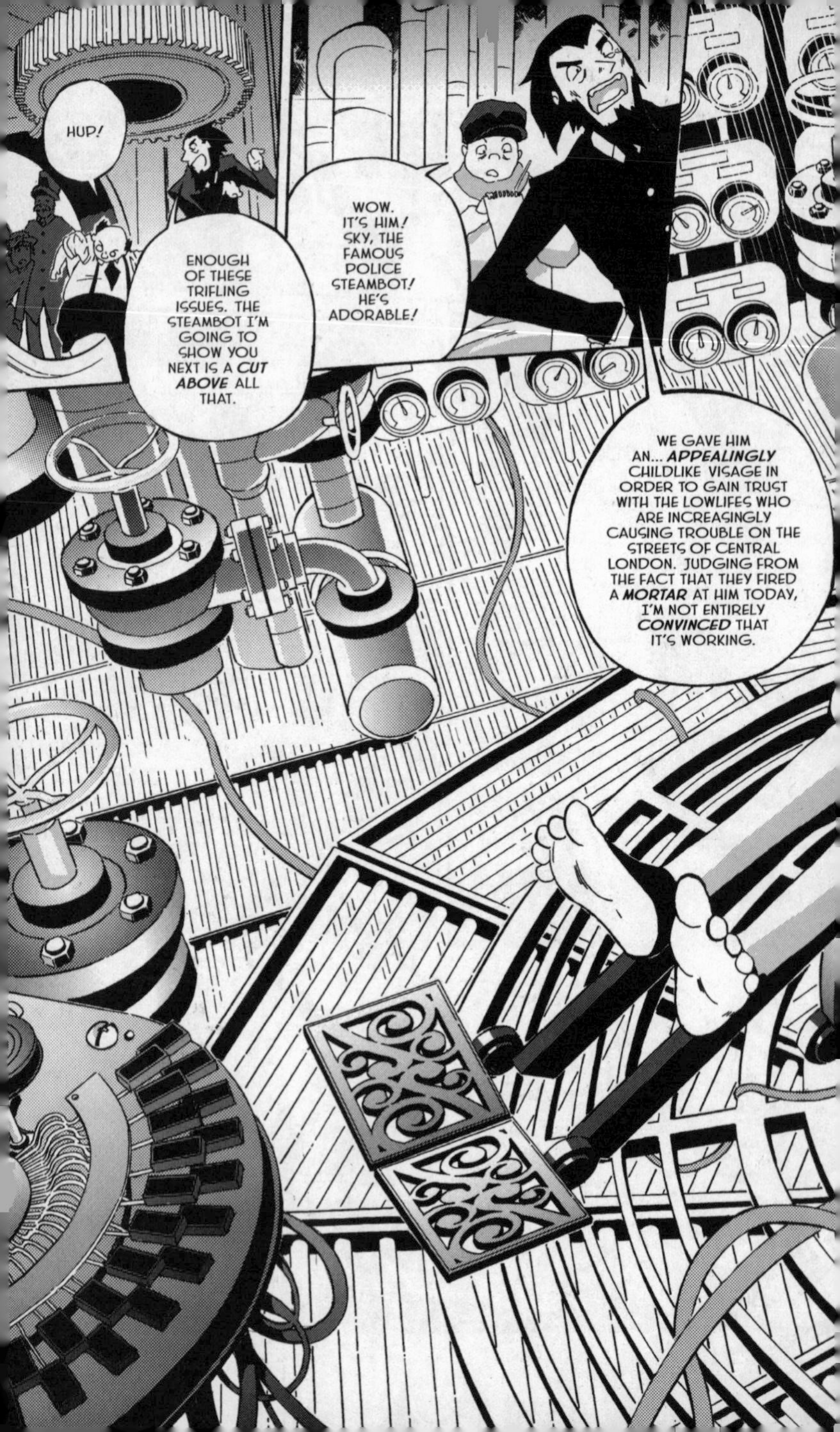
HUP!
ENOUGH OF THESE TRIFLING ISSUES. THE STEAMBOT I'M GOING TO SHOW YOU NEXT IS A *CUT ABOVE* ALL THAT.
WOW. IT'S HIM! SKY, THE FAMOUS POLICE STEAMBOT! HE'S ADORABLE!
WE GAVE HIM AN... *APPEALINGLY* CHILDLIKE VISAGE IN ORDER TO GAIN TRUST WITH THE LOWLIFES WHO ARE INCREASINGLY CAUSING TROUBLE ON THE STREETS OF CENTRAL LONDON. JUDGING FROM THE FACT THAT THEY FIRED A *MORTAR* AT HIM TODAY, I'M NOT ENTIRELY *CONVINCED* THAT IT'S WORKING.

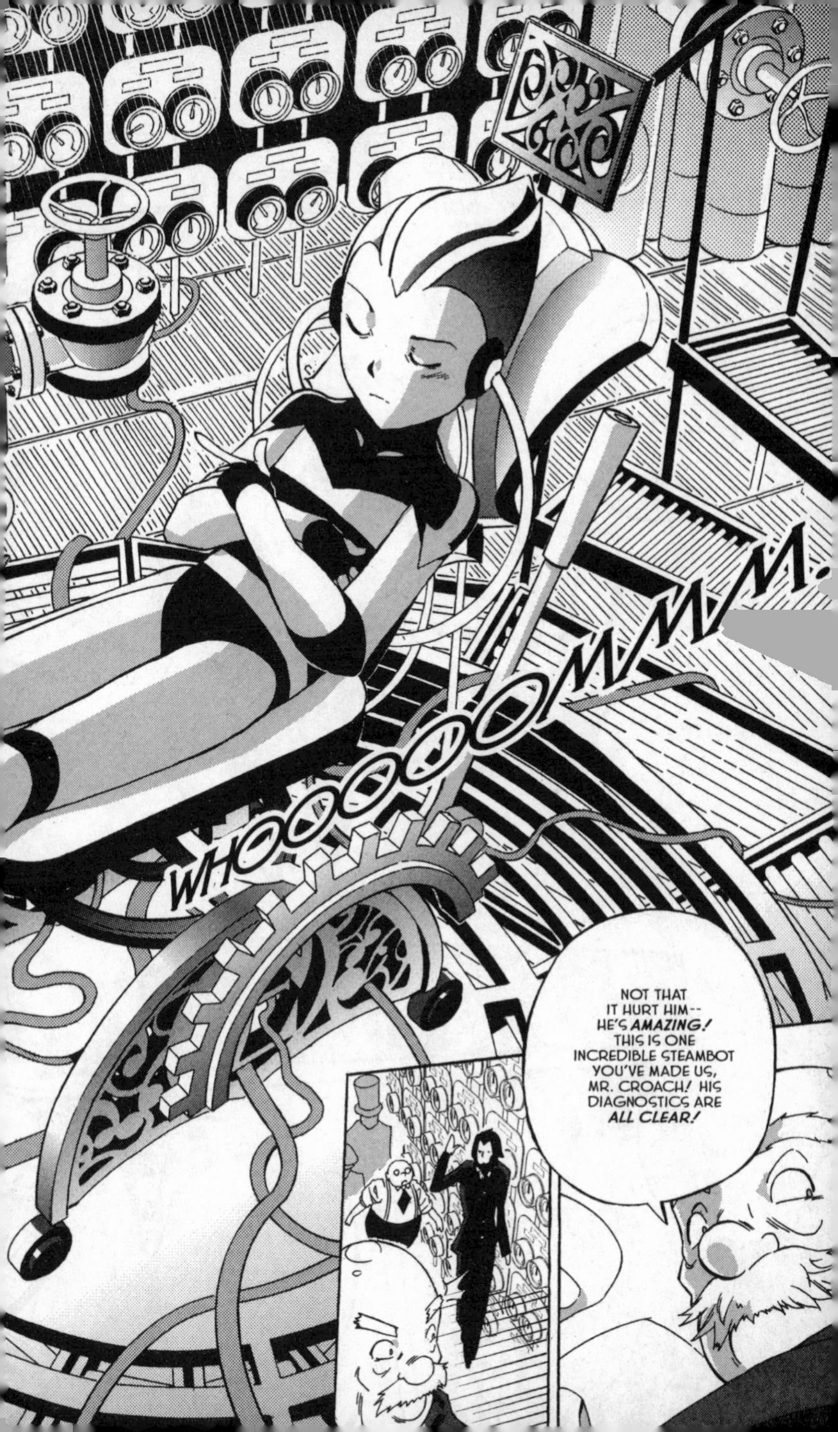
WHOOOOOOMMMM...
NOT THAT IT HURT HIM-- HE'S **AMAZING!** THIS IS ONE INCREDIBLE STEAMBOT YOU'VE MADE US, MR. CROACH! HIS DIAGNOSTICS ARE **ALL CLEAR!**

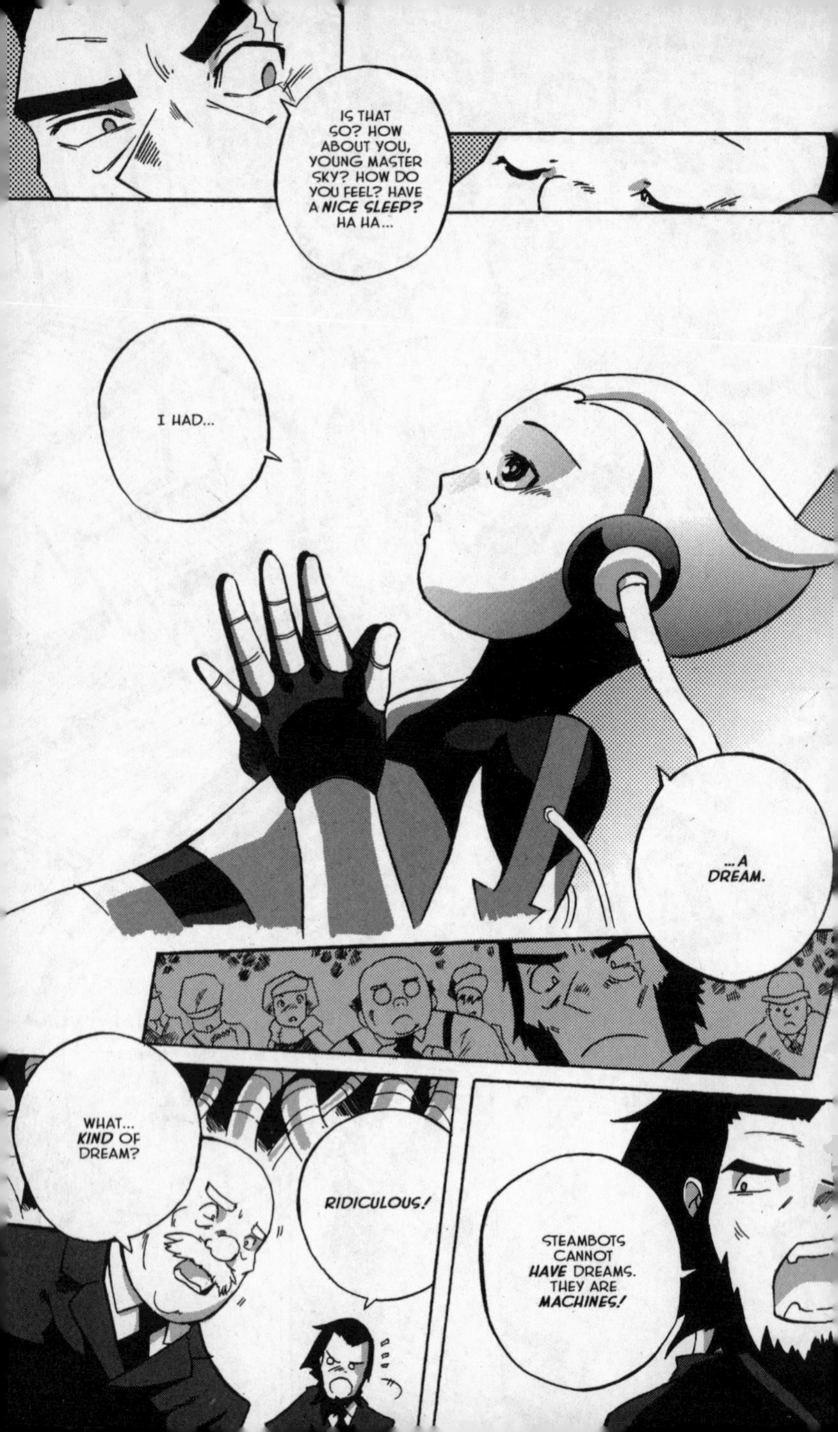
IS THAT SO? HOW ABOUT YOU, YOUNG MASTER SKY? HOW DO YOU FEEL? HAVE A **NICE SLEEP?** HA HA...
I HAD...
...A **DREAM.**
WHAT... **KIND** OF DREAM?
RIDICULOUS!
STEAMBOTS CANNOT **HAVE** DREAMS. THEY ARE **MACHINES!**

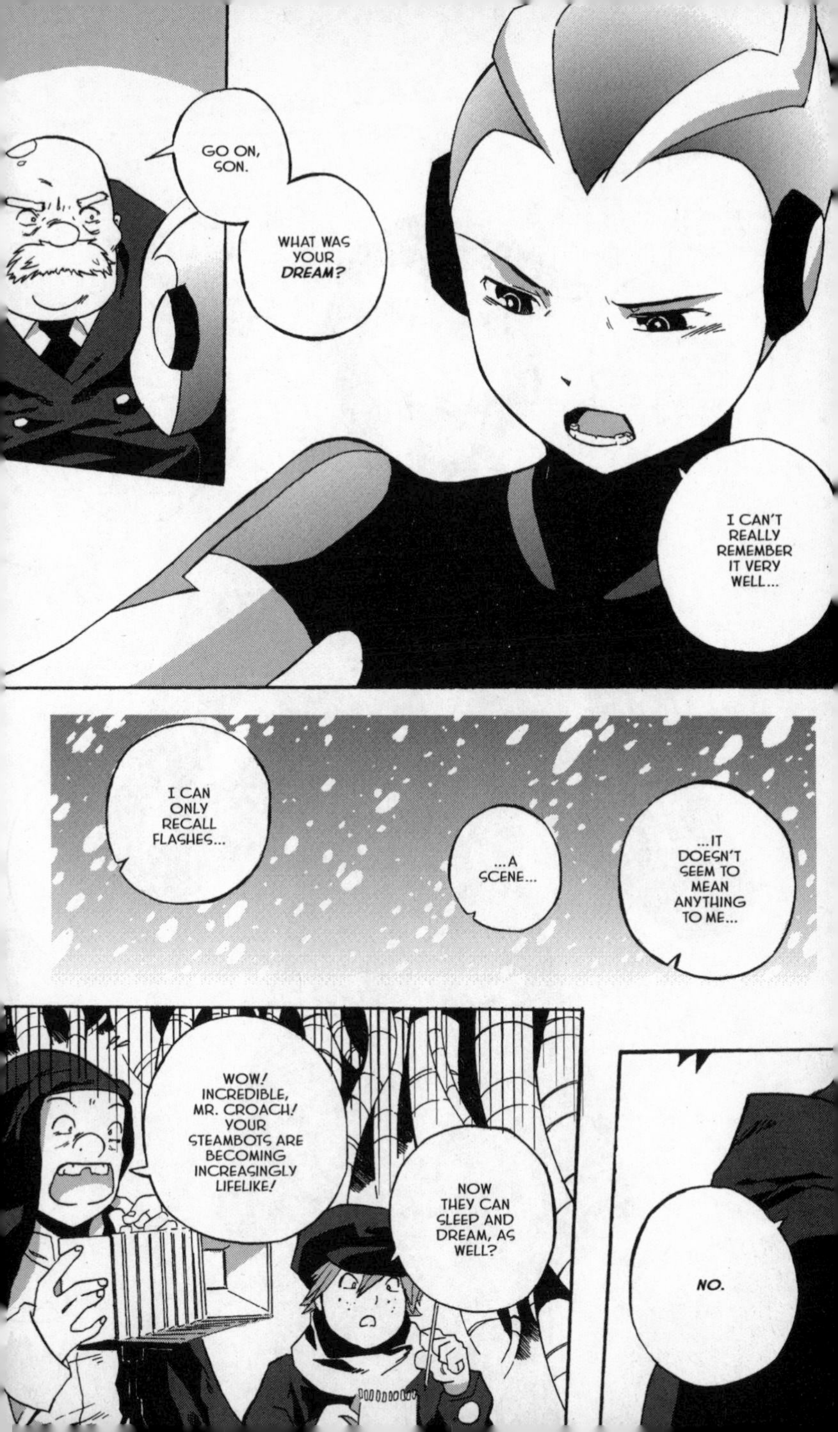
GO ON, SON.
WHAT WAS YOUR *DREAM?*
I CAN'T REALLY REMEMBER IT VERY WELL...
I CAN ONLY RECALL FLASHES...
...A SCENE...
...IT DOESN'T SEEM TO MEAN ANYTHING TO ME...
WOW! INCREDIBLE, MR. CROACH! YOUR STEAMBOTS ARE BECOMING INCREASINGLY LIFELIKE!
NOW THEY CAN SLEEP AND DREAM, AS WELL?
NO.

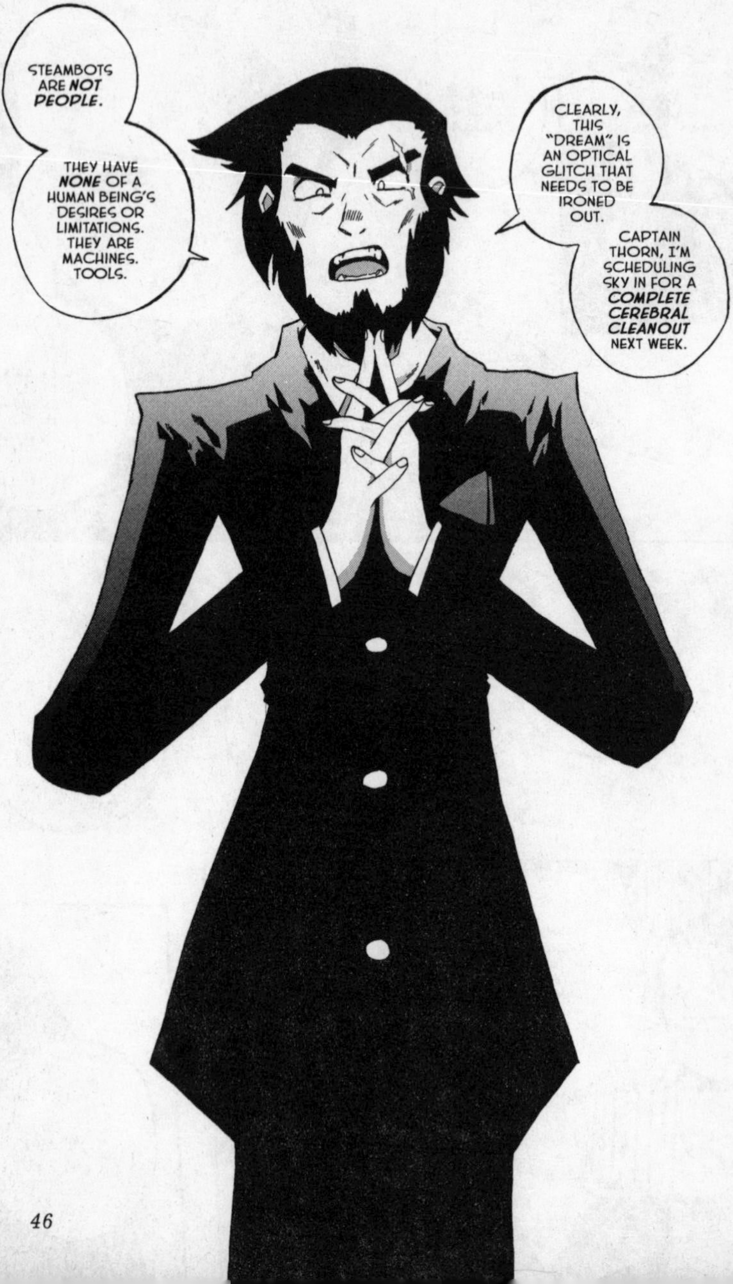
STEAMBOTS ARE ***NOT PEOPLE***.
THEY HAVE ***NONE*** OF A HUMAN BEING'S DESIRES OR LIMITATIONS. THEY ARE MACHINES. TOOLS.
CLEARLY, THIS "DREAM" IS AN OPTICAL GLITCH THAT NEEDS TO BE IRONED OUT.
CAPTAIN THORN, I'M SCHEDULING SKY IN FOR A ***COMPLETE CEREBRAL CLEANOUT*** NEXT WEEK.

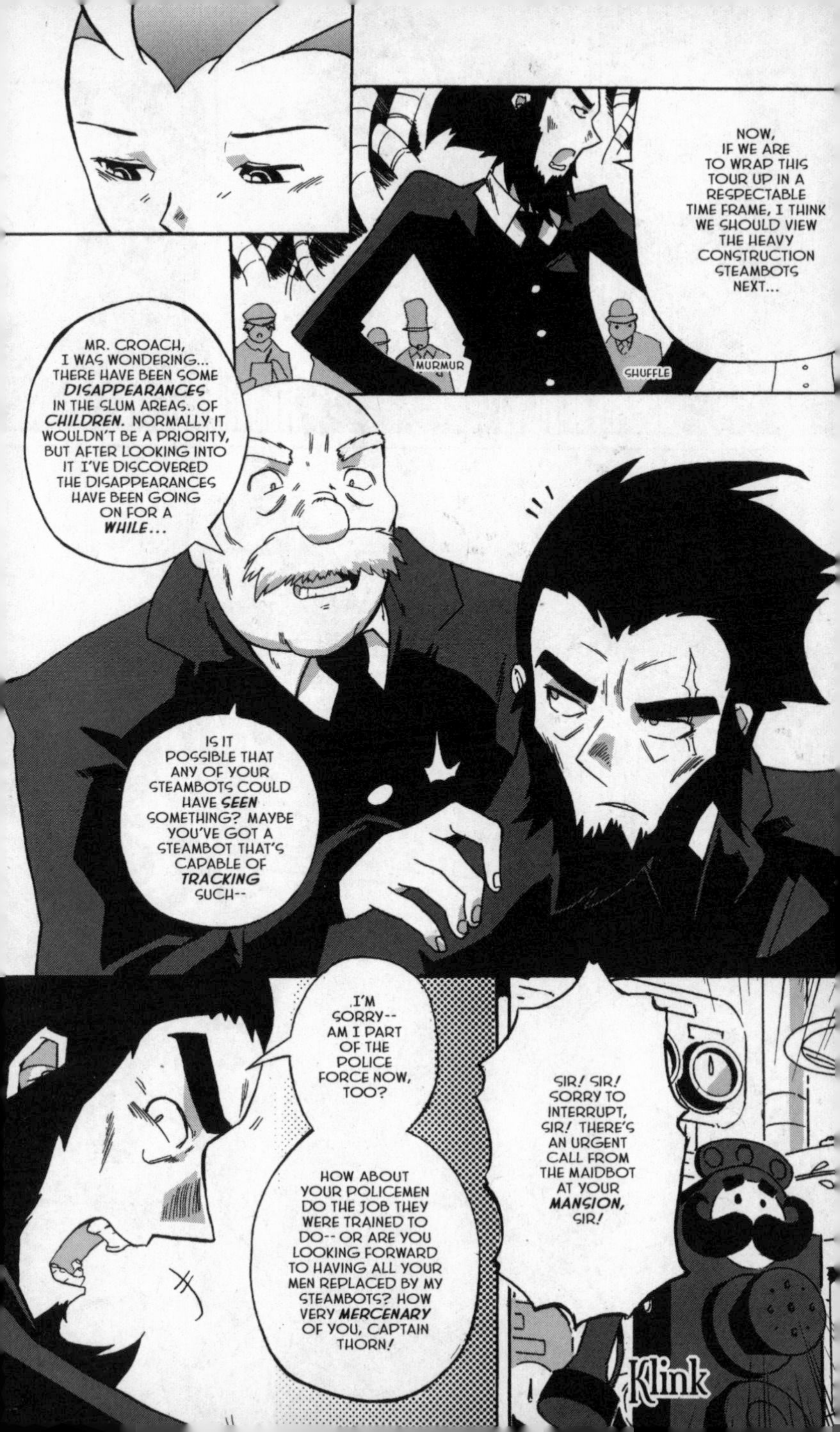
NOW, IF WE ARE TO WRAP THIS TOUR UP IN A RESPECTABLE TIME FRAME, I THINK WE SHOULD VIEW THE HEAVY CONSTRUCTION STEAMBOTS NEXT...
MURMUR
SHUFFLE
MR. CROACH, I WAS WONDERING... THERE HAVE BEEN SOME DISAPPEARANCES IN THE SLUM AREAS. OF CHILDREN. NORMALLY IT WOULDN'T BE A PRIORITY, BUT AFTER LOOKING INTO IT I'VE DISCOVERED THE DISAPPEARANCES HAVE BEEN GOING ON FOR A WHILE...
IS IT POSSIBLE THAT ANY OF YOUR STEAMBOTS COULD HAVE SEEN SOMETHING? MAYBE YOU'VE GOT A STEAMBOT THAT'S CAPABLE OF TRACKING SUCH--
I'M SORRY-- AM I PART OF THE POLICE FORCE NOW, TOO?
HOW ABOUT YOUR POLICEMEN DO THE JOB THEY WERE TRAINED TO DO-- OR ARE YOU LOOKING FORWARD TO HAVING ALL YOUR MEN REPLACED BY MY STEAMBOTS? HOW VERY MERCENARY OF YOU, CAPTAIN THORN!
SIR! SIR! SORRY TO INTERRUPT, SIR! THERE'S AN URGENT CALL FROM THE MAIDBOT AT YOUR MANSION, SIR!
Klink

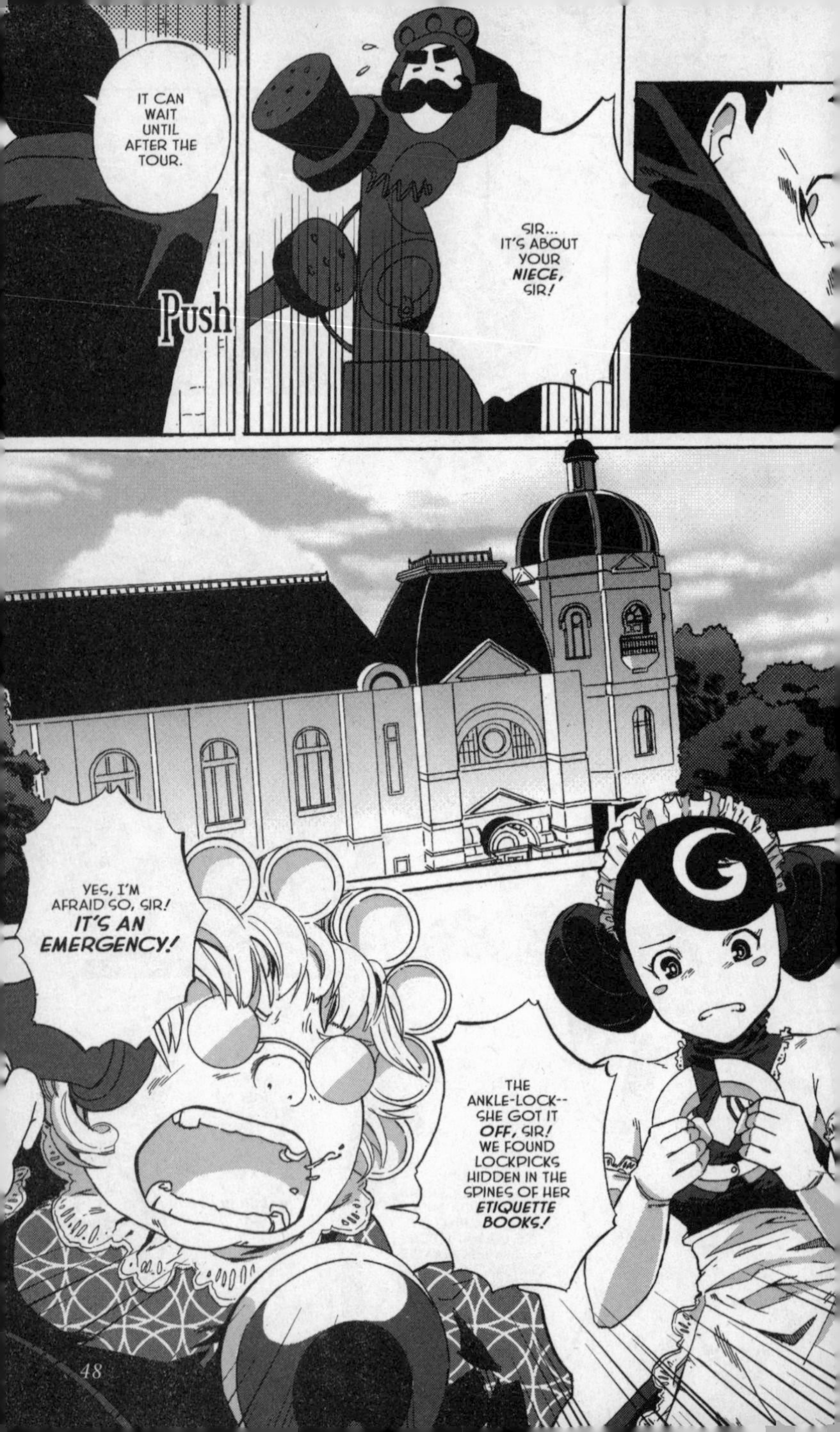
IT CAN WAIT UNTIL AFTER THE TOUR.
Push
SIR... IT'S ABOUT YOUR NIECE, SIR!
YES, I'M AFRAID SO, SIR! IT'S AN EMERGENCY!
THE ANKLE-LOCK--SHE GOT IT OFF, SIR! WE FOUND LOCKPICKS HIDDEN IN THE SPINES OF HER ETIQUETTE BOOKS!

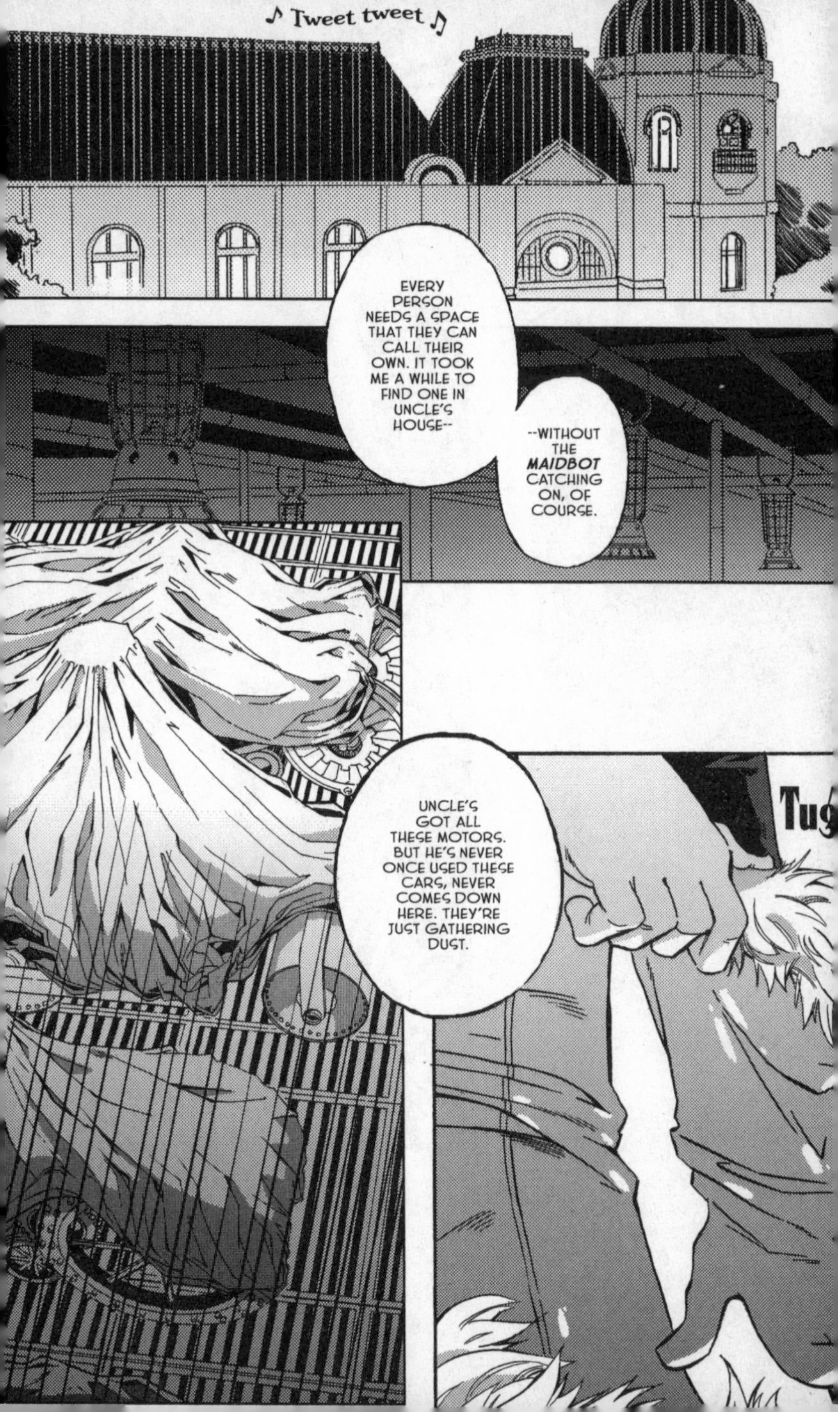
♪ Tweet tweet ♪
EVERY PERSON NEEDS A SPACE THAT THEY CAN CALL THEIR OWN. IT TOOK ME A WHILE TO FIND ONE IN UNCLE'S HOUSE--
--WITHOUT THE *MAIDBOT* CATCHING ON, OF COURSE.
UNCLE'S GOT ALL THESE MOTORS. BUT HE'S NEVER ONCE USED THESE CARS, NEVER COMES DOWN HERE. THEY'RE JUST GATHERING DUST.
Tug

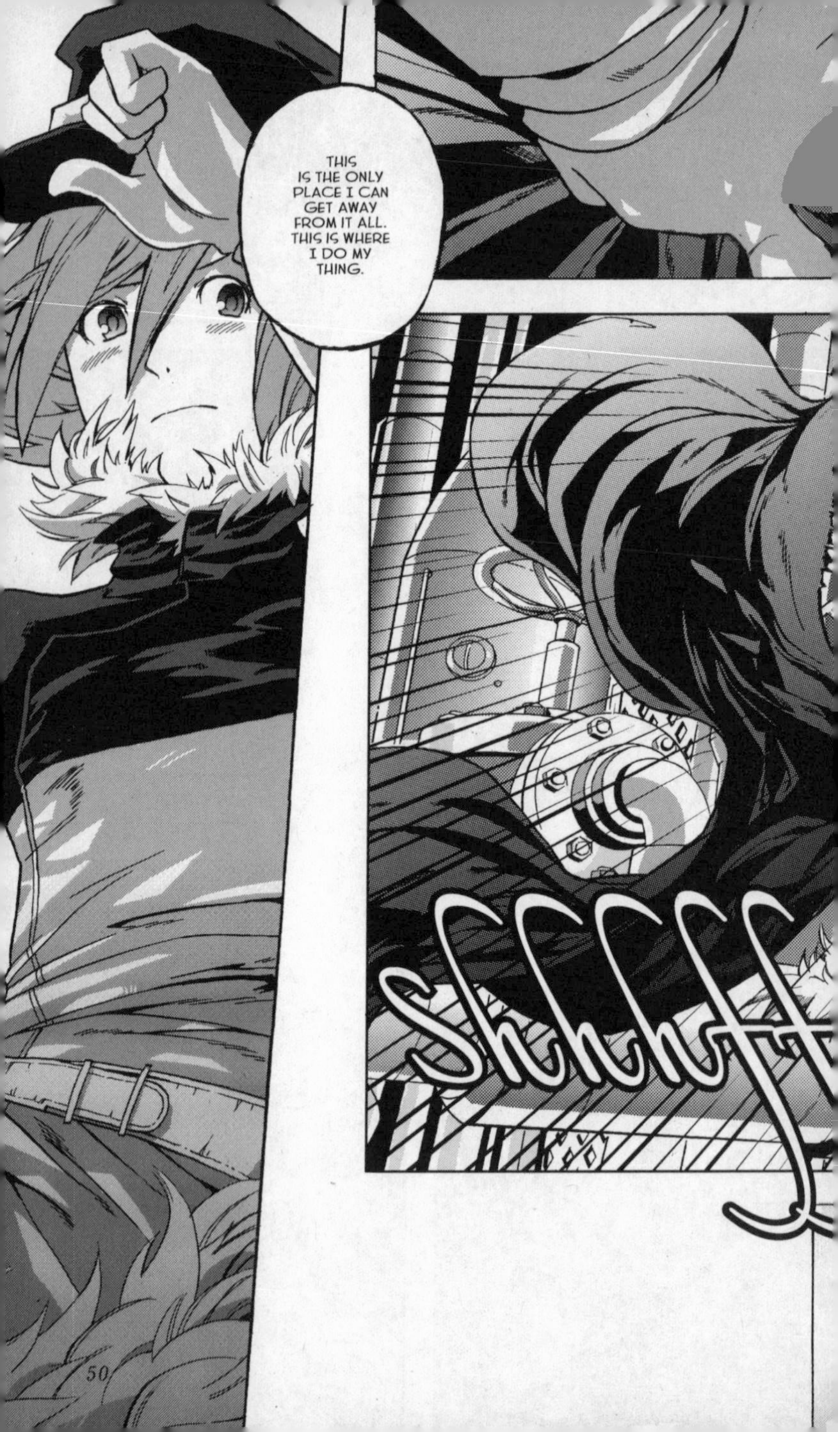
THIS IS THE ONLY PLACE I CAN GET AWAY FROM IT ALL. THIS IS WHERE I DO MY THING.
SHHHFF

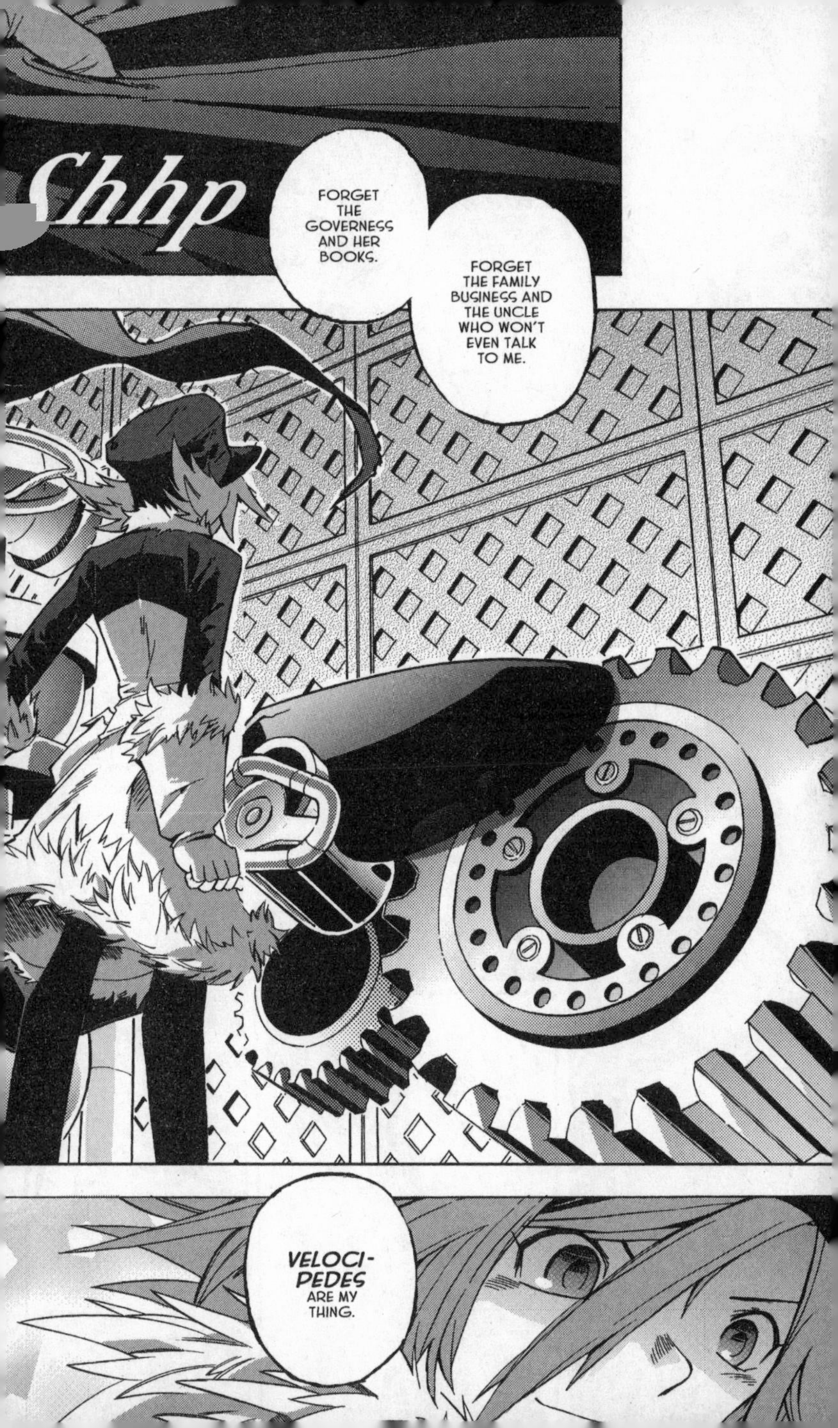
Chhp
FORGET THE GOVERNESS AND HER BOOKS.
FORGET THE FAMILY BUSINESS AND THE UNCLE WHO WON'T EVEN TALK TO ME.
VELOCI-PEDES ARE MY THING.

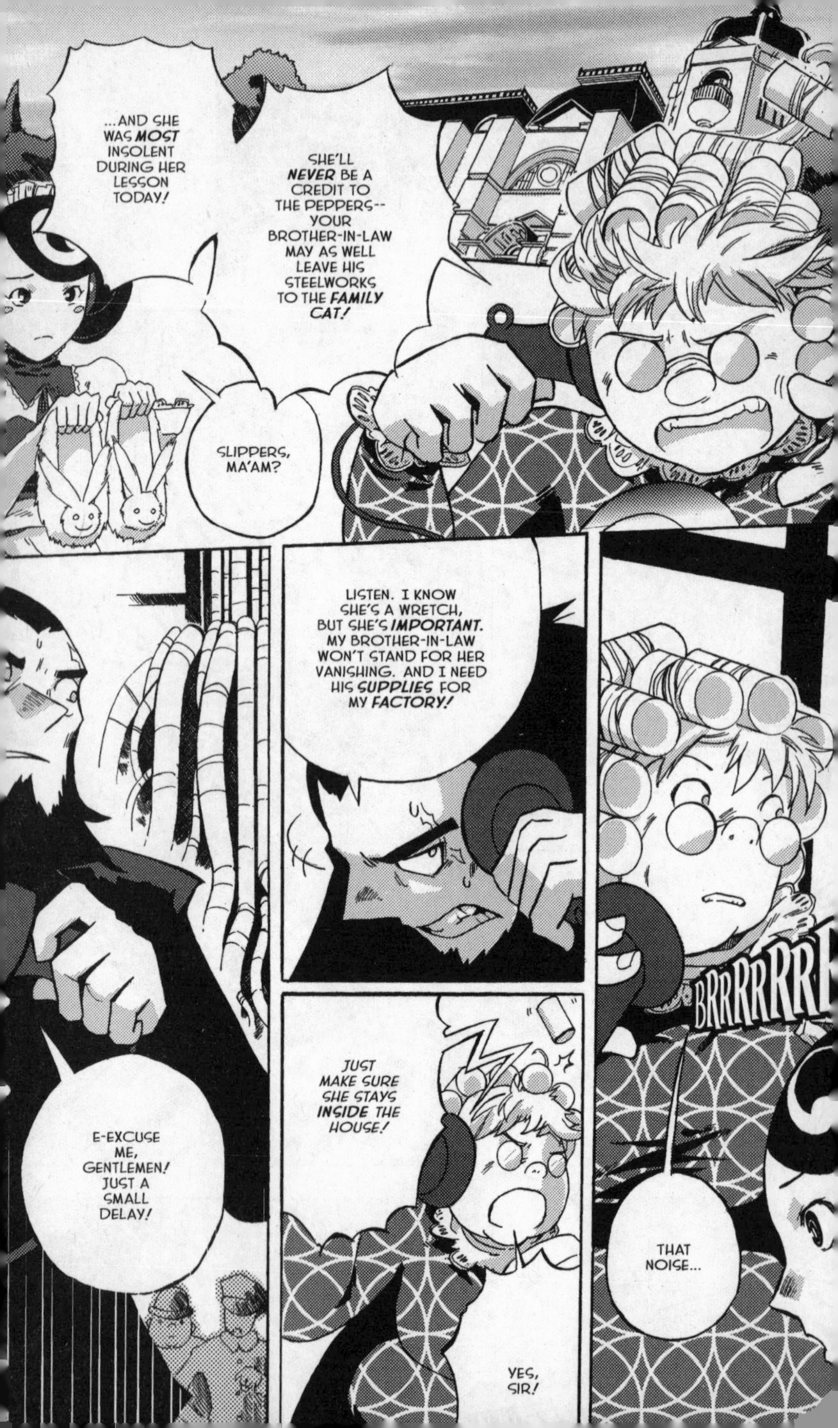
...AND SHE WAS MOST INSOLENT DURING HER LESSON TODAY!
SHE'LL NEVER BE A CREDIT TO THE PEPPERS-- YOUR BROTHER-IN-LAW MAY AS WELL LEAVE HIS STEELWORKS TO THE FAMILY CAT!
SLIPPERS, MA'AM?
E-EXCUSE ME, GENTLEMEN! JUST A SMALL DELAY!
LISTEN. I KNOW SHE'S A WRETCH, BUT SHE'S IMPORTANT. MY BROTHER-IN-LAW WON'T STAND FOR HER VANISHING. AND I NEED HIS SUPPLIES FOR MY FACTORY!
JUST MAKE SURE SHE STAYS INSIDE THE HOUSE!
YES, SIR!
BRRRRRRR
THAT NOISE...

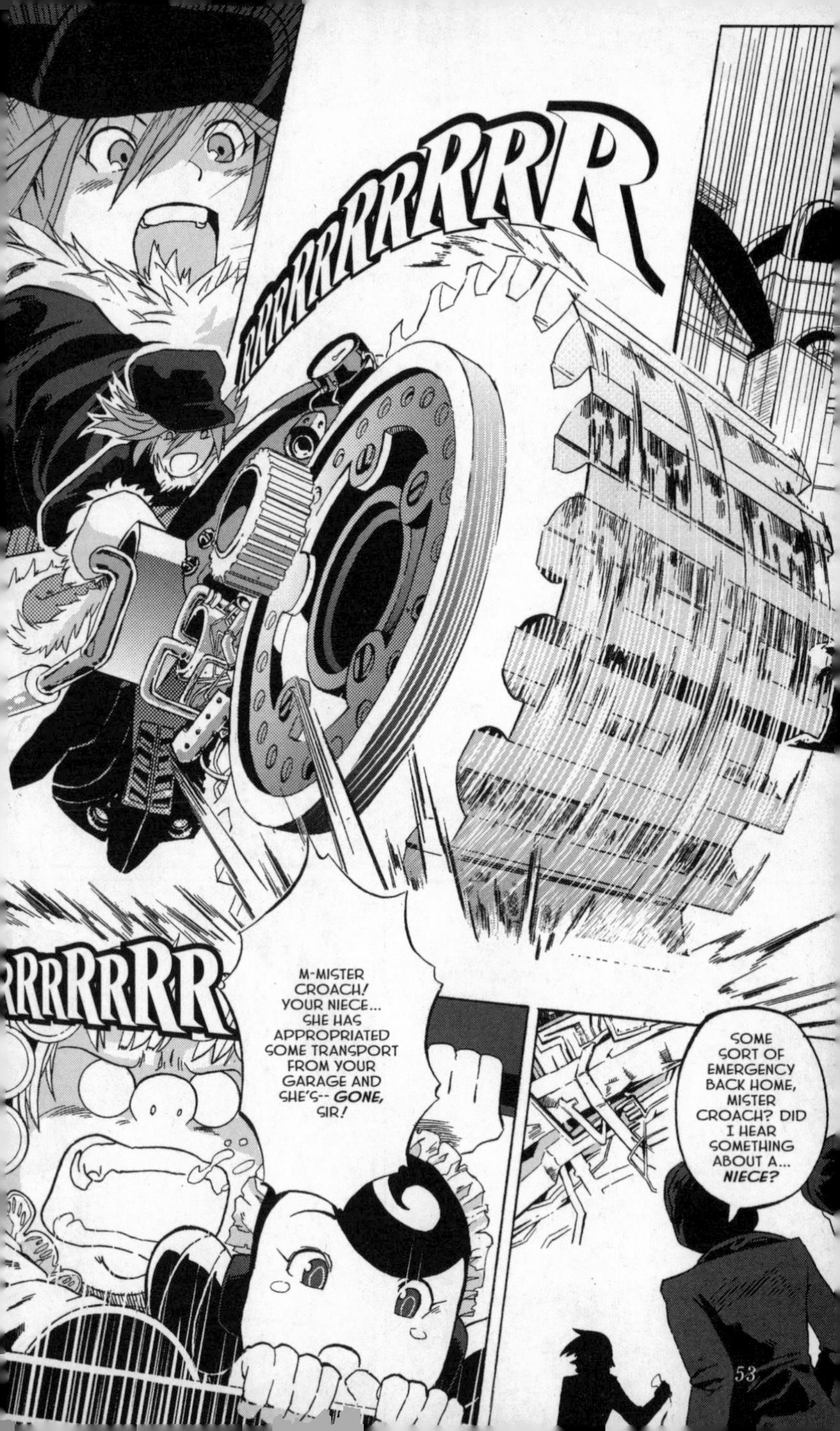

RRRRRRRRRRRRR
RRRRRRR
M-MISTER CROACH! YOUR NIECE... SHE HAS APPROPRIATED SOME TRANSPORT FROM YOUR GARAGE AND SHE'S-- *GONE,* SIR!
SOME SORT OF EMERGENCY BACK HOME, MISTER CROACH? DID I HEAR SOMETHING ABOUT A... ***NIECE?***

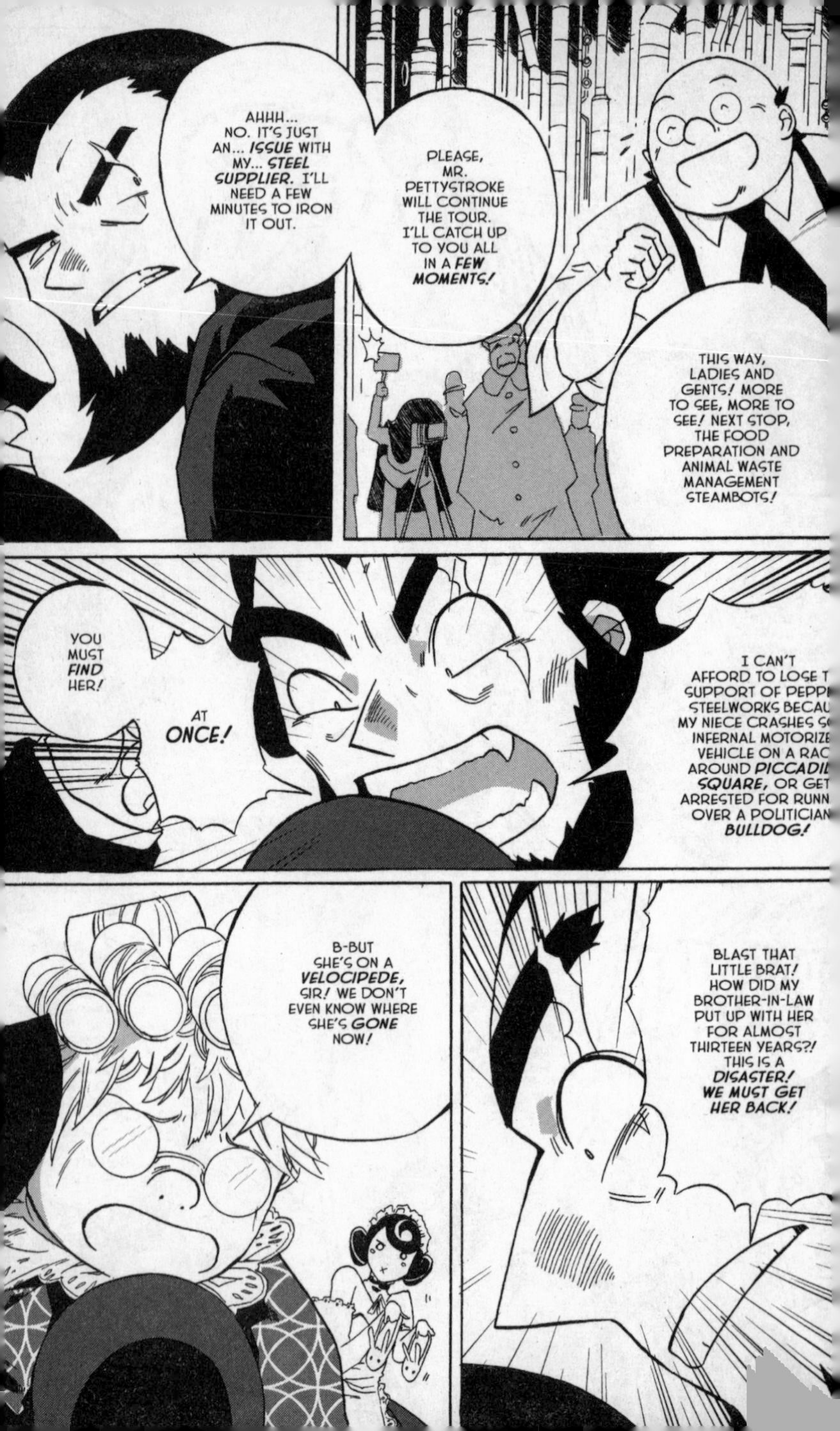
AHHH... NO. IT'S JUST AN... **ISSUE** WITH MY... **STEEL SUPPLIER.** I'LL NEED A FEW MINUTES TO IRON IT OUT.
PLEASE, MR. PETTYSTROKE WILL CONTINUE THE TOUR. I'LL CATCH UP TO YOU ALL IN A **FEW MOMENTS!**
THIS WAY, LADIES AND GENTS! MORE TO SEE, MORE TO SEE! NEXT STOP, THE FOOD PREPARATION AND ANIMAL WASTE MANAGEMENT STEAMBOTS!
YOU MUST **FIND** HER!
AT **ONCE!**
I CAN'T AFFORD TO LOSE T SUPPORT OF PEPP STEELWORKS BECAU MY NIECE CRASHES SO INFERNAL MOTORIZE VEHICLE ON A RAC AROUND **PICCADIL SQUARE,** OR GET ARRESTED FOR RUNN OVER A POLITICIAN **BULLDOG!**
B-BUT SHE'S ON A **VELOCIPEDE,** SIR! WE DON'T EVEN KNOW WHERE SHE'S **GONE** NOW!
BLAST THAT LITTLE BRAT! HOW DID MY BROTHER-IN-LAW PUT UP WITH HER FOR ALMOST THIRTEEN YEARS?! THIS IS A **DISASTER! WE MUST GET HER BACK!**

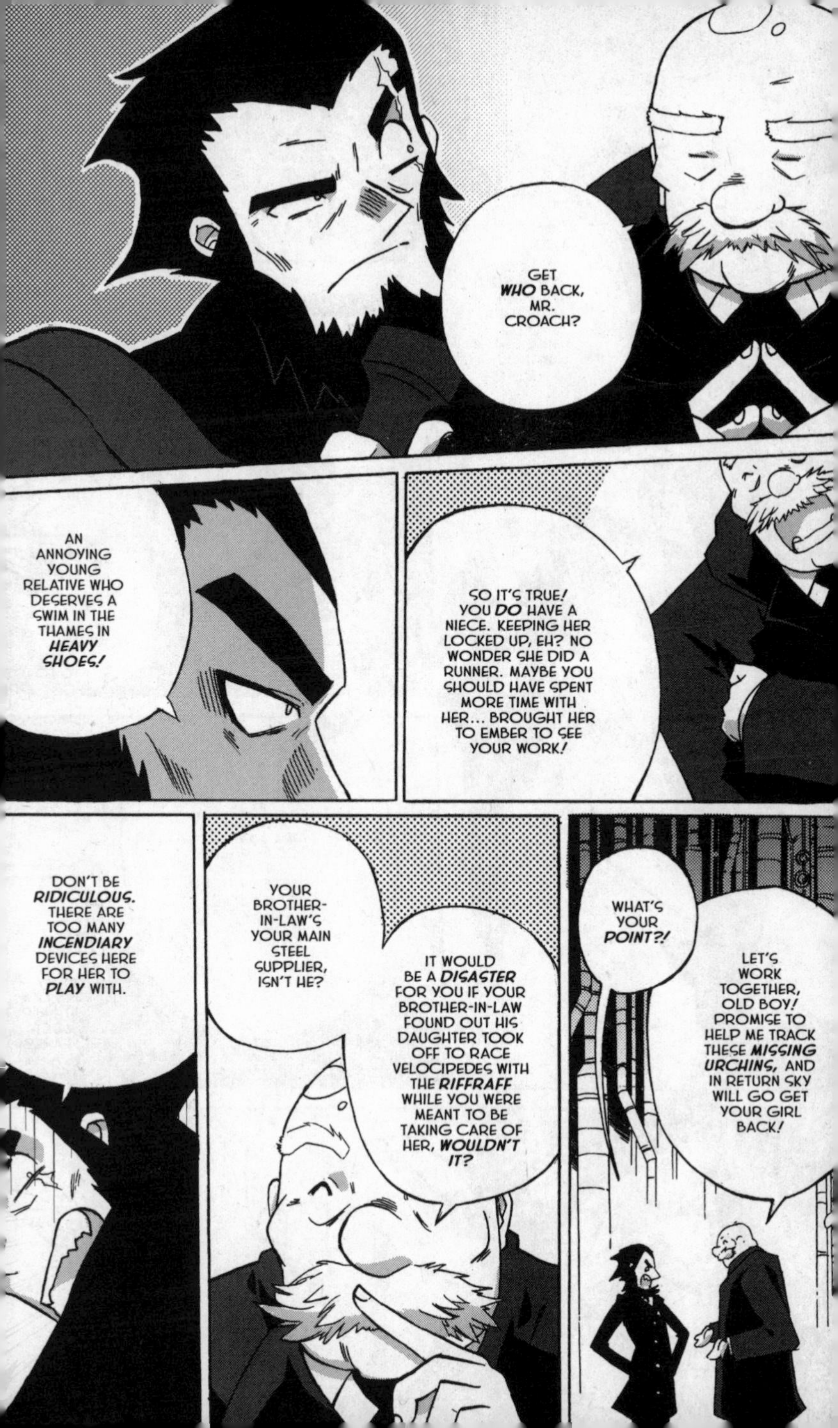

GET ***WHO*** BACK, MR. CROACH?
AN ANNOYING YOUNG RELATIVE WHO DESERVES A SWIM IN THE THAMES IN ***HEAVY SHOES!***
SO IT'S TRUE! YOU ***DO*** HAVE A NIECE. KEEPING HER LOCKED UP, EH? NO WONDER SHE DID A RUNNER. MAYBE YOU SHOULD HAVE SPENT MORE TIME WITH HER... BROUGHT HER TO EMBER TO SEE YOUR WORK!
DON'T BE ***RIDICULOUS.*** THERE ARE TOO MANY ***INCENDIARY*** DEVICES HERE FOR HER TO ***PLAY*** WITH.
YOUR BROTHER-IN-LAW'S YOUR MAIN STEEL SUPPLIER, ISN'T HE?
IT WOULD BE A ***DISASTER*** FOR YOU IF YOUR BROTHER-IN-LAW FOUND OUT HIS DAUGHTER TOOK OFF TO RACE VELOCIPEDES WITH THE ***RIFFRAFF*** WHILE YOU WERE MEANT TO BE TAKING CARE OF HER, ***WOULDN'T IT?***
WHAT'S YOUR ***POINT?!***
LET'S WORK TOGETHER, OLD BOY! PROMISE TO HELP ME TRACK THESE ***MISSING URCHINS,*** AND IN RETURN SKY WILL GO GET YOUR GIRL BACK!

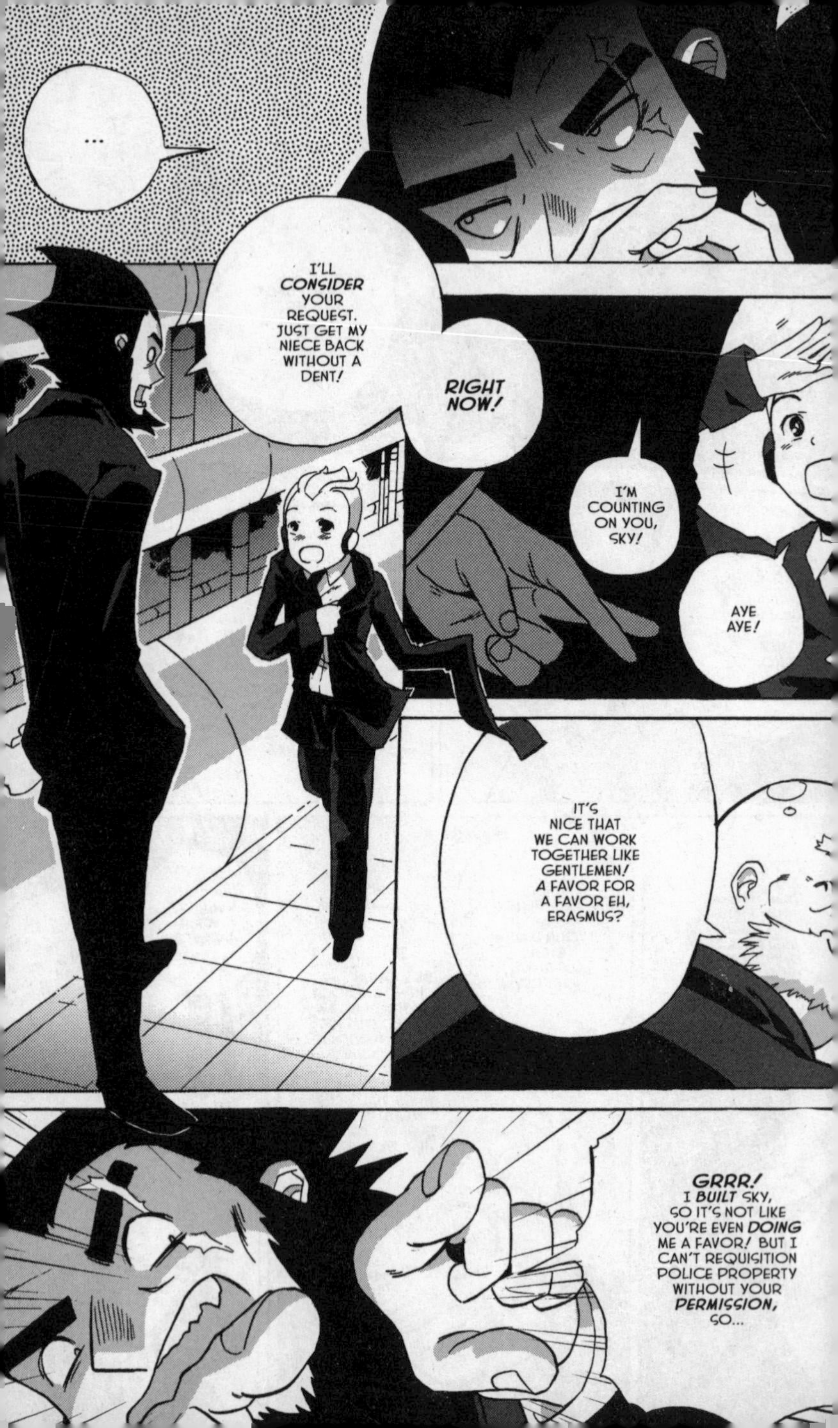
...
I'LL CONSIDER YOUR REQUEST. JUST GET MY NIECE BACK WITHOUT A DENT!
RIGHT NOW!
I'M COUNTING ON YOU, SKY!
AYE AYE!
IT'S NICE THAT WE CAN WORK TOGETHER LIKE GENTLEMEN! A FAVOR FOR A FAVOR EH, ERASMUS?
GRRR! I BUILT SKY, SO IT'S NOT LIKE YOU'RE EVEN DOING ME A FAVOR! BUT I CAN'T REQUISITION POLICE PROPERTY WITHOUT YOUR PERMISSION, SO...

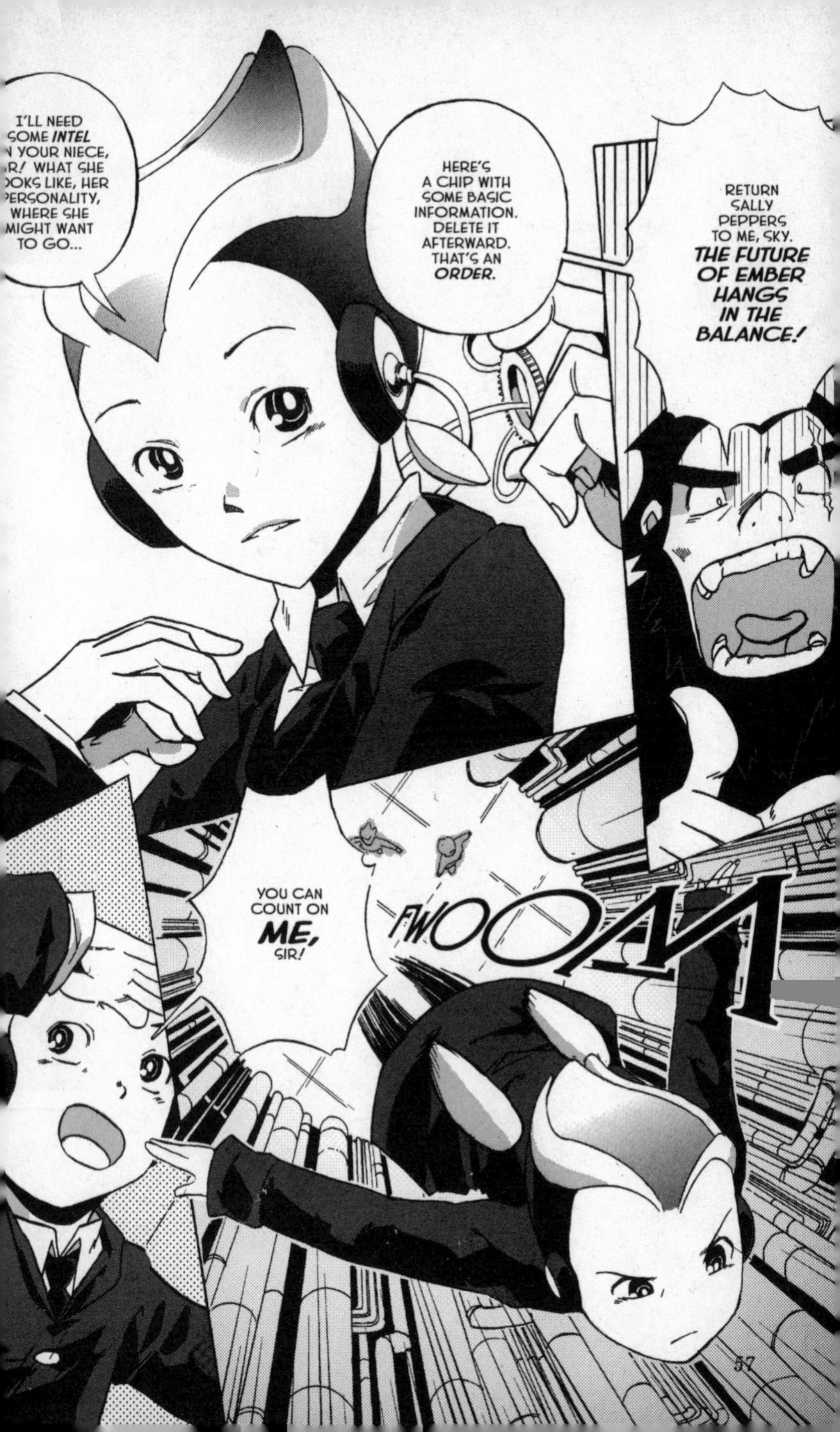
I'LL NEED SOME INTEL N YOUR NIECE, R! WHAT SHE OOKS LIKE, HER ERSONALITY, WHERE SHE MIGHT WANT TO GO...
HERE'S A CHIP WITH SOME BASIC INFORMATION. DELETE IT AFTERWARD. THAT'S AN ORDER.
RETURN SALLY PEPPERS TO ME, SKY. THE FUTURE OF EMBER HANGS IN THE BALANCE!
YOU CAN COUNT ON ME, SIR!
FWOOM

CHAPTER 3

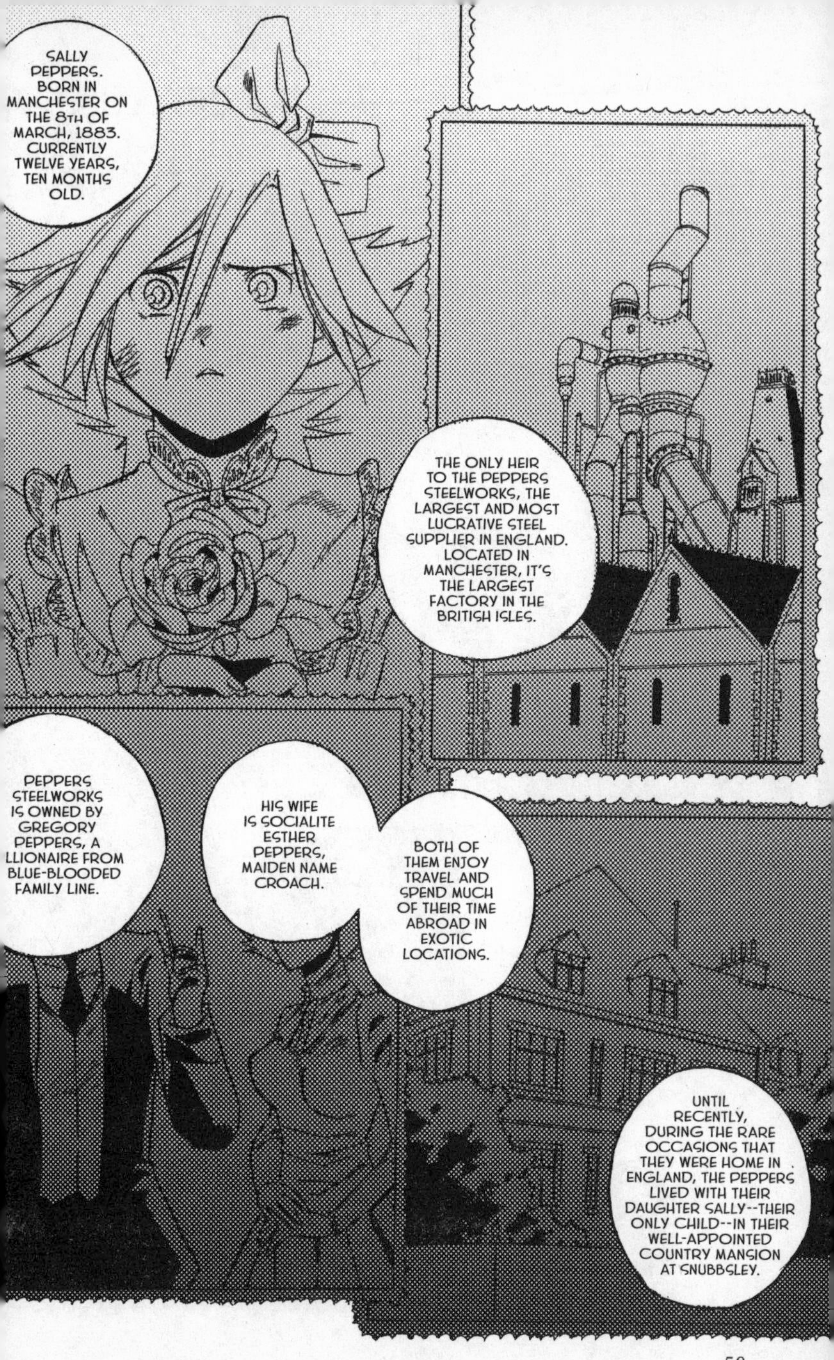
SALLY PEPPERS. BORN IN MANCHESTER ON THE 8TH OF MARCH, 1883. CURRENTLY TWELVE YEARS, TEN MONTHS OLD.
THE ONLY HEIR TO THE PEPPERS STEELWORKS, THE LARGEST AND MOST LUCRATIVE STEEL SUPPLIER IN ENGLAND. LOCATED IN MANCHESTER, IT'S THE LARGEST FACTORY IN THE BRITISH ISLES.
PEPPERS STEELWORKS IS OWNED BY GREGORY PEPPERS, A LLIONAIRE FROM BLUE-BLOODED FAMILY LINE.
HIS WIFE IS SOCIALITE ESTHER PEPPERS, MAIDEN NAME CROACH.
BOTH OF THEM ENJOY TRAVEL AND SPEND MUCH OF THEIR TIME ABROAD IN EXOTIC LOCATIONS.
UNTIL RECENTLY, DURING THE RARE OCCASIONS THAT THEY WERE HOME IN ENGLAND, THE PEPPERS LIVED WITH THEIR DAUGHTER SALLY--THEIR ONLY CHILD--IN THEIR WELL-APPOINTED COUNTRY MANSION AT SNUBBSLEY.

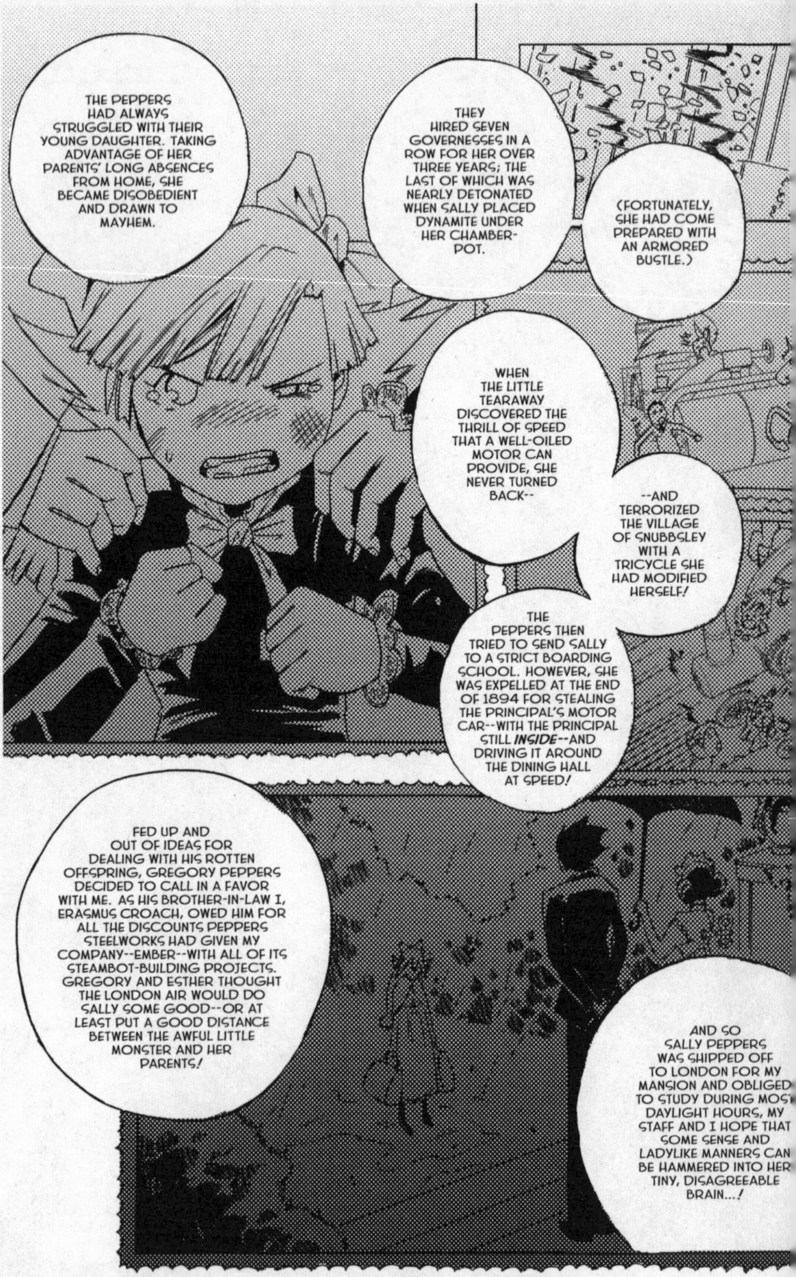
THE PEPPERS HAD ALWAYS STRUGGLED WITH THEIR YOUNG DAUGHTER. TAKING ADVANTAGE OF HER PARENTS' LONG ABSENCES FROM HOME, SHE BECAME DISOBEDIENT AND DRAWN TO MAYHEM.
THEY HIRED SEVEN GOVERNESSES IN A ROW FOR HER OVER THREE YEARS; THE LAST OF WHICH WAS NEARLY DETONATED WHEN SALLY PLACED DYNAMITE UNDER HER CHAMBER-POT.
(FORTUNATELY, SHE HAD COME PREPARED WITH AN ARMORED BUSTLE.)
WHEN THE LITTLE TEARAWAY DISCOVERED THE THRILL OF SPEED THAT A WELL-OILED MOTOR CAN PROVIDE, SHE NEVER TURNED BACK--
--AND TERRORIZED THE VILLAGE OF SNUBBSLEY WITH A TRICYCLE SHE HAD MODIFIED HERSELF!
THE PEPPERS THEN TRIED TO SEND SALLY TO A STRICT BOARDING SCHOOL. HOWEVER, SHE WAS EXPELLED AT THE END OF 1894 FOR STEALING THE PRINCIPAL'S MOTOR CAR--WITH THE PRINCIPAL STILL *INSIDE*--AND DRIVING IT AROUND THE DINING HALL AT SPEED!
FED UP AND OUT OF IDEAS FOR DEALING WITH HIS ROTTEN OFFSPRING, GREGORY PEPPERS DECIDED TO CALL IN A FAVOR WITH ME. AS HIS BROTHER-IN-LAW I, ERASMUS CROACH, OWED HIM FOR ALL THE DISCOUNTS PEPPERS STEELWORKS HAD GIVEN MY COMPANY--EMBER--WITH ALL OF ITS STEAMBOT-BUILDING PROJECTS. GREGORY AND ESTHER THOUGHT THE LONDON AIR WOULD DO SALLY SOME GOOD--OR AT LEAST PUT A GOOD DISTANCE BETWEEN THE AWFUL LITTLE MONSTER AND HER PARENTS!
AND SO SALLY PEPPERS WAS SHIPPED OFF TO LONDON FOR MY MANSION AND OBLIGED TO STUDY DURING MOST DAYLIGHT HOURS, MY STAFF AND I HOPE THAT SOME SENSE AND LADYLIKE MANNERS CAN BE HAMMERED INTO HER TINY, DISAGREEABLE BRAIN...!

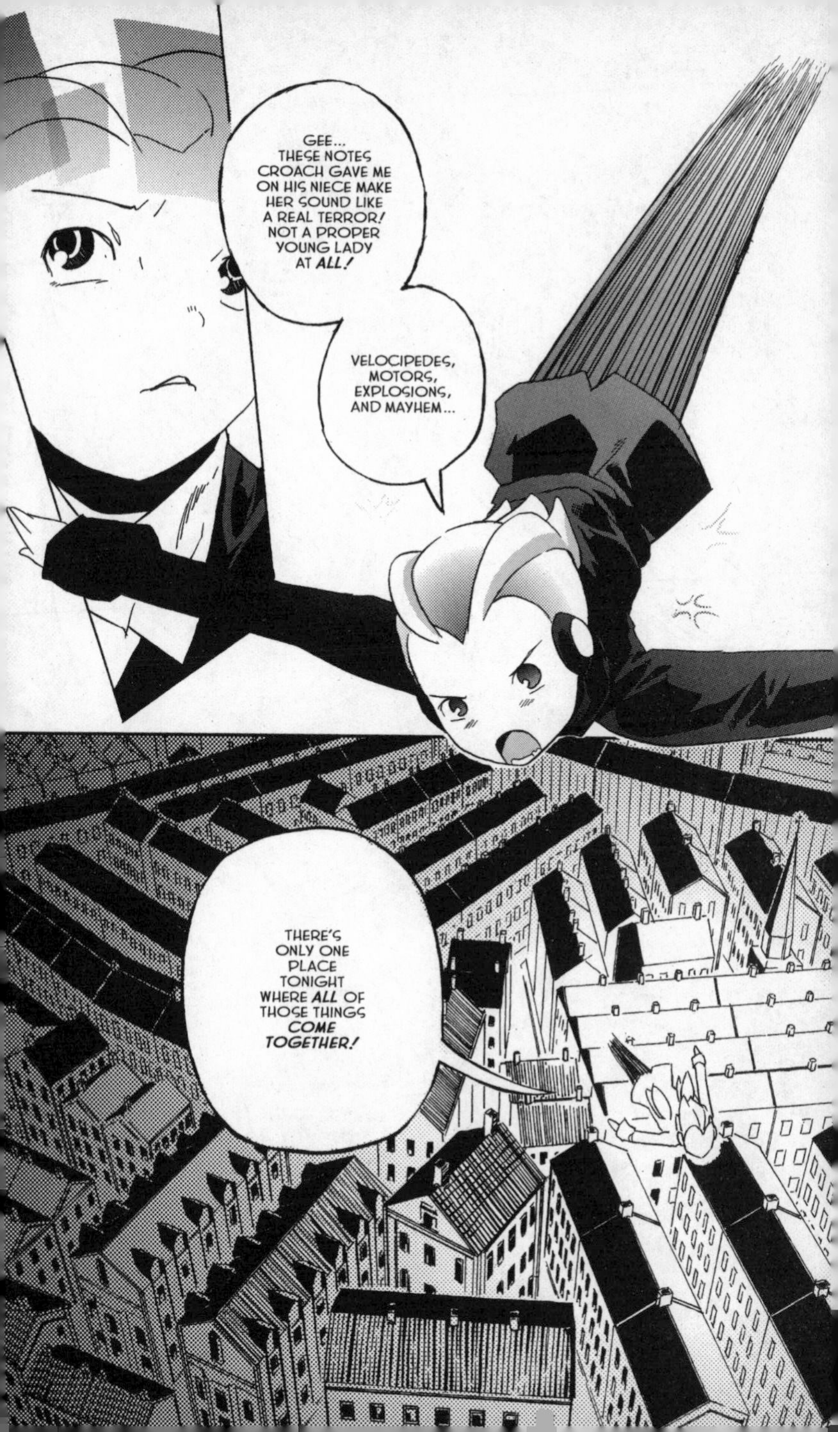
GEE... THESE NOTES CROACH GAVE ME ON HIS NIECE MAKE HER SOUND LIKE A REAL TERROR! NOT A PROPER YOUNG LADY AT *ALL!*
VELOCIPEDES, MOTORS, EXPLOSIONS, AND MAYHEM...
THERE'S ONLY ONE PLACE TONIGHT WHERE *ALL* OF THOSE THINGS *COME TOGETHER!*

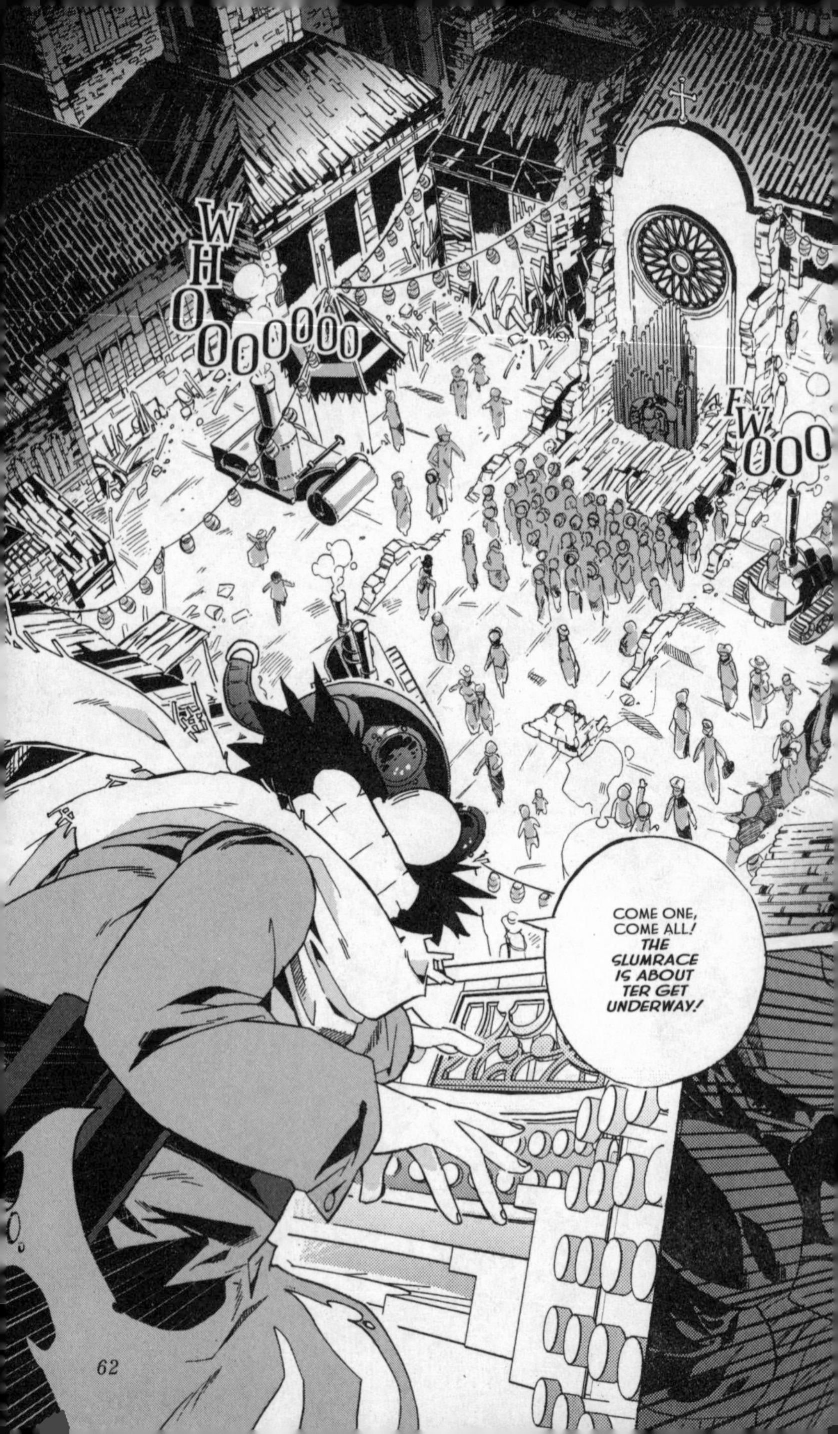
WHOOOOOOOO
FWOOO
COME ONE, COME ALL! THE SLUMRACE IS ABOUT TER GET UNDERWAY!

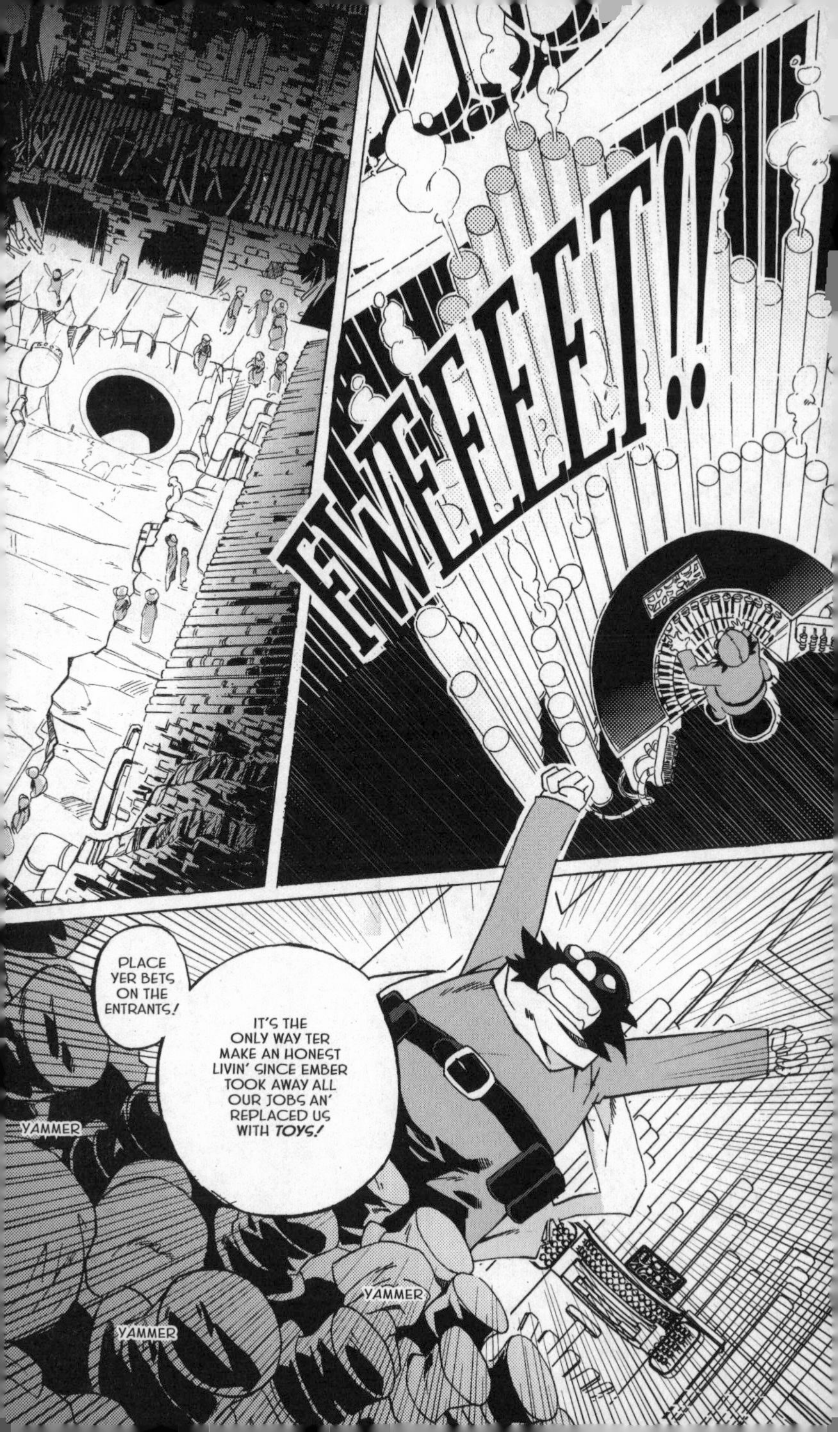

FWEEEET!!
PLACE YER BETS ON THE ENTRANTS!
IT'S THE ONLY WAY TER MAKE AN HONEST LIVIN' SINCE EMBER TOOK AWAY ALL OUR JOBS AN' REPLACED US WITH *TOYS!*
YAMMER
YAMMER
YAMMER

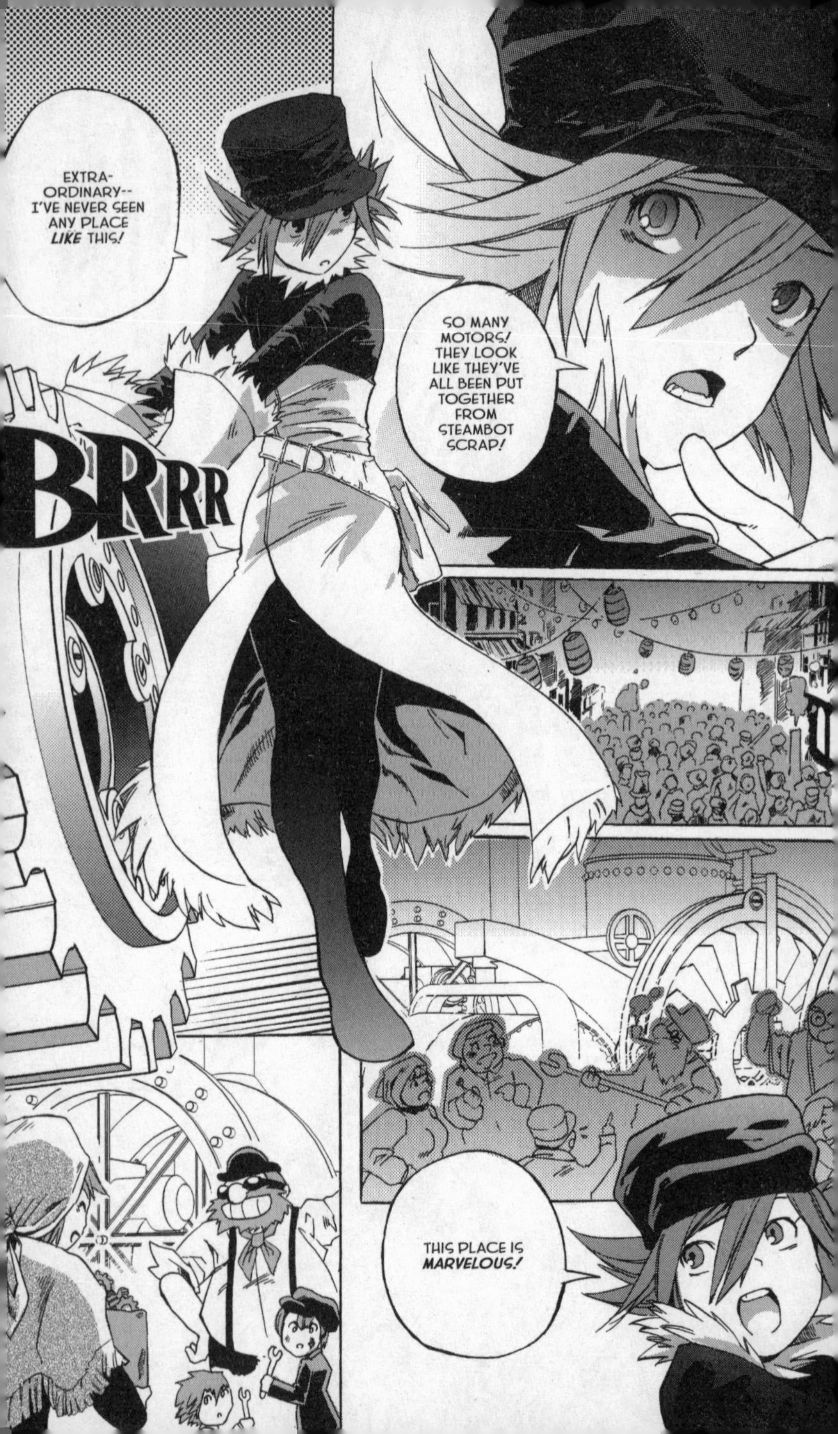
EXTRA-ORDINARY-- I'VE NEVER SEEN ANY PLACE *LIKE* THIS!
BRRRR
SO MANY MOTORS! THEY LOOK LIKE THEY'VE ALL BEEN PUT TOGETHER FROM STEAMBOT SCRAP!
THIS PLACE IS *MARVELOUS!*

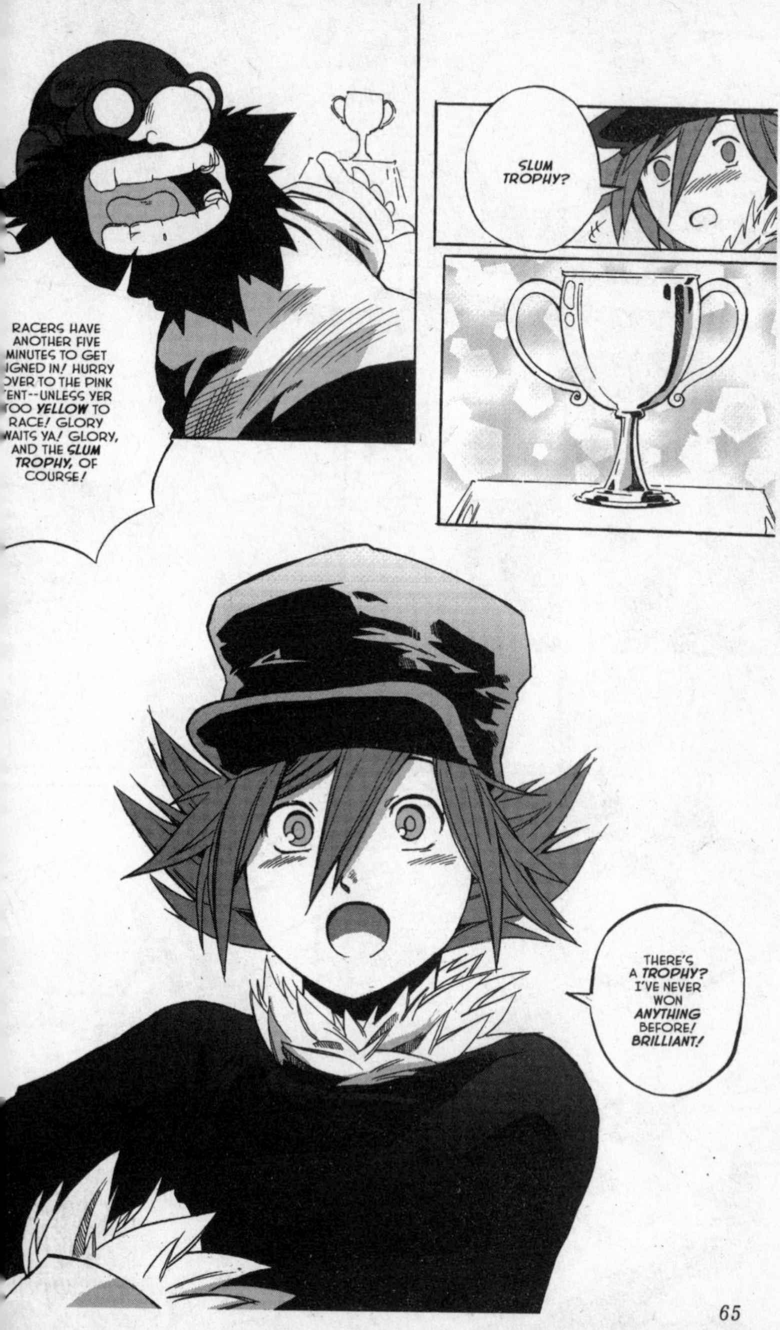
RACERS HAVE ANOTHER FIVE MINUTES TO GET SIGNED IN! HURRY OVER TO THE PINK TENT--UNLESS YER TOO YELLOW TO RACE! GLORY WAITS YA! GLORY, AND THE SLUM TROPHY, OF COURSE!
SLUM TROPHY?
THERE'S A TROPHY? I'VE NEVER WON ANYTHING BEFORE! BRILLIANT!

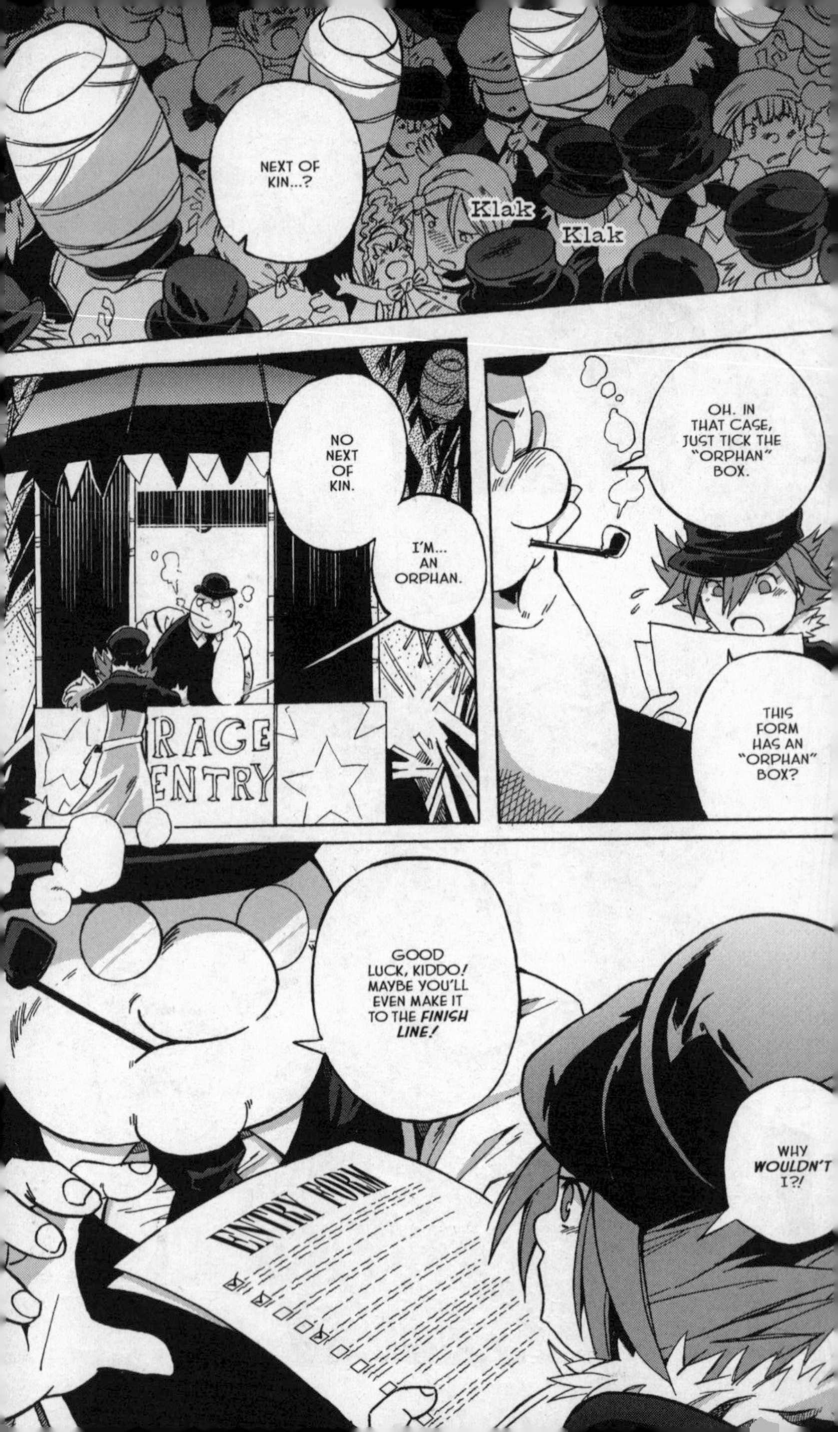
NEXT OF KIN...?
Klak
Klak
NO NEXT OF KIN.
I'M... AN ORPHAN.
RACE ENTRY
OH. IN THAT CASE, JUST TICK THE "ORPHAN" BOX.
THIS FORM HAS AN "ORPHAN" BOX?
GOOD LUCK, KIDDO! MAYBE YOU'LL EVEN MAKE IT TO THE *FINISH LINE!*
WHY *WOULDN'T* I?!
ENTRY FORM

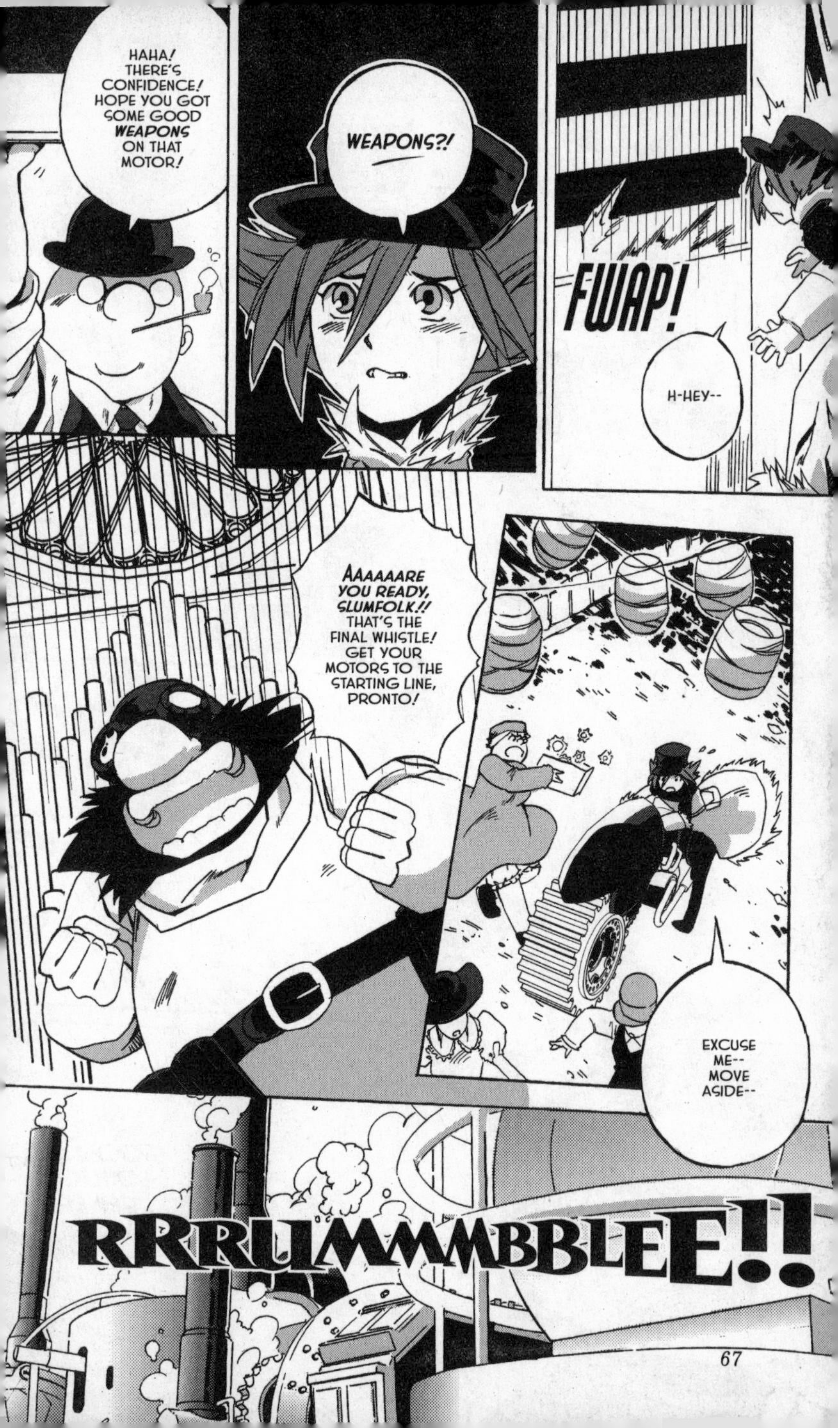
HAHA! THERE'S CONFIDENCE! HOPE YOU GOT SOME GOOD WEAPONS ON THAT MOTOR!
WEAPONS?!
FWAP!
H-HEY--
AAAAAARE YOU READY, SLUMFOLK!! THAT'S THE FINAL WHISTLE! GET YOUR MOTORS TO THE STARTING LINE, PRONTO!
EXCUSE ME-- MOVE ASIDE--
RRRUMMMBBLEE!!

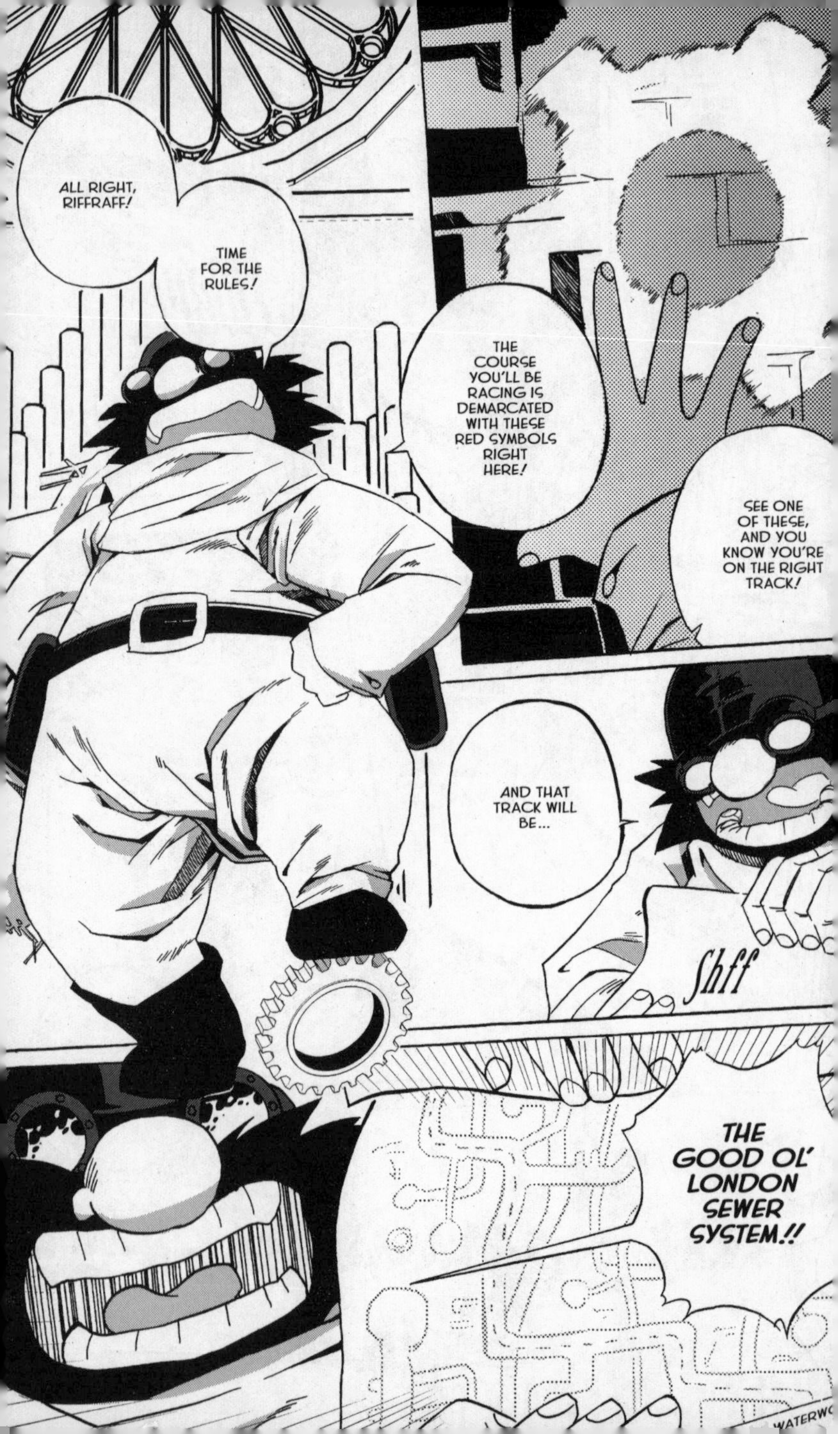

ALL RIGHT, RIFFRAFF!
TIME FOR THE RULES!
THE COURSE YOU'LL BE RACING IS DEMARCATED WITH THESE RED SYMBOLS RIGHT HERE!
SEE ONE OF THESE, AND YOU KNOW YOU'RE ON THE RIGHT TRACK!
AND THAT TRACK WILL BE...
Shff
THE GOOD OL' LONDON SEWER SYSTEM!!
WATERWO

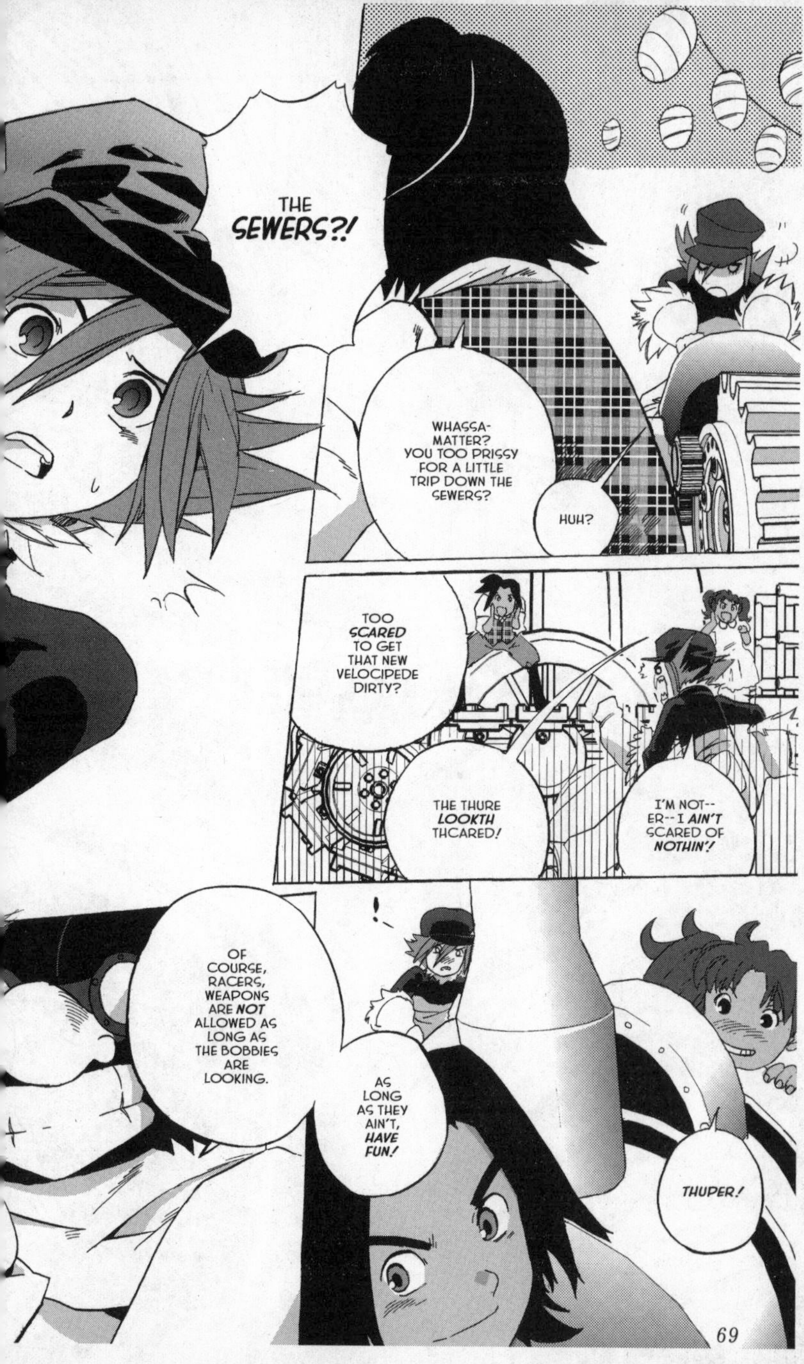
THE SEWERS?!
WHASSA-MATTER? YOU TOO PRISSY FOR A LITTLE TRIP DOWN THE SEWERS?
HUH?
TOO SCARED TO GET THAT NEW VELOCIPEDE DIRTY?
THE THURE LOOKTH THCARED!
I'M NOT-- ER-- I AIN'T SCARED OF NOTHIN'!
OF COURSE, RACERS, WEAPONS ARE NOT ALLOWED AS LONG AS THE BOBBIES ARE LOOKING.
!
AS LONG AS THEY AIN'T, HAVE FUN!
THUPER!

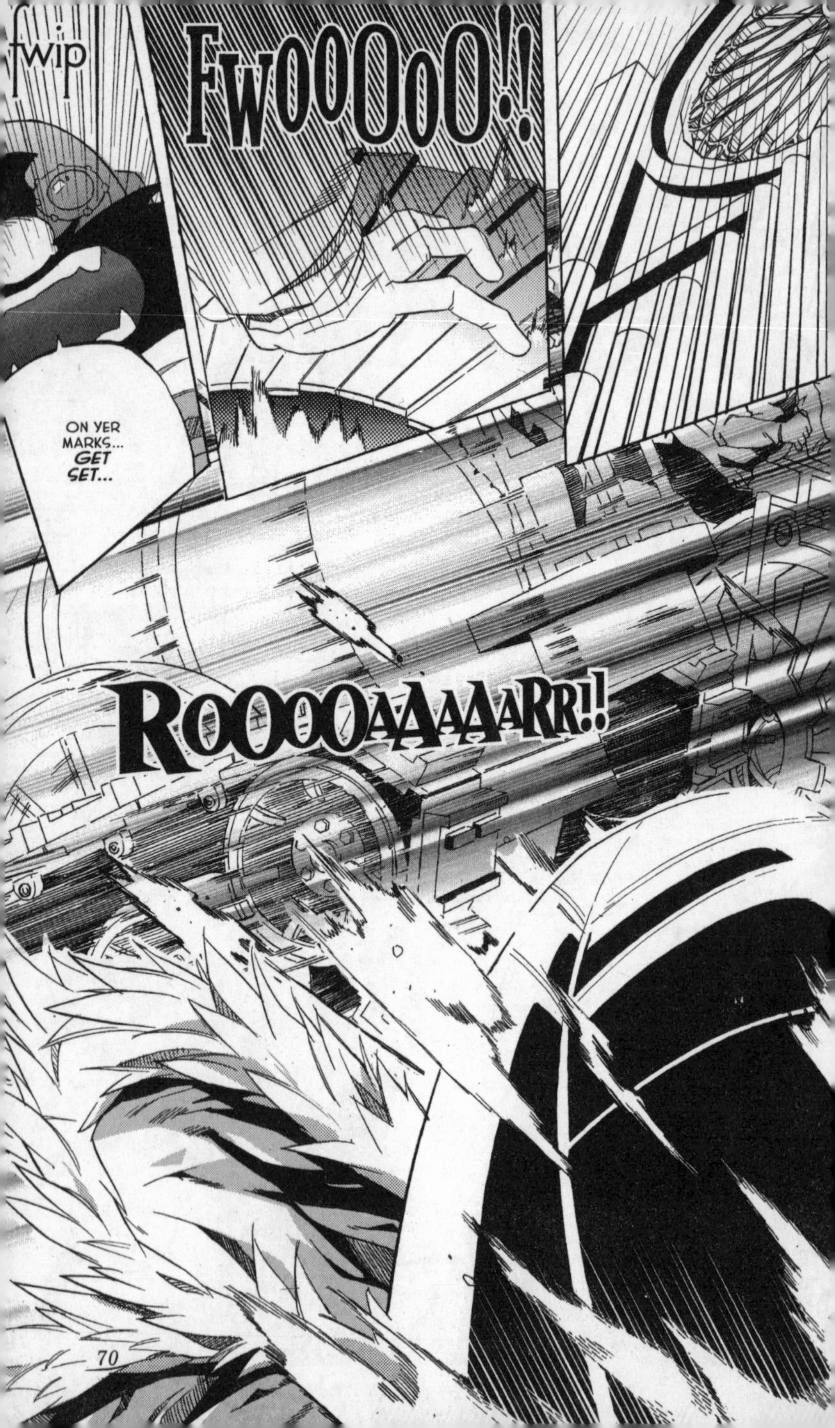
fwip
FWOOOOOO!!
ON YER MARKS... GET SET...
ROOOOAAAAARR!!

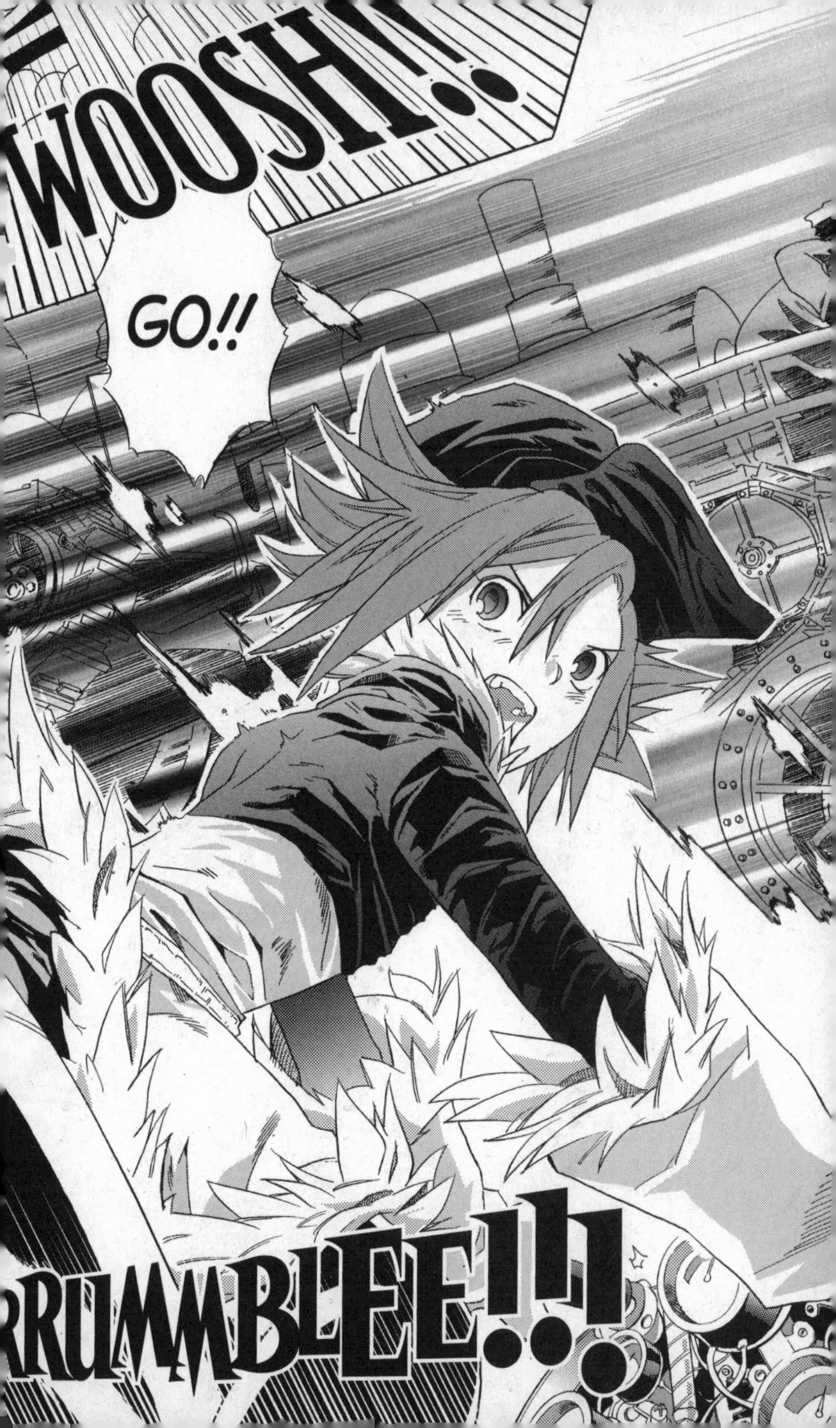
WOOSH!!
GO!!
RUMMBLEE!!!

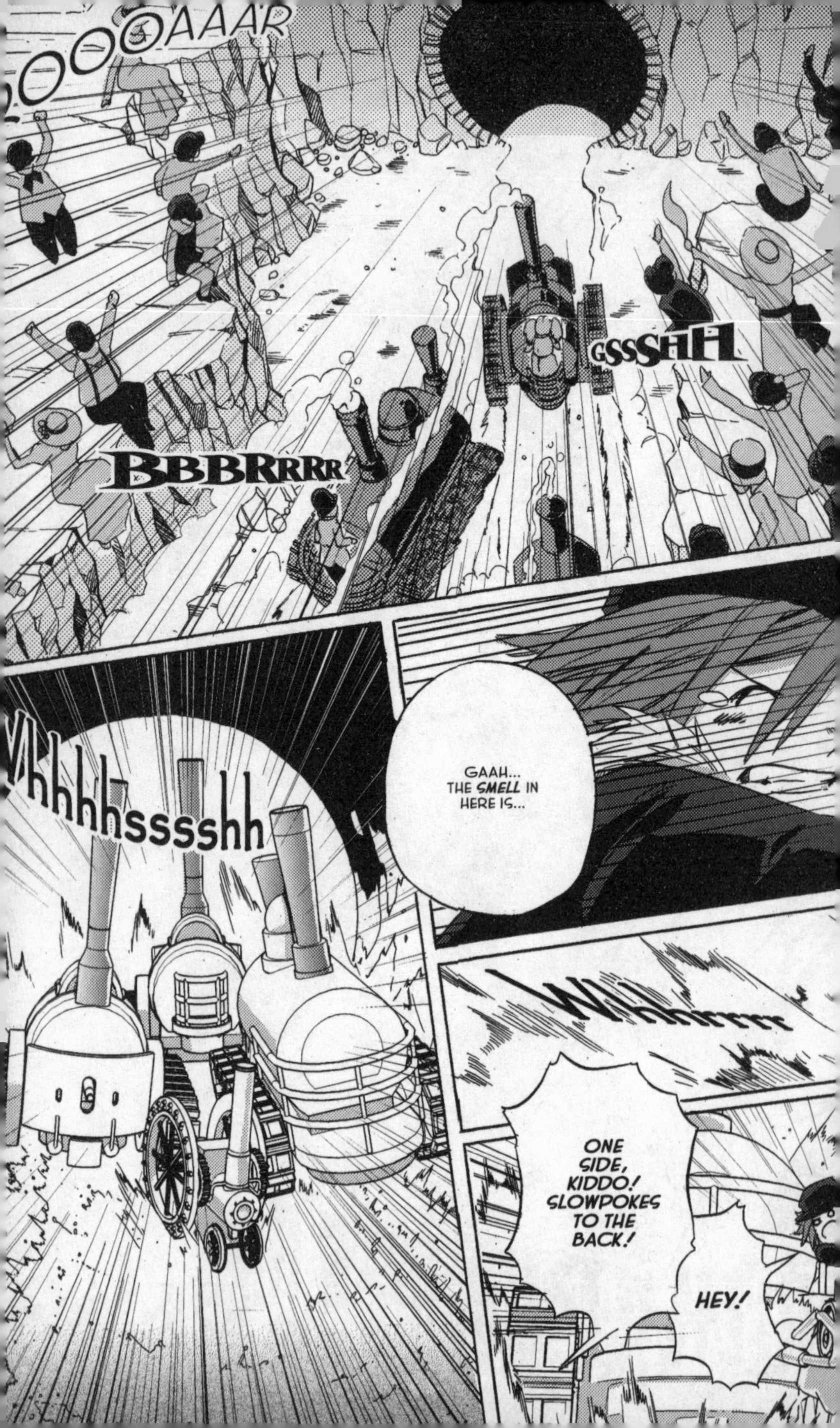

OOOOAAAR
GSSSHH
BBBRRRR
Whhhhhssssshh
GAAH... THE *SMELL* IN HERE IS...
Whhrrrr
ONE SIDE, KIDDO! SLOWPOKES TO THE BACK!
HEY!

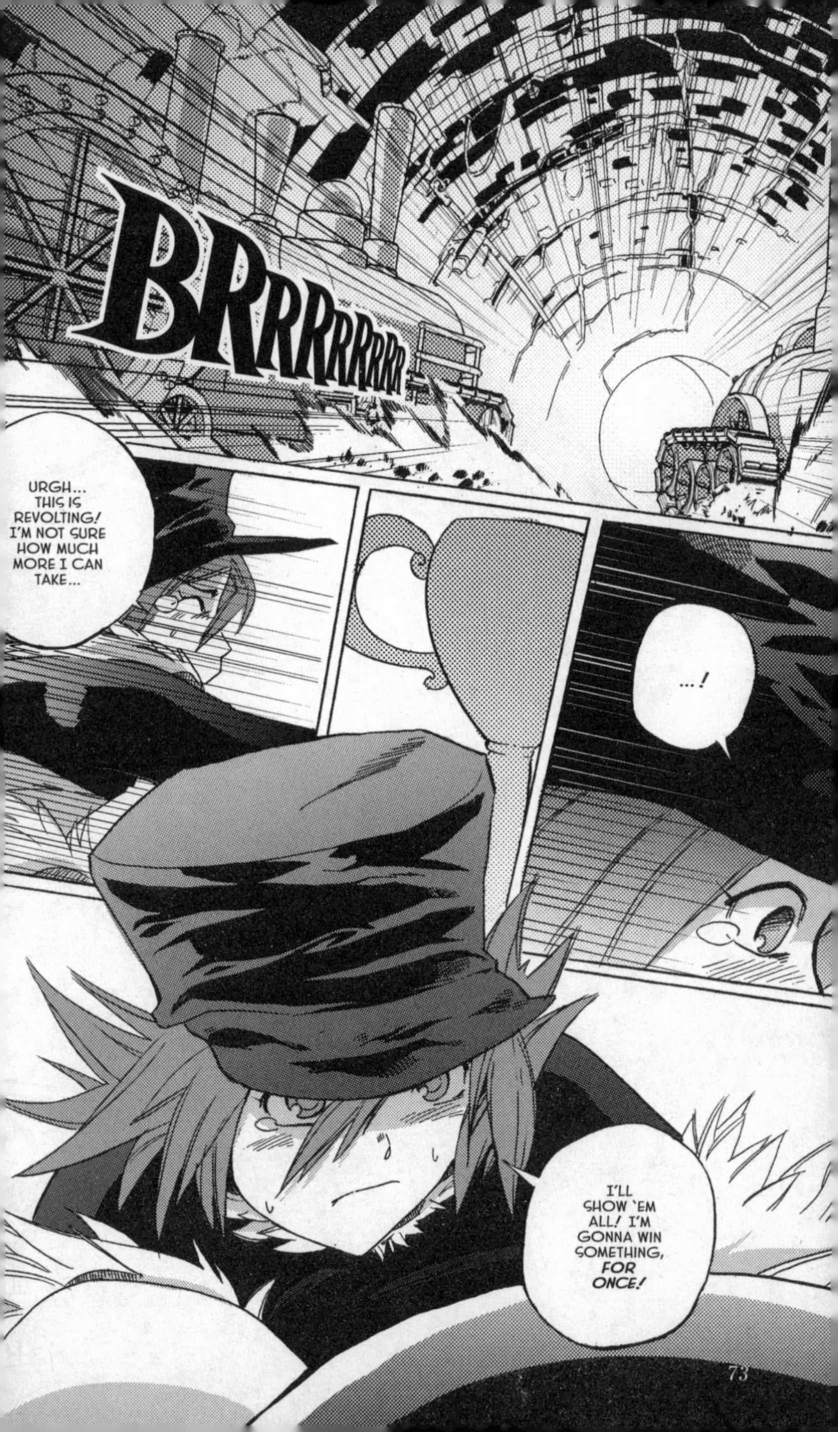

BRRRRRRRRR
URGH... THIS IS REVOLTING! I'M NOT SURE HOW MUCH MORE I CAN TAKE...
...!
I'LL SHOW 'EM ALL! I'M GONNA WIN SOMETHING, **FOR ONCE!**

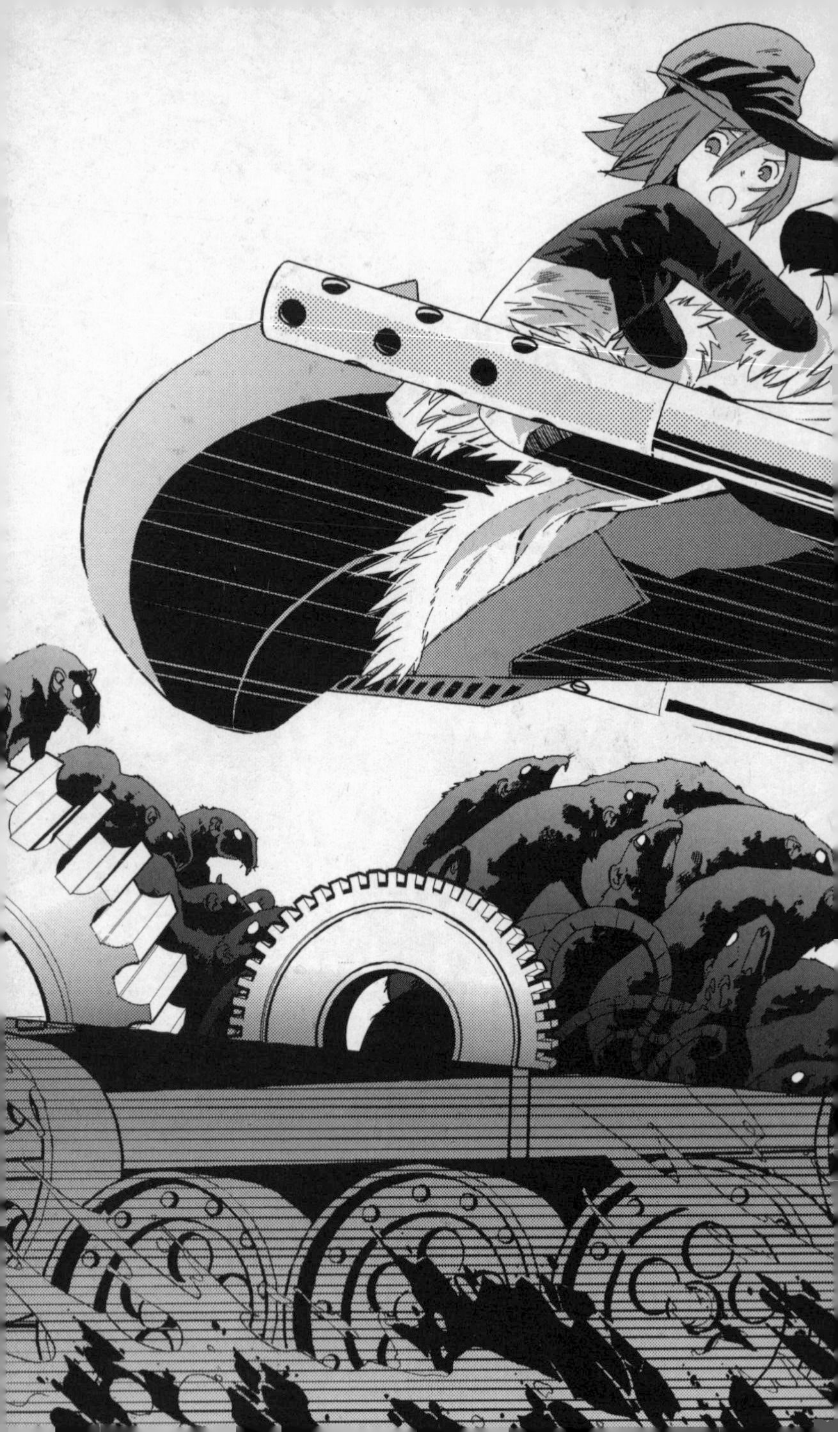

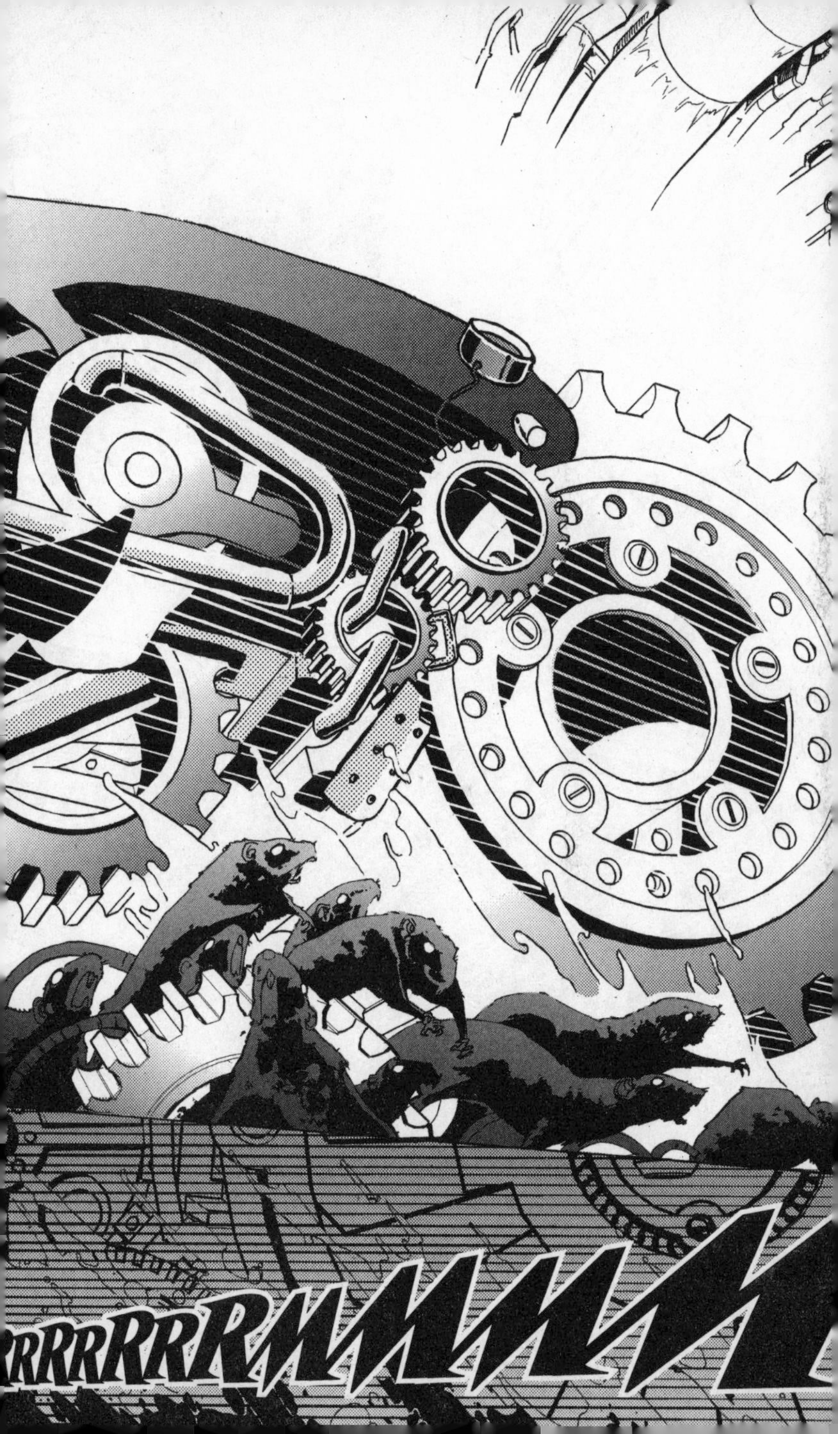
RRRRRRRRWWWWW

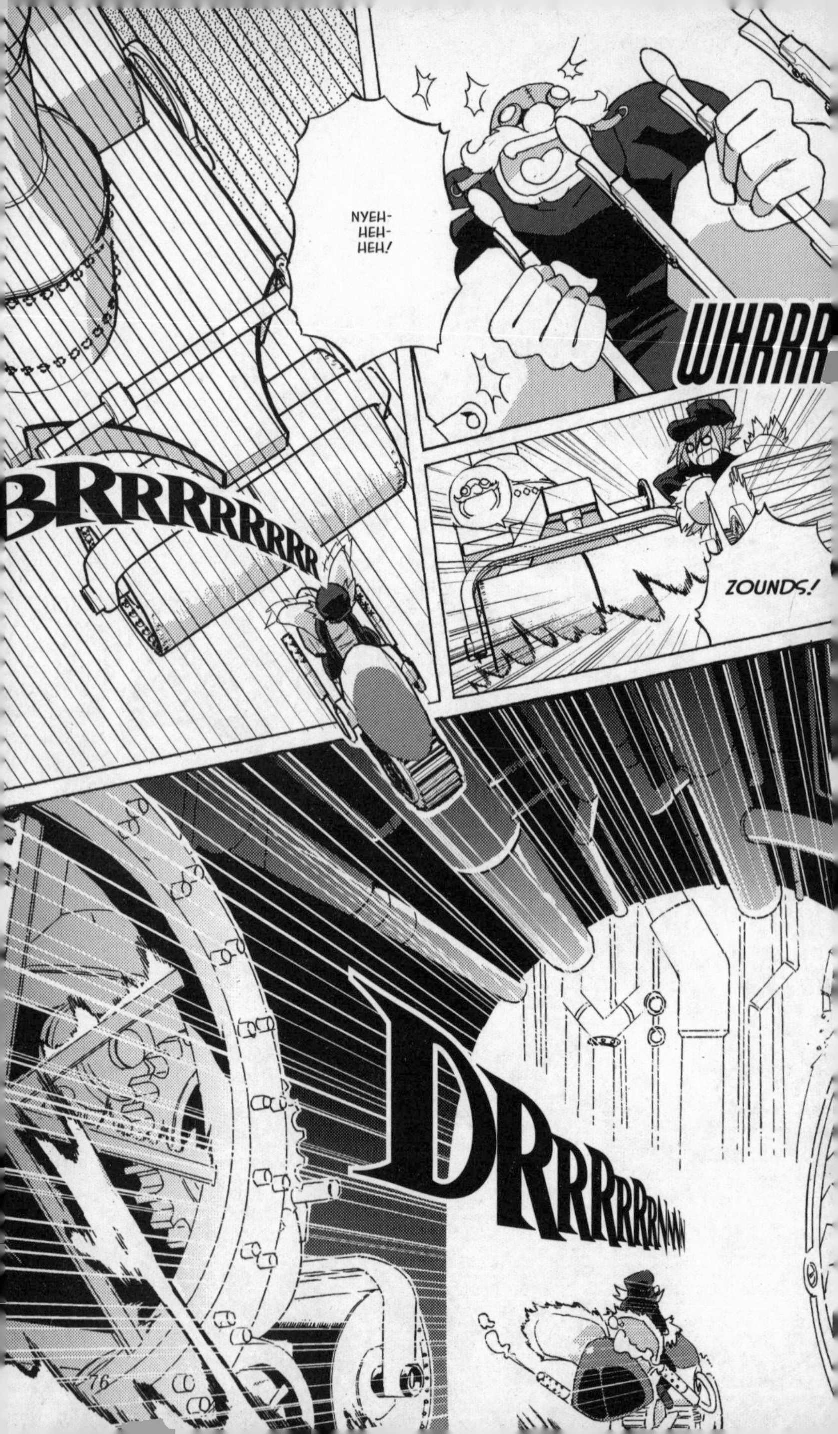
NYEH-
HEH-
HEH!
BRRRRRRRRR
WHRRR
ZOUNDS!
DRRRRRRRNNN

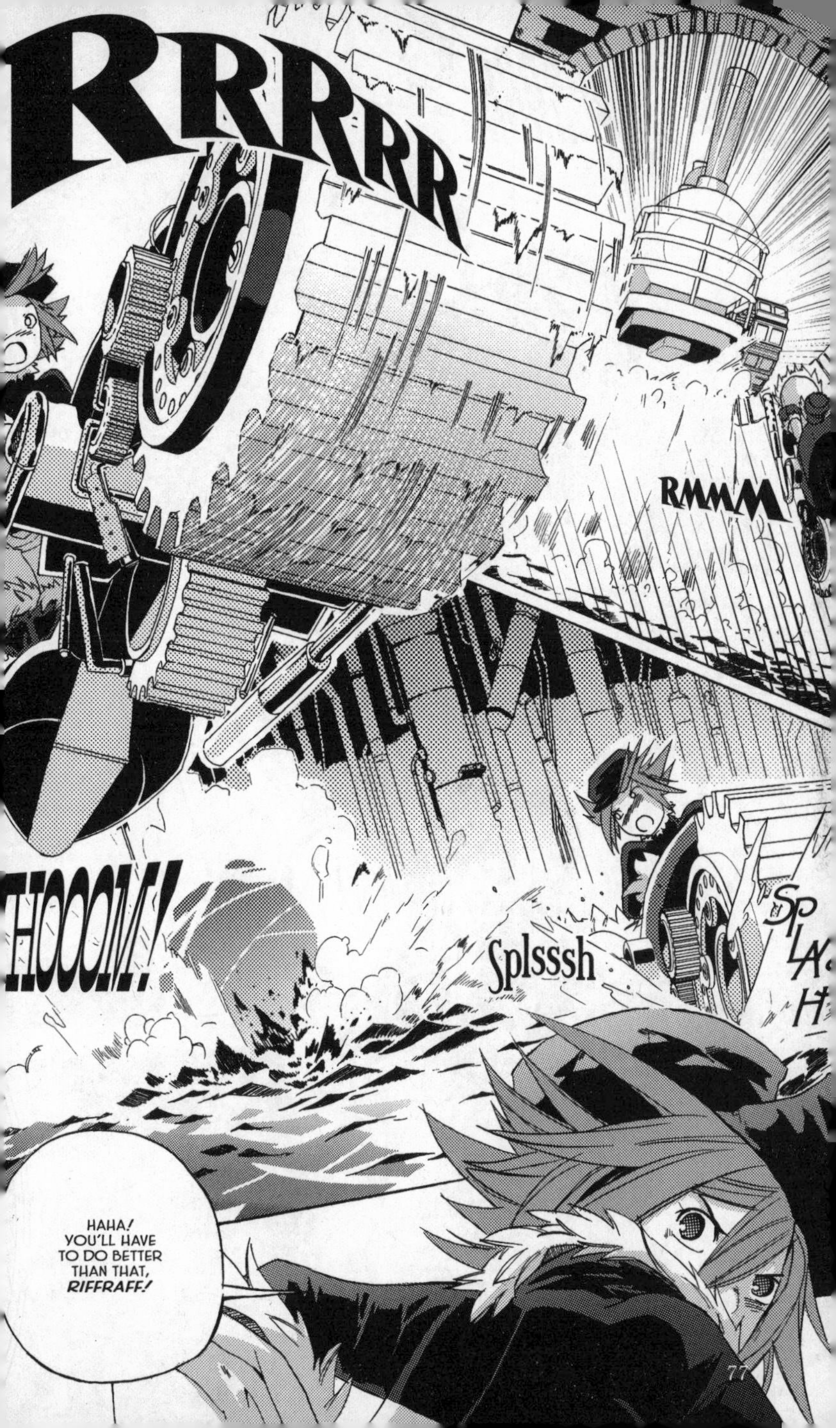
RRRRRR
RMMM
THOOOM!
Splsssh
SPLASH
HAHA! YOU'LL HAVE TO DO BETTER THAN THAT, ***RIFFRAFF!***

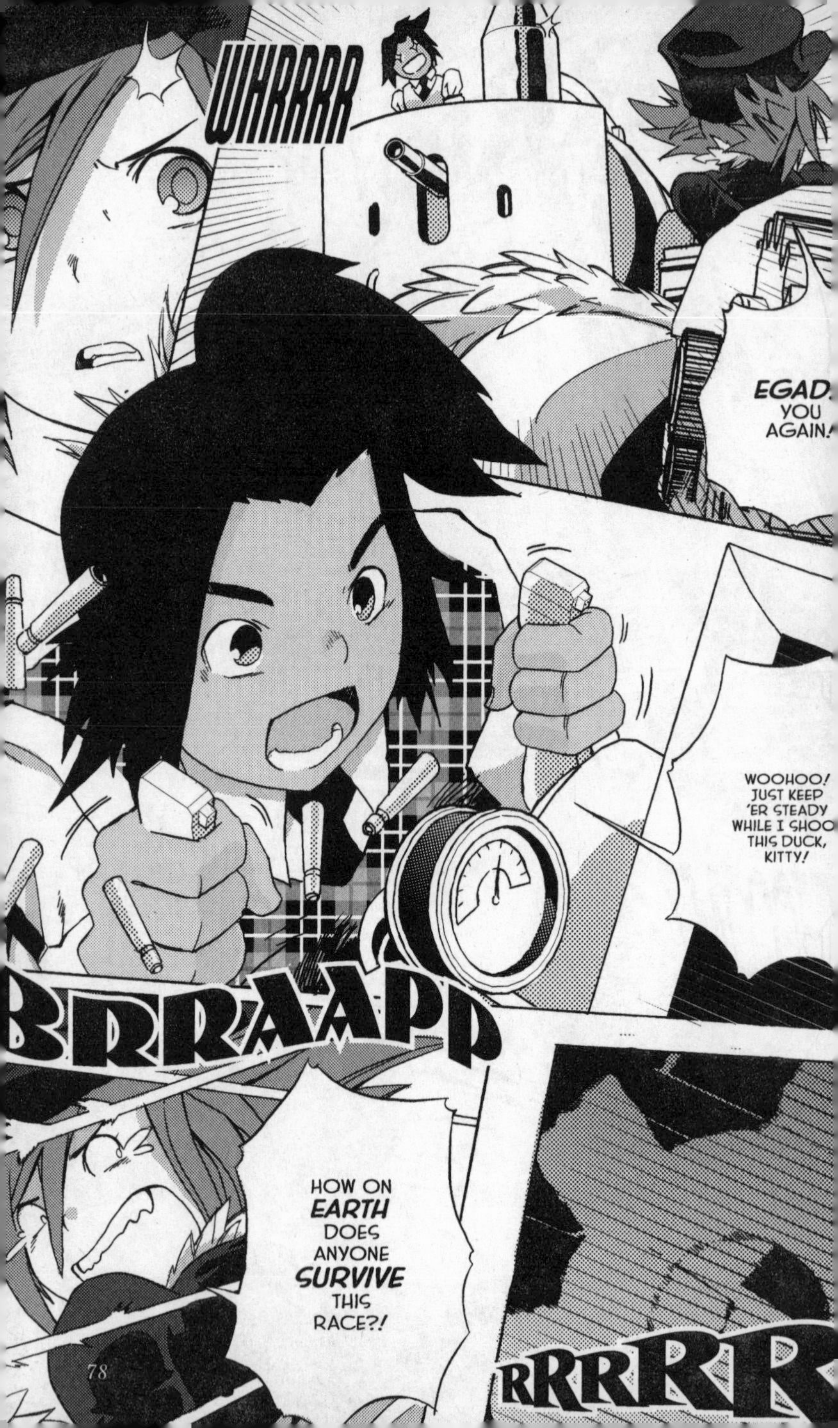
WHRRRR
EGAD! YOU AGAIN!
WOOHOO! JUST KEEP 'ER STEADY WHILE I SHOO THIS DUCK, KITTY!
BRRAAPP
HOW ON EARTH DOES ANYONE SURVIVE THIS RACE?!
RRRRR

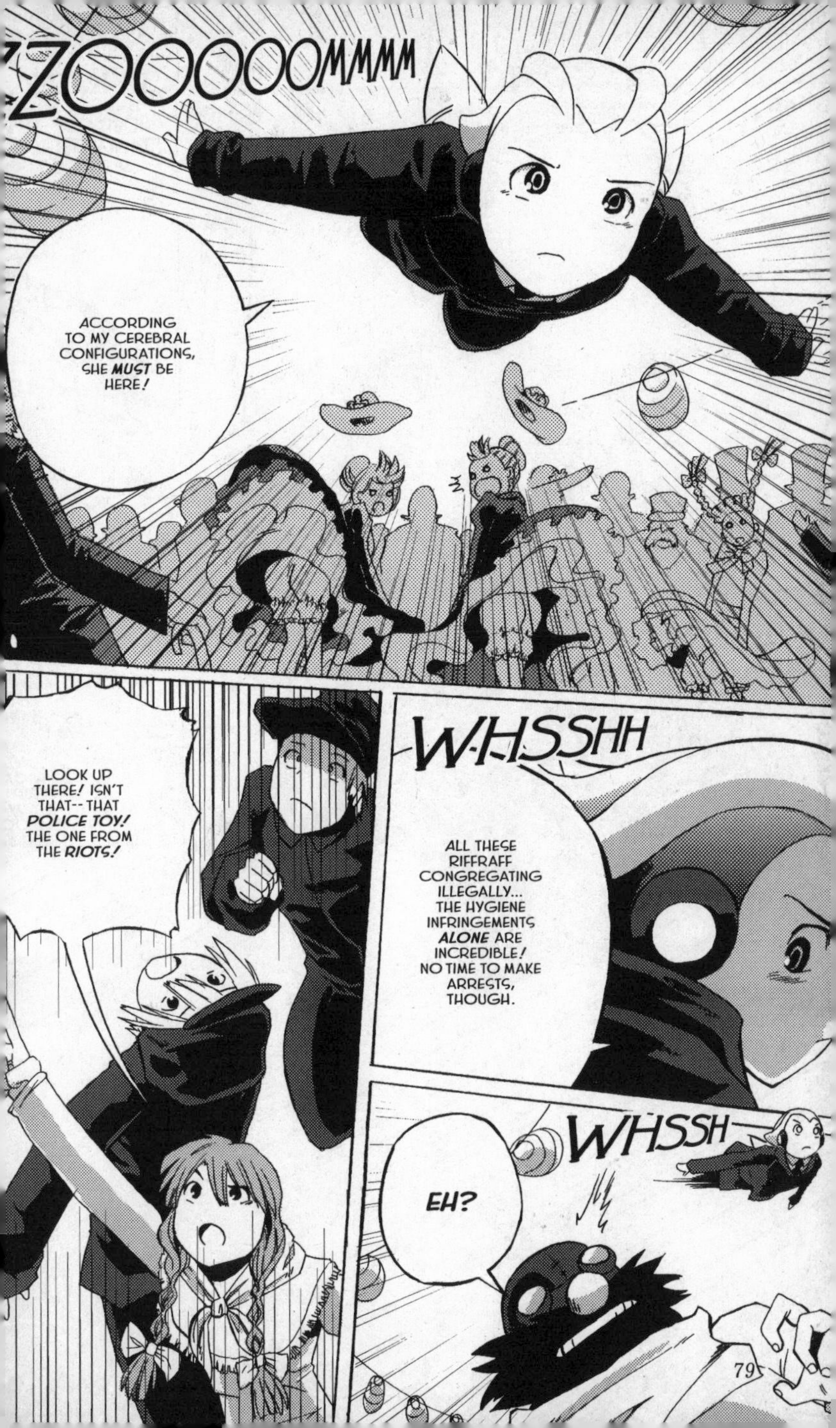

ZOOOOOMMMM
ACCORDING TO MY CEREBRAL CONFIGURATIONS, SHE *MUST* BE HERE!
LOOK UP THERE! ISN'T THAT-- THAT *POLICE TOY!* THE ONE FROM THE *RIOTS!*
W-HSSHH
ALL THESE RIFFRAFF CONGREGATING ILLEGALLY... THE HYGIENE INFRINGEMENTS *ALONE* ARE INCREDIBLE! NO TIME TO MAKE ARRESTS, THOUGH.
WHSSH
EH?

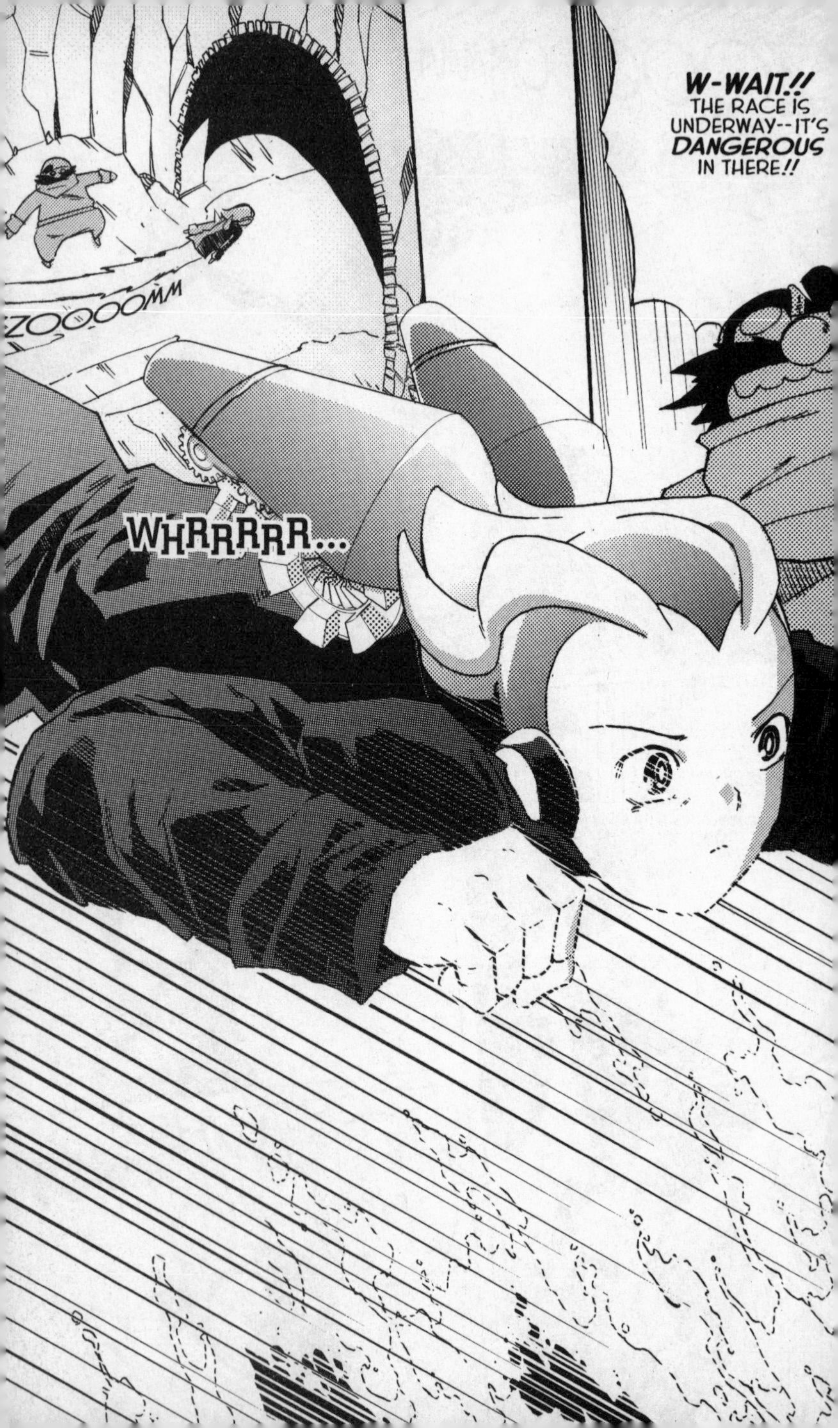
ZOOOOOMM
W-WAIT!! THE RACE IS UNDERWAY--IT'S DANGEROUS IN THERE!!
WHRRRRR...

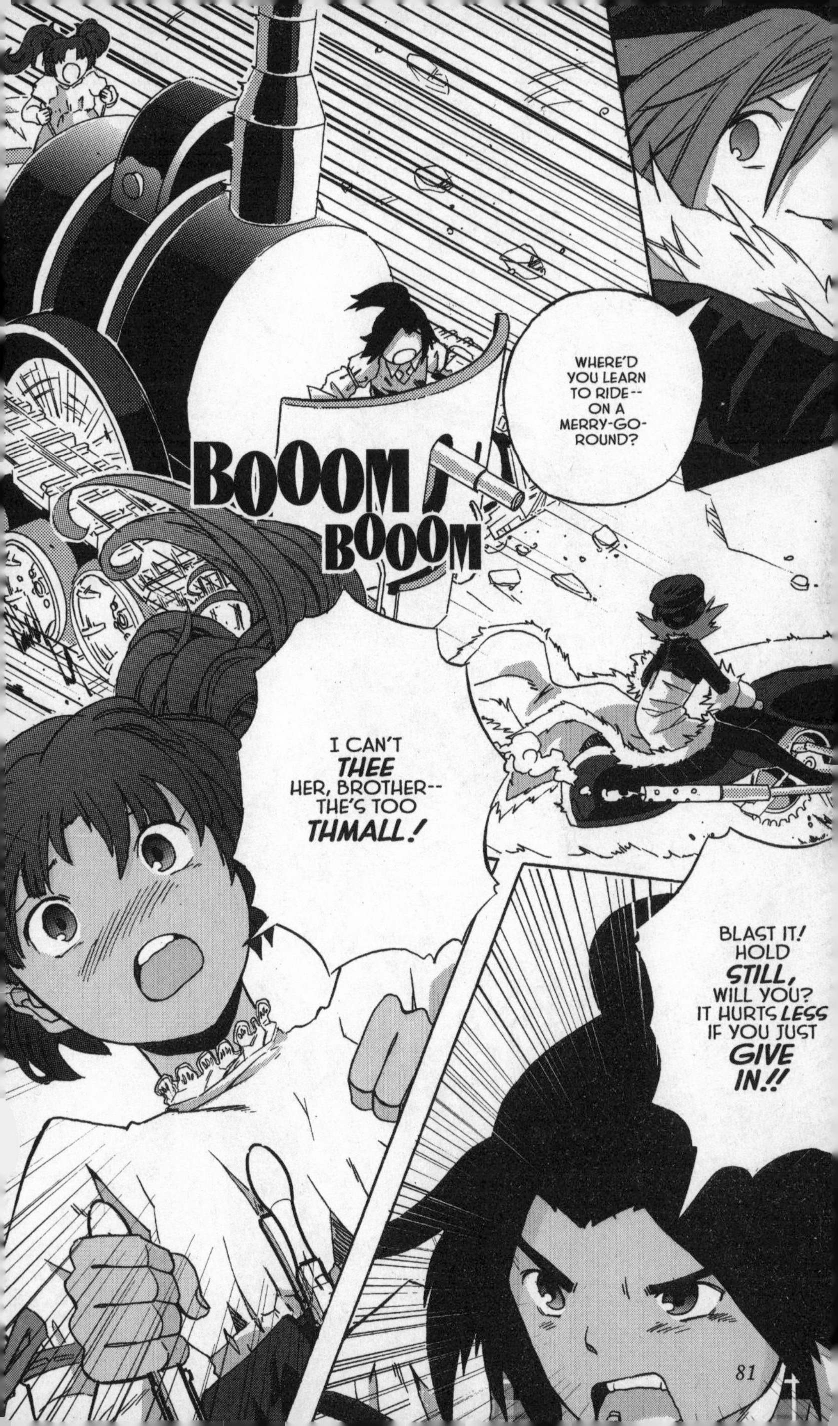
WHERE'D YOU LEARN TO RIDE-- ON A MERRY-GO-ROUND?
BOOOM
BOOOM
I CAN'T **THEE** HER, BROTHER-- THE'S TOO **THMALL!**
BLAST IT! HOLD **STILL,** WILL YOU? IT HURTS **LESS** IF YOU JUST **GIVE IN!!**

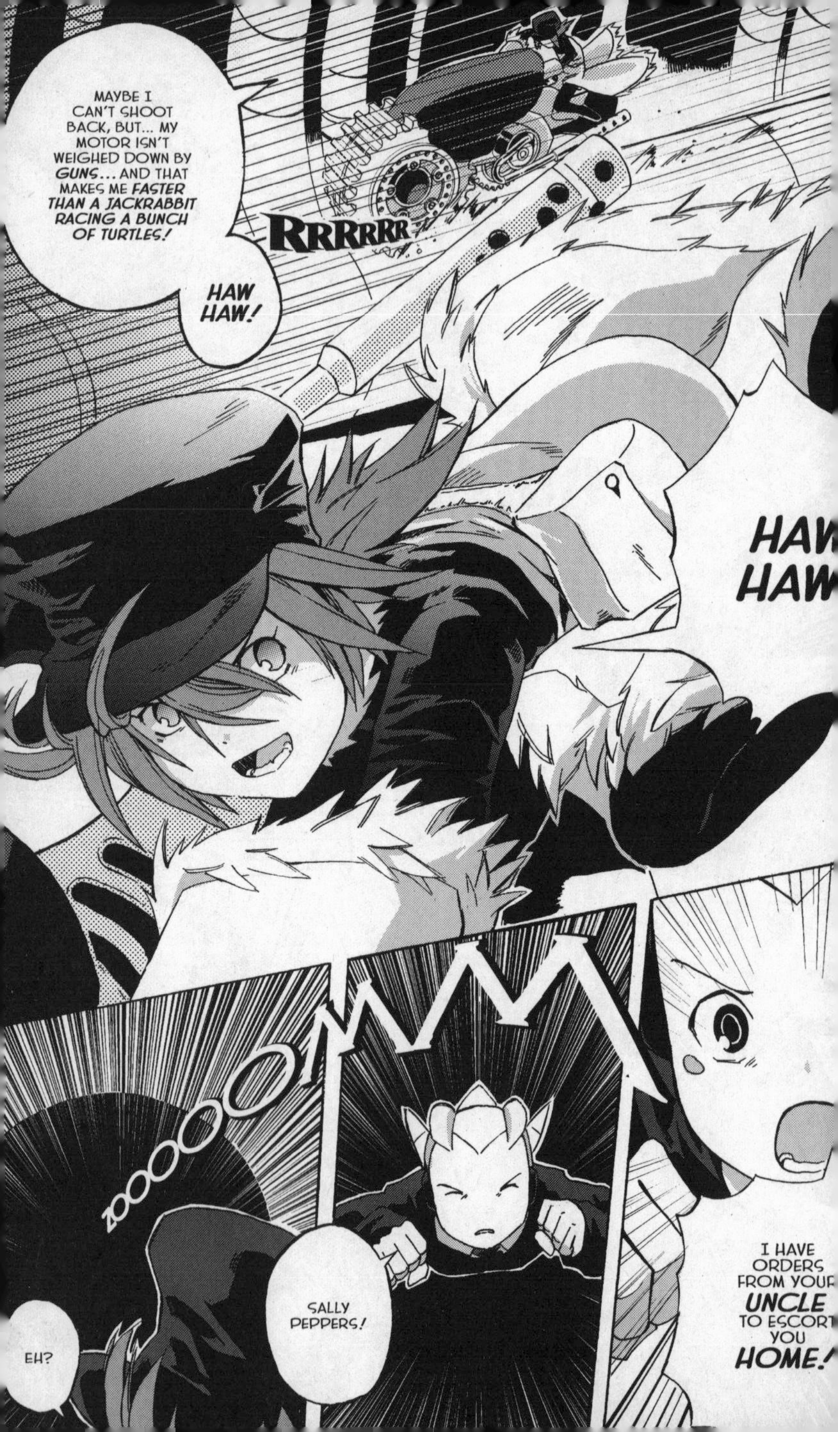

MAYBE I CAN'T SHOOT BACK, BUT... MY MOTOR ISN'T WEIGHED DOWN BY GUNS... AND THAT MAKES ME FASTER THAN A JACKRABBIT RACING A BUNCH OF TURTLES!
RRRRRR
HAW HAW!
HAW HAW
ZOOOOOMMM
EH?
SALLY PEPPERS!
I HAVE ORDERS FROM YOUR UNCLE TO ESCORT YOU HOME!

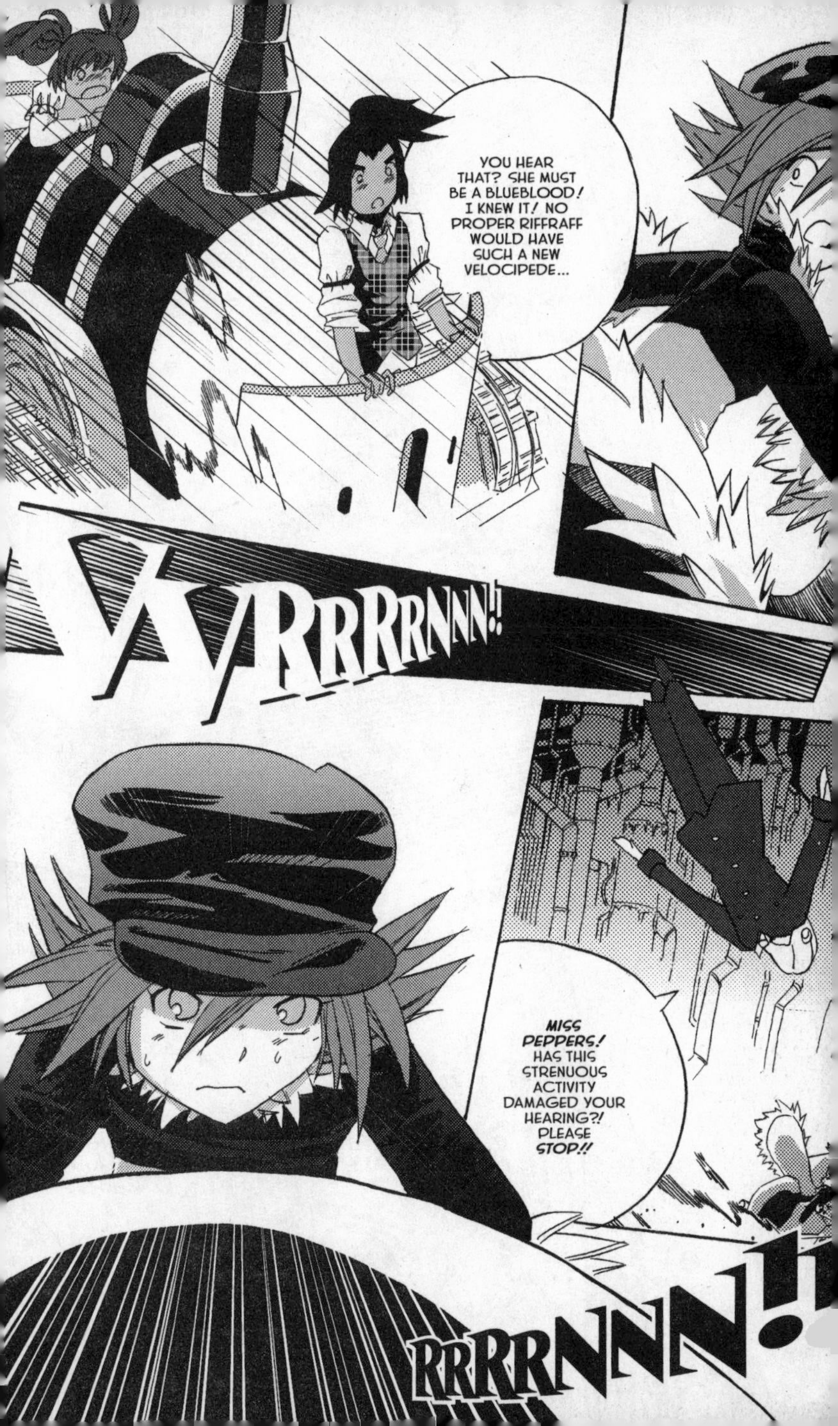
YOU HEAR THAT? SHE MUST BE A BLUEBLOOD! I KNEW IT! NO PROPER RIFFRAFF WOULD HAVE SUCH A NEW VELOCIPEDE...
VVRRRRRNNN!!
MISS PEPPERS! HAS THIS STRENUOUS ACTIVITY DAMAGED YOUR HEARING?! PLEASE STOP!!
RRRRRNNNN!!

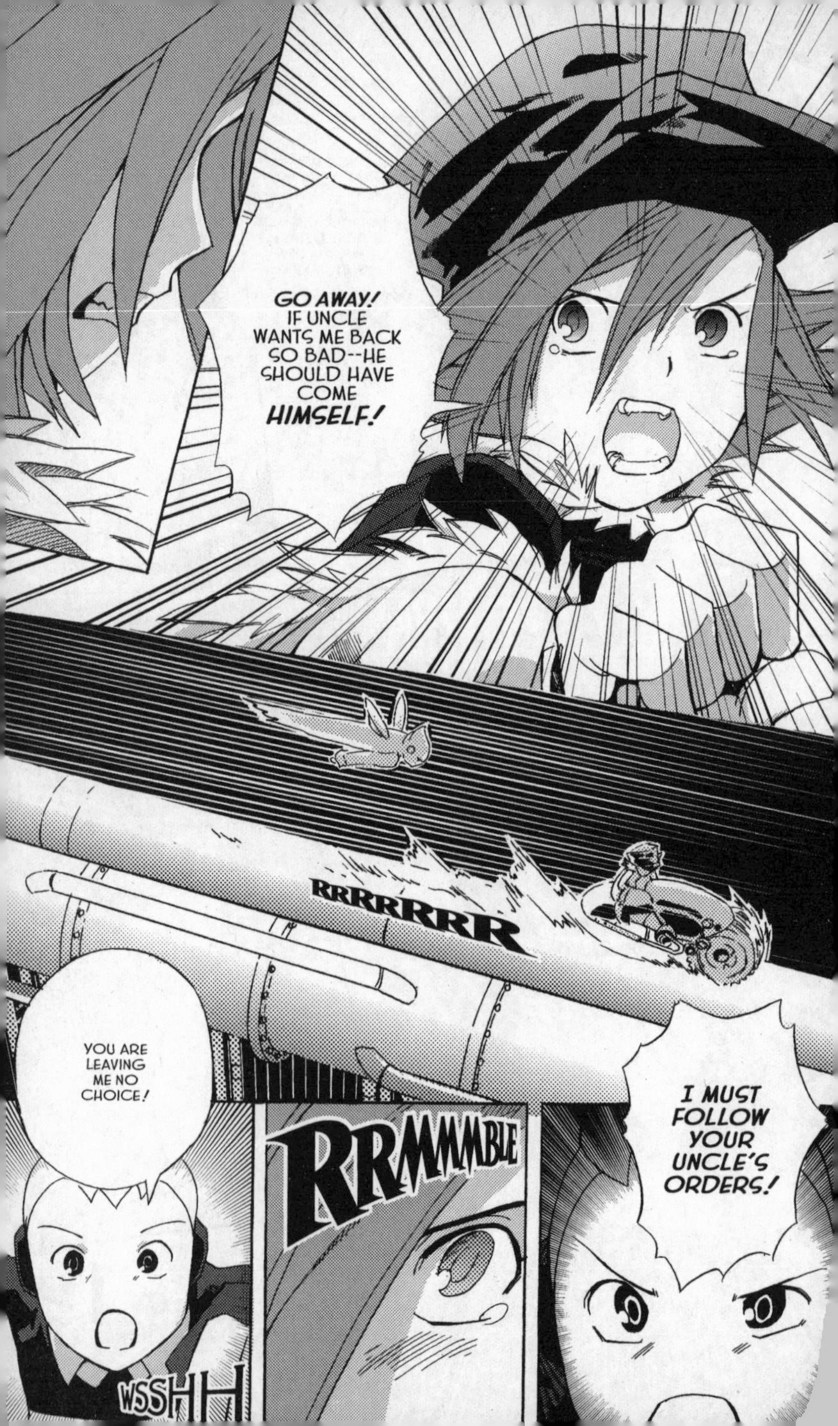
GO AWAY! IF UNCLE WANTS ME BACK SO BAD--HE SHOULD HAVE COME HIMSELF!
RRRRRRRR
YOU ARE LEAVING ME NO CHOICE!
RRMMMBLE
I MUST FOLLOW YOUR UNCLE'S ORDERS!
WSSHH

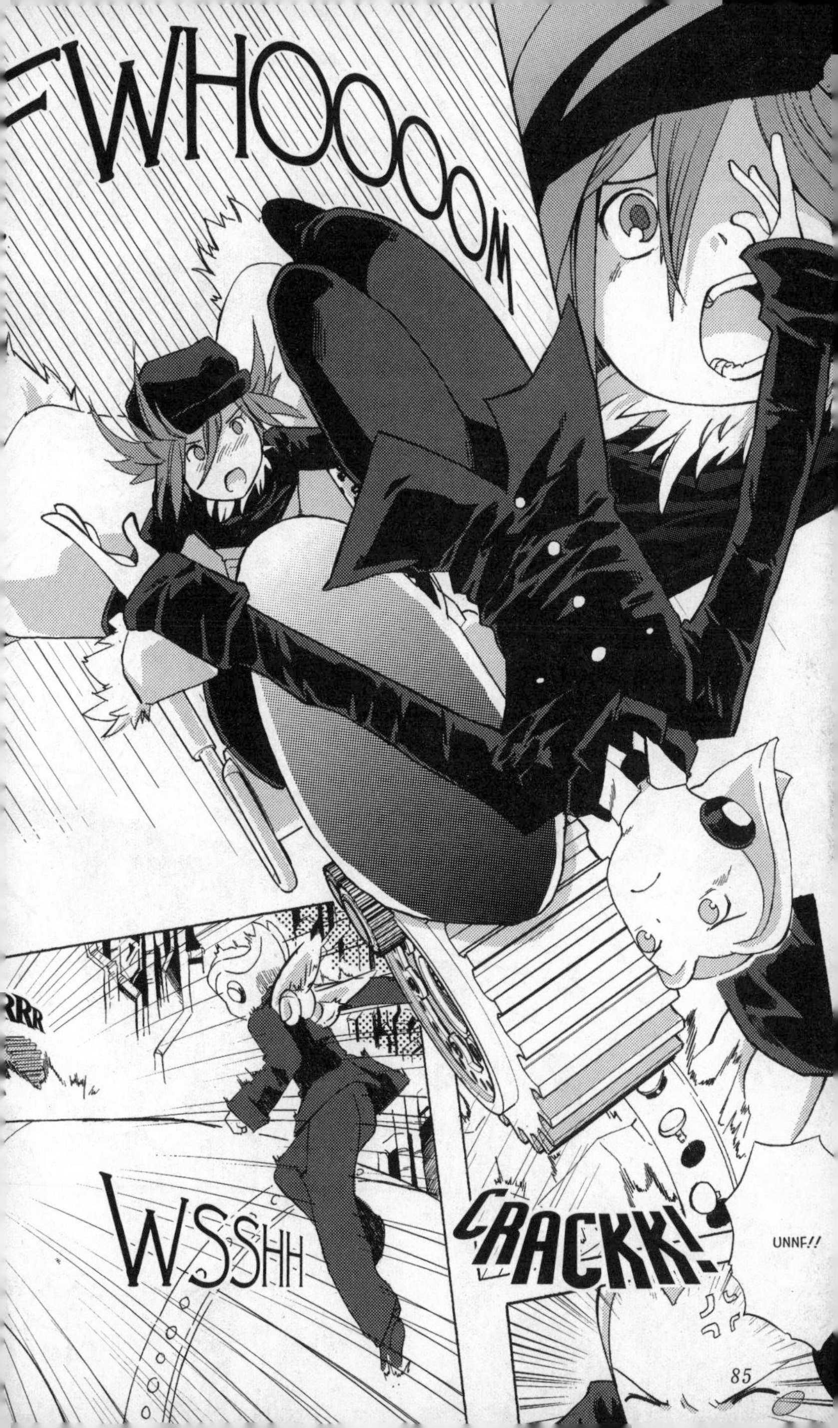
WHOOOOOM
RRR
WSSHH
CRACKK!
UNNF!!

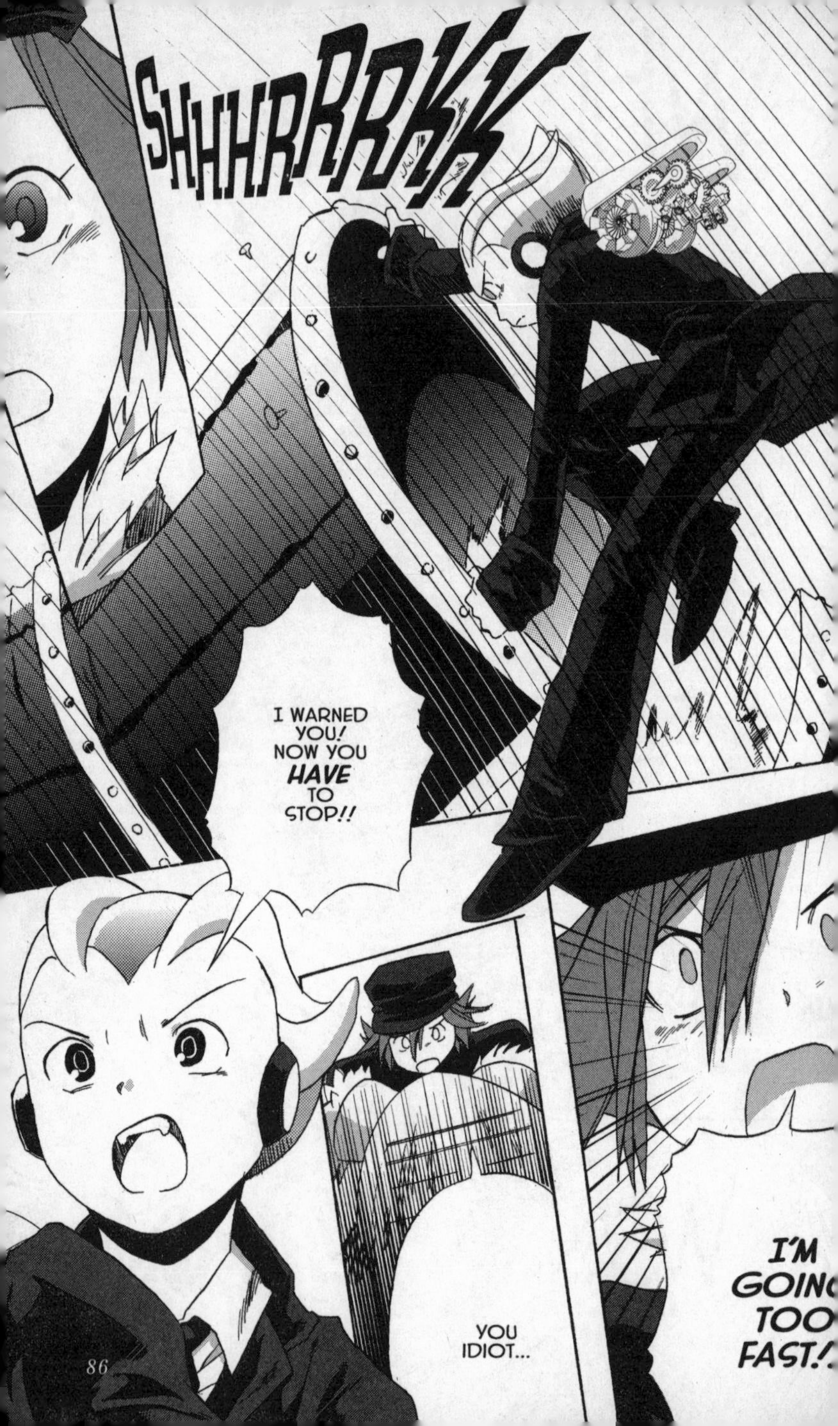
SHHHRRRKK
I WARNED YOU! NOW YOU *HAVE* TO STOP!!
YOU IDIOT...
I'M GOING TOO FAST!!

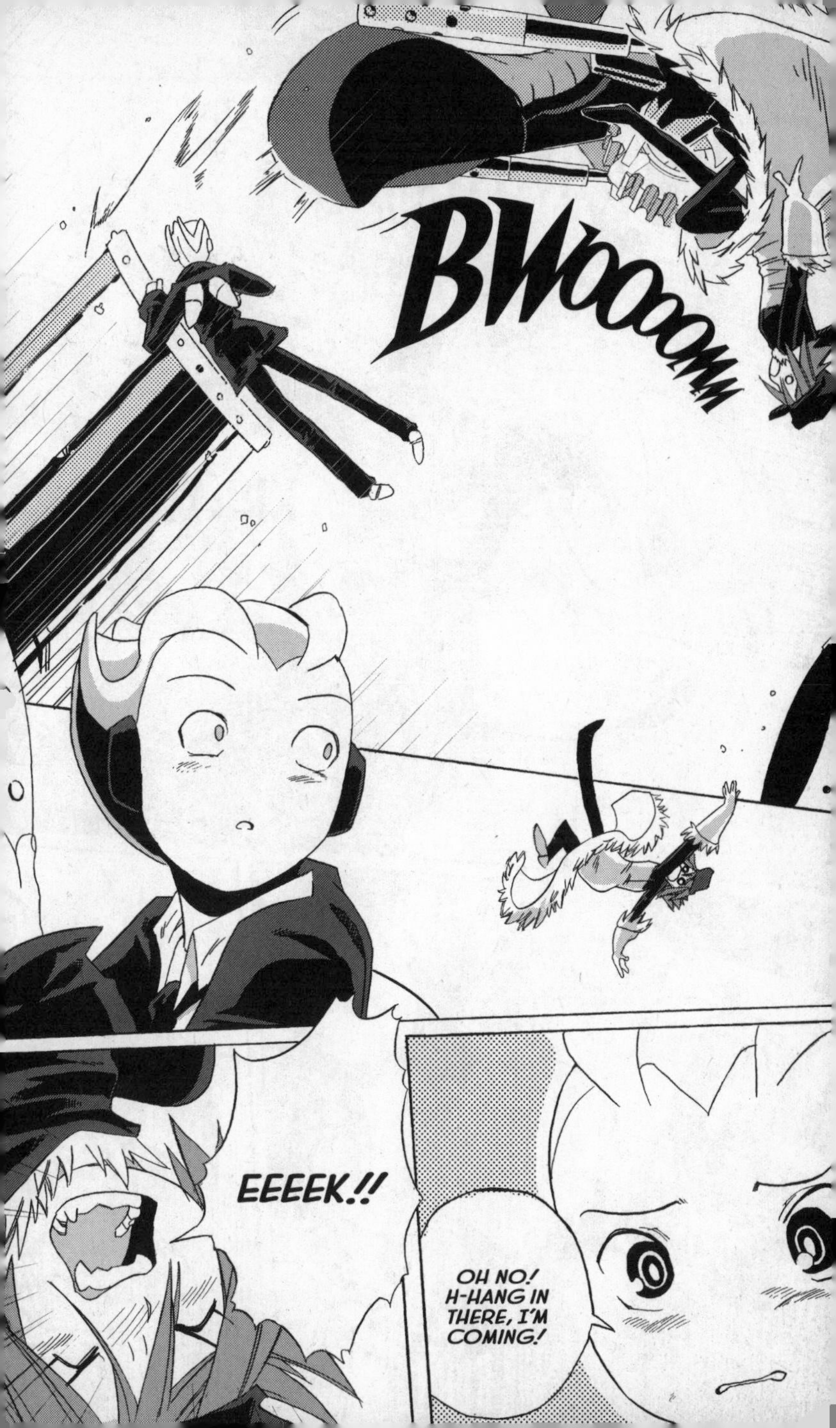
BWOOOOMM
EEEEK.!!
OH NO!
H-HANG IN
THERE, I'M
COMING!

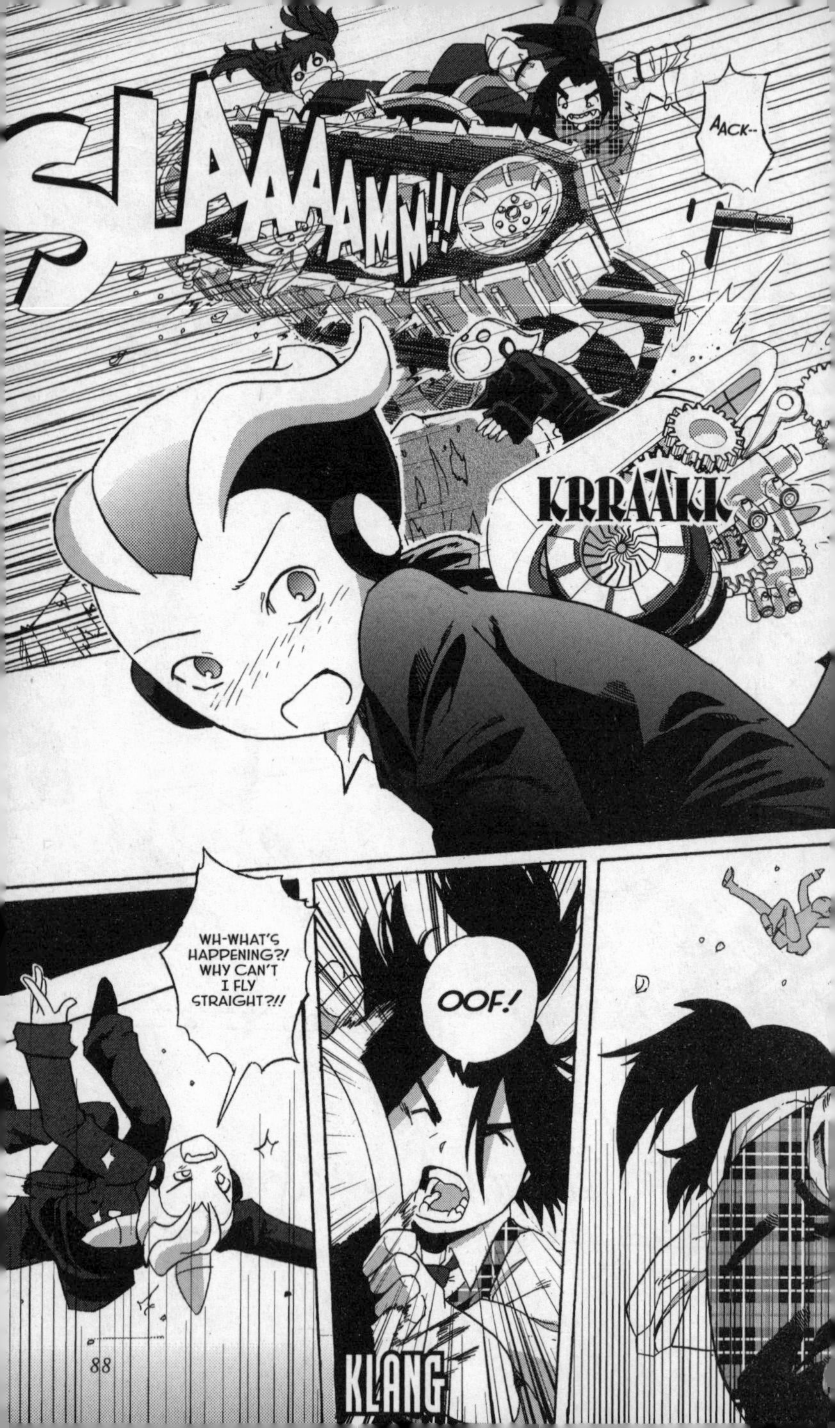
SLAAAAMM!!
AACK--
KRRAAKK
WH-WHAT'S HAPPENING?! WHY CAN'T I FLY STRAIGHT?!!
OOF!
KLANG

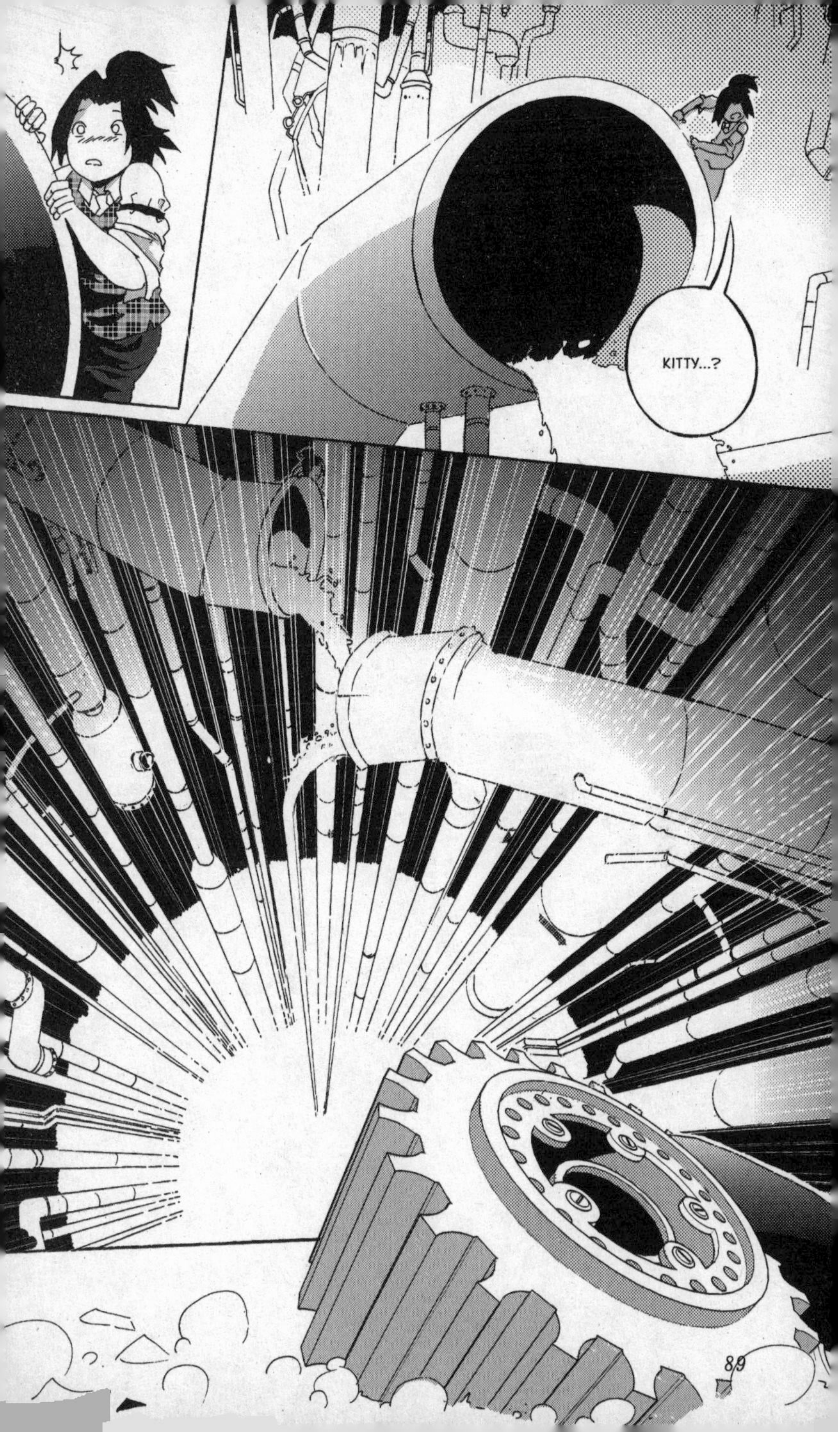
KITTY...?

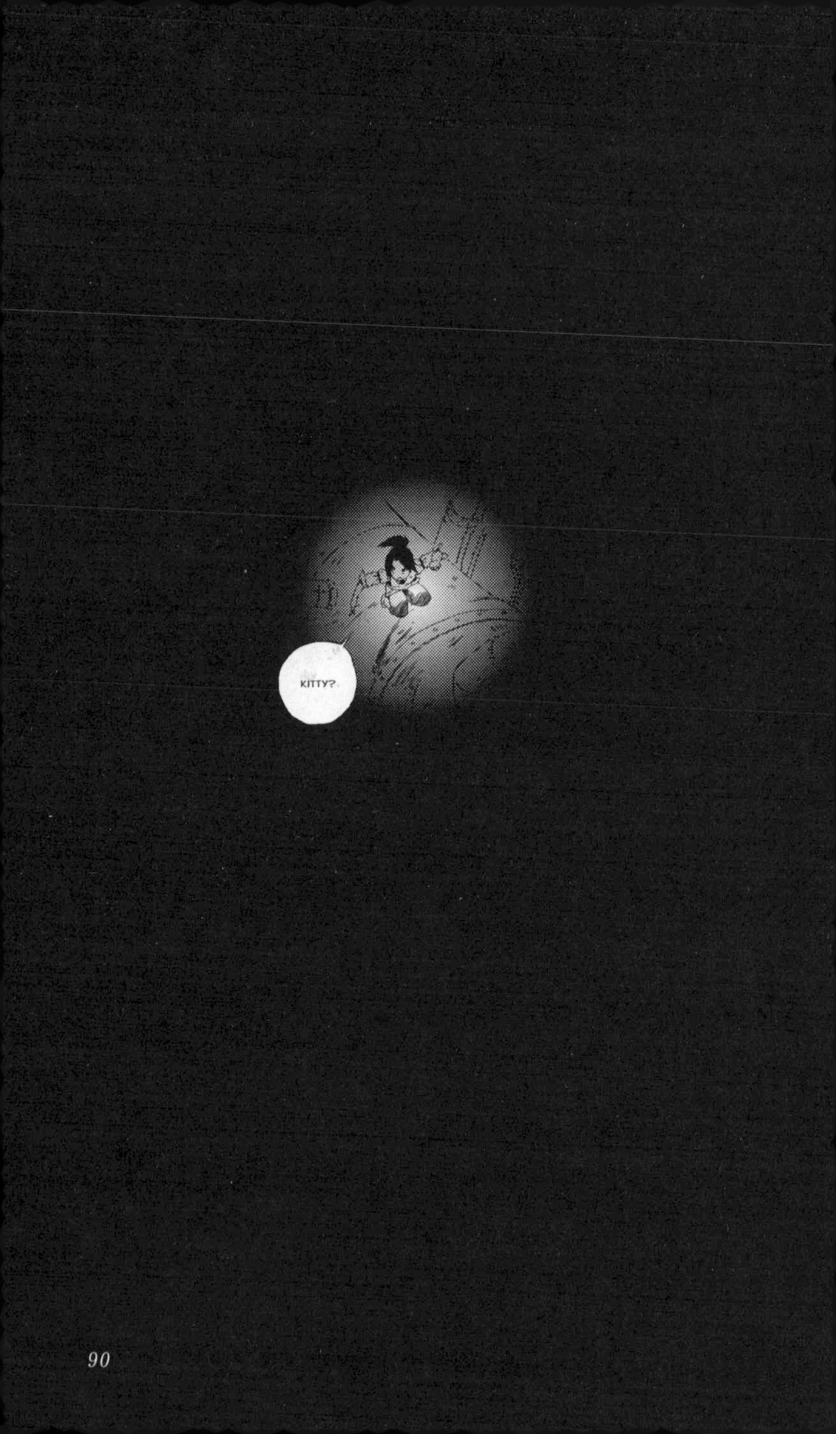
KITTY?

CHAPTER 4

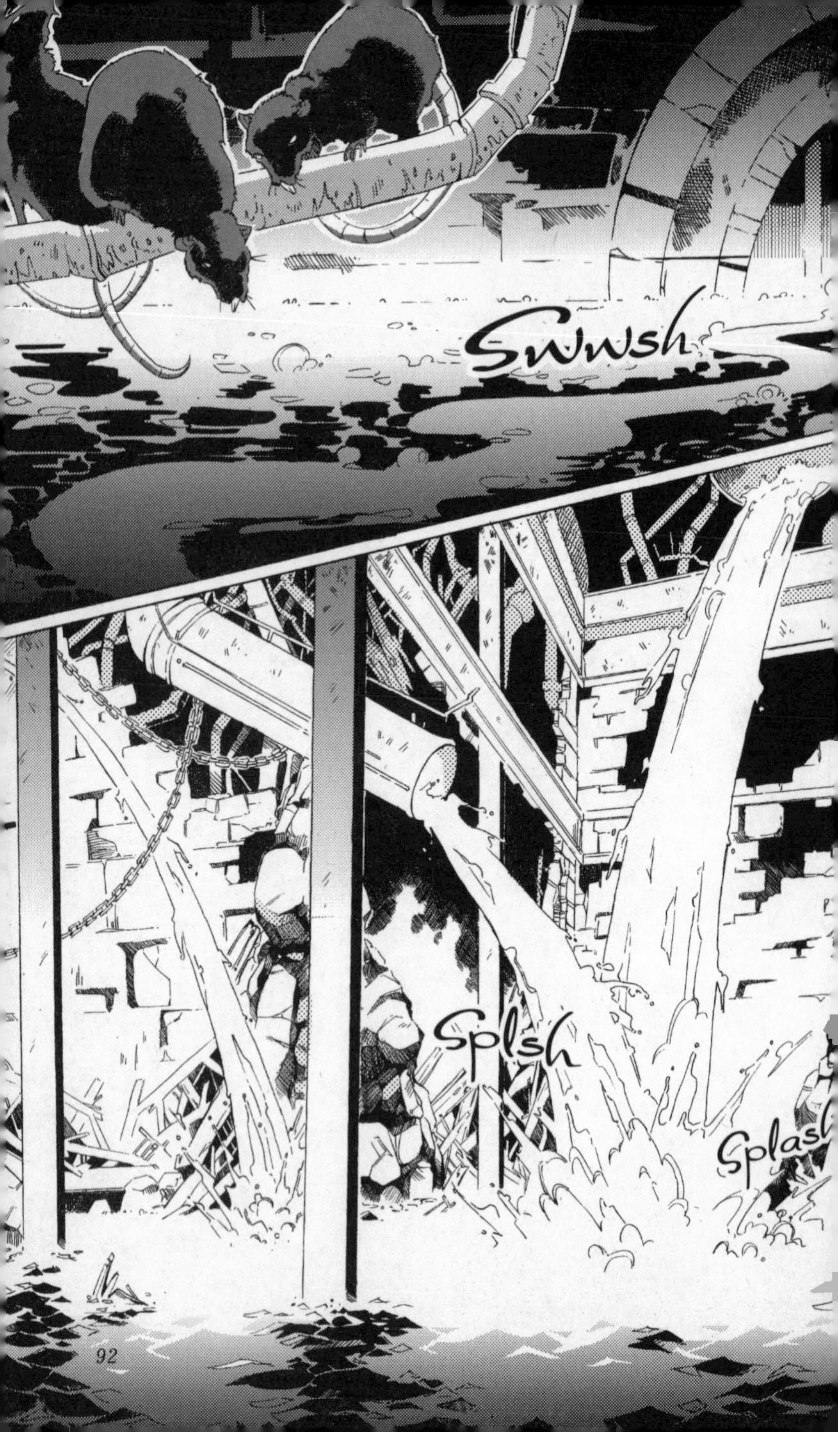
Swwsh
Splsh
Splas

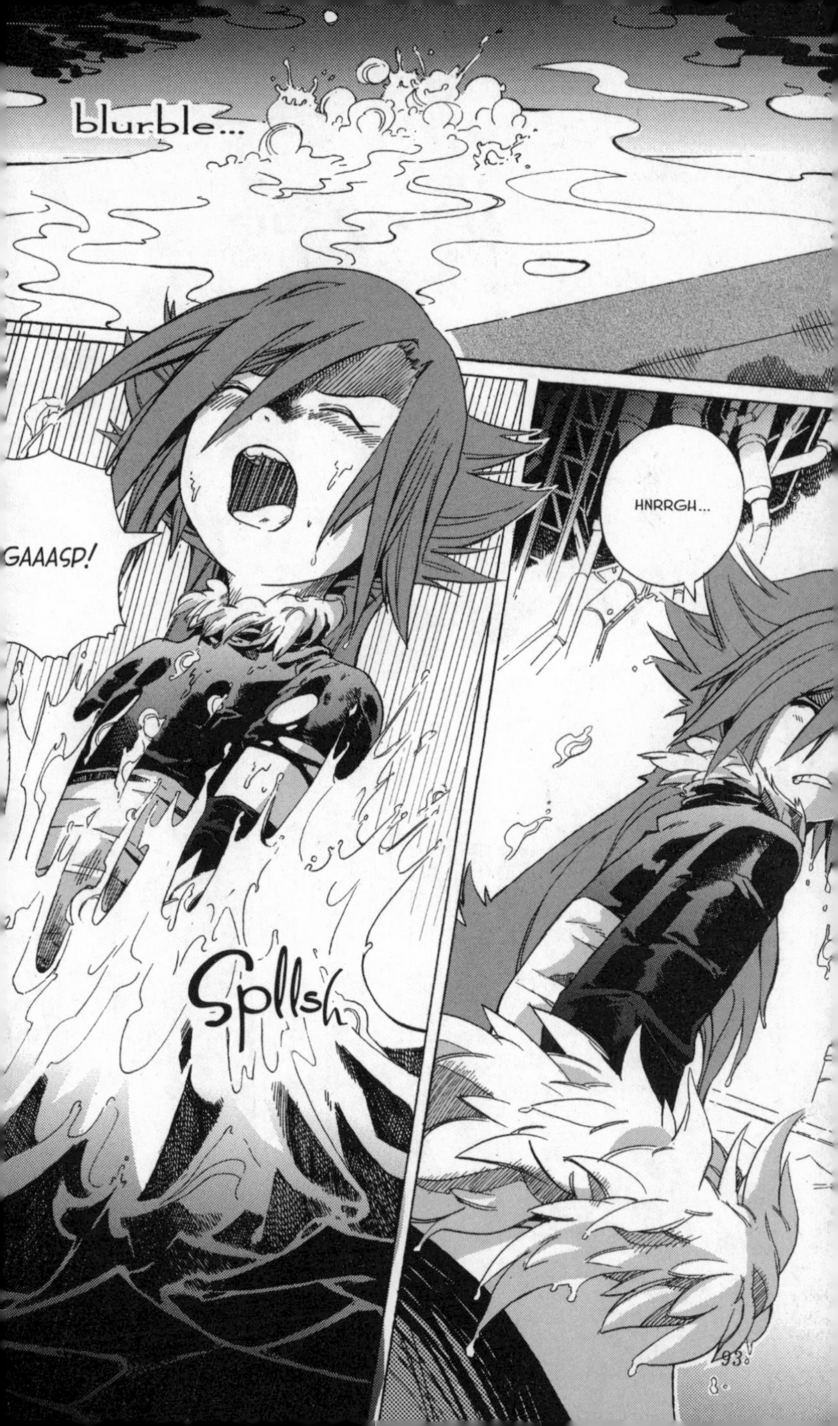
blurble...
GAAASP!
Spllsh
HNRRGH...

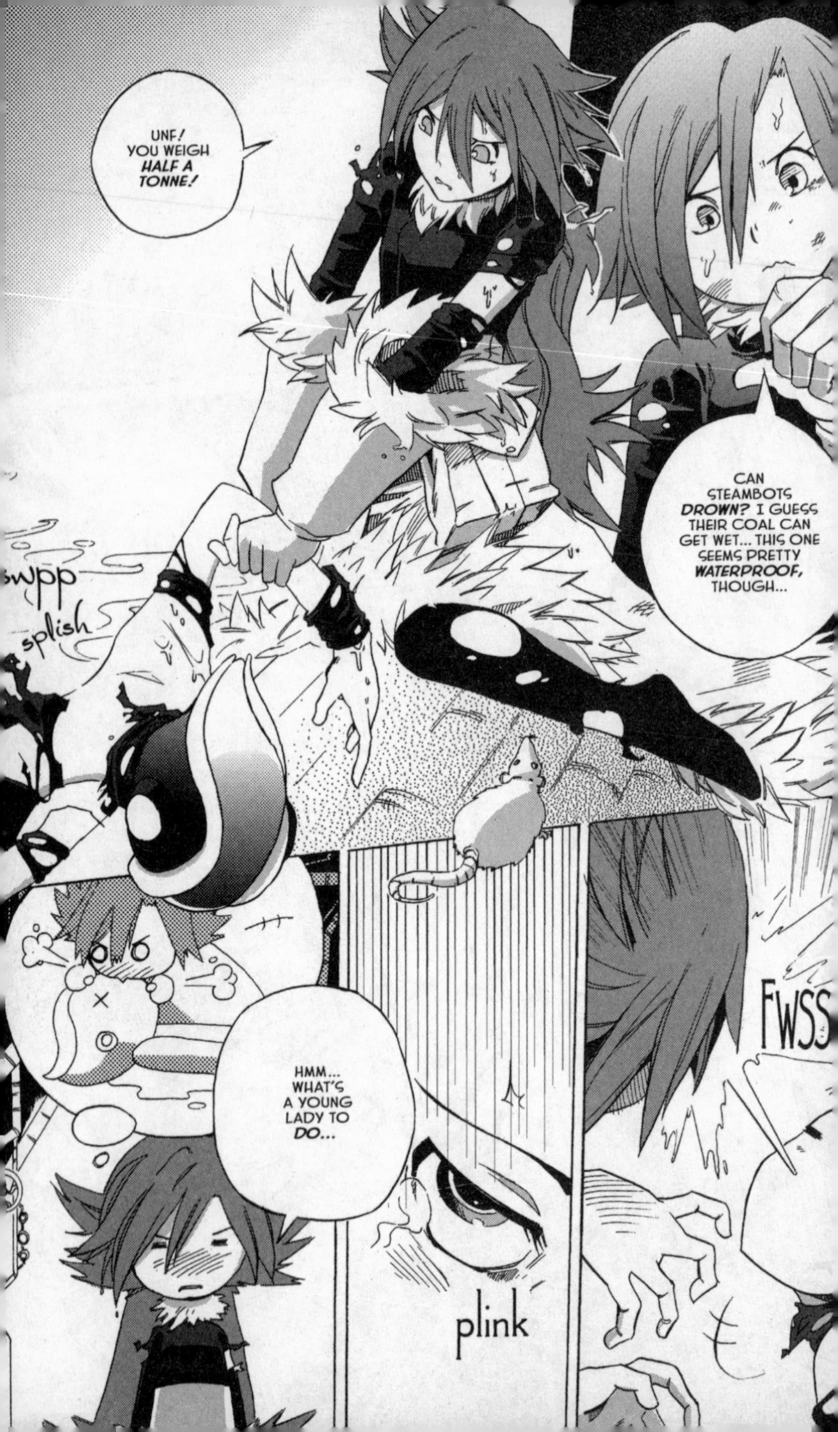

UNF! YOU WEIGH *HALF A TONNE!*
swpp
splish
CAN STEAMBOTS *DROWN?* I GUESS THEIR COAL CAN GET WET... THIS ONE SEEMS PRETTY *WATERPROOF,* THOUGH...
FWSS
HMM... WHAT'S A YOUNG LADY TO *DO...*
plink

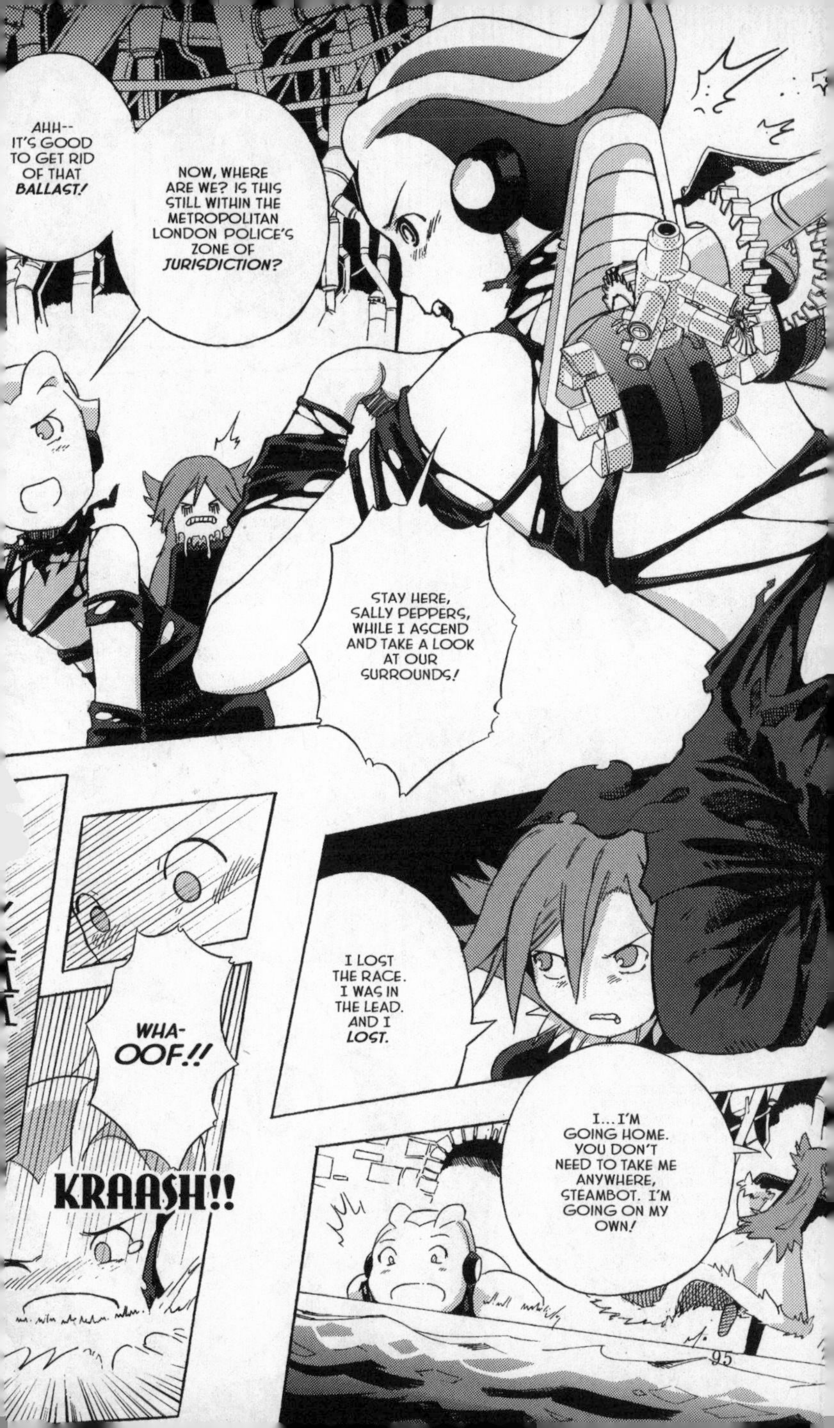
AHH-- IT'S GOOD TO GET RID OF THAT BALLAST!
NOW, WHERE ARE WE? IS THIS STILL WITHIN THE METROPOLITAN LONDON POLICE'S ZONE OF JURISDICTION?
STAY HERE, SALLY PEPPERS, WHILE I ASCEND AND TAKE A LOOK AT OUR SURROUNDS!
WHA-OOF!!
KRAASH!!
I LOST THE RACE. I WAS IN THE LEAD. AND I LOST.
I...I'M GOING HOME. YOU DON'T NEED TO TAKE ME ANYWHERE, STEAMBOT. I'M GOING ON MY OWN!

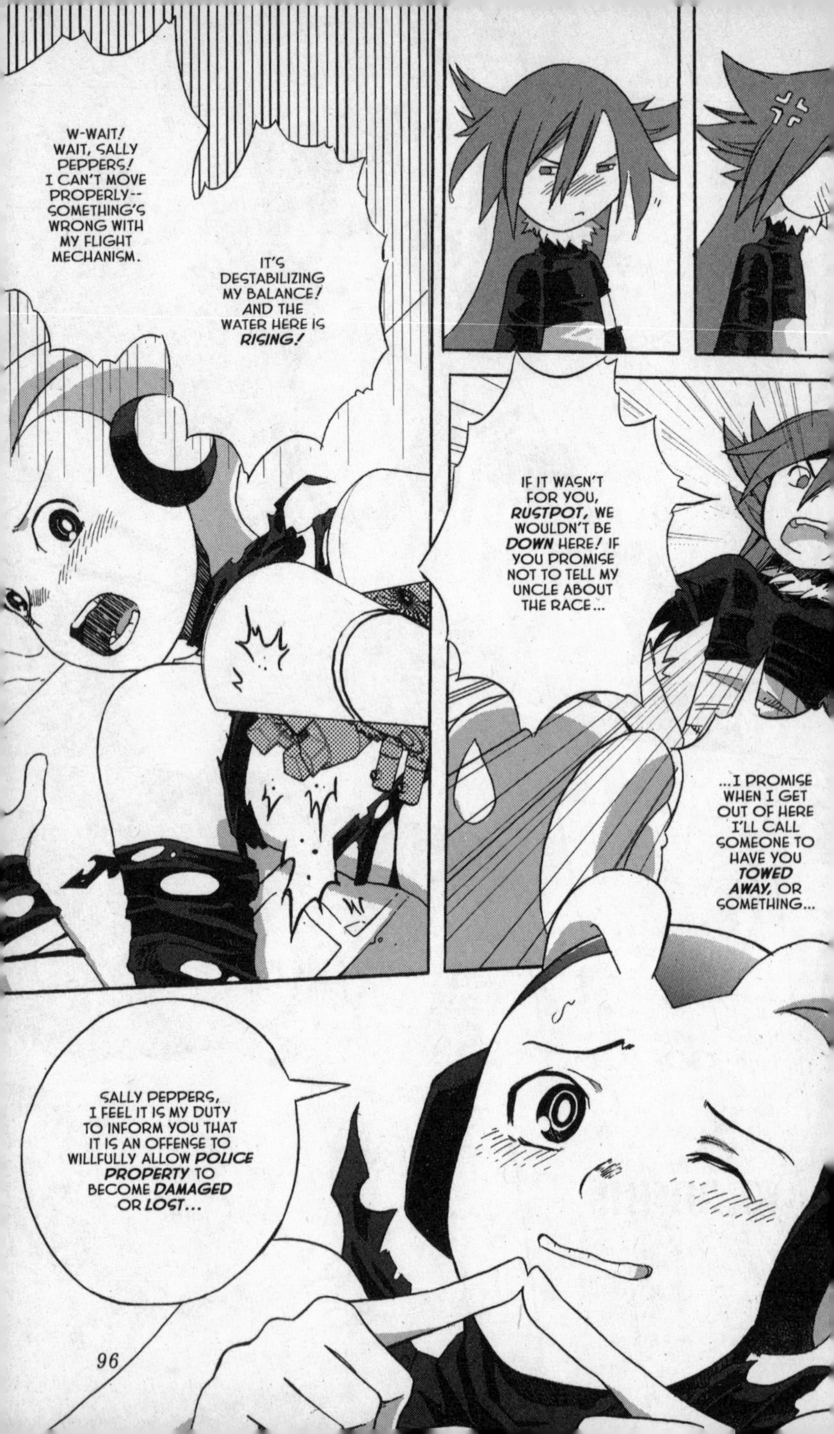
W-WAIT! WAIT, SALLY PEPPERS! I CAN'T MOVE PROPERLY-- SOMETHING'S WRONG WITH MY FLIGHT MECHANISM.
IT'S DESTABILIZING MY BALANCE! AND THE WATER HERE IS *RISING!*
IF IT WASN'T FOR YOU, *RUSTPOT,* WE WOULDN'T BE *DOWN* HERE! IF YOU PROMISE NOT TO TELL MY UNCLE ABOUT THE RACE...
...I PROMISE WHEN I GET OUT OF HERE I'LL CALL SOMEONE TO HAVE YOU *TOWED AWAY,* OR SOMETHING...
SALLY PEPPERS, I FEEL IT IS MY DUTY TO INFORM YOU THAT IT IS AN OFFENSE TO WILLFULLY ALLOW *POLICE PROPERTY* TO BECOME *DAMAGED* OR *LOST*...

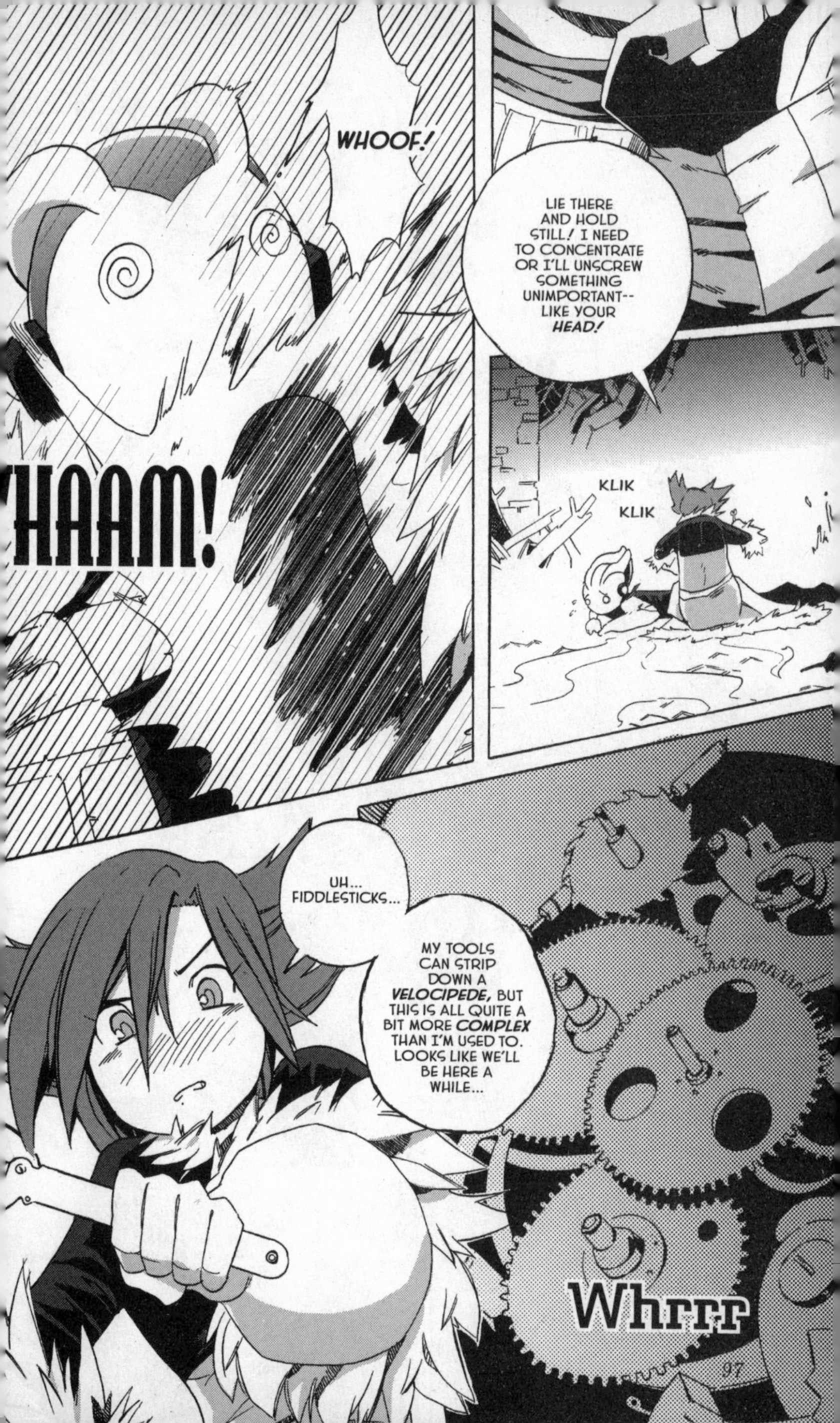
WHOOF!
HAAM!
LIE THERE AND HOLD STILL! I NEED TO CONCENTRATE OR I'LL UNSCREW SOMETHING UNIMPORTANT--LIKE YOUR HEAD!
KLIK
KLIK
UH... FIDDLESTICKS...
MY TOOLS CAN STRIP DOWN A VELOCIPEDE, BUT THIS IS ALL QUITE A BIT MORE COMPLEX THAN I'M USED TO. LOOKS LIKE WE'LL BE HERE A WHILE...
Whrrr

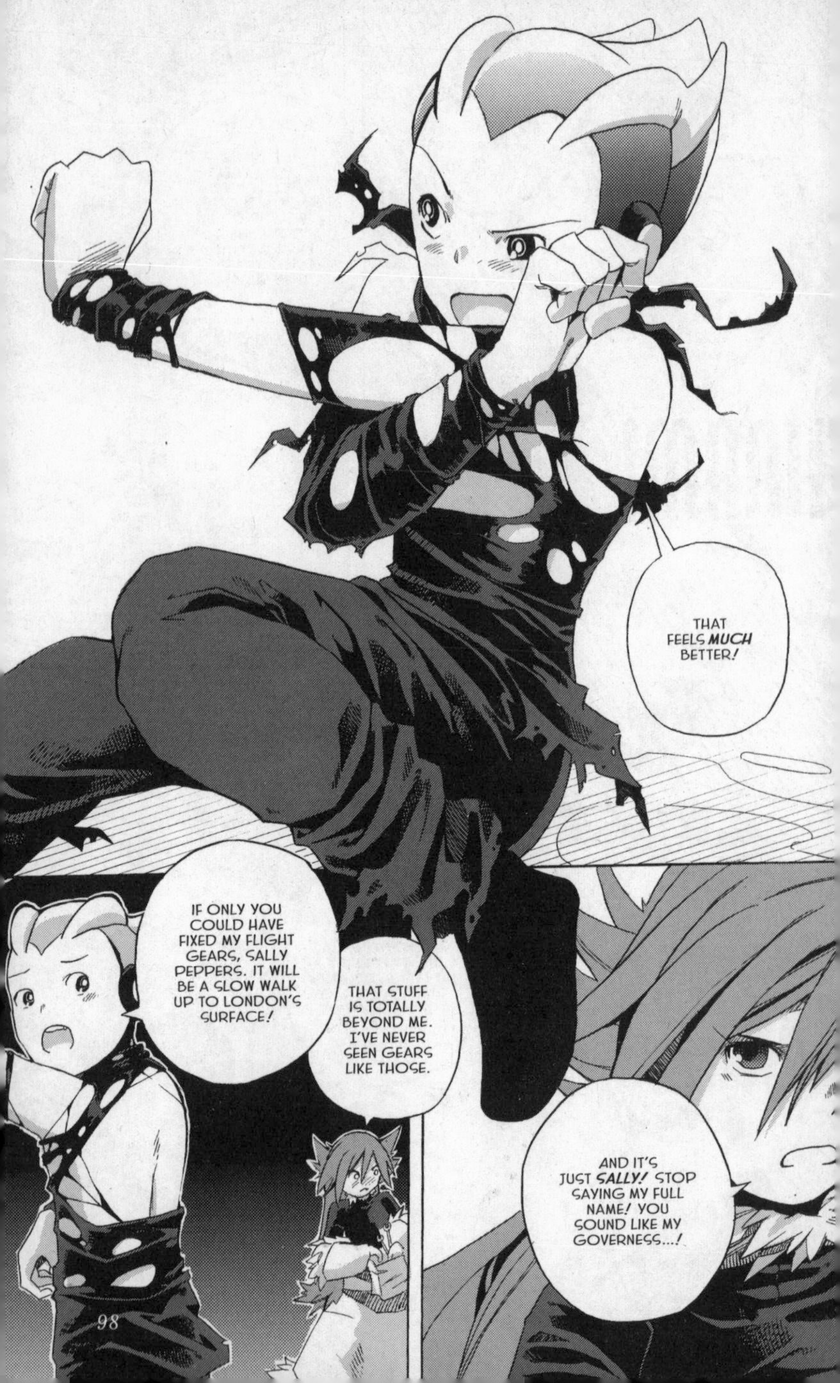
THAT FEELS ***MUCH*** BETTER!
IF ONLY YOU COULD HAVE FIXED MY FLIGHT GEARS, SALLY PEPPERS. IT WILL BE A SLOW WALK UP TO LONDON'S SURFACE!
THAT STUFF IS TOTALLY BEYOND ME. I'VE NEVER SEEN GEARS LIKE THOSE.
AND IT'S JUST ***SALLY!*** STOP SAYING MY FULL NAME! YOU SOUND LIKE MY GOVERNESS...!

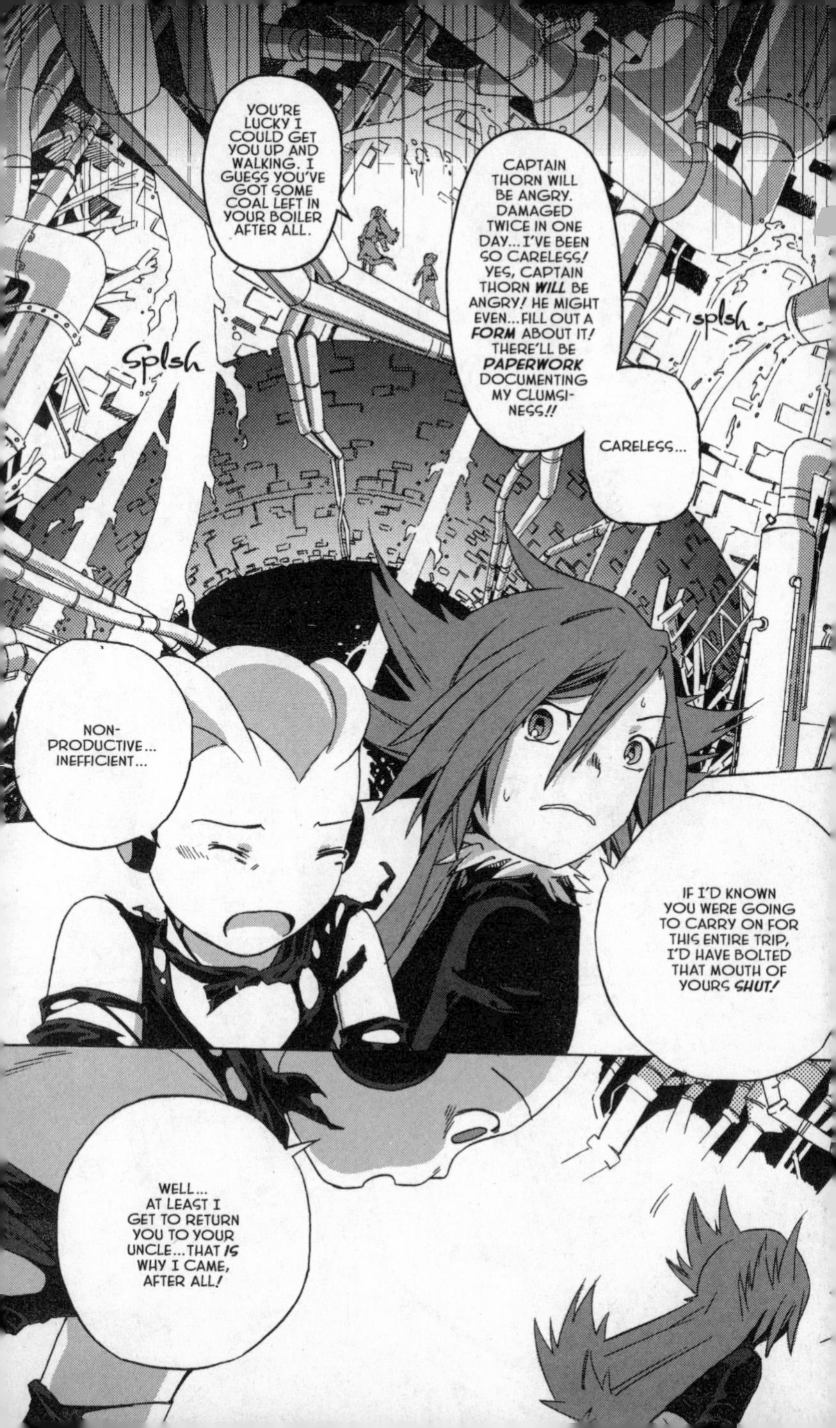

YOU'RE LUCKY I COULD GET YOU UP AND WALKING. I GUESS YOU'VE GOT SOME COAL LEFT IN YOUR BOILER AFTER ALL.
CAPTAIN THORN WILL BE ANGRY. DAMAGED TWICE IN ONE DAY... I'VE BEEN SO CARELESS! YES, CAPTAIN THORN **WILL** BE ANGRY! HE MIGHT EVEN... FILL OUT A **FORM** ABOUT IT! THERE'LL BE **PAPERWORK** DOCUMENTING MY CLUMSI-NESS!!
splsh
Splsh
CARELESS...
NON-PRODUCTIVE... INEFFICIENT...
IF I'D KNOWN YOU WERE GOING TO CARRY ON FOR THIS ENTIRE TRIP, I'D HAVE BOLTED THAT MOUTH OF YOURS ***SHUT!***
WELL... AT LEAST I GET TO RETURN YOU TO YOUR UNCLE... THAT *IS* WHY I CAME, AFTER ALL!

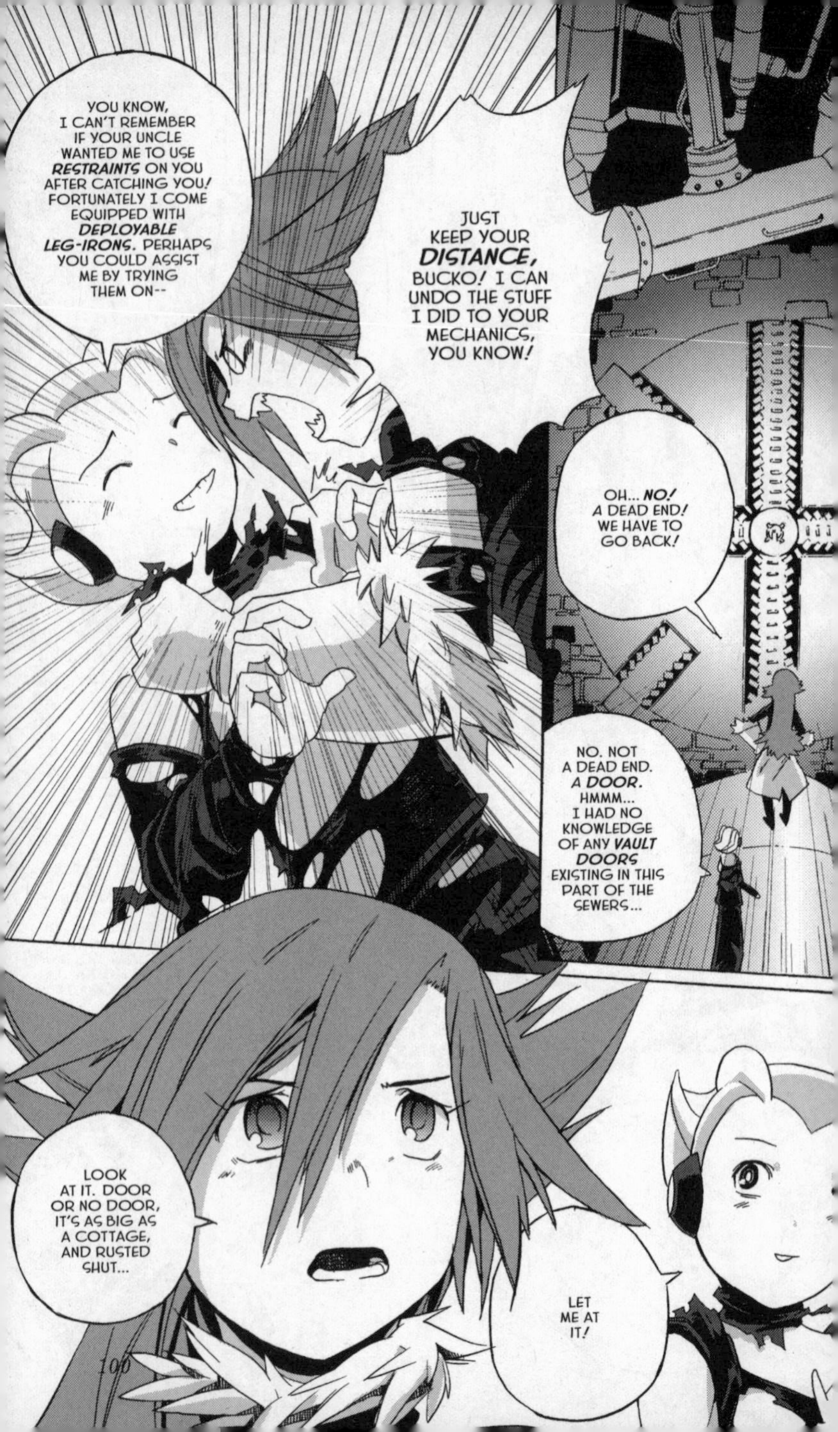
YOU KNOW, I CAN'T REMEMBER IF YOUR UNCLE WANTED ME TO USE **RESTRAINTS** ON YOU AFTER CATCHING YOU! FORTUNATELY I COME EQUIPPED WITH **DEPLOYABLE LEG-IRONS**. PERHAPS YOU COULD ASSIST ME BY TRYING THEM ON--
JUST KEEP YOUR **DISTANCE,** BUCKO! I CAN UNDO THE STUFF I DID TO YOUR MECHANICS, YOU KNOW!
OH... **NO!** A DEAD END! WE HAVE TO GO BACK!
NO. NOT A DEAD END. A **DOOR.** HMMM... I HAD NO KNOWLEDGE OF ANY **VAULT DOORS** EXISTING IN THIS PART OF THE SEWERS...
LOOK AT IT. DOOR OR NO DOOR, IT'S AS BIG AS A COTTAGE, AND RUSTED SHUT...
LET ME AT IT!

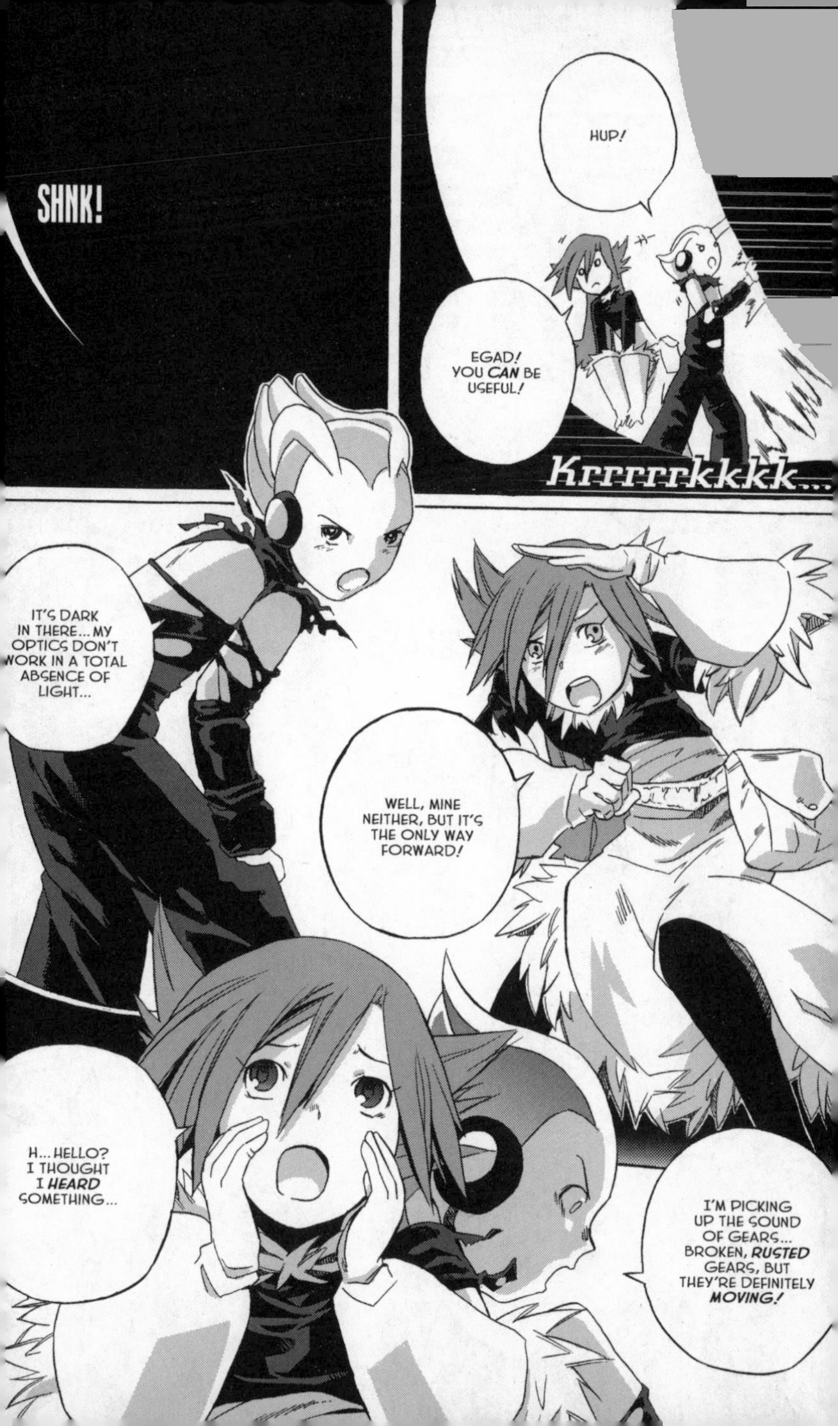
SHNK!
HUP!
EGAD! YOU *CAN* BE USEFUL!
Krrrrrkkkk...
IT'S DARK IN THERE... MY OPTICS DON'T WORK IN A TOTAL ABSENCE OF LIGHT...
WELL, MINE NEITHER, BUT IT'S THE ONLY WAY FORWARD!
H... HELLO? I THOUGHT I *HEARD* SOMETHING...
I'M PICKING UP THE SOUND OF GEARS... BROKEN, *RUSTED* GEARS, BUT THEY'RE DEFINITELY *MOVING!*

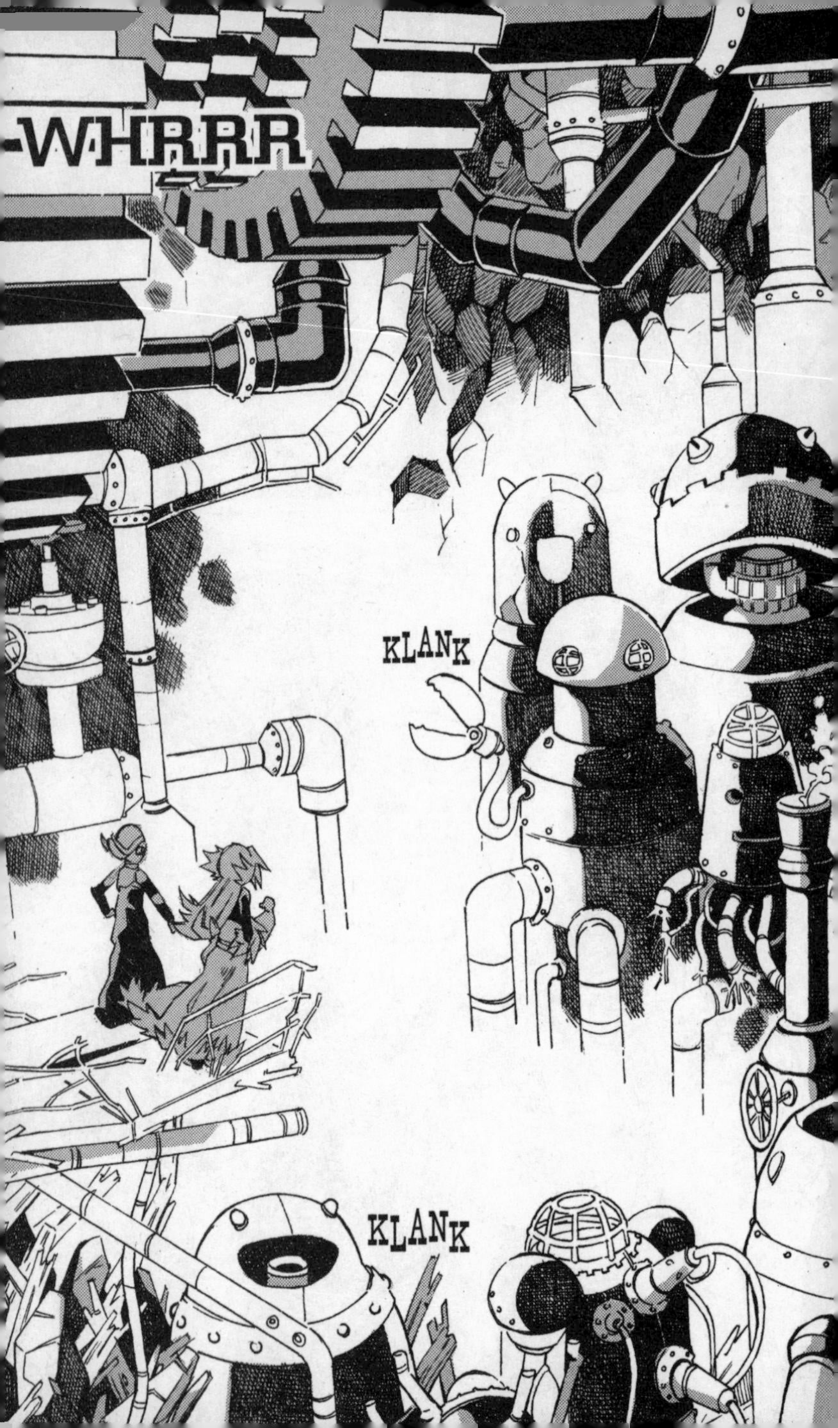
WHRRR
KLANK
KLANK

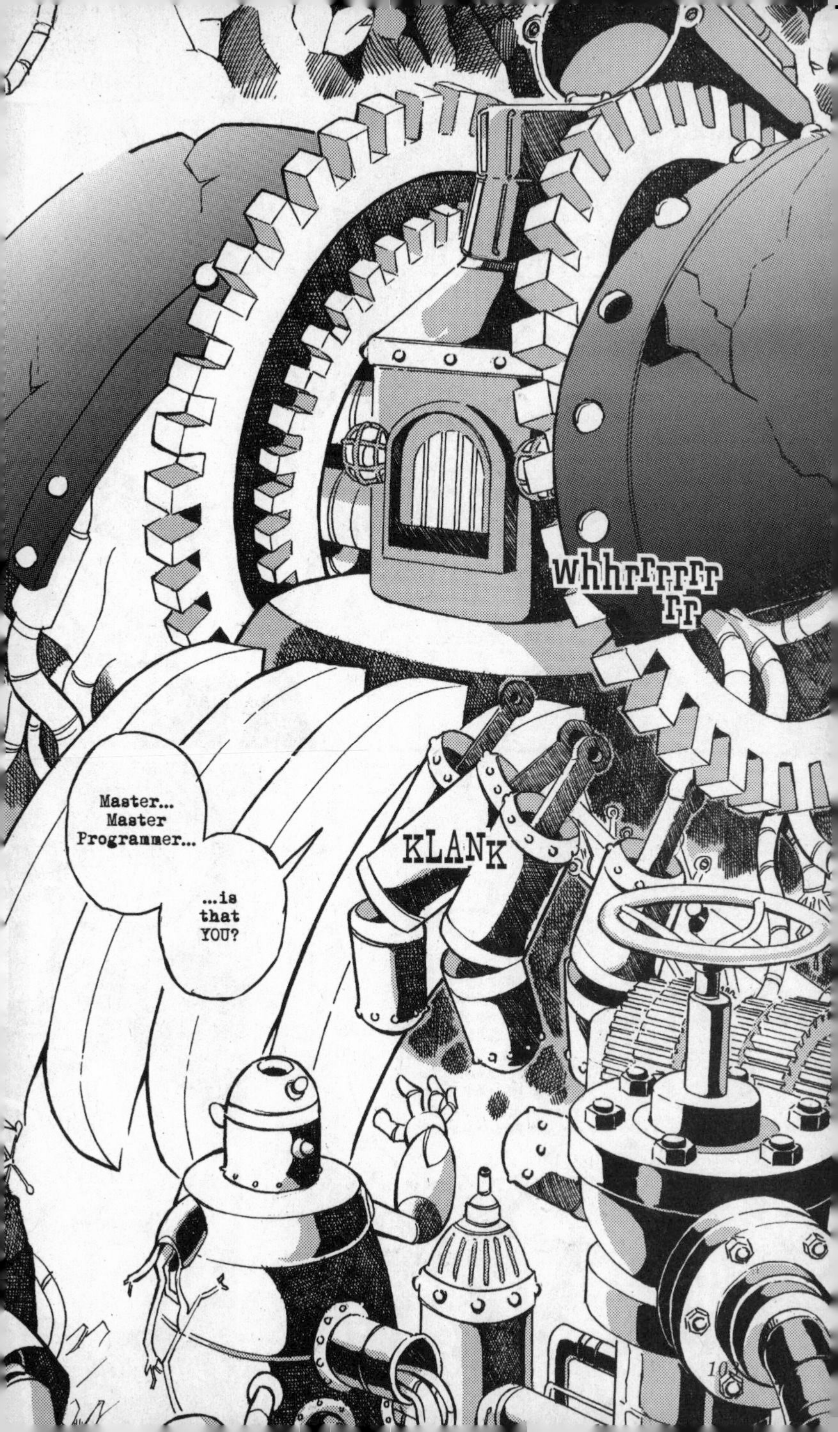
whhrrrrrrr
Master... Master Programmer...
...is that YOU?
KLANK

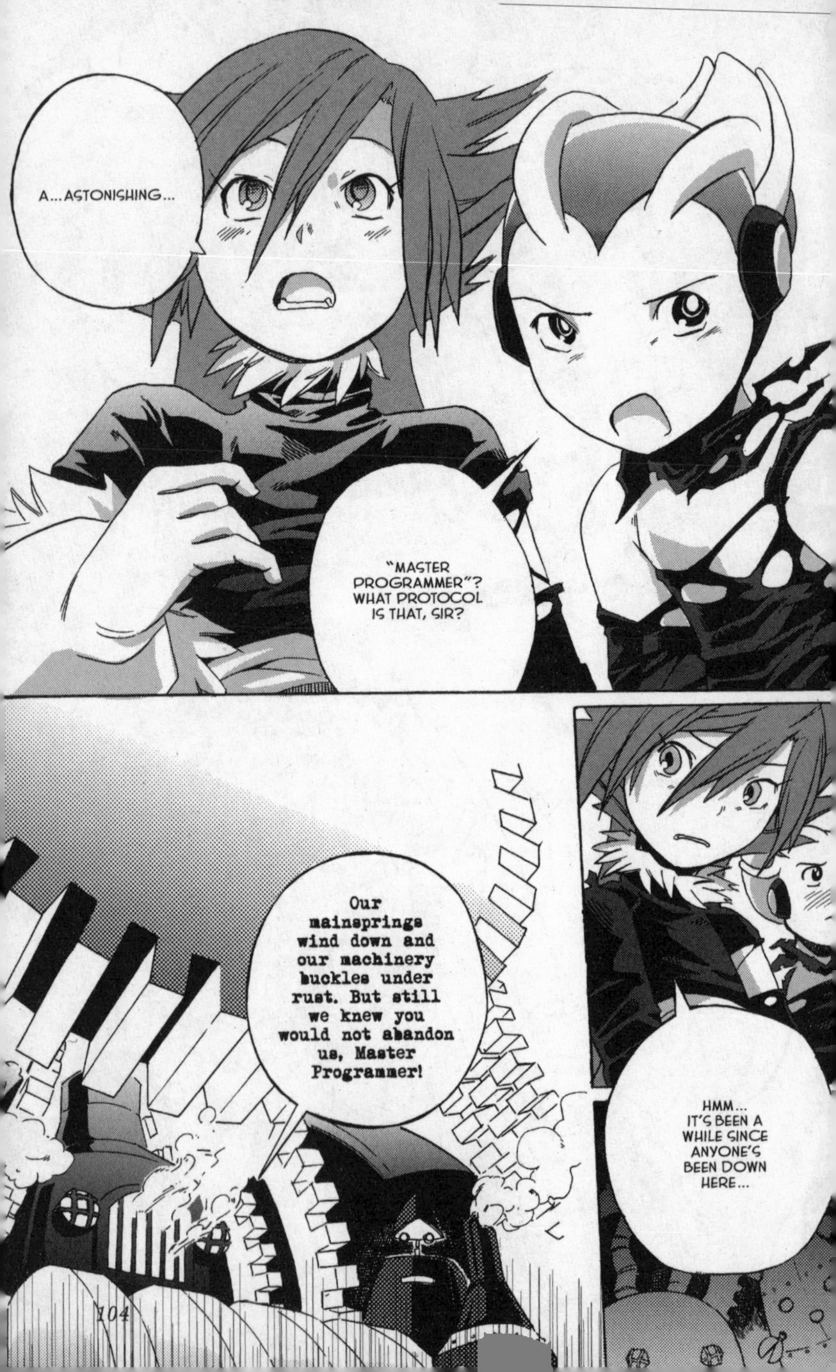
A...ASTONISHING...
"MASTER PROGRAMMER"? WHAT PROTOCOL IS THAT, SIR?
Our mainsprings wind down and our machinery buckles under rust. But still we knew you would not abandon us, Master Programmer!
HMM... IT'S BEEN A WHILE SINCE ANYONE'S BEEN DOWN HERE...

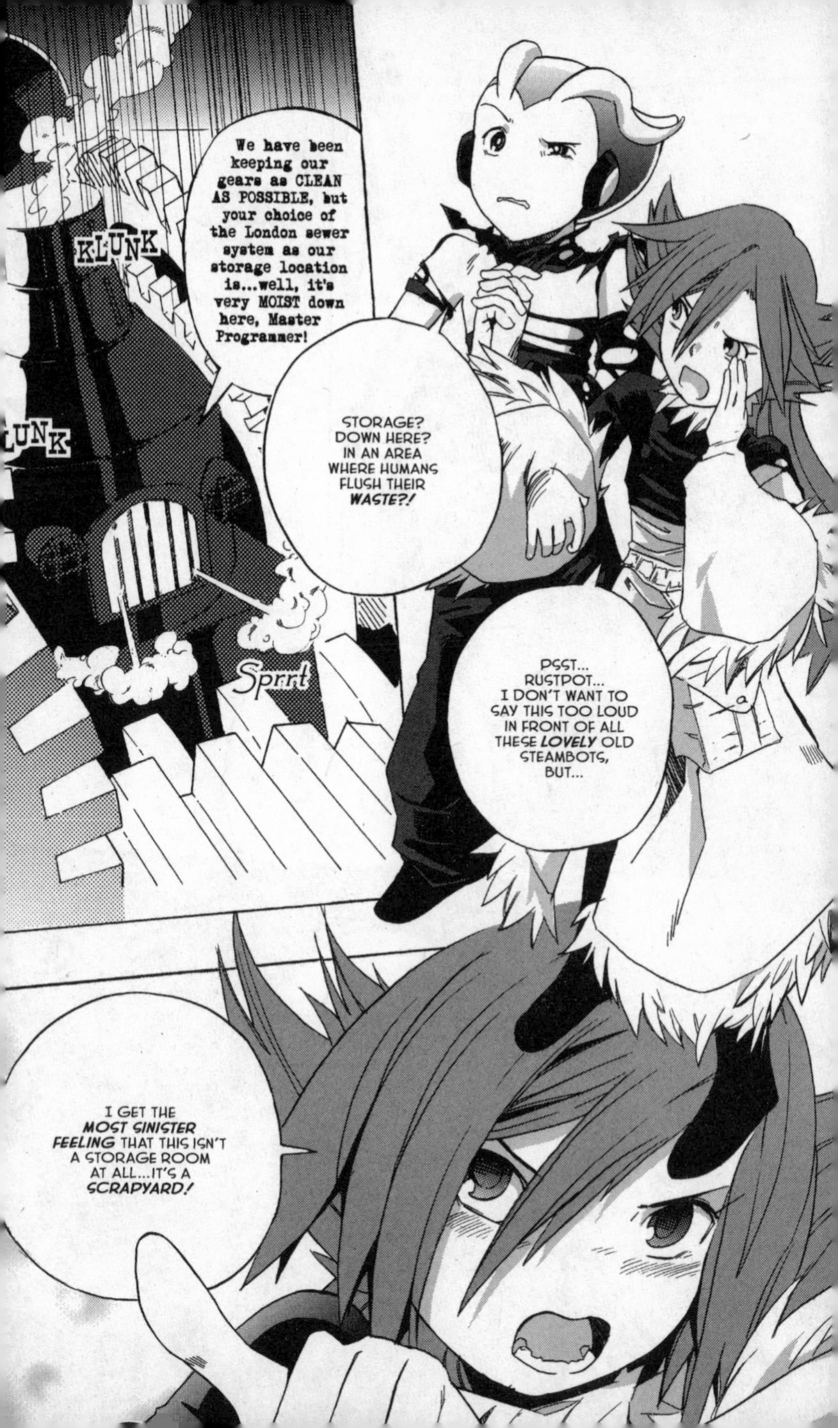
We have been keeping our gears as CLEAN AS POSSIBLE, but your choice of the London sewer system as our storage location is...well, it's very MOIST down here, Master Programmer!
KLUNK
LUNK
STORAGE? DOWN HERE? IN AN AREA WHERE HUMANS FLUSH THEIR *WASTE?!*
Sprrt
PSST... RUSTPOT... I DON'T WANT TO SAY THIS TOO LOUD IN FRONT OF ALL THESE *LOVELY* OLD STEAMBOTS, BUT...
I GET THE *MOST SINISTER FEELING* THAT THIS ISN'T A STORAGE ROOM AT ALL...IT'S A *SCRAPYARD!*

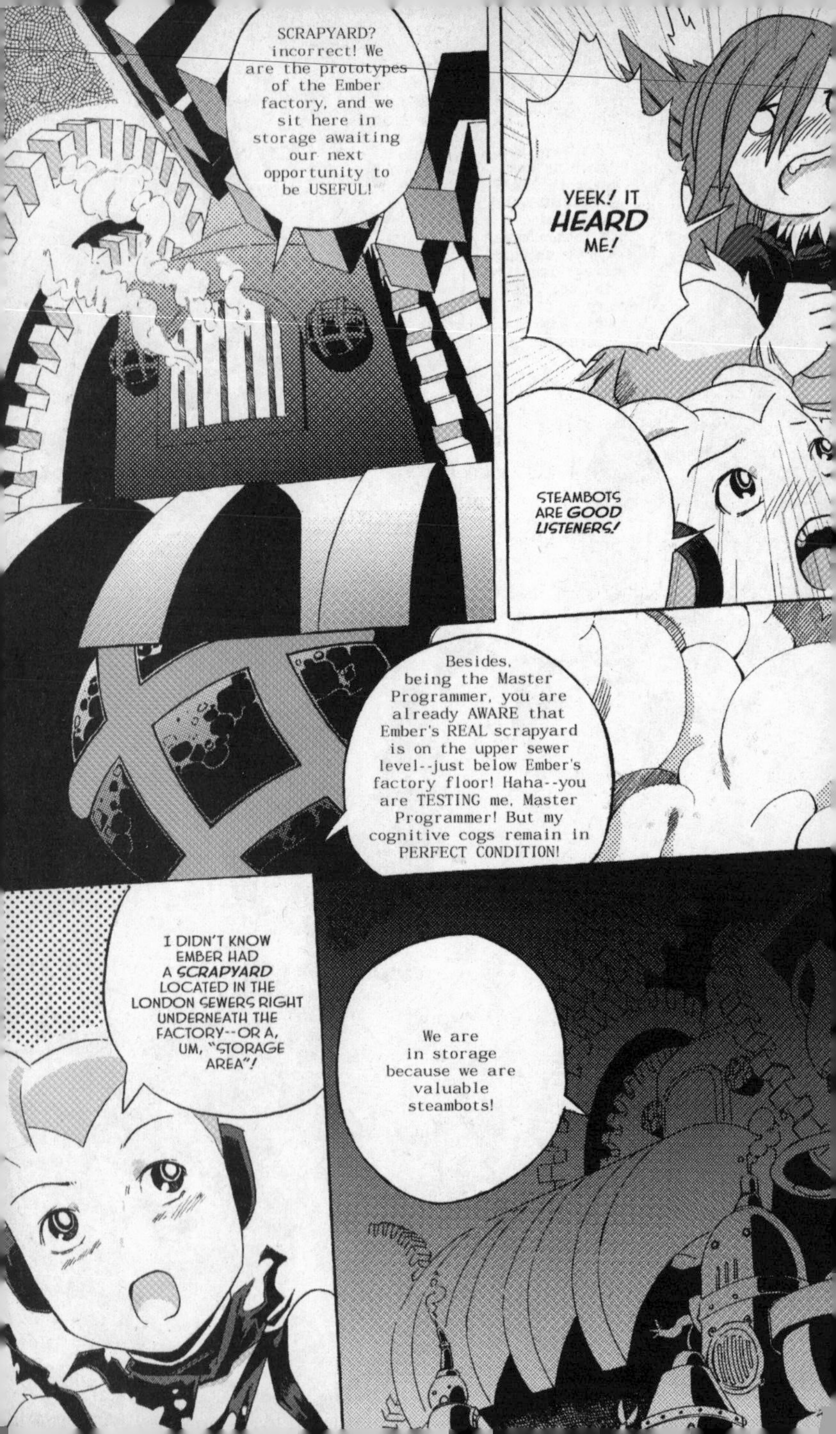

SCRAPYARD? incorrect! We are the prototypes of the Ember factory, and we sit here in storage awaiting our next opportunity to be USEFUL!
YEEK! IT **HEARD** ME!
STEAMBOTS ARE ***GOOD*** ***LISTENERS!***
Besides, being the Master Programmer, you are already AWARE that Ember's REAL scrapyard is on the upper sewer level--just below Ember's factory floor! Haha--you are TESTING me, Master Programmer! But my cognitive cogs remain in PERFECT CONDITION!
I DIDN'T KNOW EMBER HAD A ***SCRAPYARD*** LOCATED IN THE LONDON SEWERS RIGHT UNDERNEATH THE FACTORY--OR A, UM, "STORAGE AREA"!
We are in storage because we are valuable steambots!

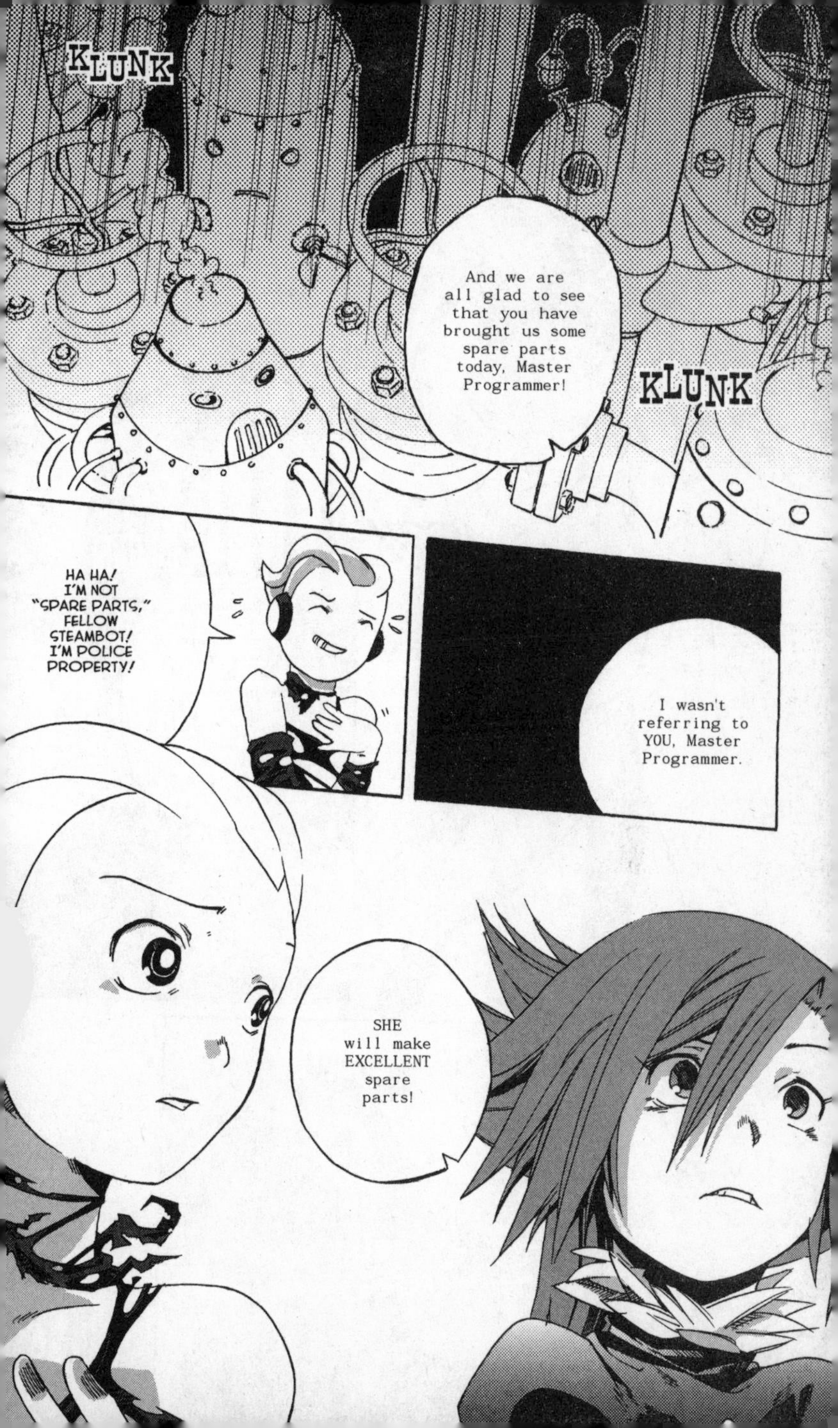
KLUNK
And we are all glad to see that you have brought us some spare parts today, Master Programmer!
KLUNK
HA HA! I'M NOT "SPARE PARTS," FELLOW STEAMBOT! I'M POLICE PROPERTY!
I wasn't referring to YOU, Master Programmer.
SHE will make EXCELLENT spare parts!

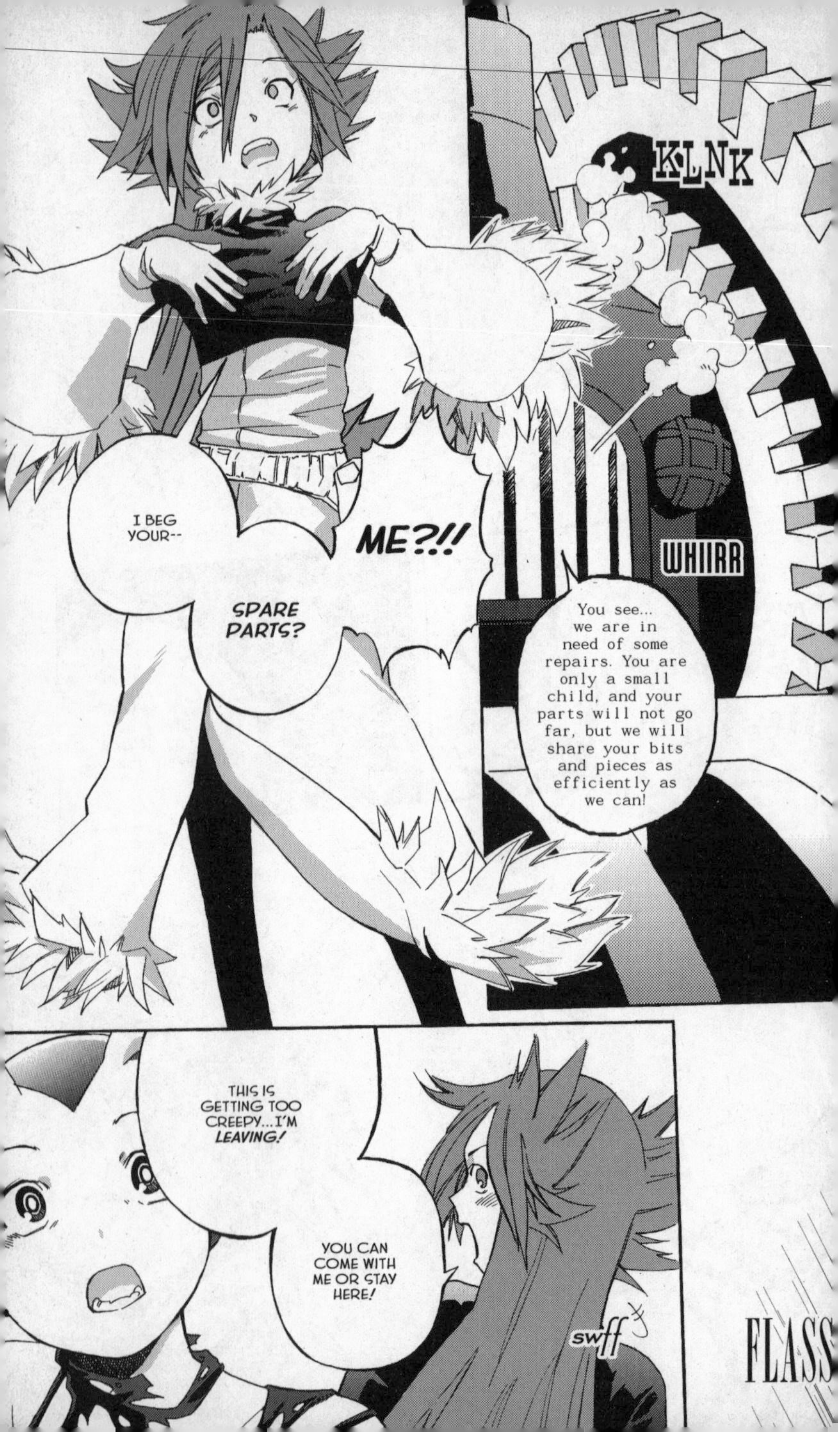
I BEG YOUR--
SPARE PARTS?
ME?!!
KLNK
WHIIRR
You see... we are in need of some repairs. You are only a small child, and your parts will not go far, but we will share your bits and pieces as efficiently as we can!
THIS IS GETTING TOO CREEPY...I'M *LEAVING!*
YOU CAN COME WITH ME OR STAY HERE!
swff
FLASS

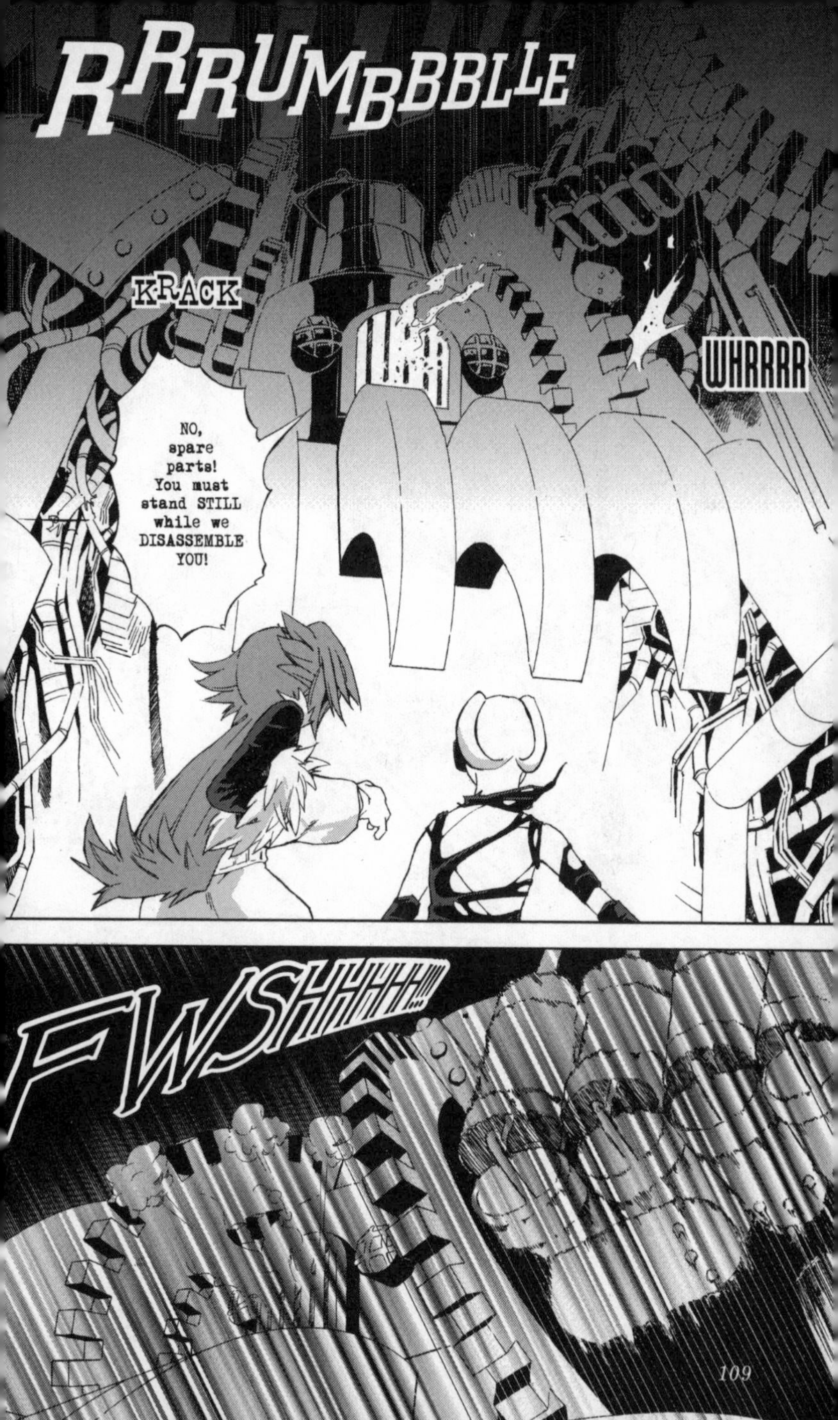
RRRUMBBBLLE
KRACK
WHRRRR
NO, spare parts! You must stand STILL while we DISASSEMBLE YOU!
FWSHHHH!!!

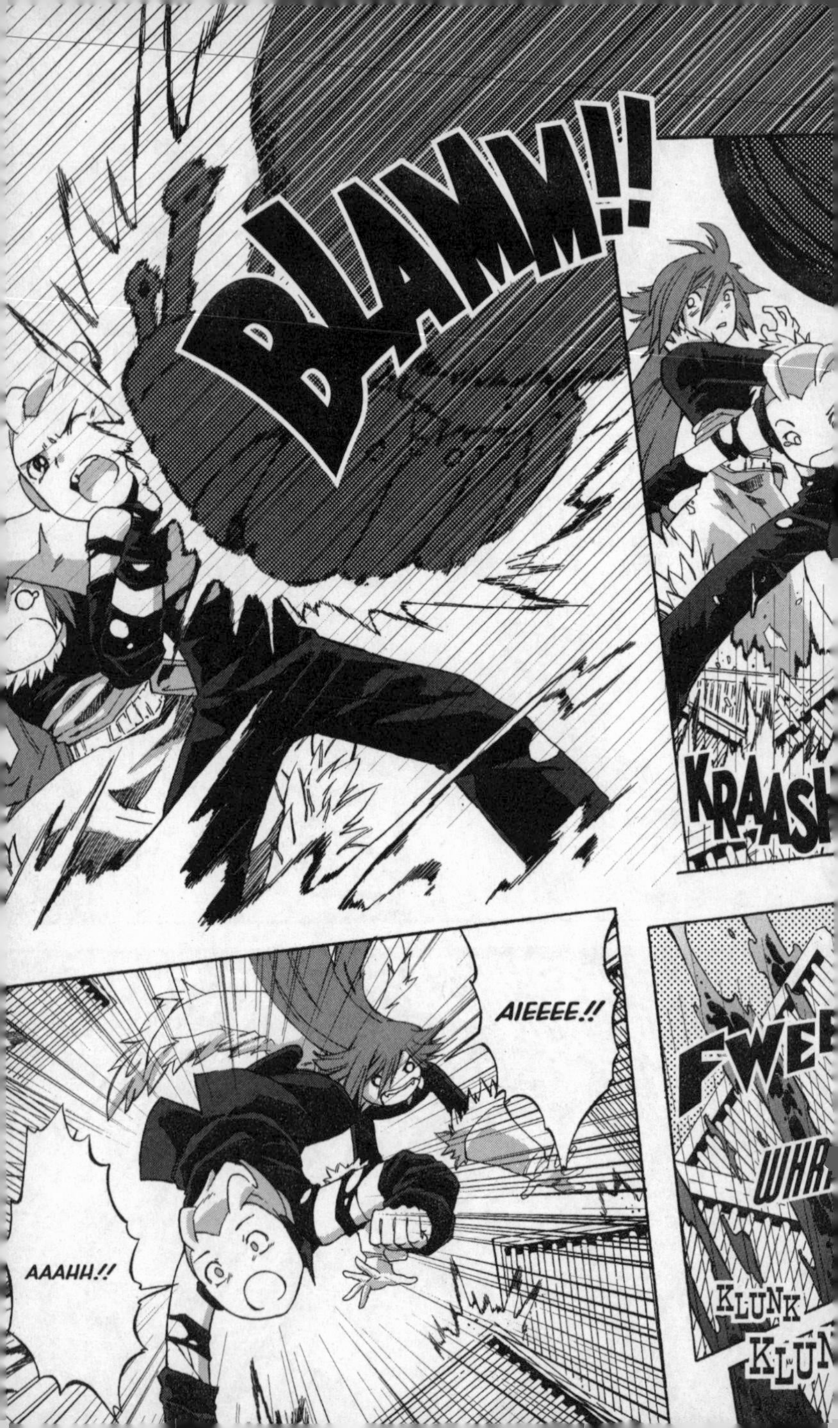
BLAMM!!
KRAAS
AIEEEE!!
AAAHH!!
FWEE
WHR
KLUNK
KLUN

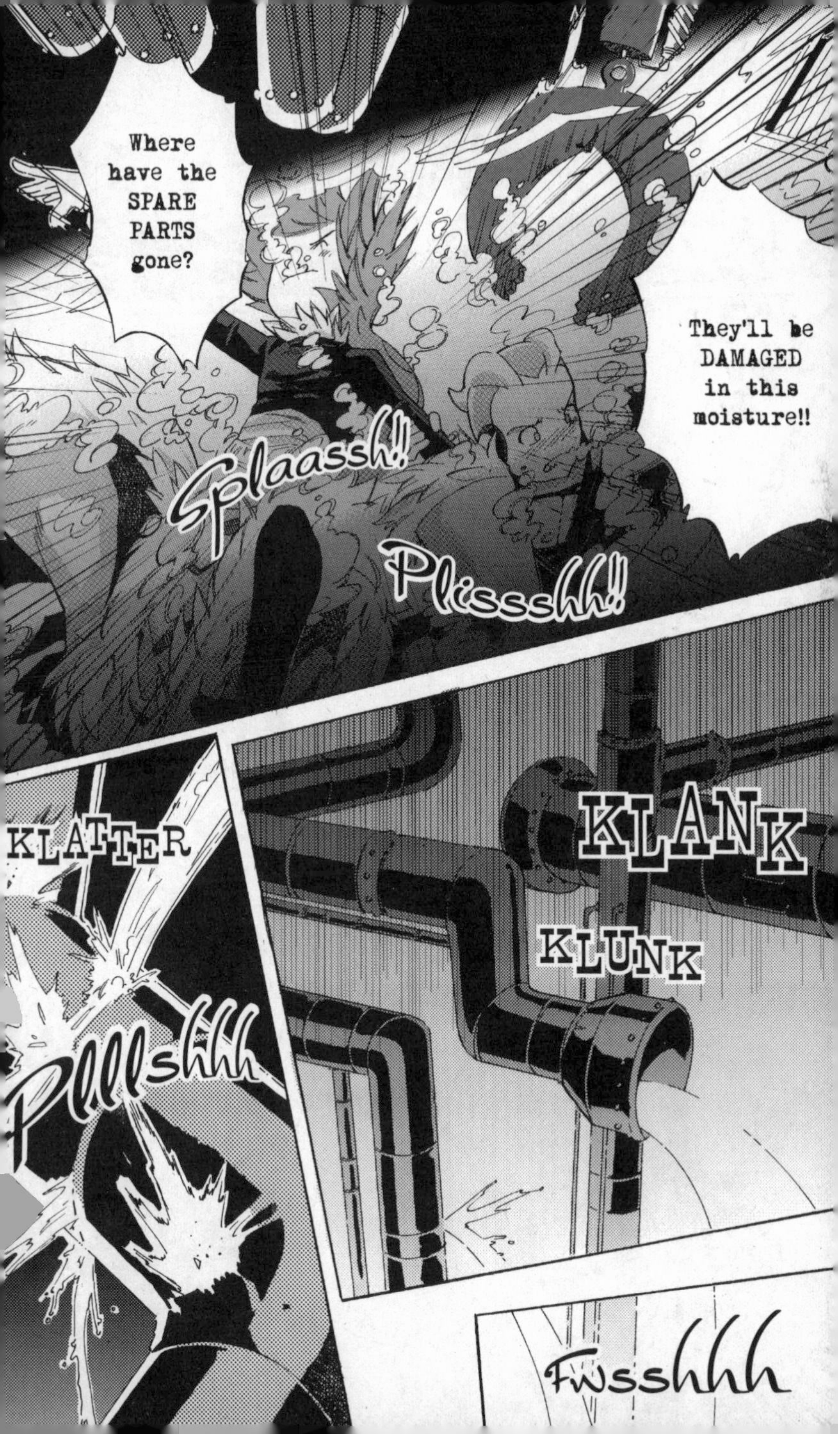

Where have the SPARE PARTS gone?
They'll be DAMAGED in this moisture!!
Splaassh!!
Plissshh!!
KLATTER
Plllshhh
KLANK
KLUNK
Fwsshhh

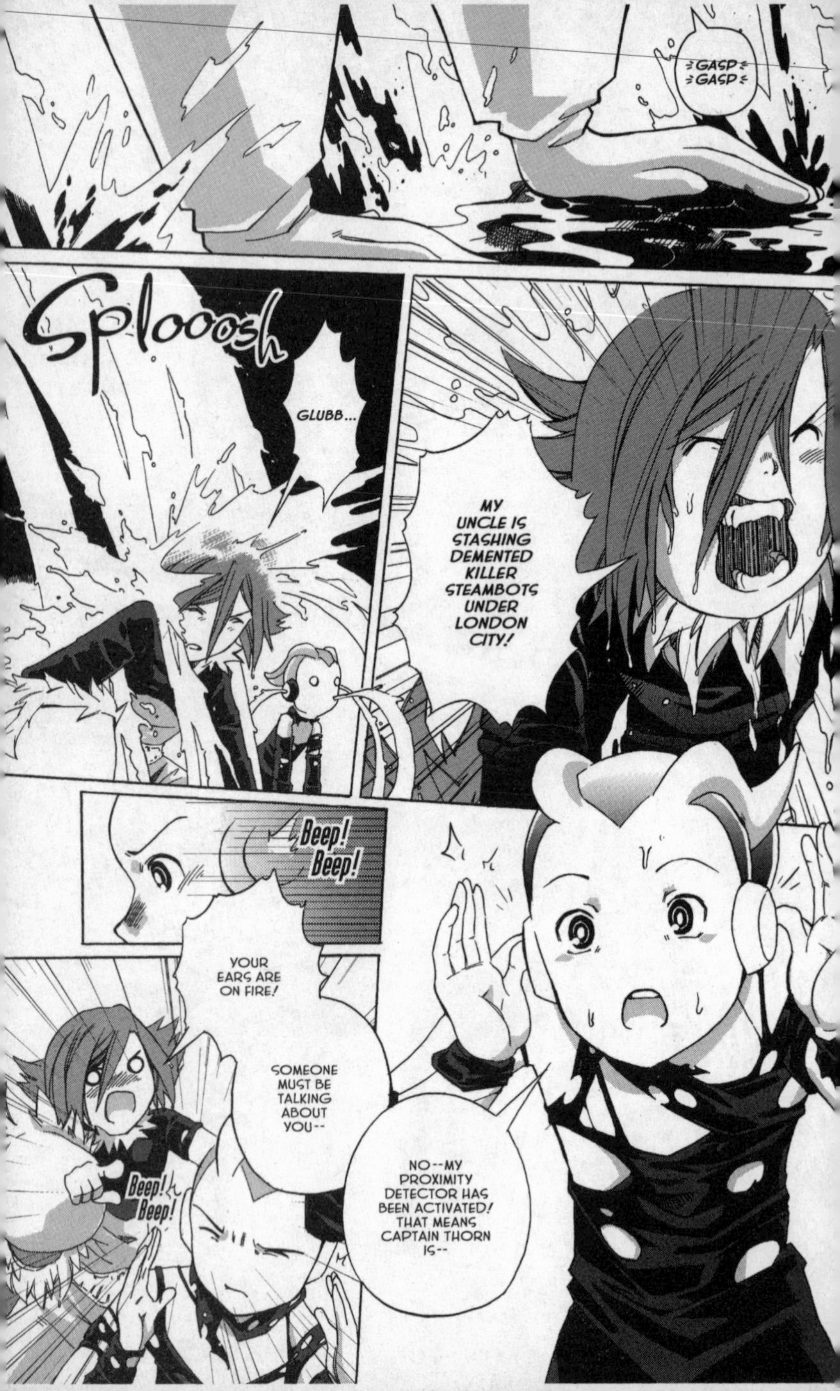
GASP GASP
Splooosh
GLUBB...
MY UNCLE IS STASHING DEMENTED KILLER STEAMBOTS UNDER LONDON CITY!
Beep! Beep!
YOUR EARS ARE ON FIRE!
SOMEONE MUST BE TALKING ABOUT YOU--
Beep! Beep!
NO--MY PROXIMITY DETECTOR HAS BEEN ACTIVATED! THAT MEANS CAPTAIN THORN IS--

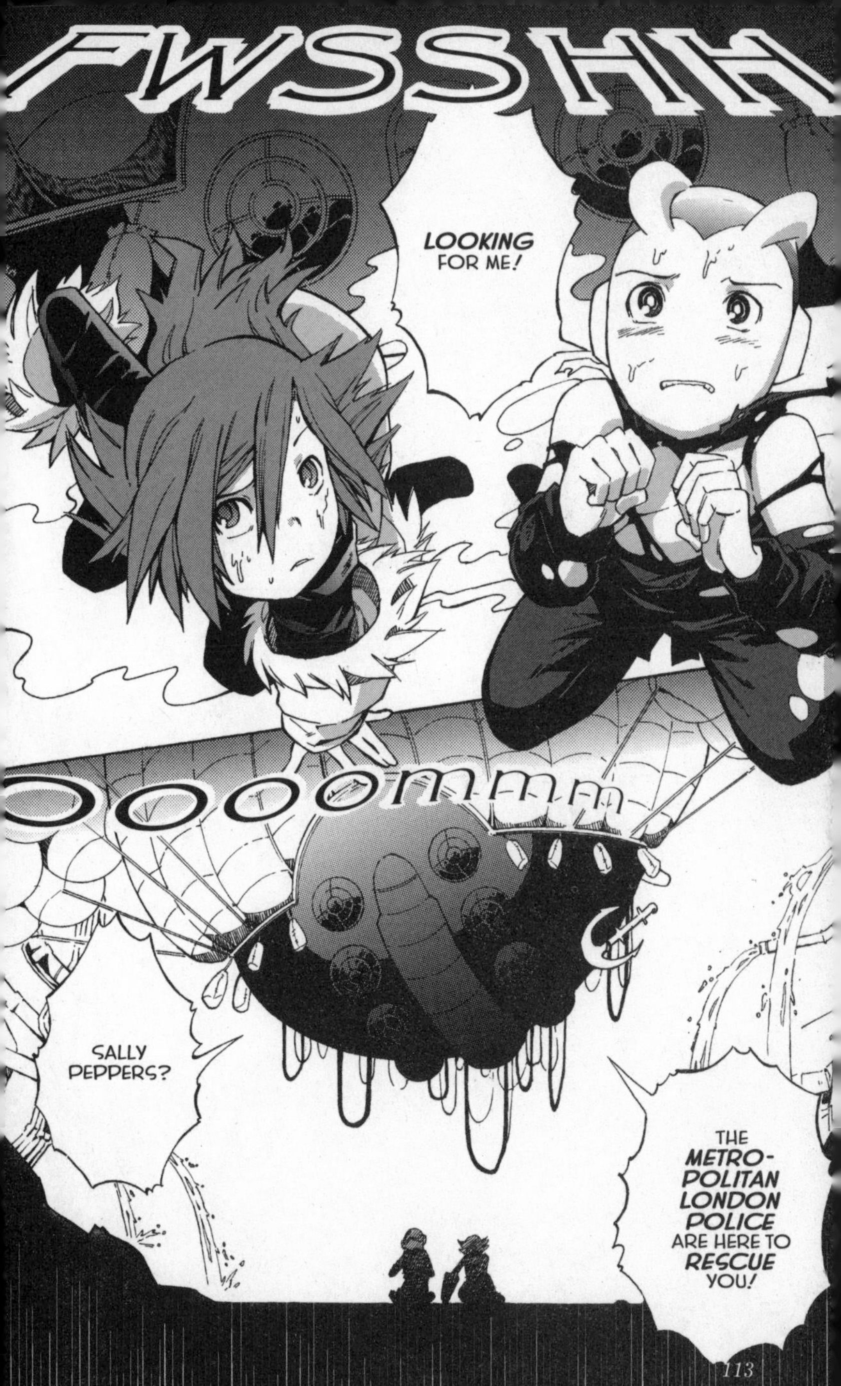
FWSSHH
LOOKING FOR ME!
OOOOMMMM
SALLY PEPPERS?
THE METRO-POLITAN LONDON POLICE ARE HERE TO RESCUE YOU!

CHAPTER 5

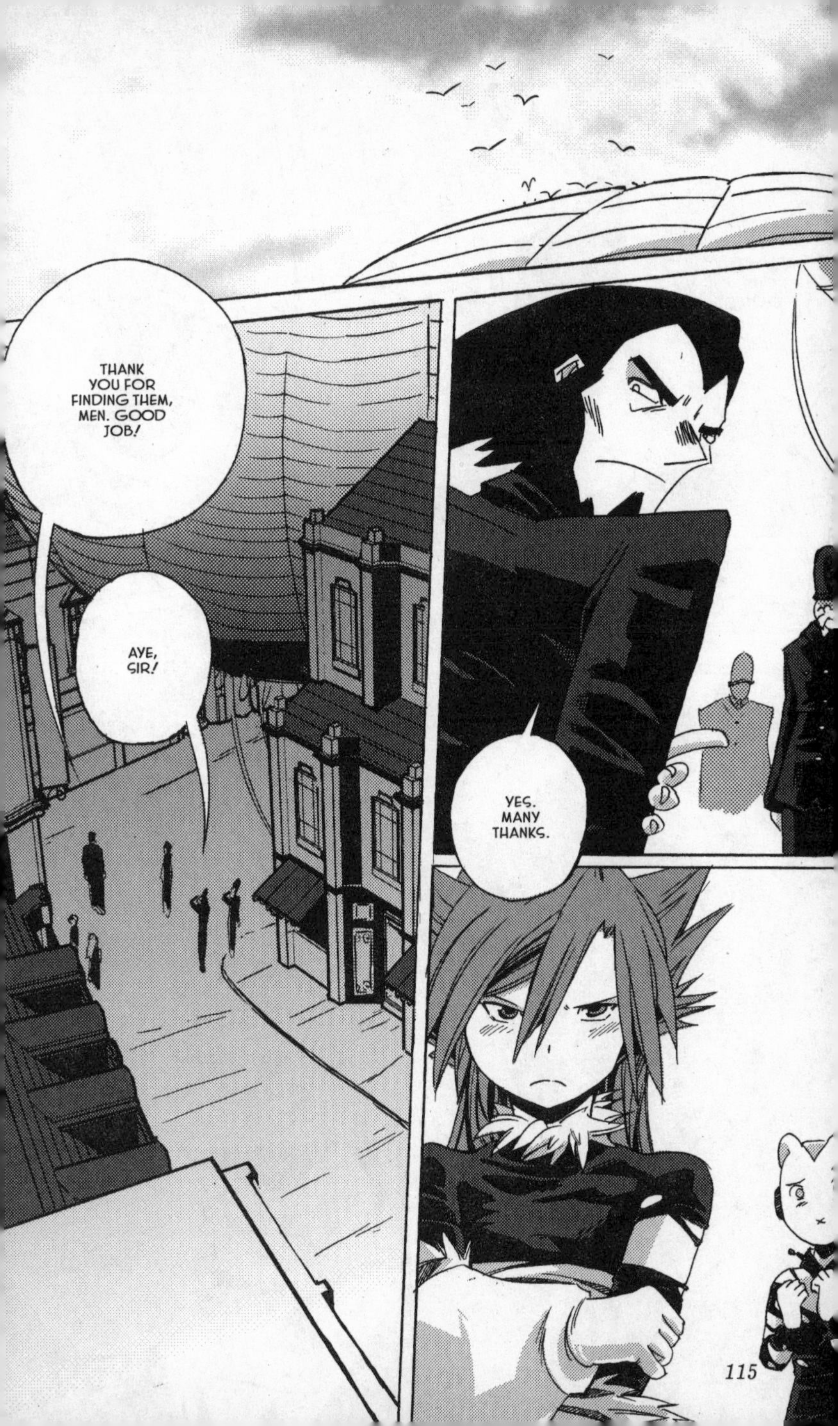
THANK YOU FOR FINDING THEM, MEN. GOOD JOB!
AYE, SIR!
YES. MANY THANKS.

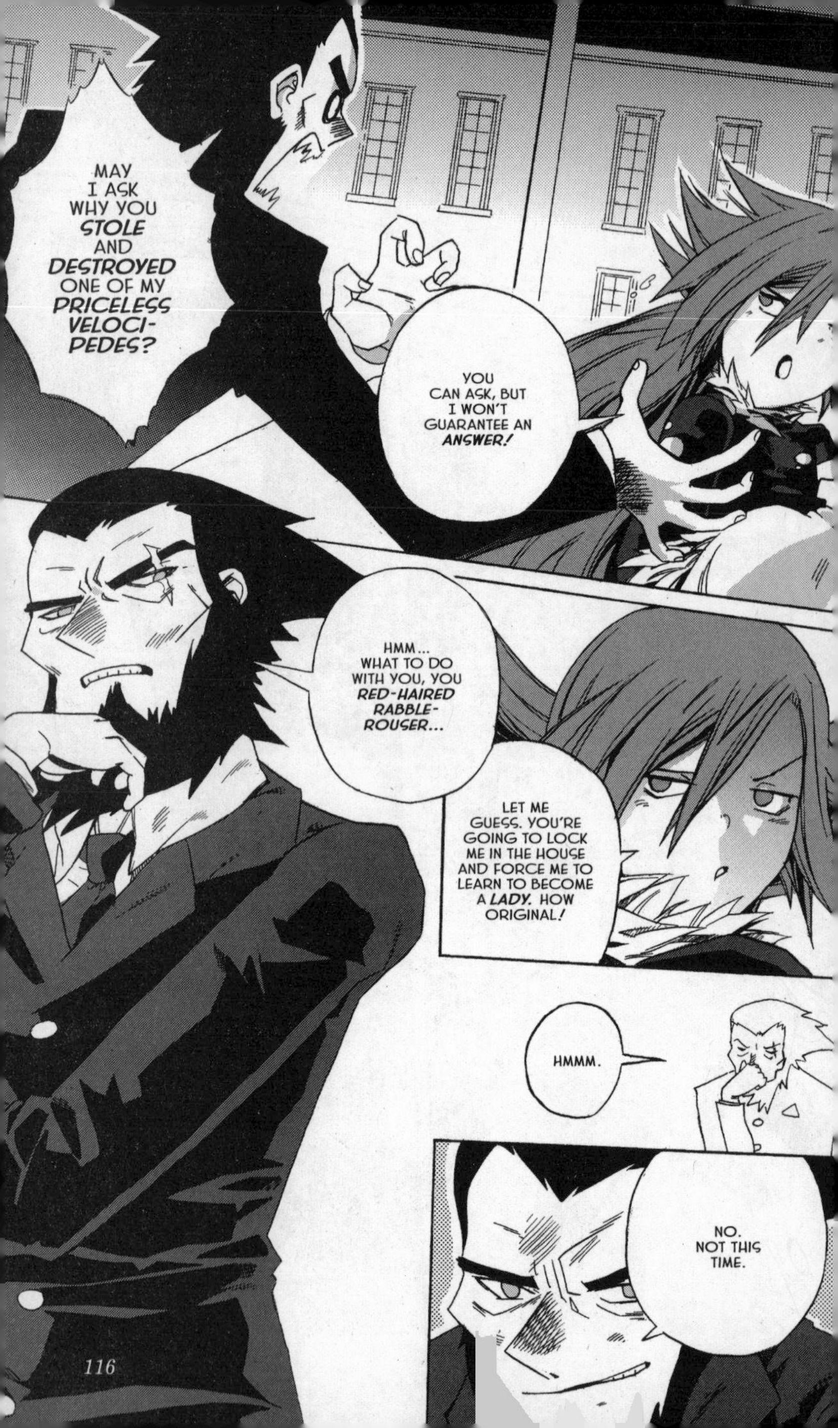
MAY I ASK WHY YOU STOLE AND DESTROYED ONE OF MY PRICELESS VELOCI-PEDES?
YOU CAN ASK, BUT I WON'T GUARANTEE AN ANSWER!
HMM... WHAT TO DO WITH YOU, YOU RED-HAIRED RABBLE-ROUSER...
LET ME GUESS. YOU'RE GOING TO LOCK ME IN THE HOUSE AND FORCE ME TO LEARN TO BECOME A LADY. HOW ORIGINAL!
HMMM.
NO. NOT THIS TIME.

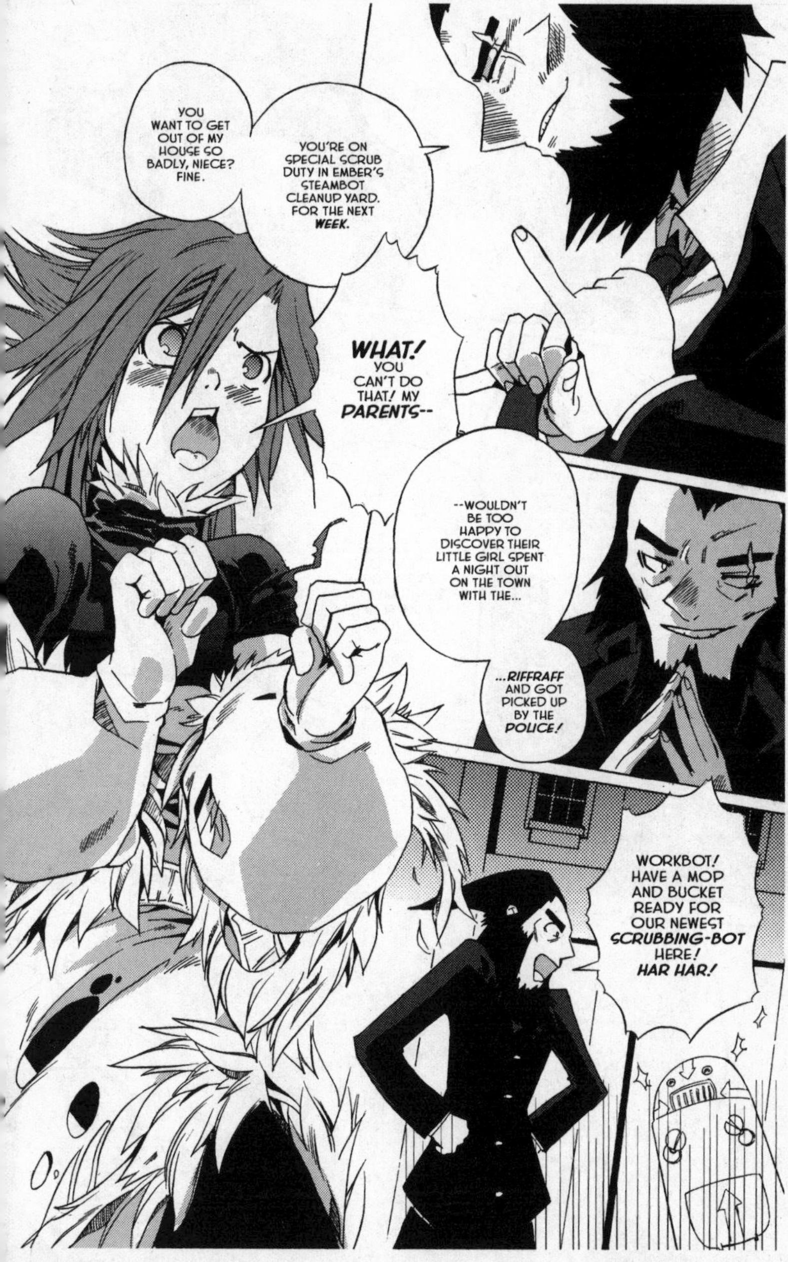
YOU WANT TO GET OUT OF MY HOUSE SO BADLY, NIECE? FINE.
YOU'RE ON SPECIAL SCRUB DUTY IN EMBER'S STEAMBOT CLEANUP YARD. FOR THE NEXT WEEK.
WHAT! YOU CAN'T DO THAT! MY PARENTS--
--WOULDN'T BE TOO HAPPY TO DISCOVER THEIR LITTLE GIRL SPENT A NIGHT OUT ON THE TOWN WITH THE...
...RIFFRAFF AND GOT PICKED UP BY THE POLICE!
WORKBOT! HAVE A MOP AND BUCKET READY FOR OUR NEWEST SCRUBBING-BOT HERE! HAR HAR!

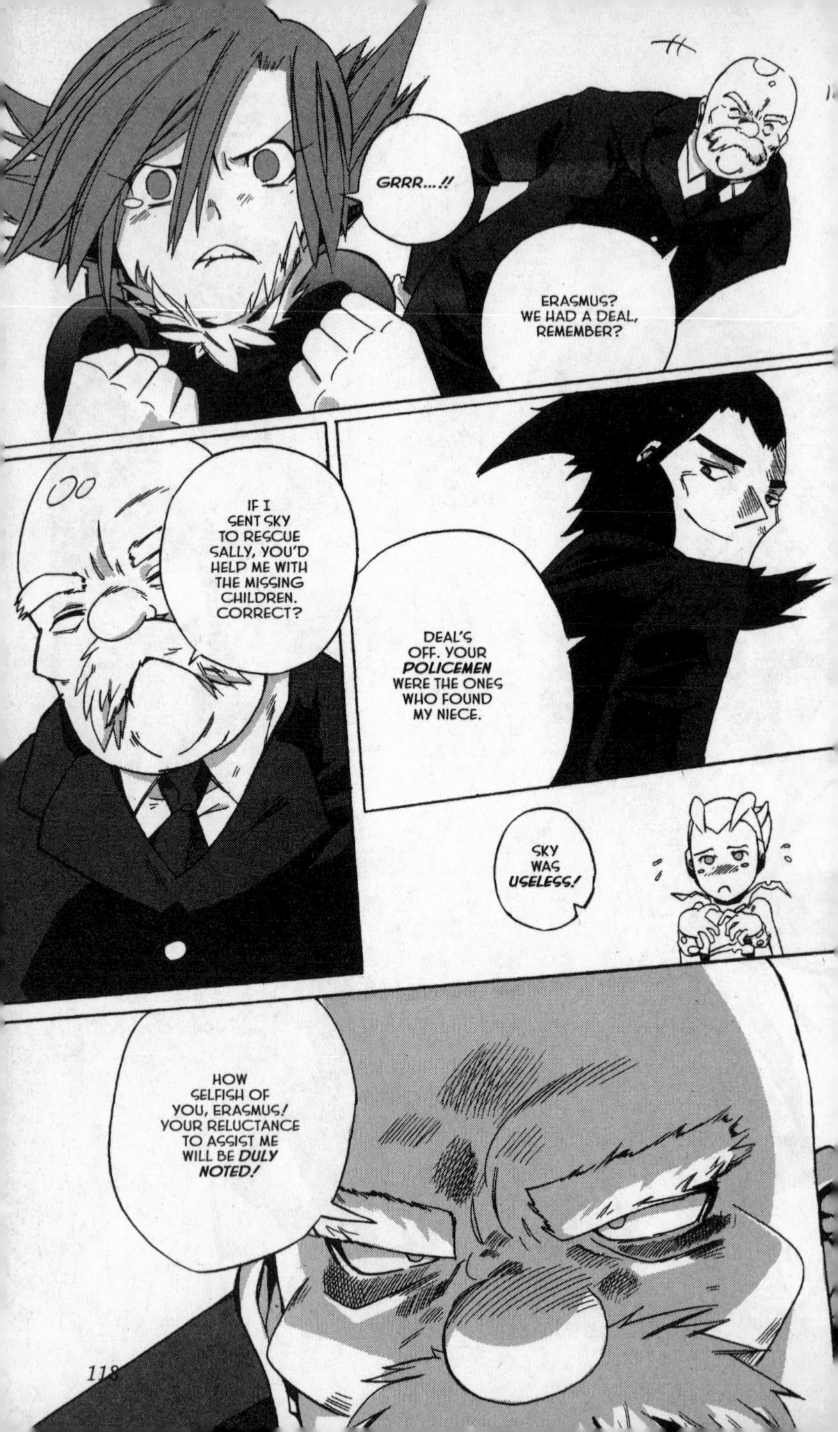
GRRR...!!
ERASMUS? WE HAD A DEAL, REMEMBER?
IF I SENT SKY TO RESCUE SALLY, YOU'D HELP ME WITH THE MISSING CHILDREN. CORRECT?
DEAL'S OFF. YOUR ***POLICEMEN*** WERE THE ONES WHO FOUND MY NIECE.
SKY WAS ***USELESS!***
HOW SELFISH OF YOU, ERASMUS! YOUR RELUCTANCE TO ASSIST ME WILL BE ***DULY NOTED!***

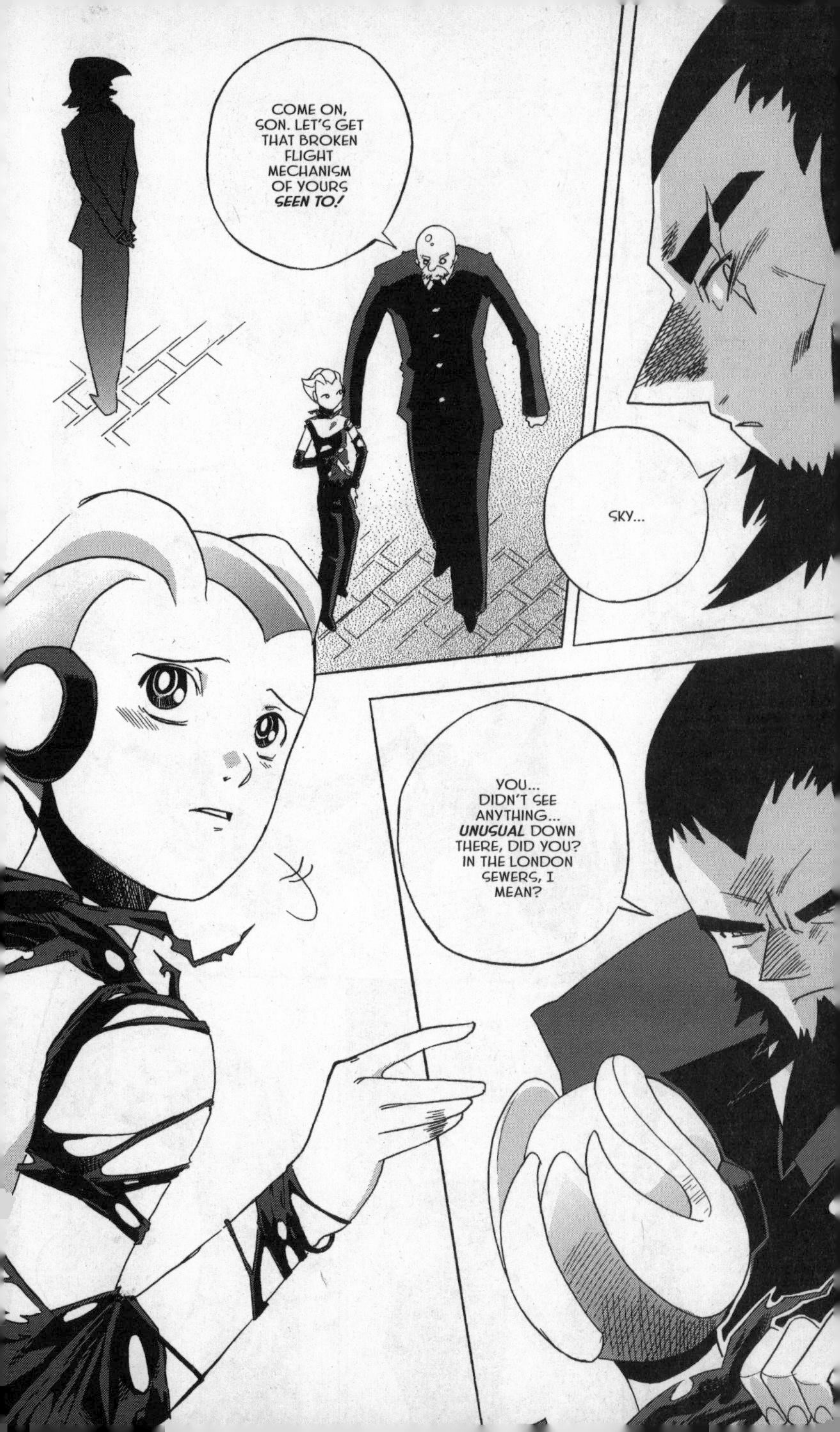
COME ON, SON. LET'S GET THAT BROKEN FLIGHT MECHANISM OF YOURS *SEEN TO!*
SKY...
YOU... DIDN'T SEE ANYTHING... *UNUSUAL* DOWN THERE, DID YOU? IN THE LONDON SEWERS, I MEAN?

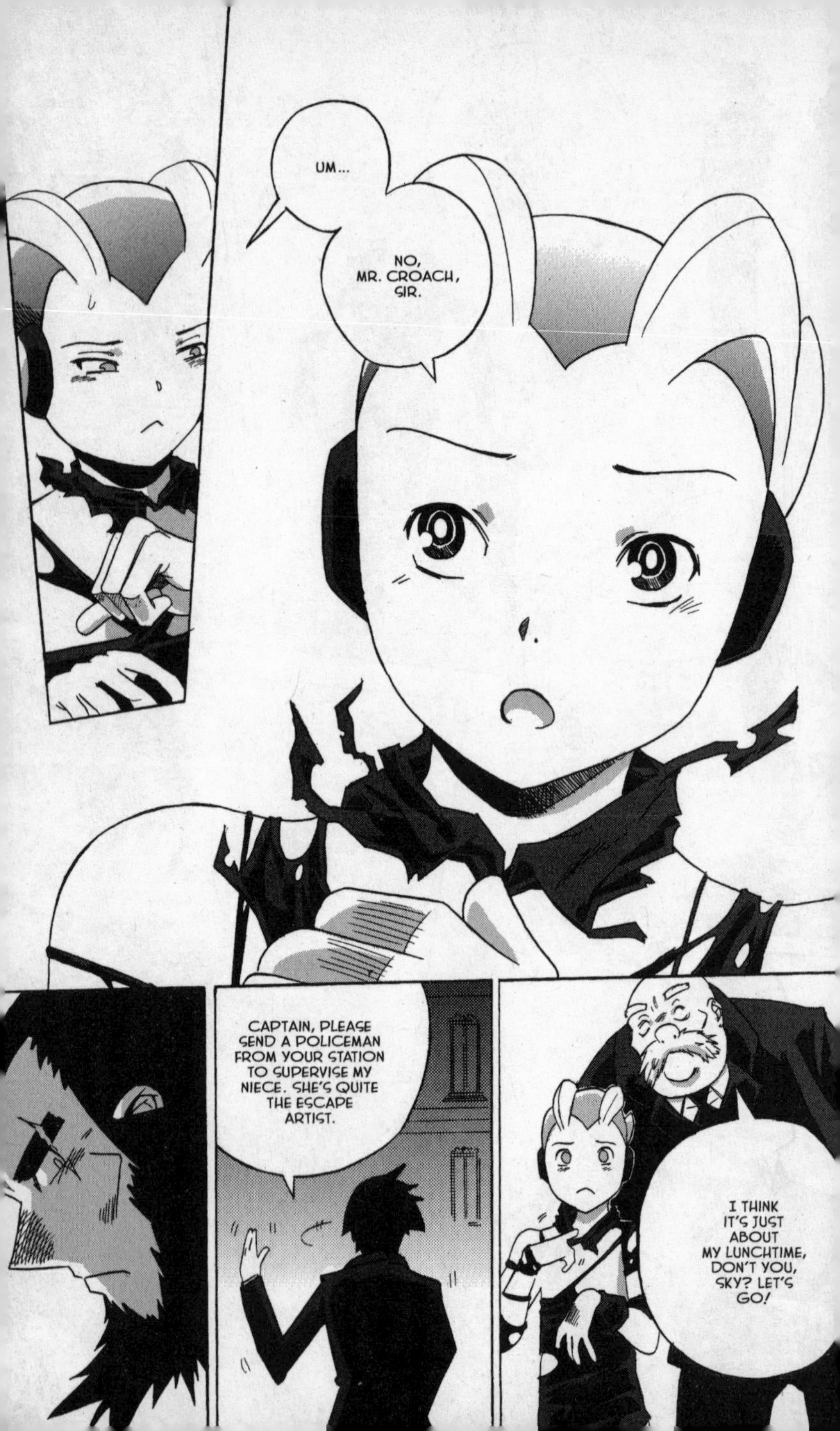
UM...
NO, MR. CROACH, SIR.
CAPTAIN, PLEASE SEND A POLICEMAN FROM YOUR STATION TO SUPERVISE MY NIECE. SHE'S QUITE THE ESCAPE ARTIST.
I THINK IT'S JUST ABOUT MY LUNCHTIME, DON'T YOU, SKY? LET'S GO!

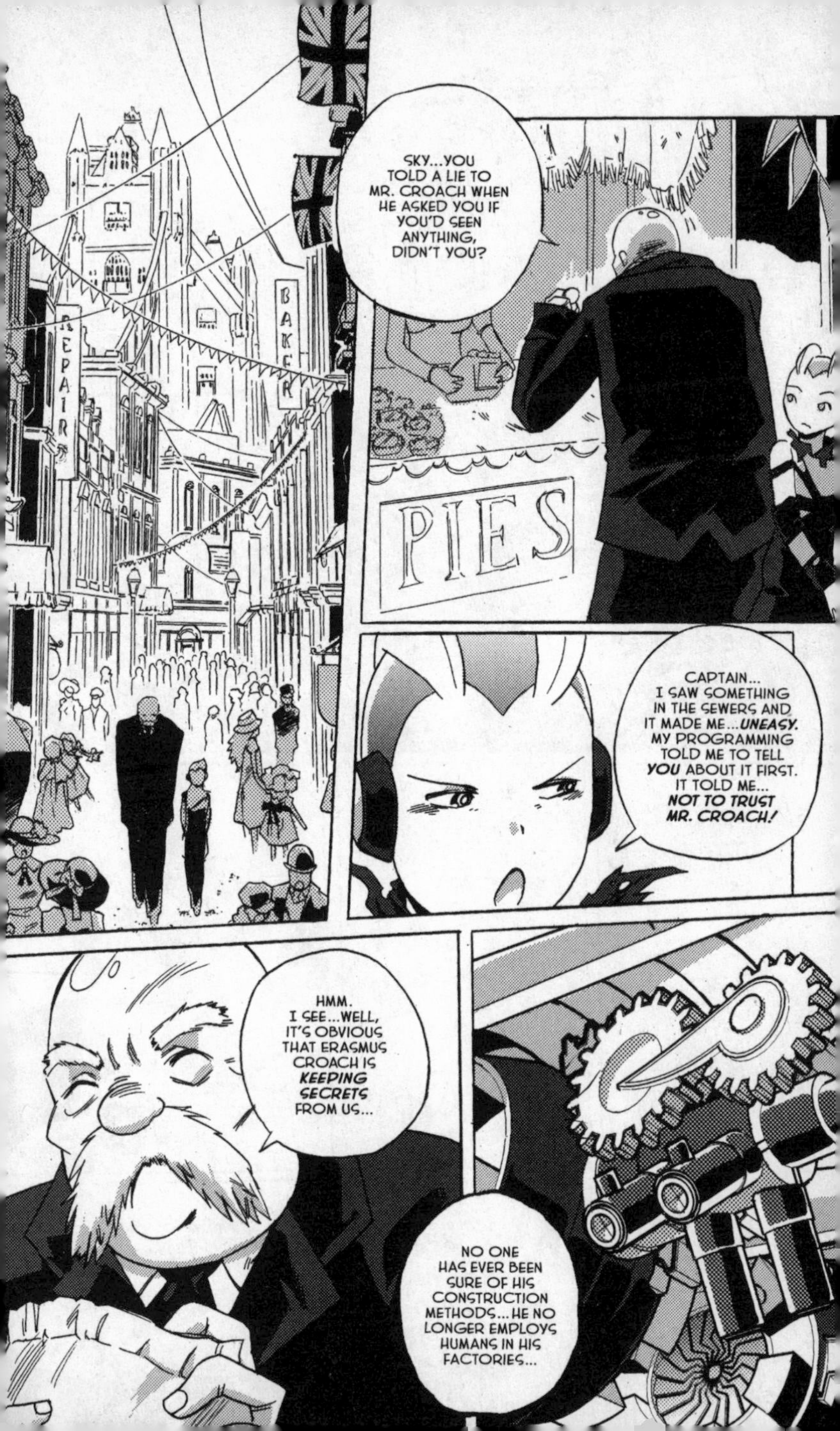
REPAIR
BAKER
SKY...YOU TOLD A LIE TO MR. CROACH WHEN HE ASKED YOU IF YOU'D SEEN ANYTHING, DIDN'T YOU?
PIES
CAPTAIN... I SAW SOMETHING IN THE SEWERS AND IT MADE ME...*UNEASY.* MY PROGRAMMING TOLD ME TO TELL *YOU* ABOUT IT FIRST. IT TOLD ME... *NOT TO TRUST MR. CROACH!*
HMM. I SEE...WELL, IT'S OBVIOUS THAT ERASMUS CROACH IS *KEEPING SECRETS* FROM US...
NO ONE HAS EVER BEEN SURE OF HIS CONSTRUCTION METHODS...HE NO LONGER EMPLOYS HUMANS IN HIS FACTORIES...

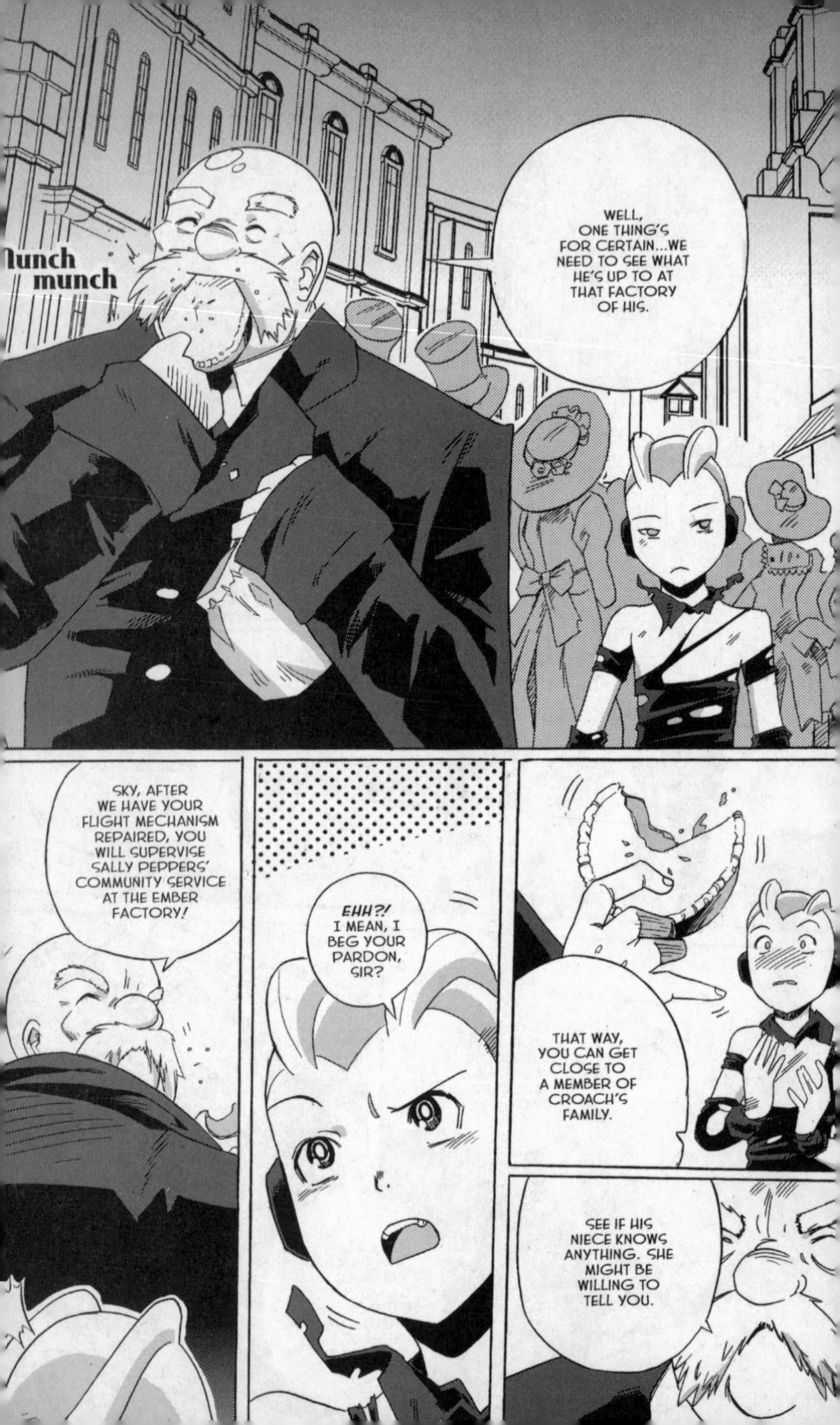
Munch munch
WELL, ONE THING'S FOR CERTAIN...WE NEED TO SEE WHAT HE'S UP TO AT THAT FACTORY OF HIS.
SKY, AFTER WE HAVE YOUR FLIGHT MECHANISM REPAIRED, YOU WILL SUPERVISE SALLY PEPPERS' COMMUNITY SERVICE AT THE EMBER FACTORY!
EHH?! I MEAN, I BEG YOUR PARDON, SIR?
THAT WAY, YOU CAN GET CLOSE TO A MEMBER OF CROACH'S FAMILY.
SEE IF HIS NIECE KNOWS ANYTHING. SHE MIGHT BE WILLING TO TELL YOU.

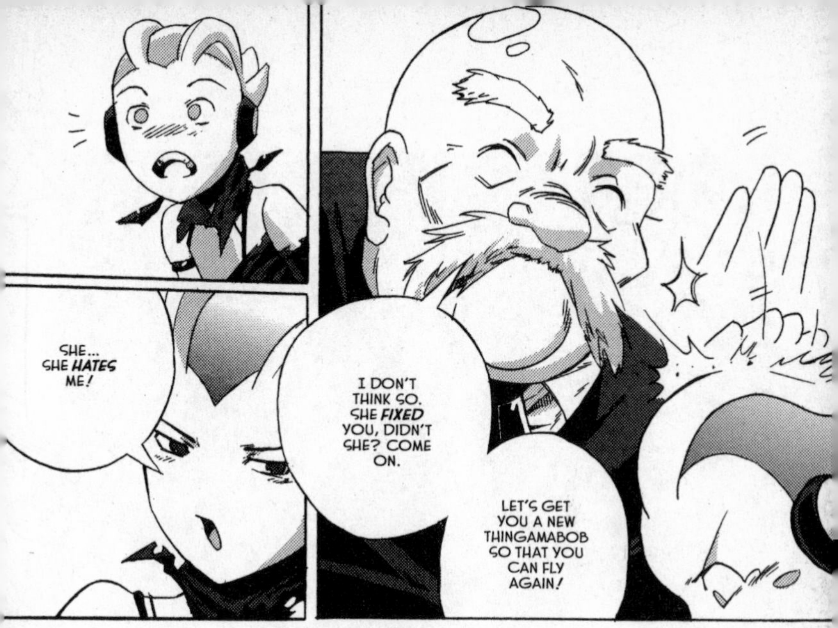
SHE... SHE HATES ME!
I DON'T THINK SO. SHE FIXED YOU, DIDN'T SHE? COME ON.
LET'S GET YOU A NEW THINGAMABOB SO THAT YOU CAN FLY AGAIN!

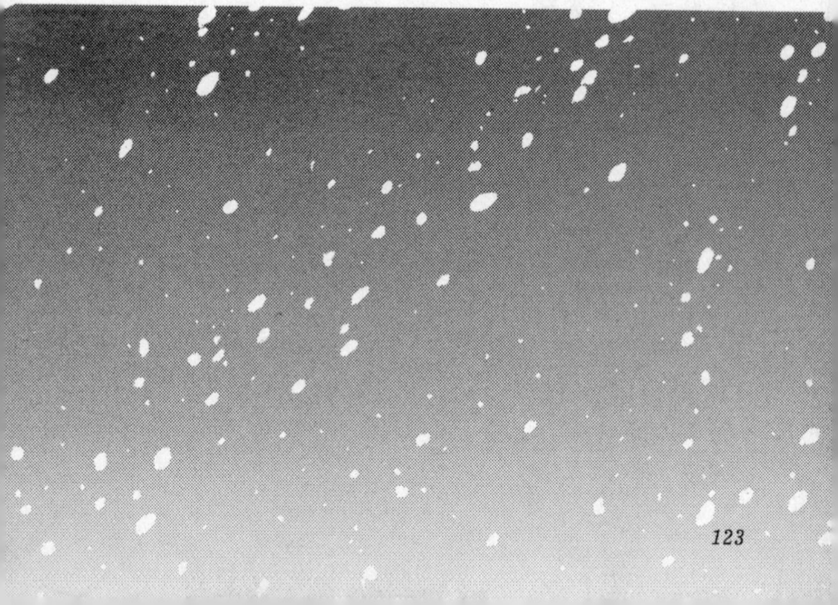

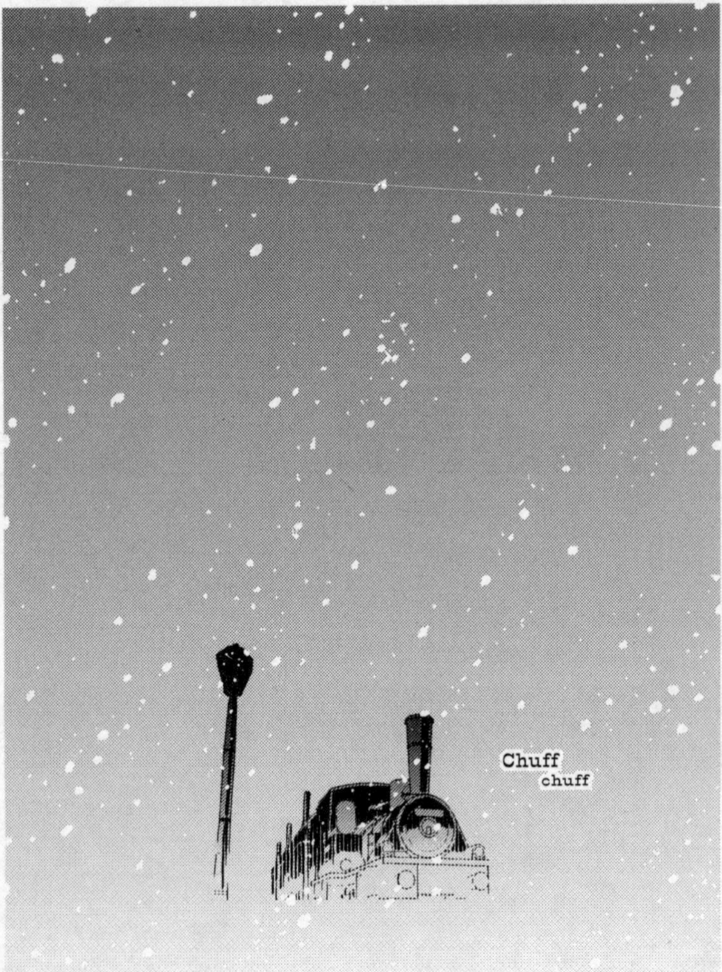
Chuff
chuff

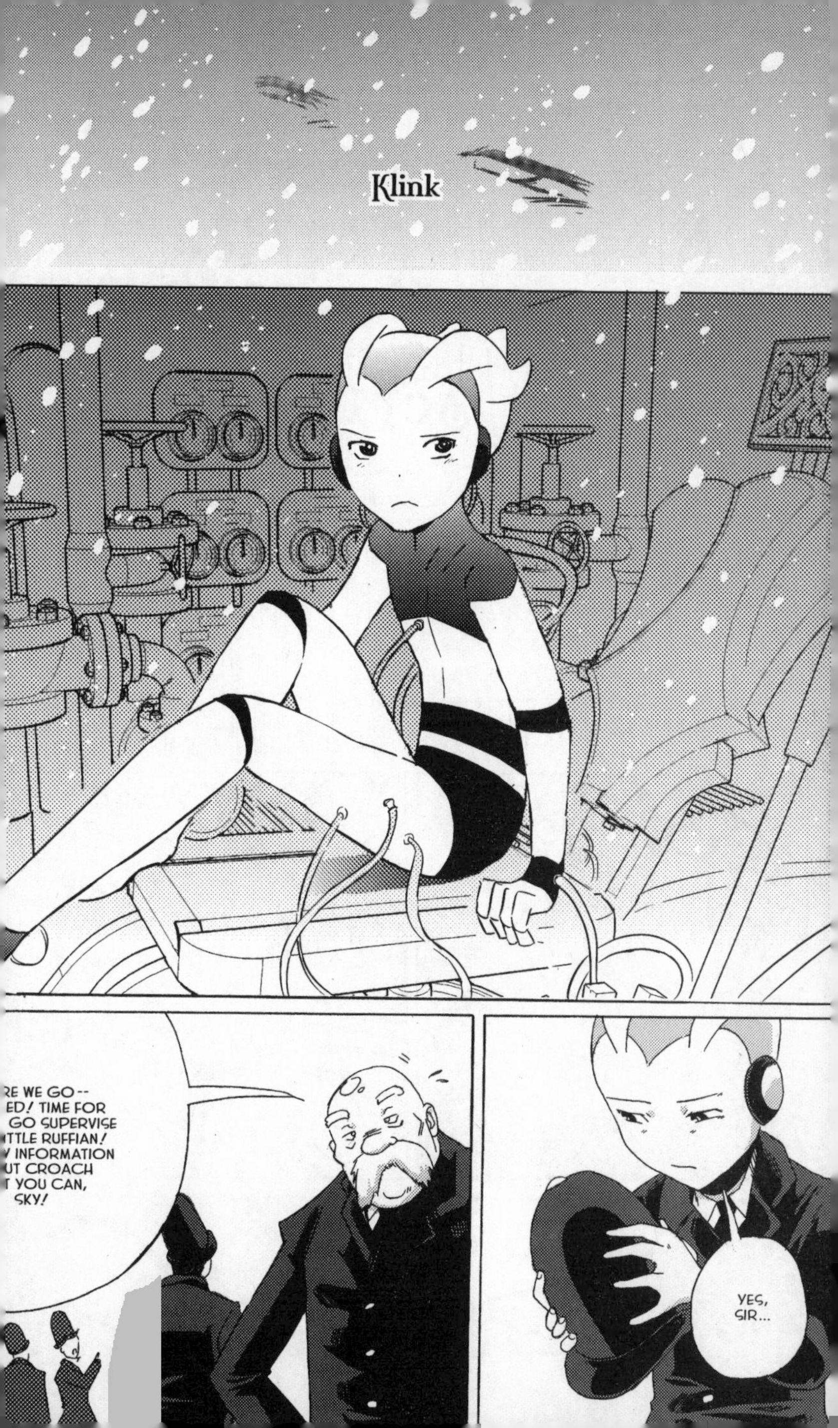
Klink
RE WE GO-- ED! TIME FOR GO SUPERVISE TTLE RUFFIAN! Y INFORMATION UT CROACH T YOU CAN, SKY!
YES, SIR...

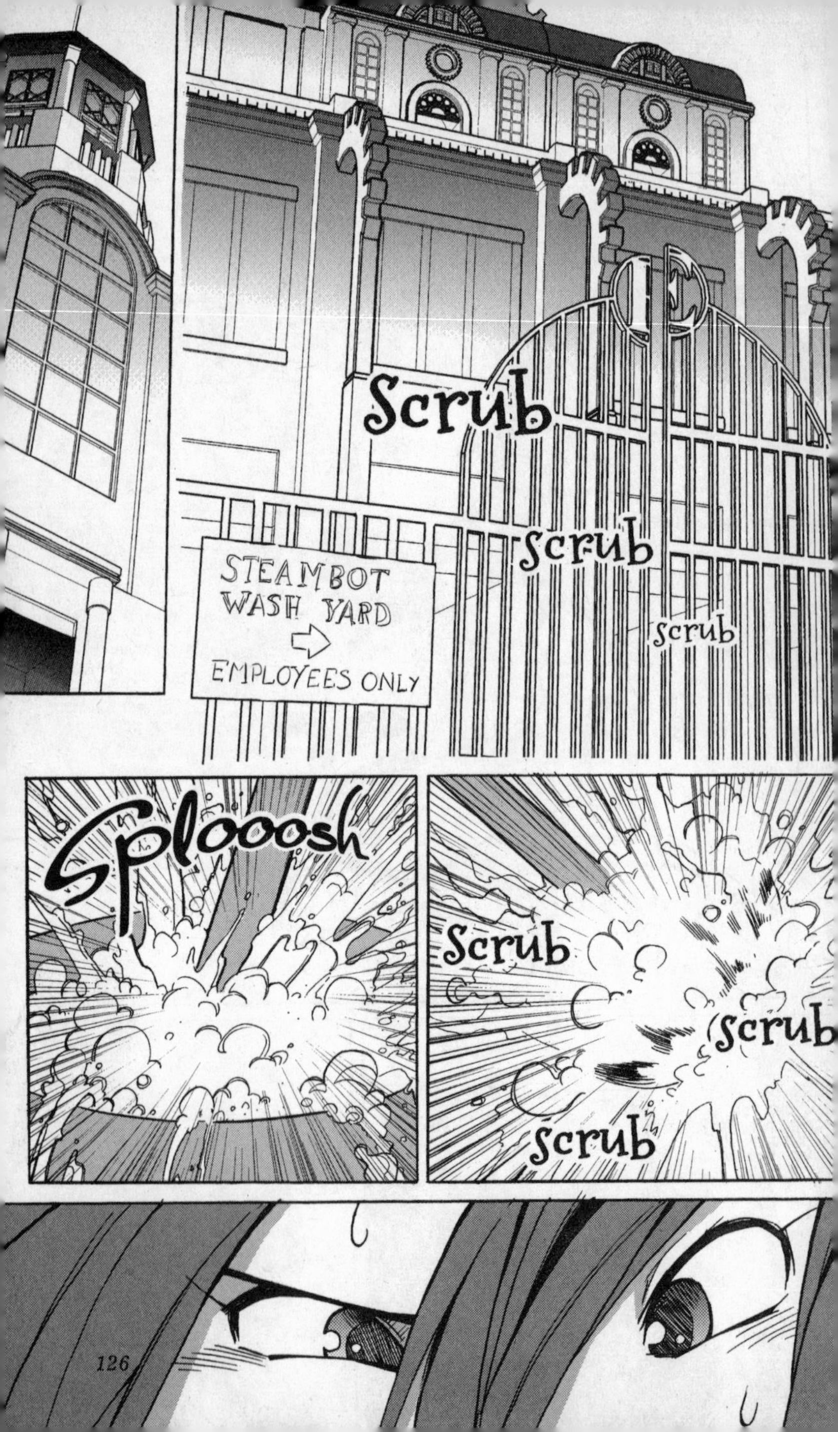
STEAMBOT
WASH YARD
EMPLOYEES ONLY
Scrub
Scrub
scrub
Splooosh
Scrub
Scrub
Scrub

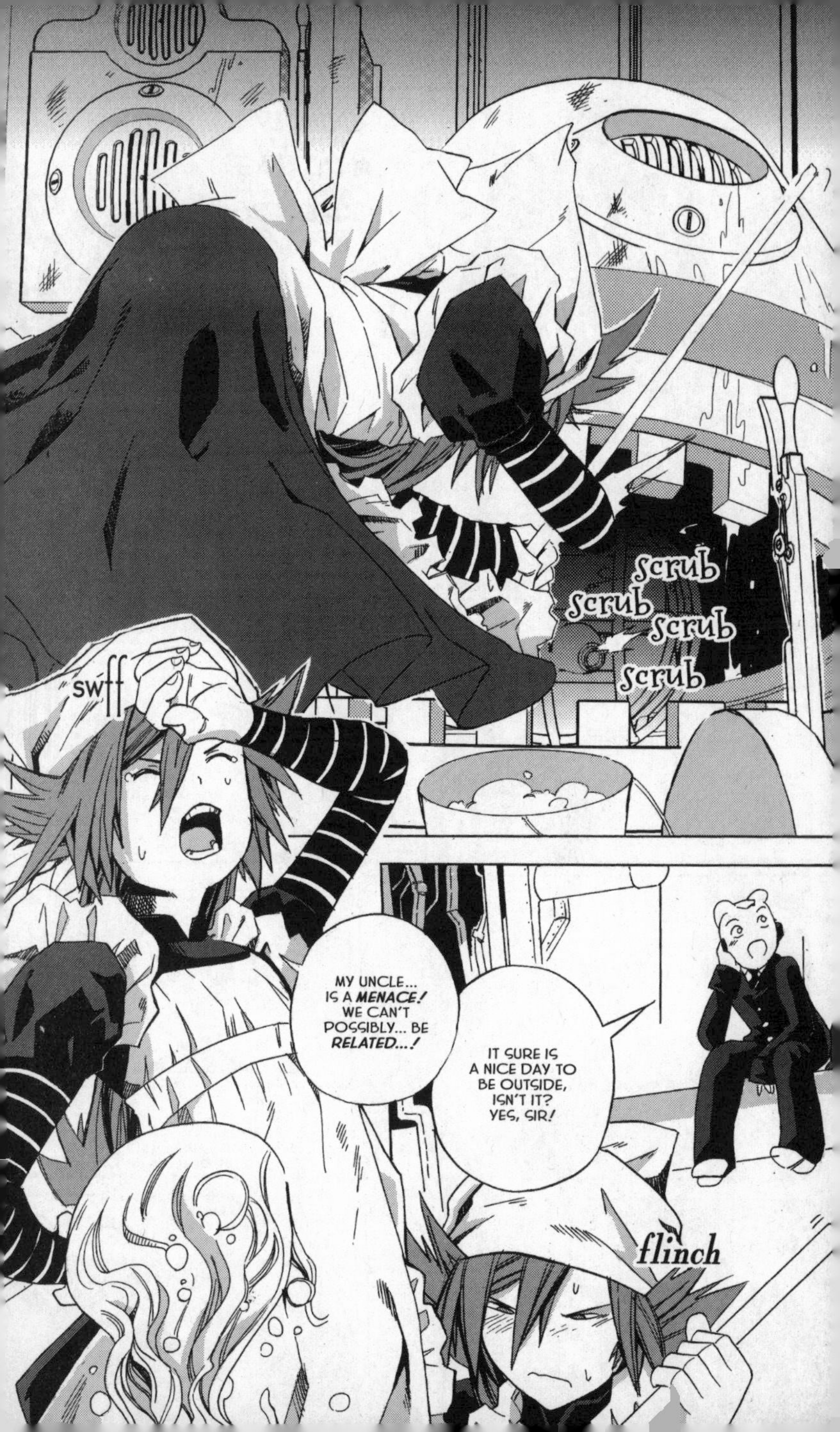
scrub
scrub
scrub
scrub
swff
MY UNCLE... IS A ***MENACE!*** WE CAN'T POSSIBLY... BE ***RELATED...!***
IT SURE IS A NICE DAY TO BE OUTSIDE, ISN'T IT? YES, SIR!
flinch

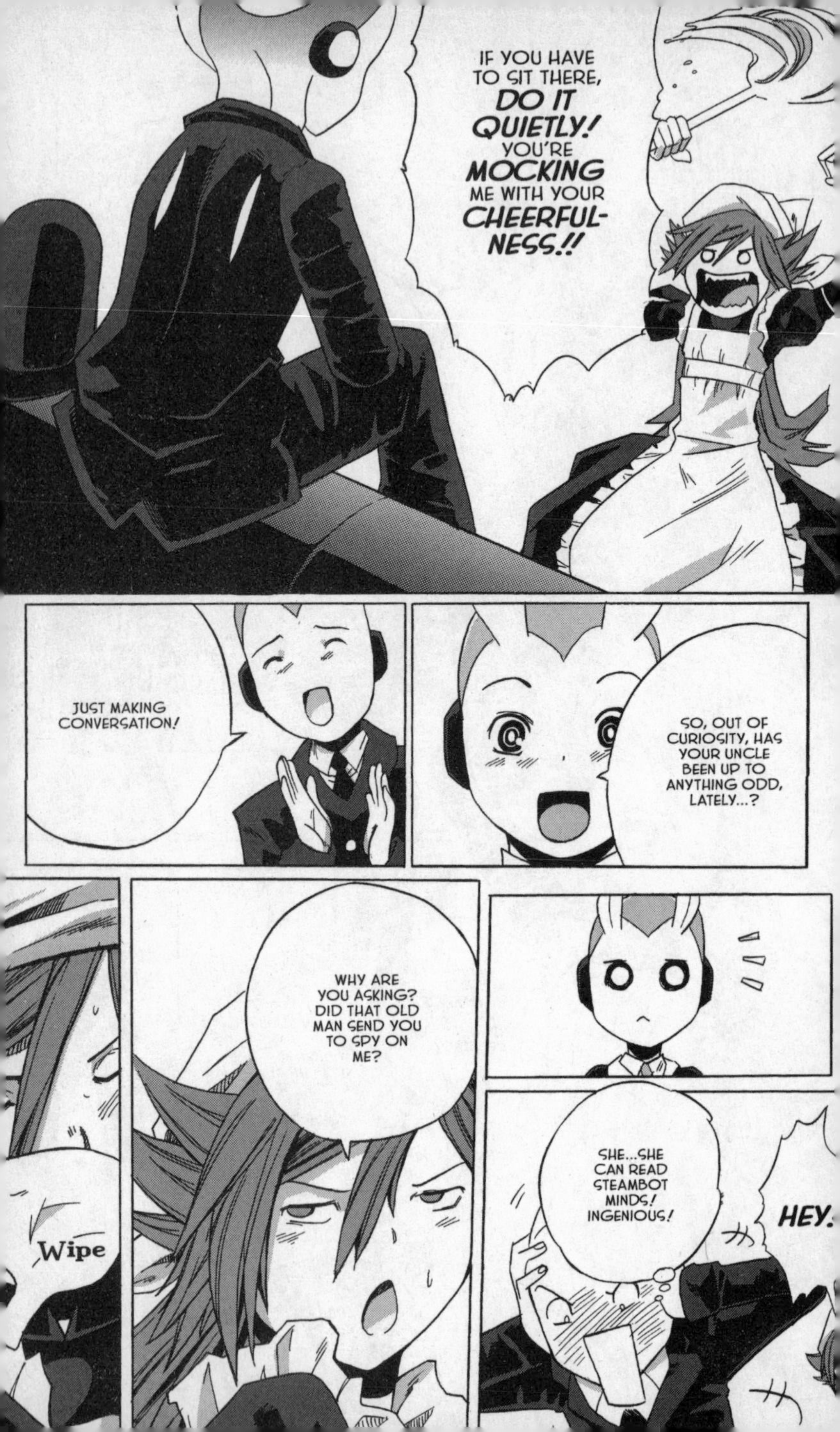
IF YOU HAVE TO SIT THERE, DO IT QUIETLY! YOU'RE MOCKING ME WITH YOUR CHEERFUL-NESS!!
JUST MAKING CONVERSATION!
SO, OUT OF CURIOSITY, HAS YOUR UNCLE BEEN UP TO ANYTHING ODD, LATELY...?
Wipe
WHY ARE YOU ASKING? DID THAT OLD MAN SEND YOU TO SPY ON ME?
SHE...SHE CAN READ STEAMBOT MINDS! INGENIOUS!
HEY.

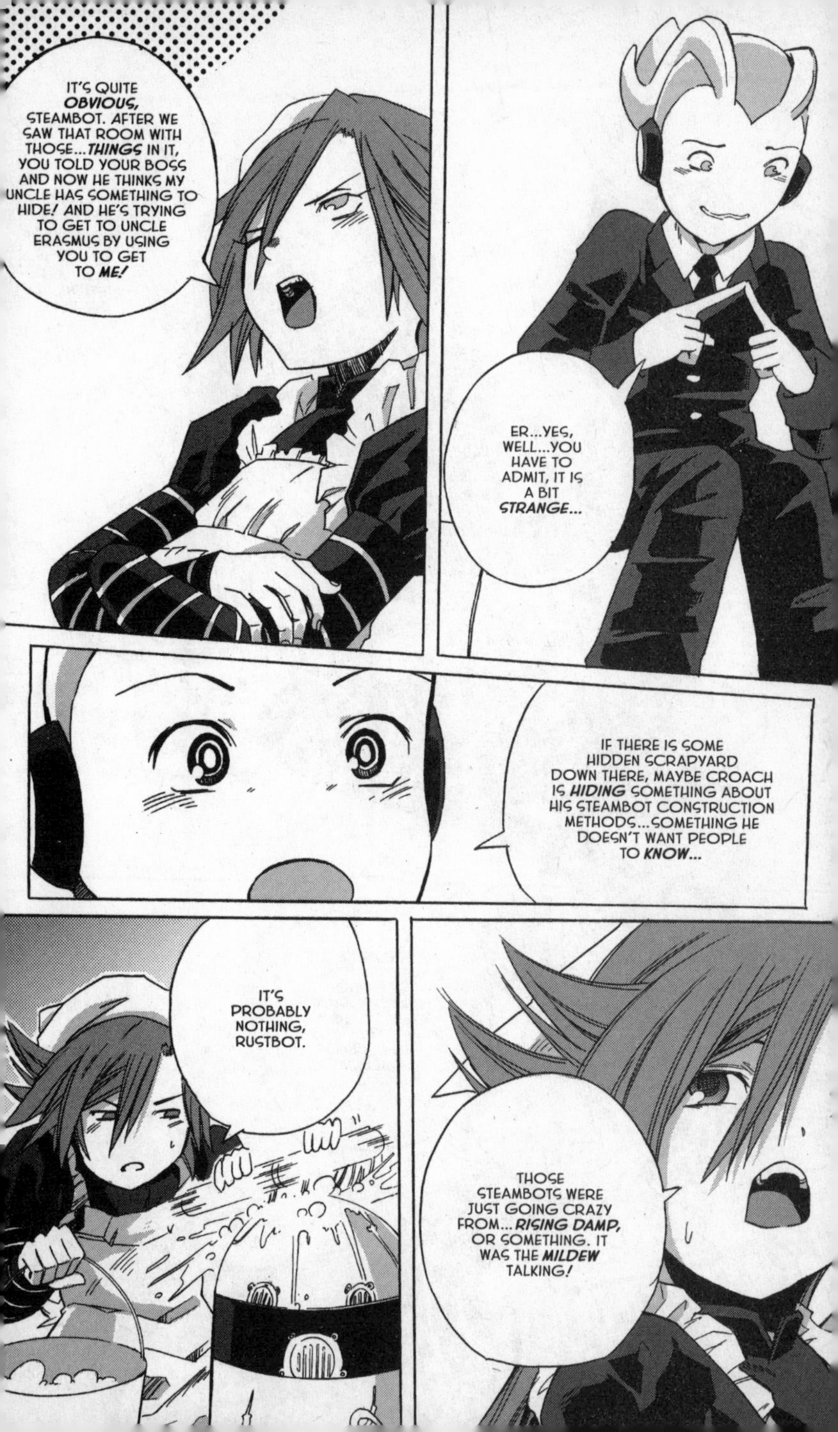
IT'S QUITE OBVIOUS, STEAMBOT. AFTER WE SAW THAT ROOM WITH THOSE...THINGS IN IT, YOU TOLD YOUR BOSS AND NOW HE THINKS MY UNCLE HAS SOMETHING TO HIDE! AND HE'S TRYING TO GET TO UNCLE ERASMUS BY USING YOU TO GET TO ME!
ER...YES, WELL...YOU HAVE TO ADMIT, IT IS A BIT STRANGE...
IF THERE IS SOME HIDDEN SCRAPYARD DOWN THERE, MAYBE CROACH IS HIDING SOMETHING ABOUT HIS STEAMBOT CONSTRUCTION METHODS...SOMETHING HE DOESN'T WANT PEOPLE TO KNOW...
IT'S PROBABLY NOTHING, RUSTBOT.
THOSE STEAMBOTS WERE JUST GOING CRAZY FROM...RISING DAMP, OR SOMETHING. IT WAS THE MILDEW TALKING!

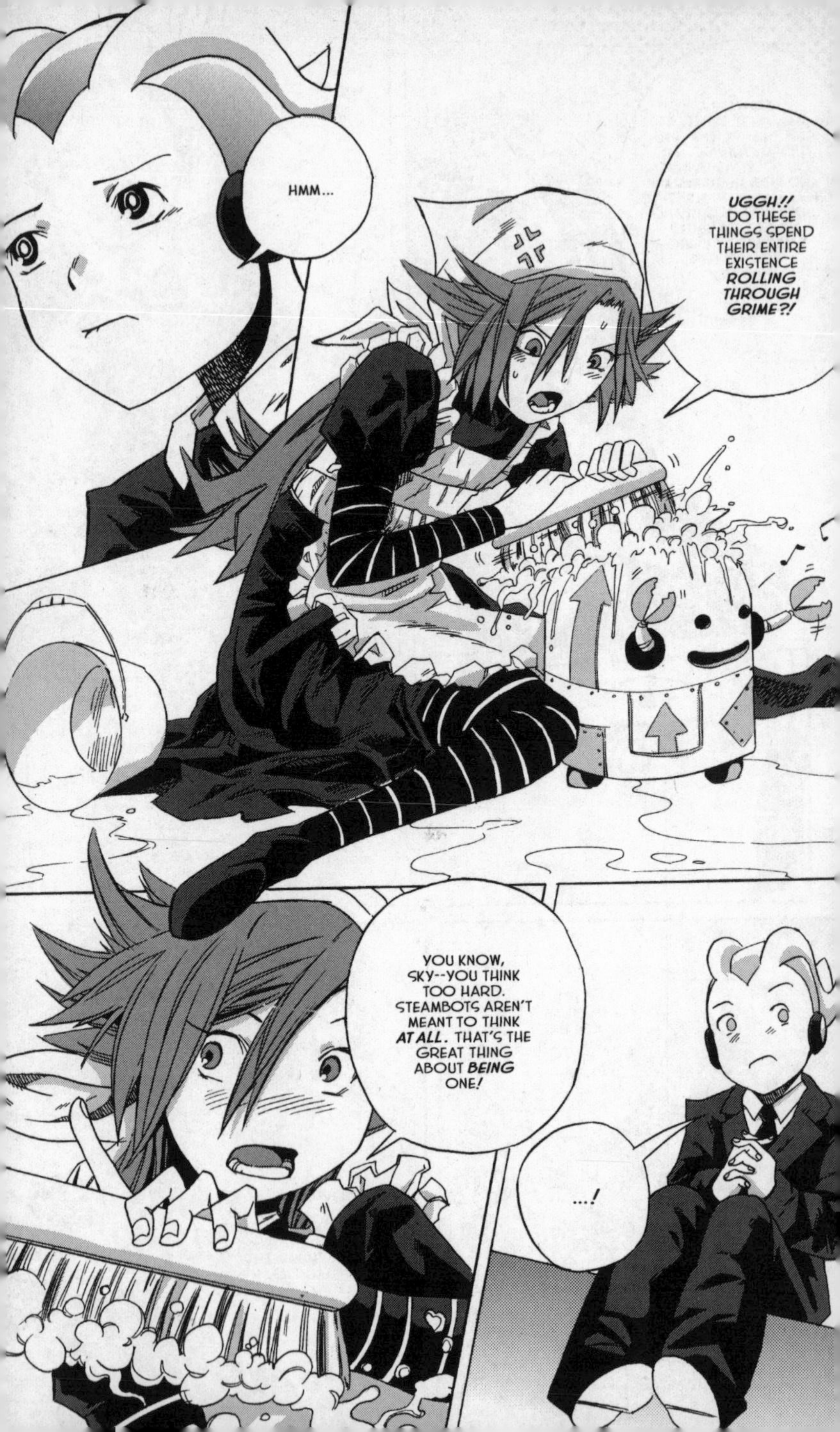
HMM...
UGGH!! DO THESE THINGS SPEND THEIR ENTIRE EXISTENCE ROLLING THROUGH GRIME?!
YOU KNOW, SKY--YOU THINK TOO HARD. STEAMBOTS AREN'T MEANT TO THINK AT ALL. THAT'S THE GREAT THING ABOUT BEING ONE!
...!

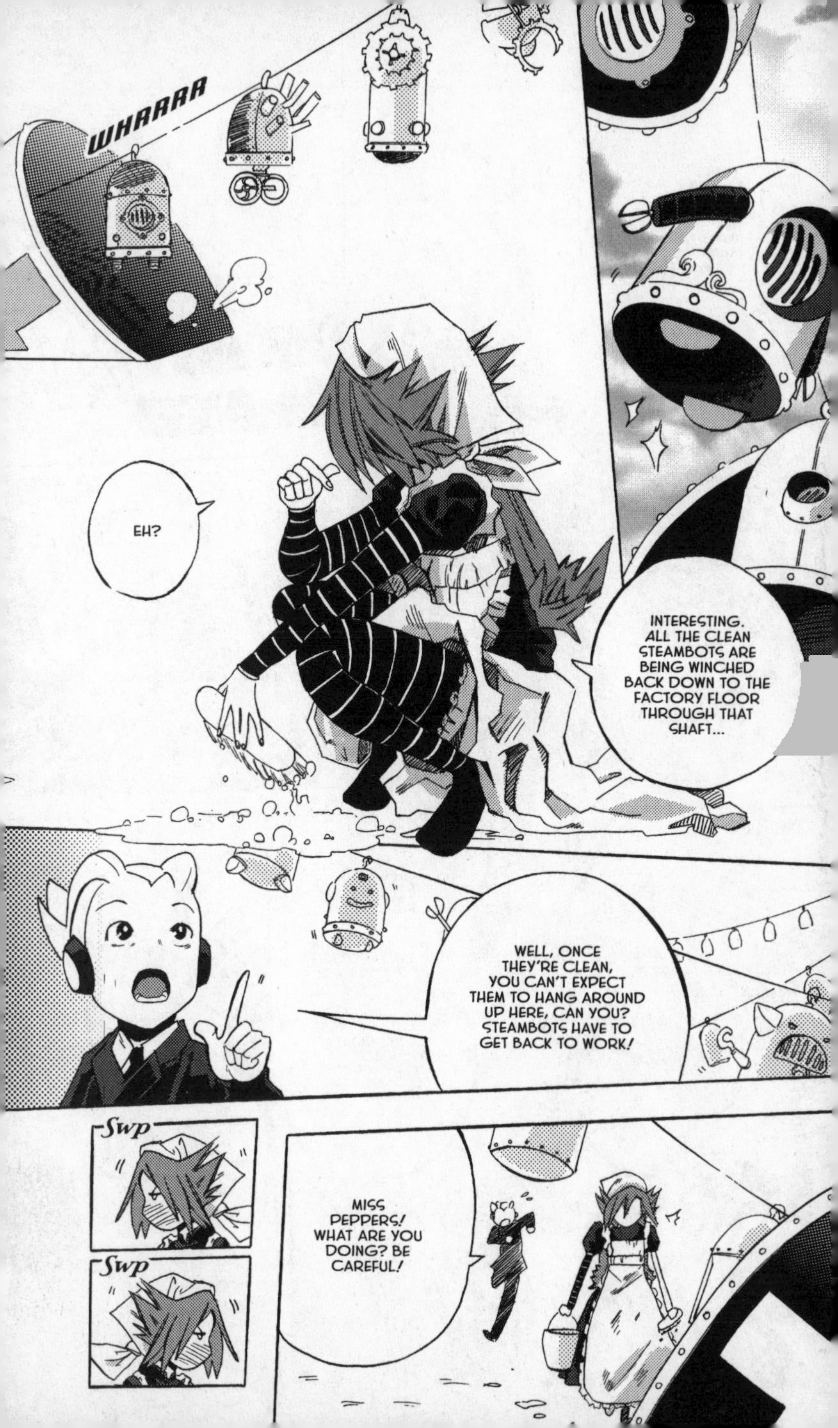

WHRRRR
EH?
INTERESTING. ALL THE CLEAN STEAMBOTS ARE BEING WINCHED BACK DOWN TO THE FACTORY FLOOR THROUGH THAT SHAFT...
WELL, ONCE THEY'RE CLEAN, YOU CAN'T EXPECT THEM TO HANG AROUND UP HERE, CAN YOU? STEAMBOTS HAVE TO GET BACK TO WORK!
Swp
Swp
MISS PEPPERS! WHAT ARE YOU DOING? BE CAREFUL!

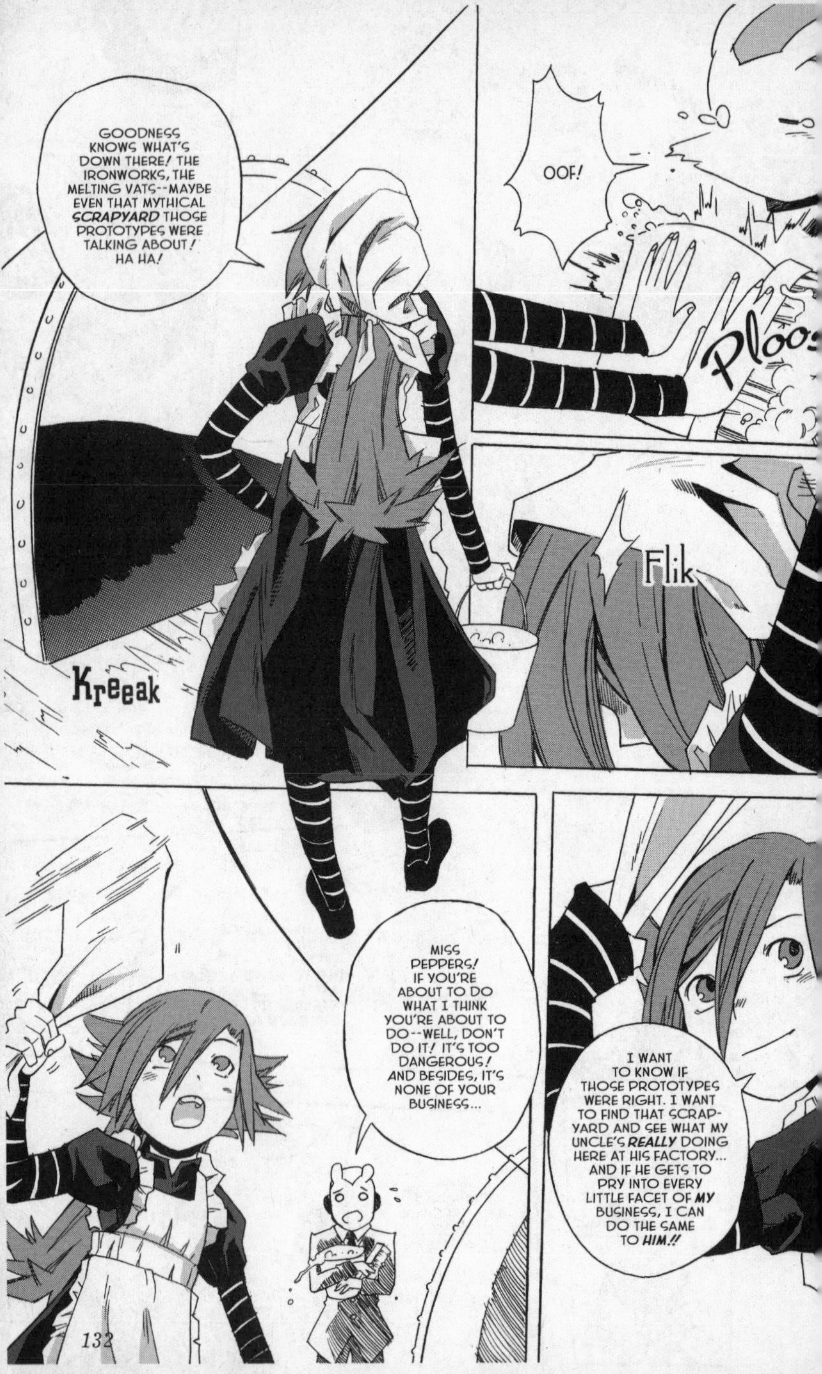
GOODNESS KNOWS WHAT'S DOWN THERE! THE IRONWORKS, THE MELTING VATS--MAYBE EVEN THAT MYTHICAL SCRAPYARD THOSE PROTOTYPES WERE TALKING ABOUT! HA HA!
Kreeak
OOF!
Ploos
Flik
MISS PEPPERS! IF YOU'RE ABOUT TO DO WHAT I THINK YOU'RE ABOUT TO DO--WELL, DON'T DO IT! IT'S TOO DANGEROUS! AND BESIDES, IT'S NONE OF YOUR BUSINESS...
I WANT TO KNOW IF THOSE PROTOTYPES WERE RIGHT. I WANT TO FIND THAT SCRAPYARD AND SEE WHAT MY UNCLE'S REALLY DOING HERE AT HIS FACTORY... AND IF HE GETS TO PRY INTO EVERY LITTLE FACET OF MY BUSINESS, I CAN DO THE SAME TO HIM!!

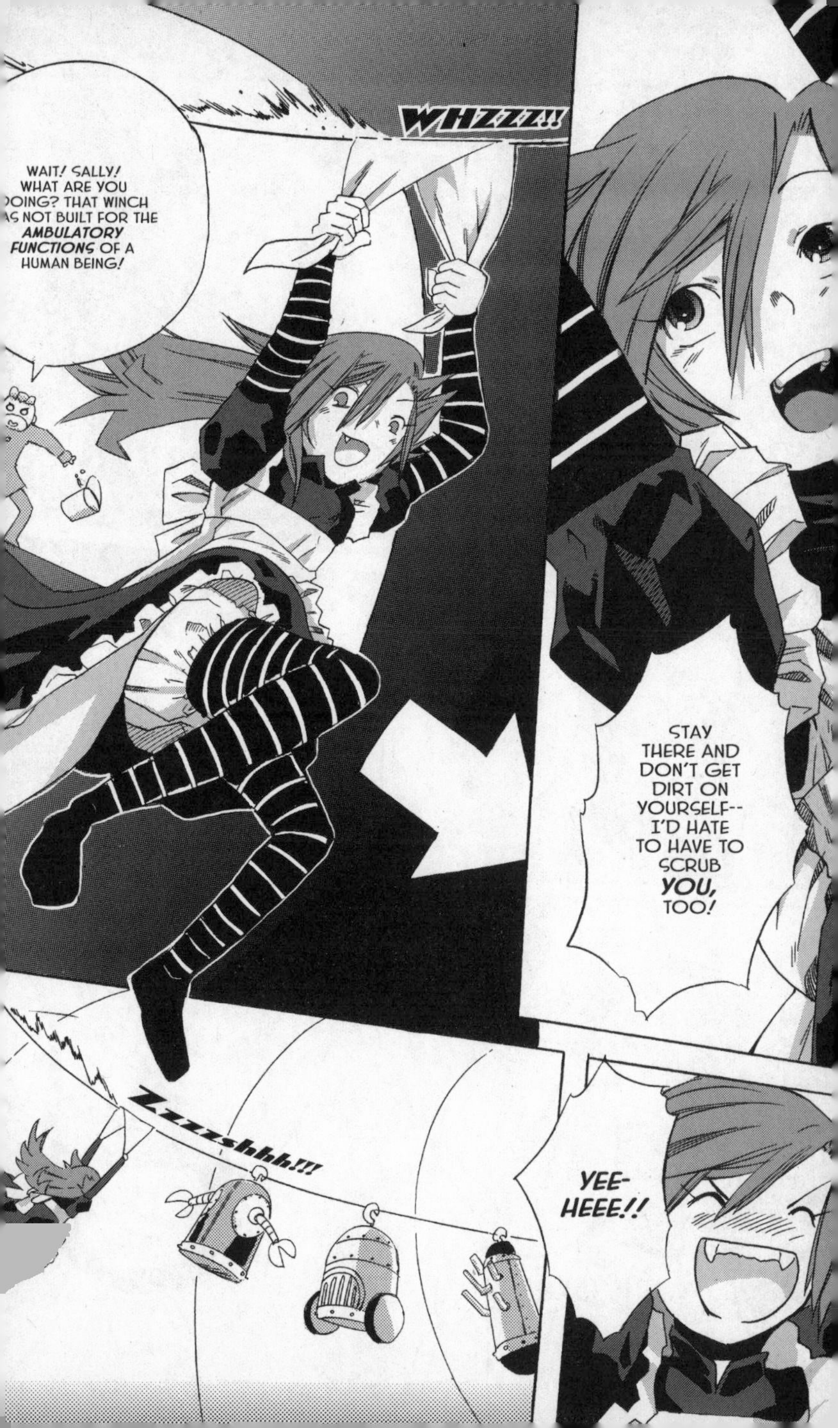

WAIT! SALLY! WHAT ARE YOU OING? THAT WINCH AS NOT BUILT FOR THE **AMBULATORY FUNCTIONS** OF A HUMAN BEING!
WHZZZZ!!
STAY THERE AND DON'T GET DIRT ON YOURSELF-- I'D HATE TO HAVE TO SCRUB **YOU,** TOO!
Zzzzzshhhh!!!
YEE-HEEE!!

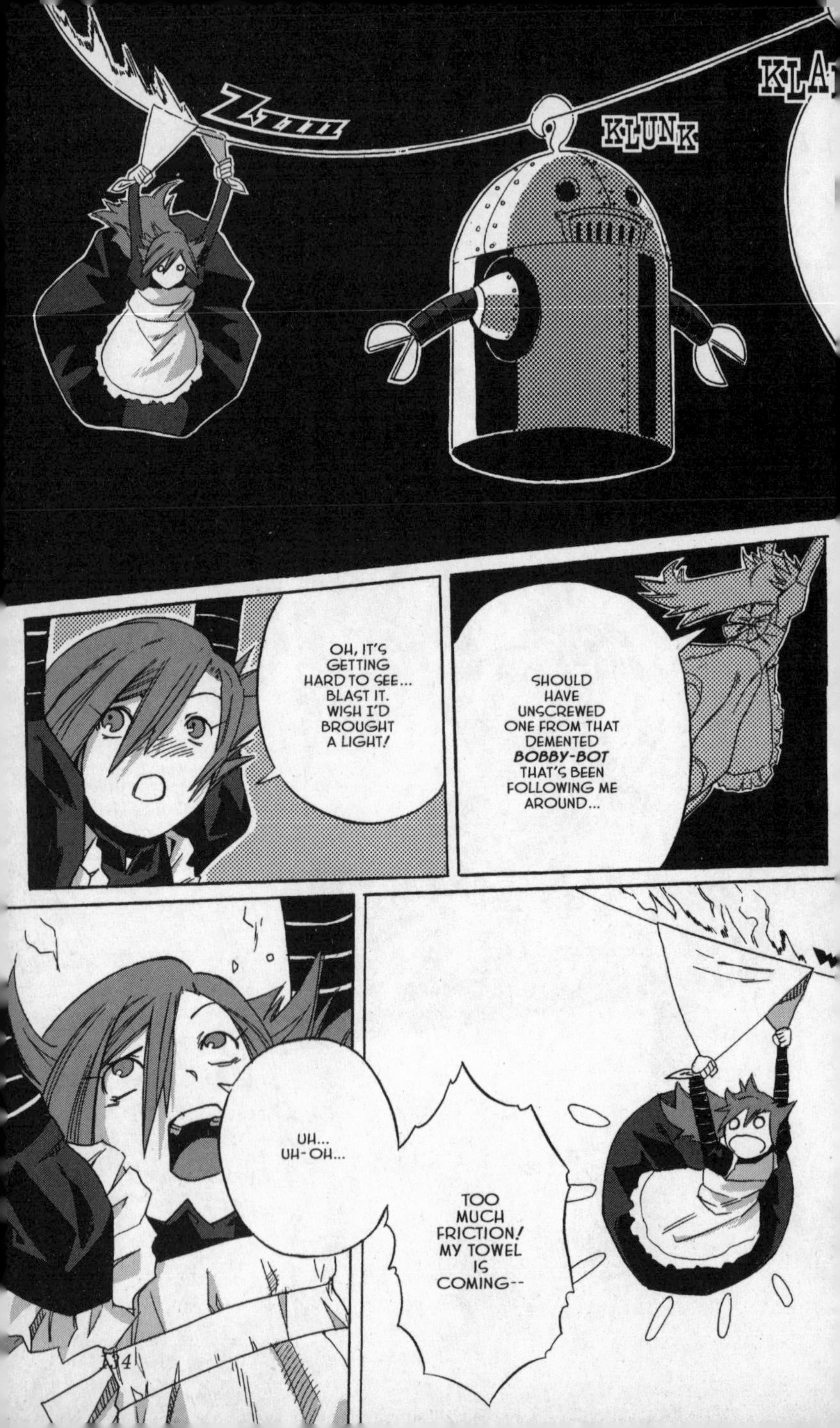

Zzzzzz
KLUNK
KLA
OH, IT'S GETTING HARD TO SEE... BLAST IT. WISH I'D BROUGHT A LIGHT!
SHOULD HAVE UNSCREWED ONE FROM THAT DEMENTED *BOBBY-BOT* THAT'S BEEN FOLLOWING ME AROUND...
UH... UH-OH...
TOO MUCH FRICTION! MY TOWEL IS COMING--

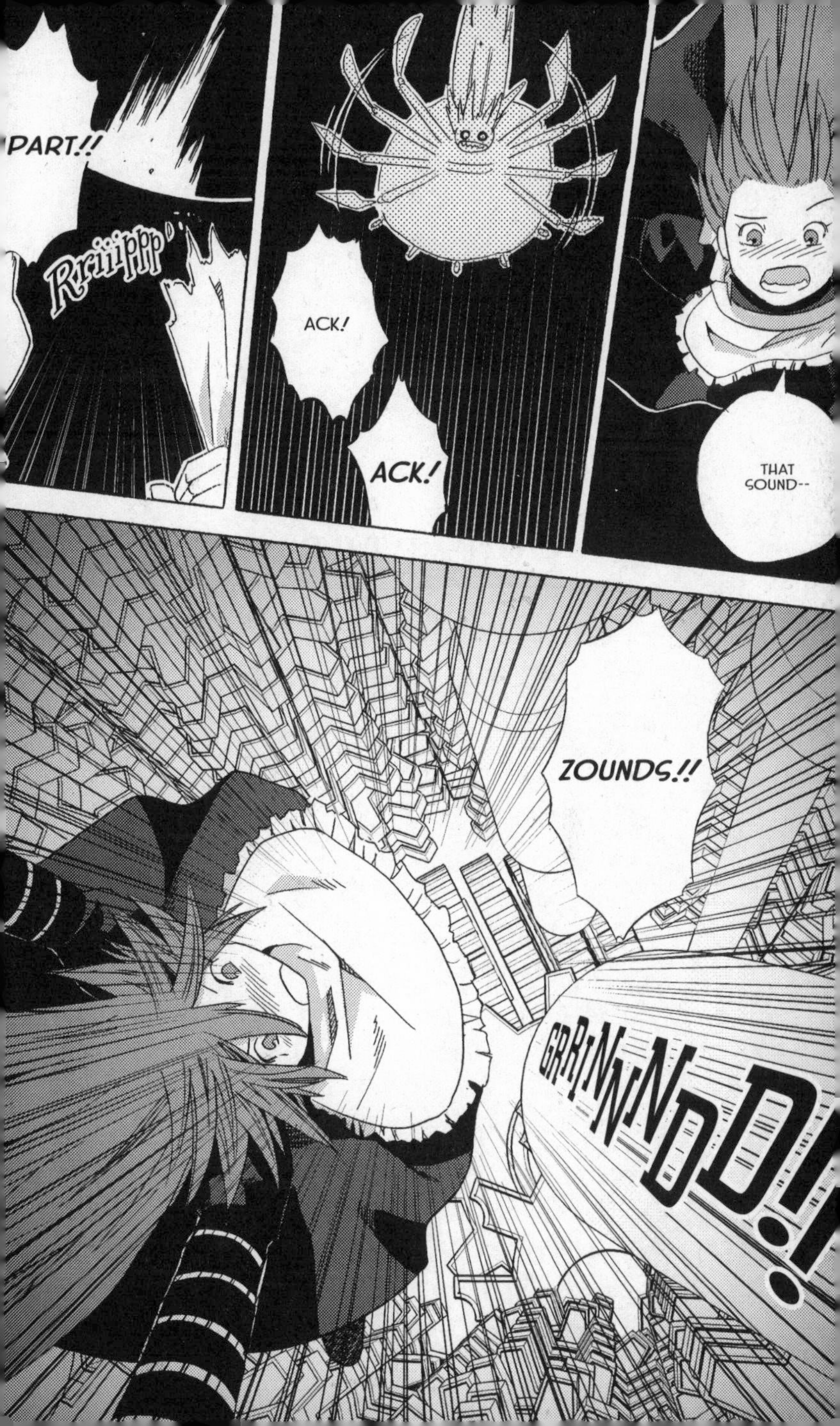
PART!!
Rriiippp
ACK!
ACK!
THAT SOUND--
ZOUNDS!!
GRRINNNDD!!

CHAPTER 6

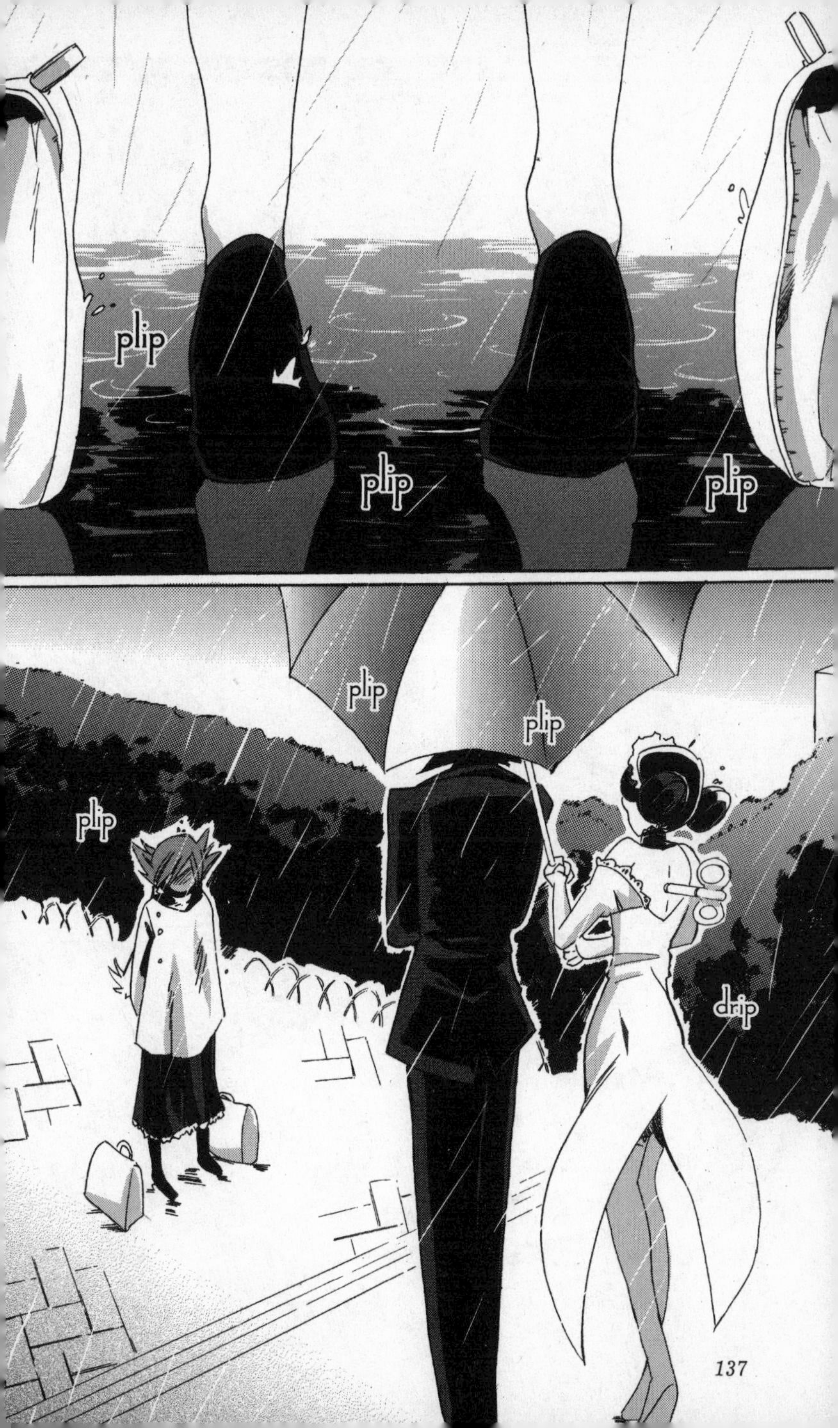
plip
plip
plip
plip
plip
plip
drip

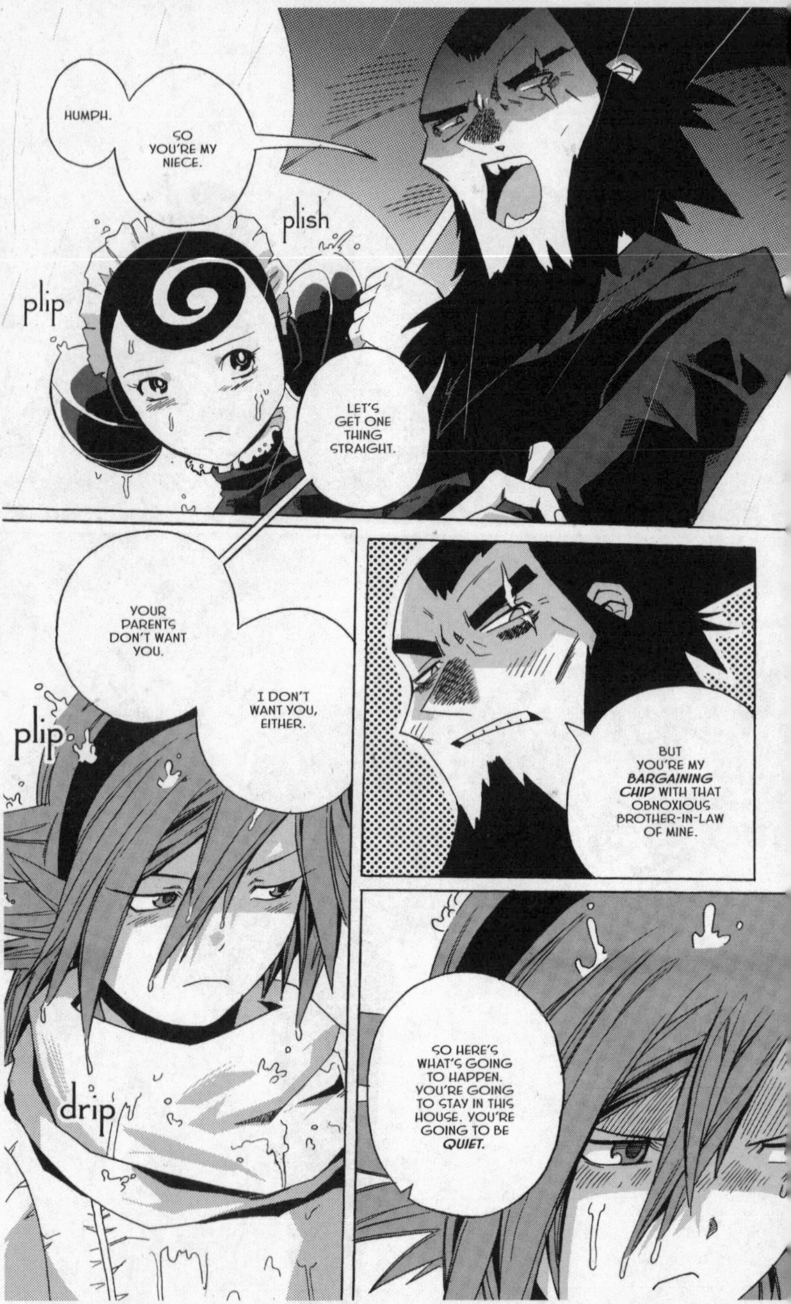
HUMPH.
SO YOU'RE MY NIECE.
plish
plip
LET'S GET ONE THING STRAIGHT.
YOUR PARENTS DON'T WANT YOU.
I DON'T WANT YOU, EITHER.
plip
BUT YOU'RE MY *BARGAINING CHIP* WITH THAT OBNOXIOUS BROTHER-IN-LAW OF MINE.
drip
SO HERE'S WHAT'S GOING TO HAPPEN. YOU'RE GOING TO STAY IN THIS HOUSE. YOU'RE GOING TO BE *QUIET.*

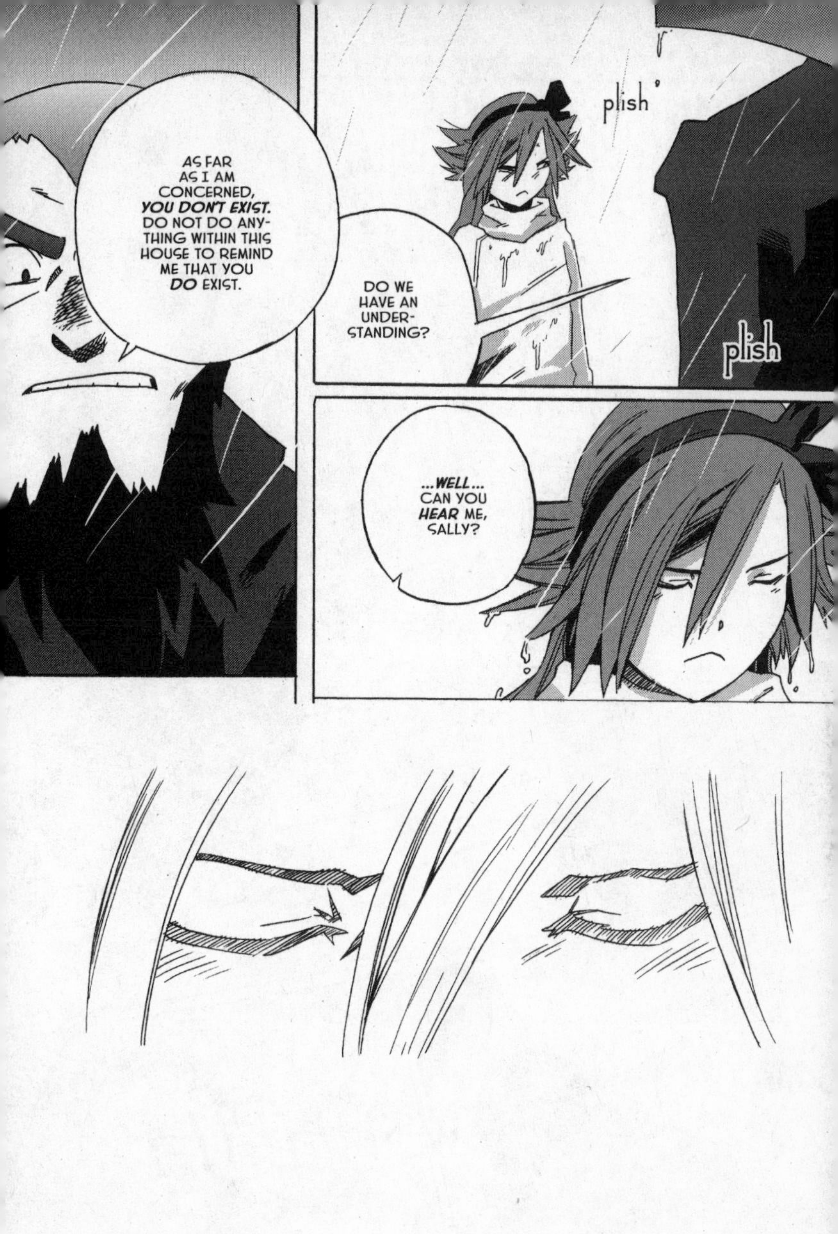
AS FAR AS I AM CONCERNED, **YOU DON'T EXIST.** DO NOT DO ANYTHING WITHIN THIS HOUSE TO REMIND ME THAT YOU **DO** EXIST.
DO WE HAVE AN UNDERSTANDING?
plish
plish
...WELL... CAN YOU **HEAR** ME, SALLY?

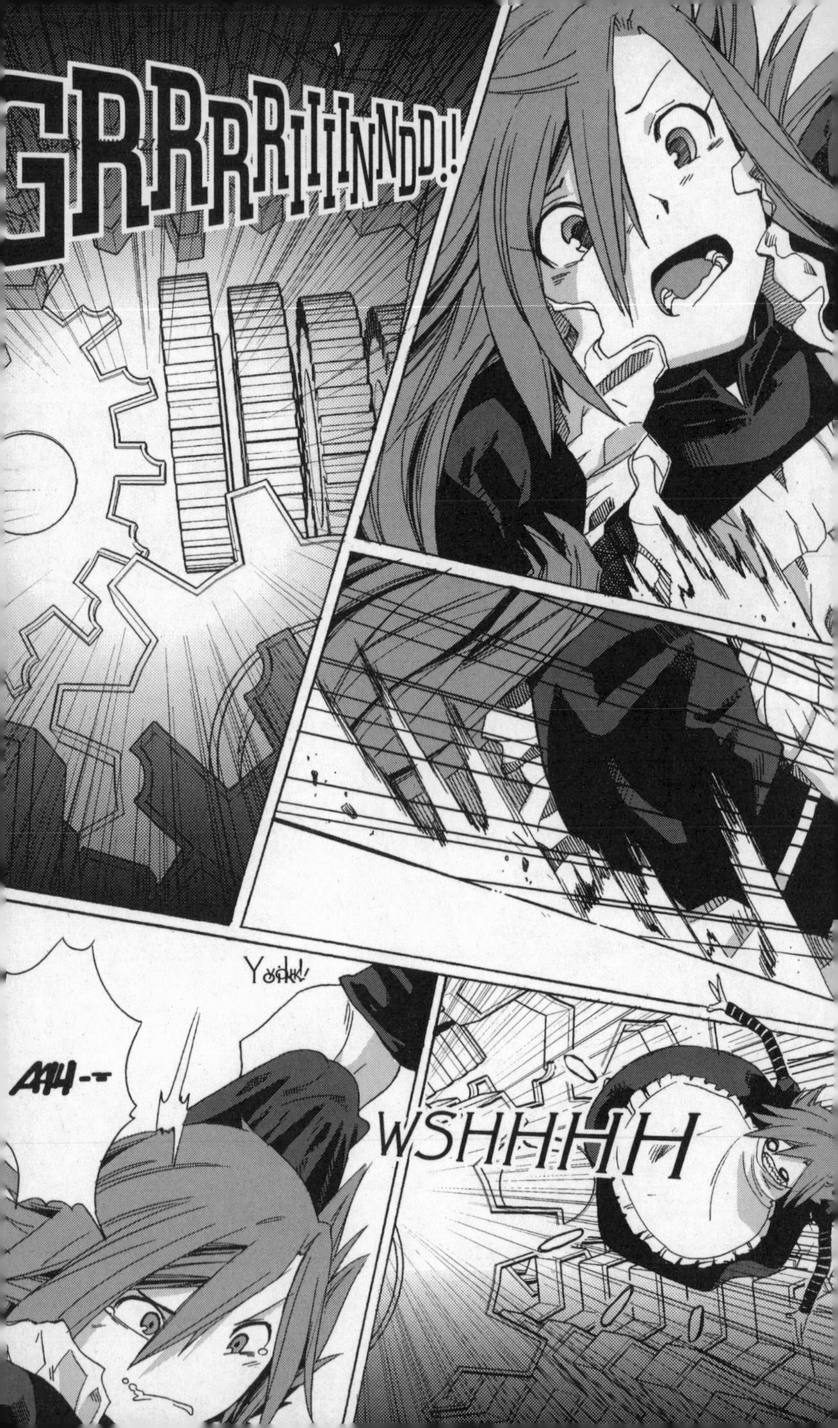
GRRRRIIINNDD!!
Yoink!
AAH--
WSHHHHH

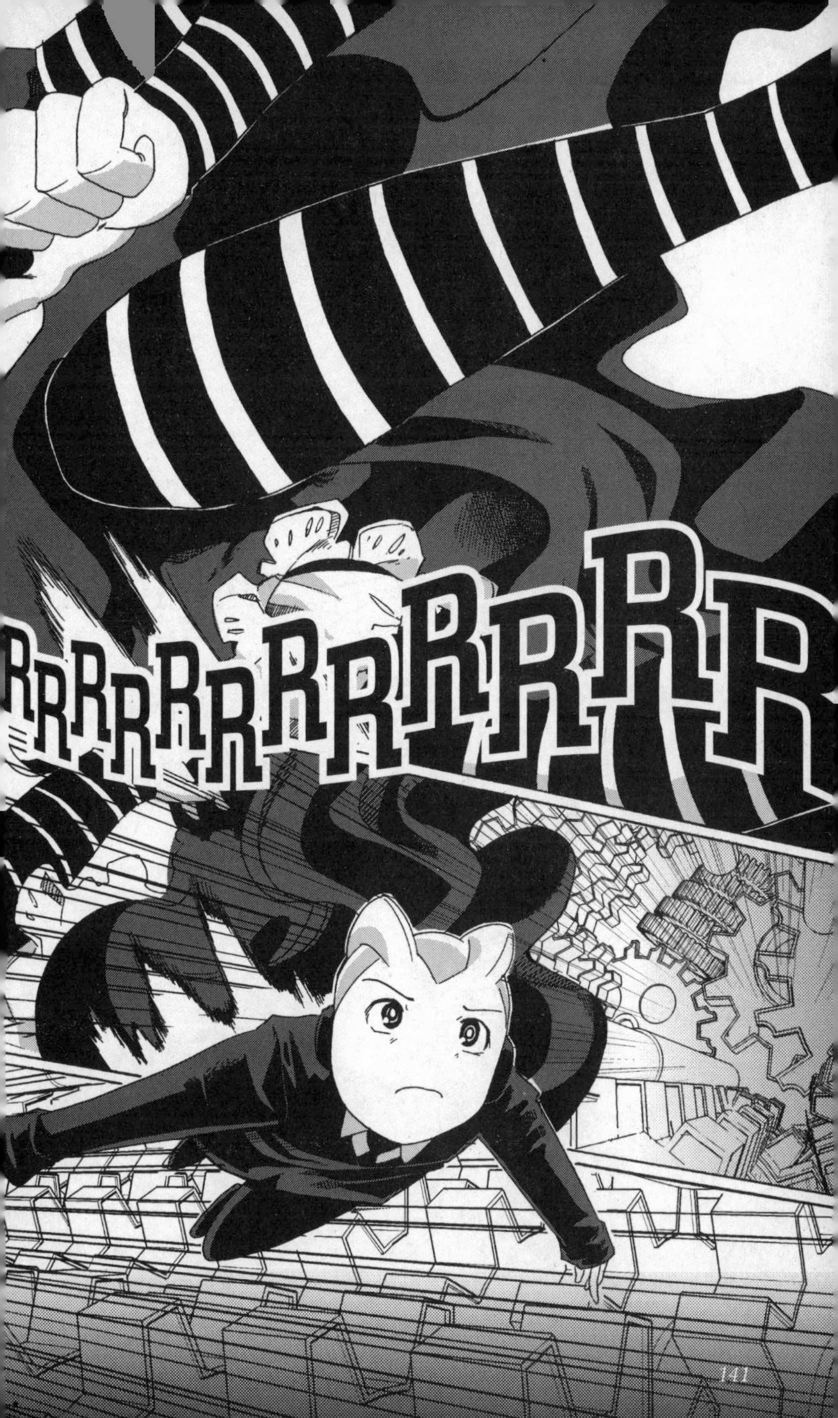
RRRRRRRRRR

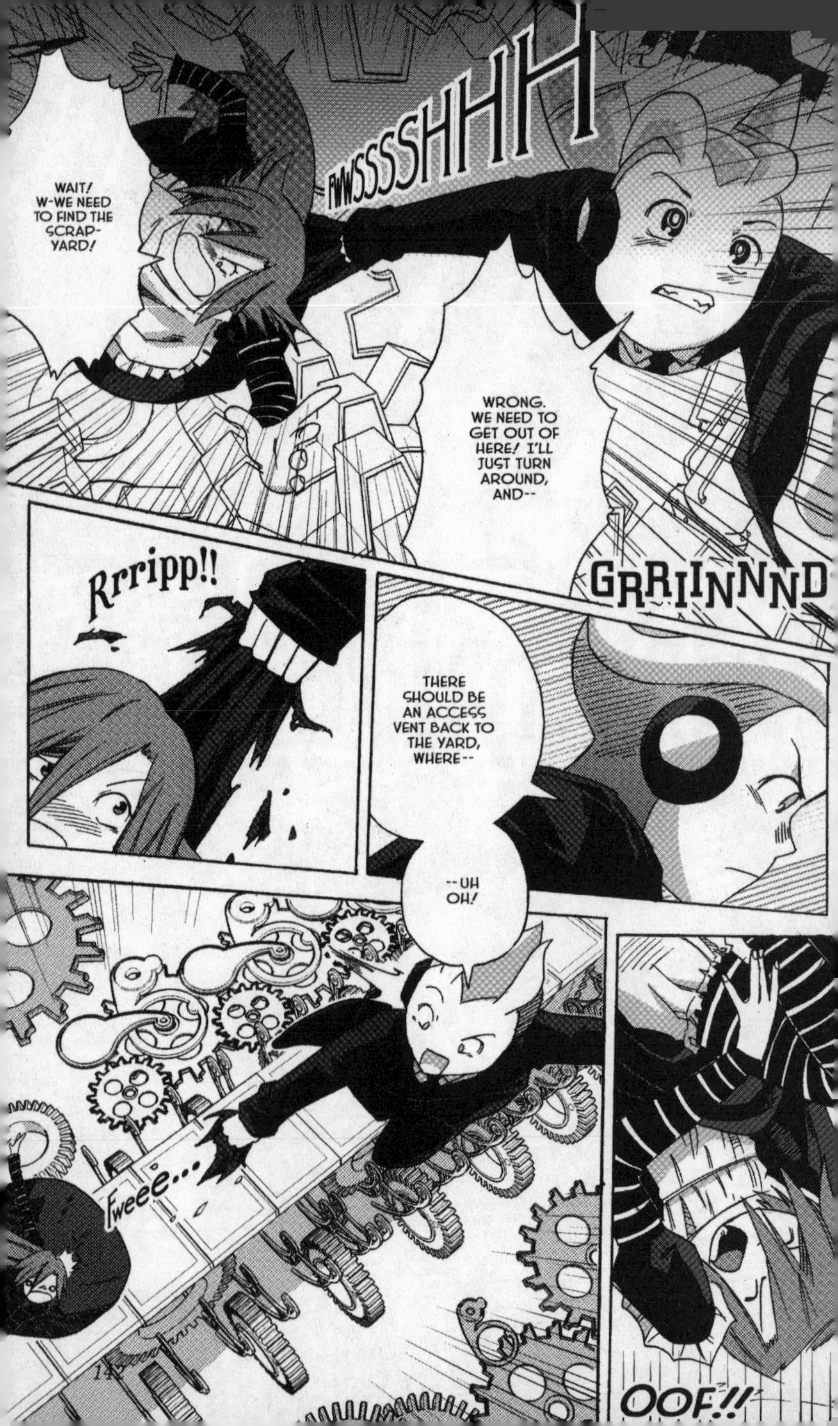
WAIT! W-WE NEED TO FIND THE SCRAP-YARD!
FWWSSSSHHH
WRONG. WE NEED TO GET OUT OF HERE! I'LL JUST TURN AROUND, AND--
Rrripp!!
GRRIINNND
THERE SHOULD BE AN ACCESS VENT BACK TO THE YARD, WHERE--
--UH OH!
Fweee...
OOF!!

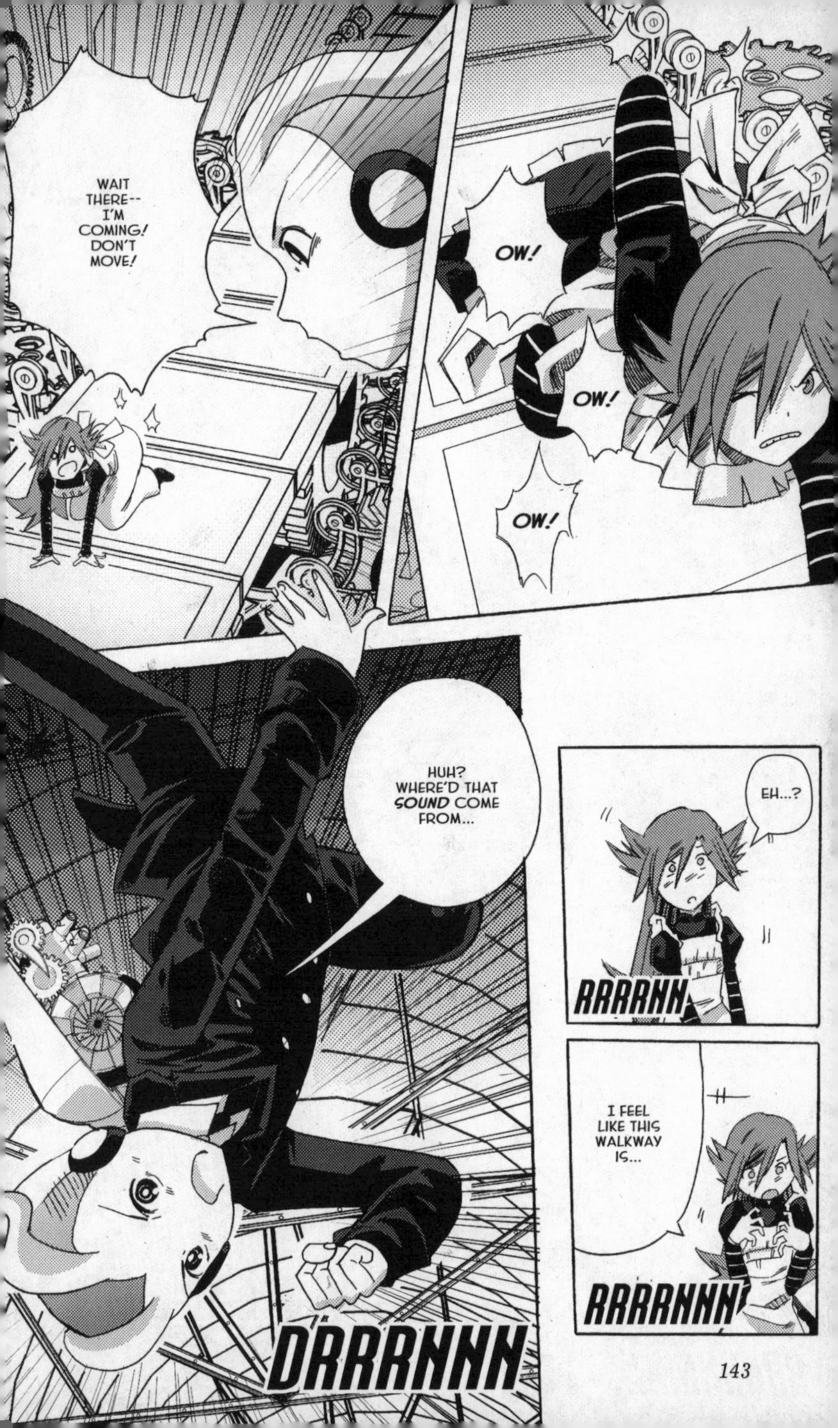

WAIT THERE-- I'M COMING! DON'T MOVE!
OW!
OW!
OW!
HUH? WHERE'D THAT SOUND COME FROM...
DRRRNNN
EH...?
RRRRNN
I FEEL LIKE THIS WALKWAY IS...
RRRRNNN

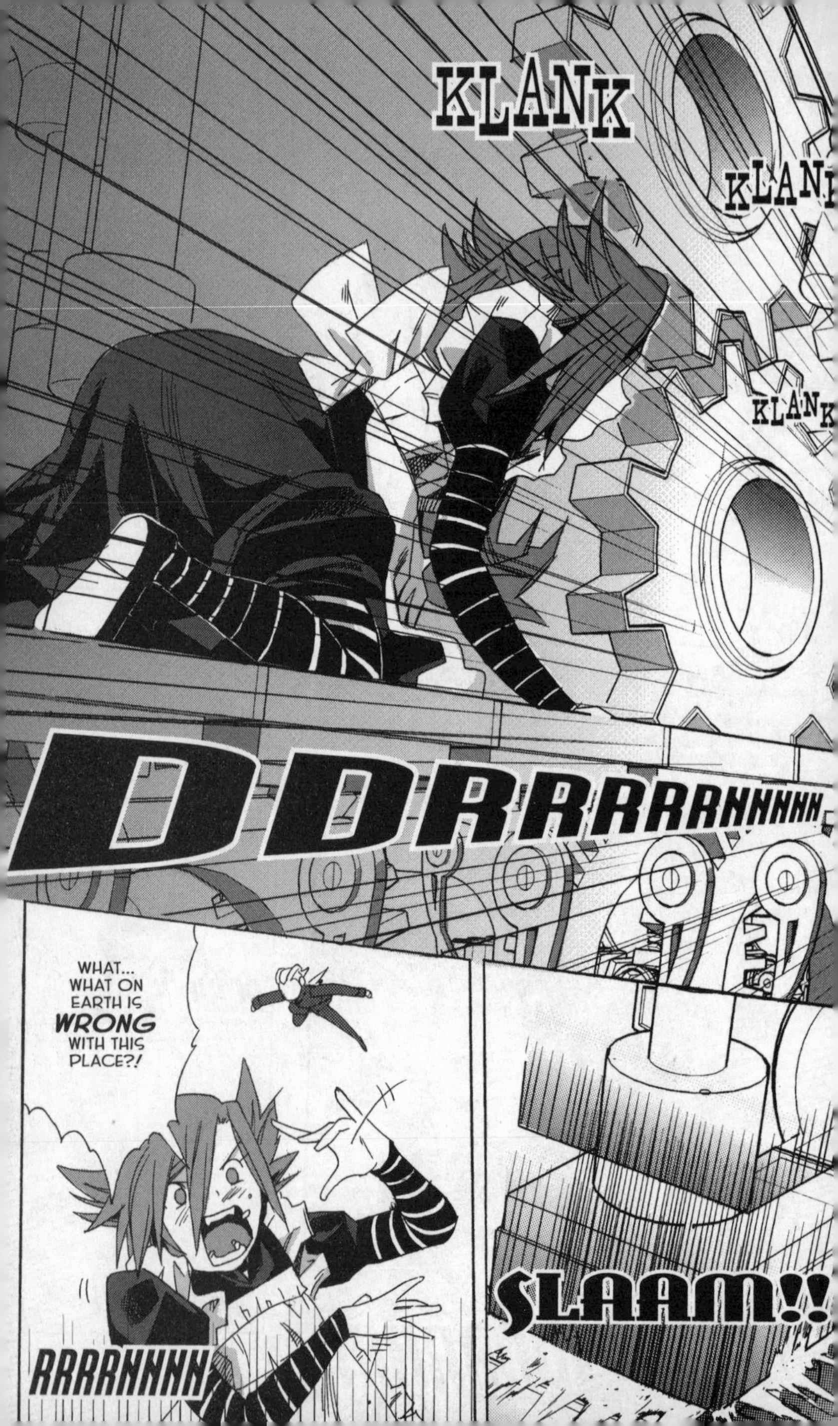
KLANK
KLANK
KLANK
DDRRRRRNNNNN
WHAT... WHAT ON EARTH IS **WRONG** WITH THIS PLACE?!
RRRRNNNN
SLAAM!!

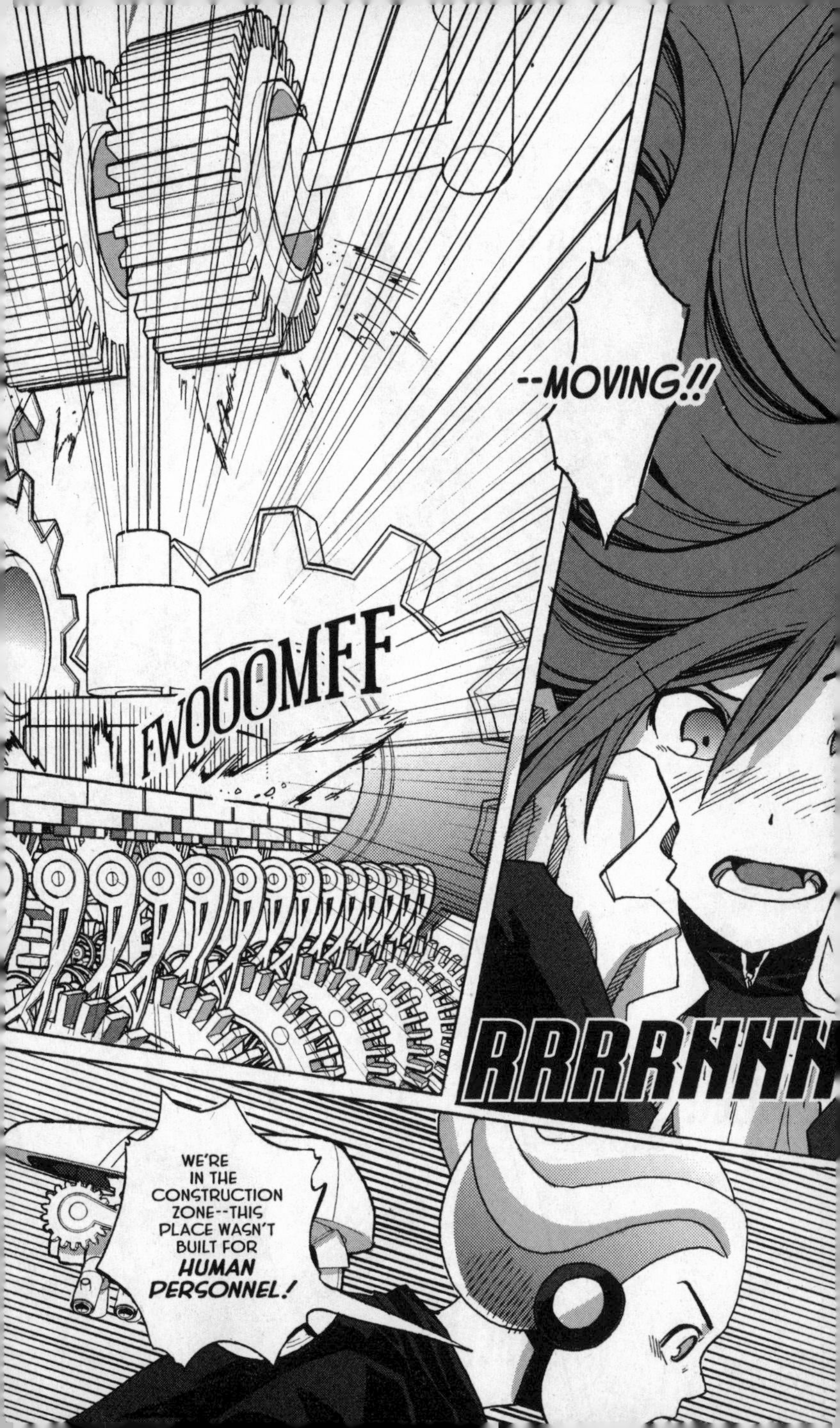

FWOOOMFF
--MOVING!!
RRRRNNN
WE'RE IN THE CONSTRUCTION ZONE--THIS PLACE WASN'T BUILT FOR HUMAN PERSONNEL!

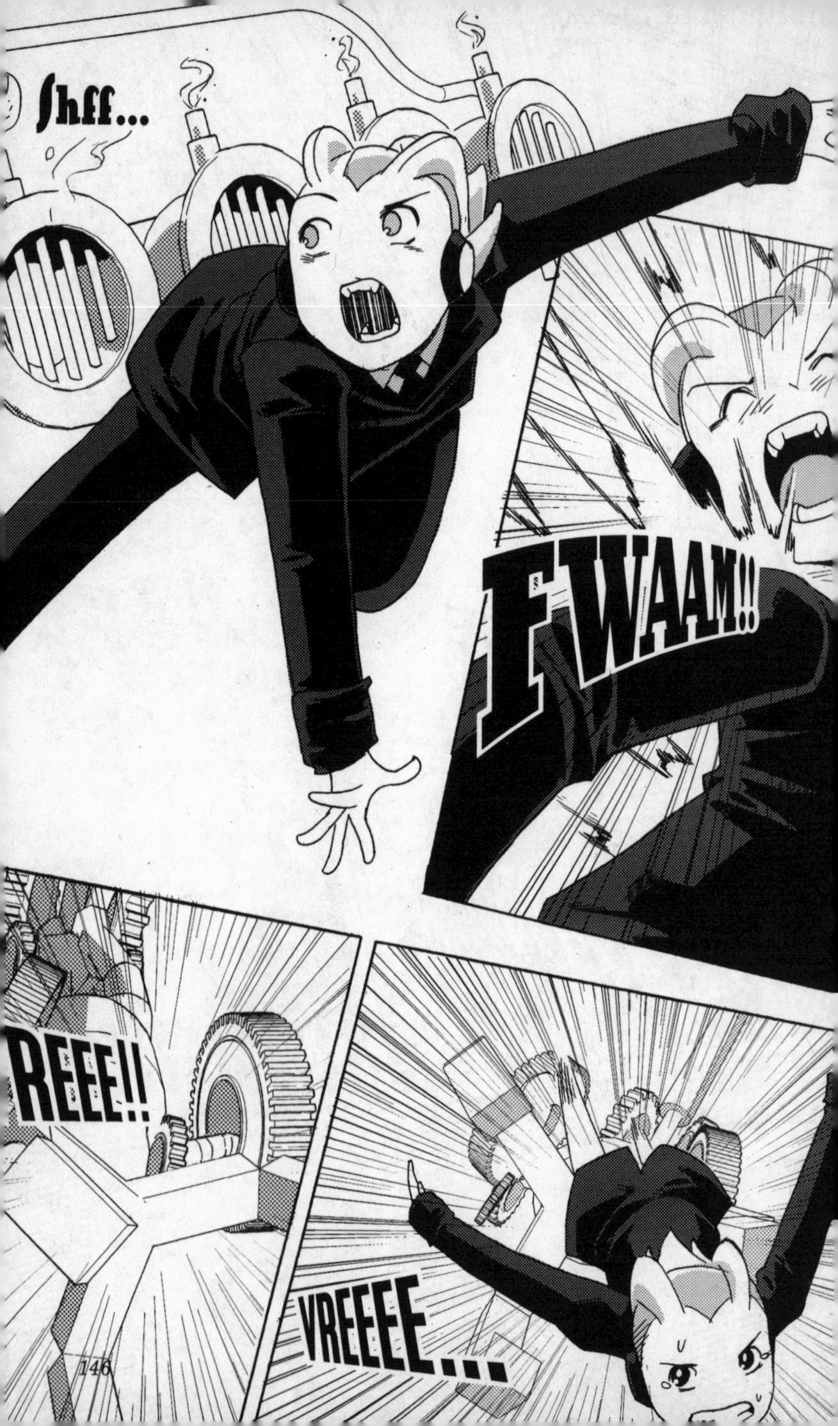

Shff...
FWAAM!!
REEE!!
VREEEE....

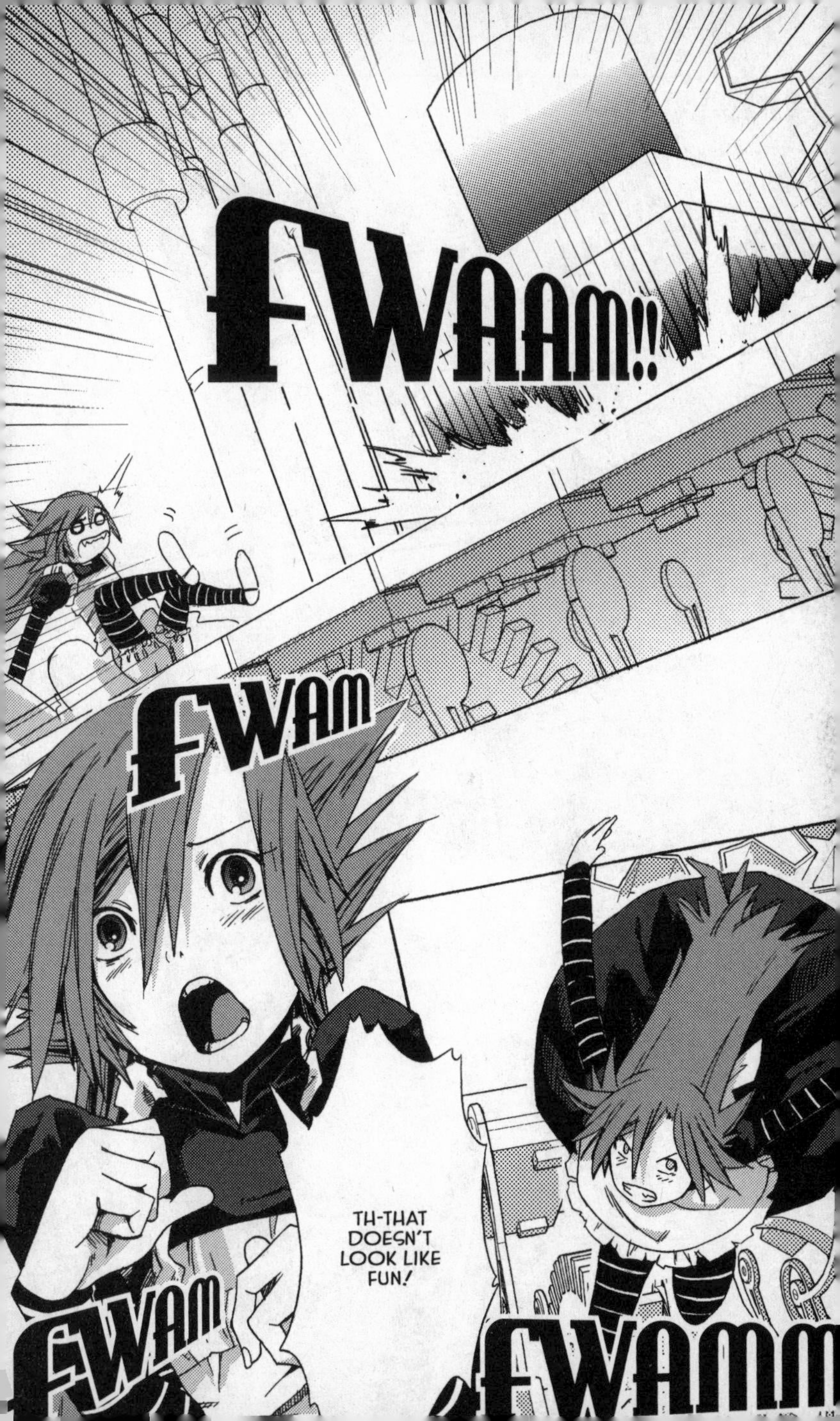
FWAAM!!
FWAM
TH-THAT DOESN'T LOOK LIKE FUN!
FWAM
FWAMM

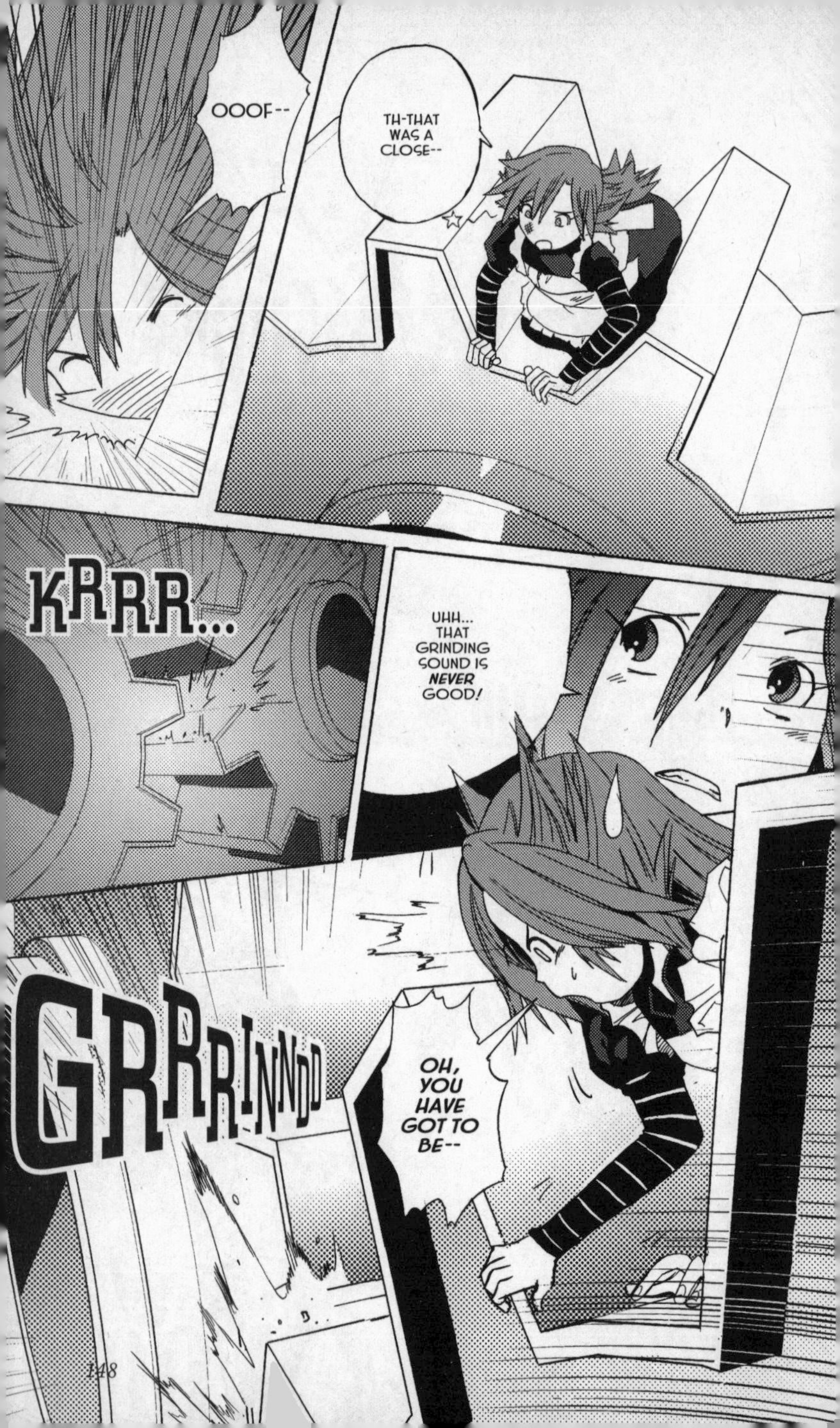
OOOF--
TH-THAT WAS A CLOSE--
KRRR...
UHH... THAT GRINDING SOUND IS *NEVER* GOOD!
GRRRINNDD
OH, YOU HAVE GOT TO BE--

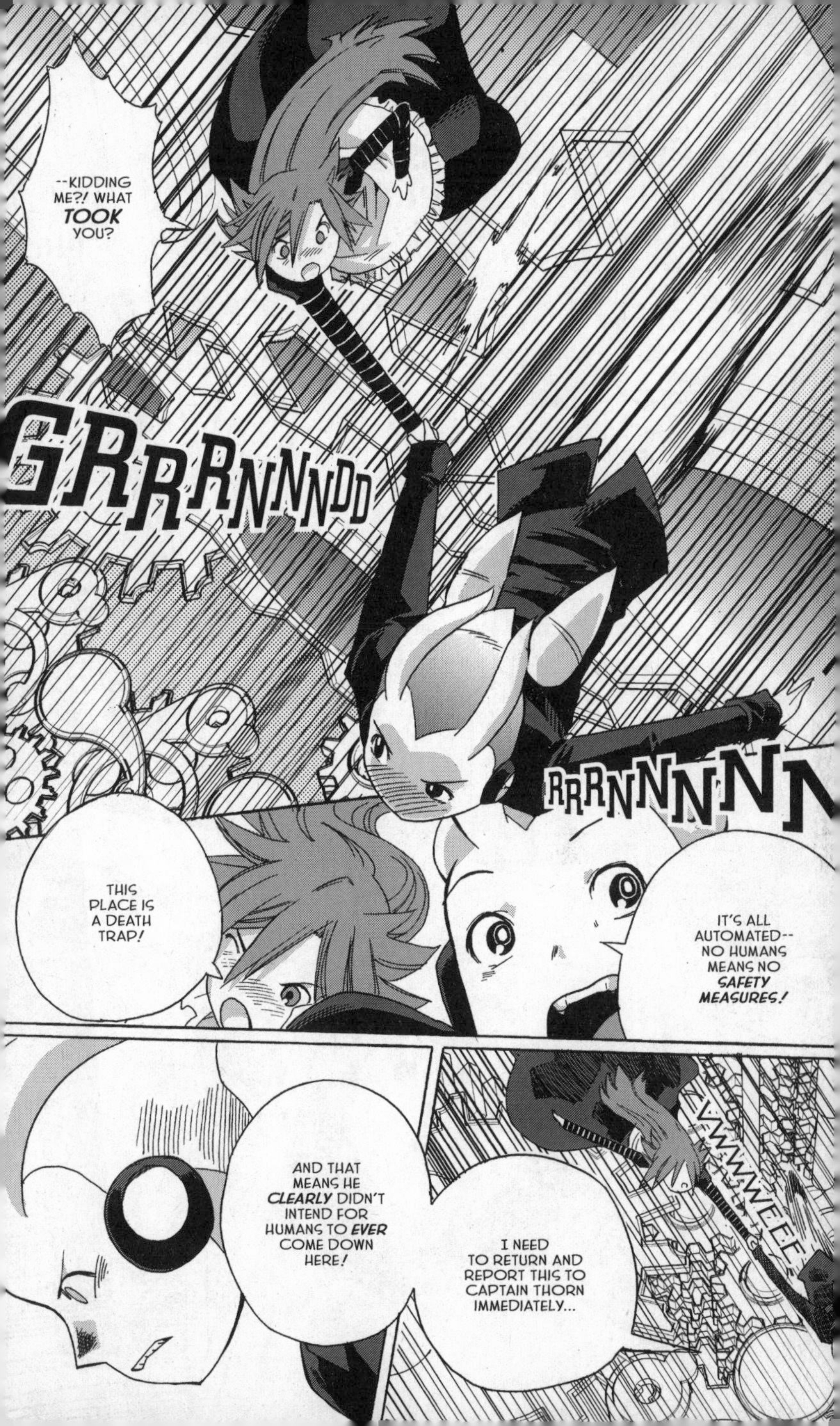
--KIDDING ME?! WHAT TOOK YOU?
GRRRNNNDD
RRRNNNNN
THIS PLACE IS A DEATH TRAP!
IT'S ALL AUTOMATED-- NO HUMANS MEANS NO SAFETY MEASURES!
AND THAT MEANS HE CLEARLY DIDN'T INTEND FOR HUMANS TO EVER COME DOWN HERE!
I NEED TO RETURN AND REPORT THIS TO CAPTAIN THORN IMMEDIATELY...
VWWWEEE

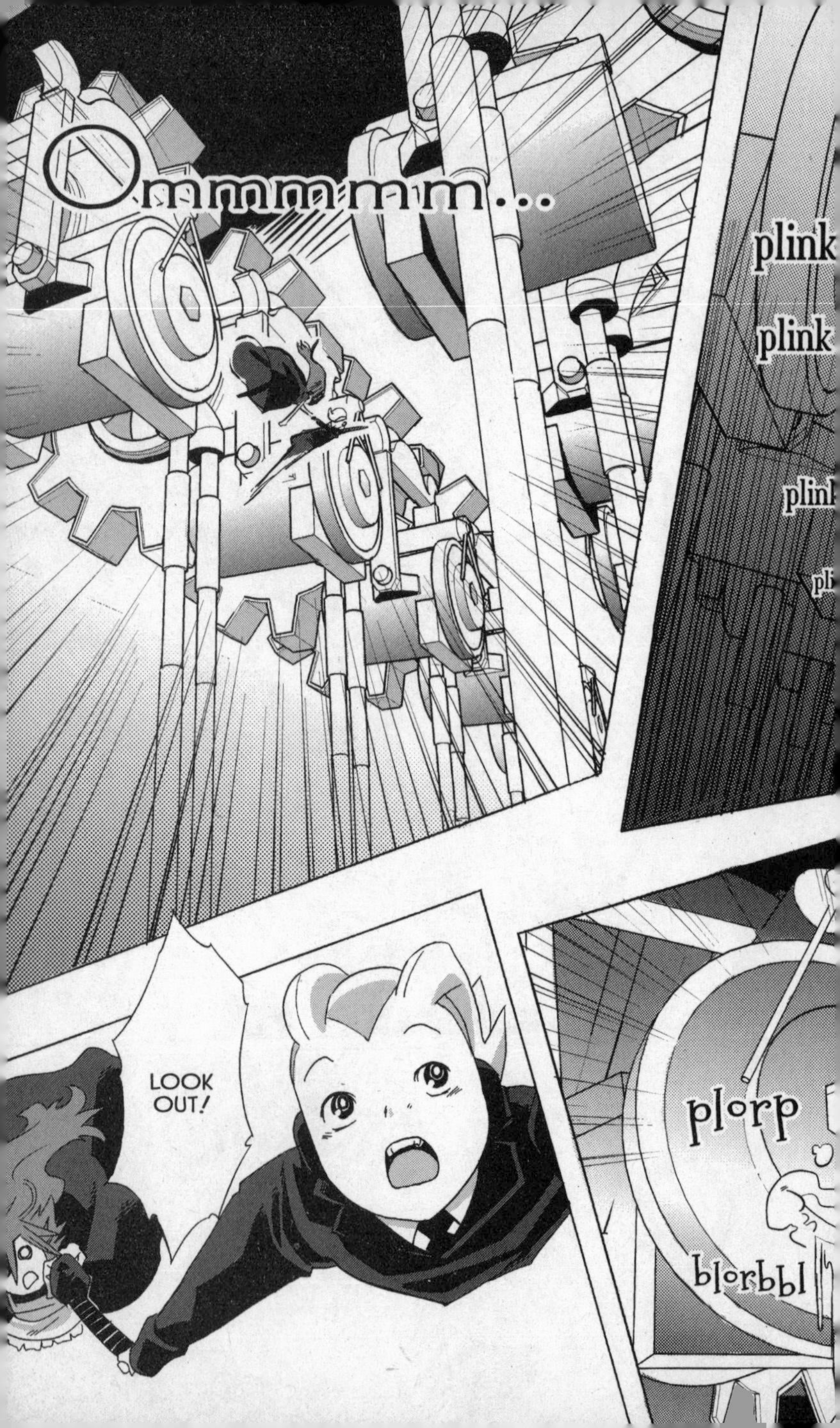
Ommmmmm...
plink
plink
LOOK OUT!
plorp
blorbbl

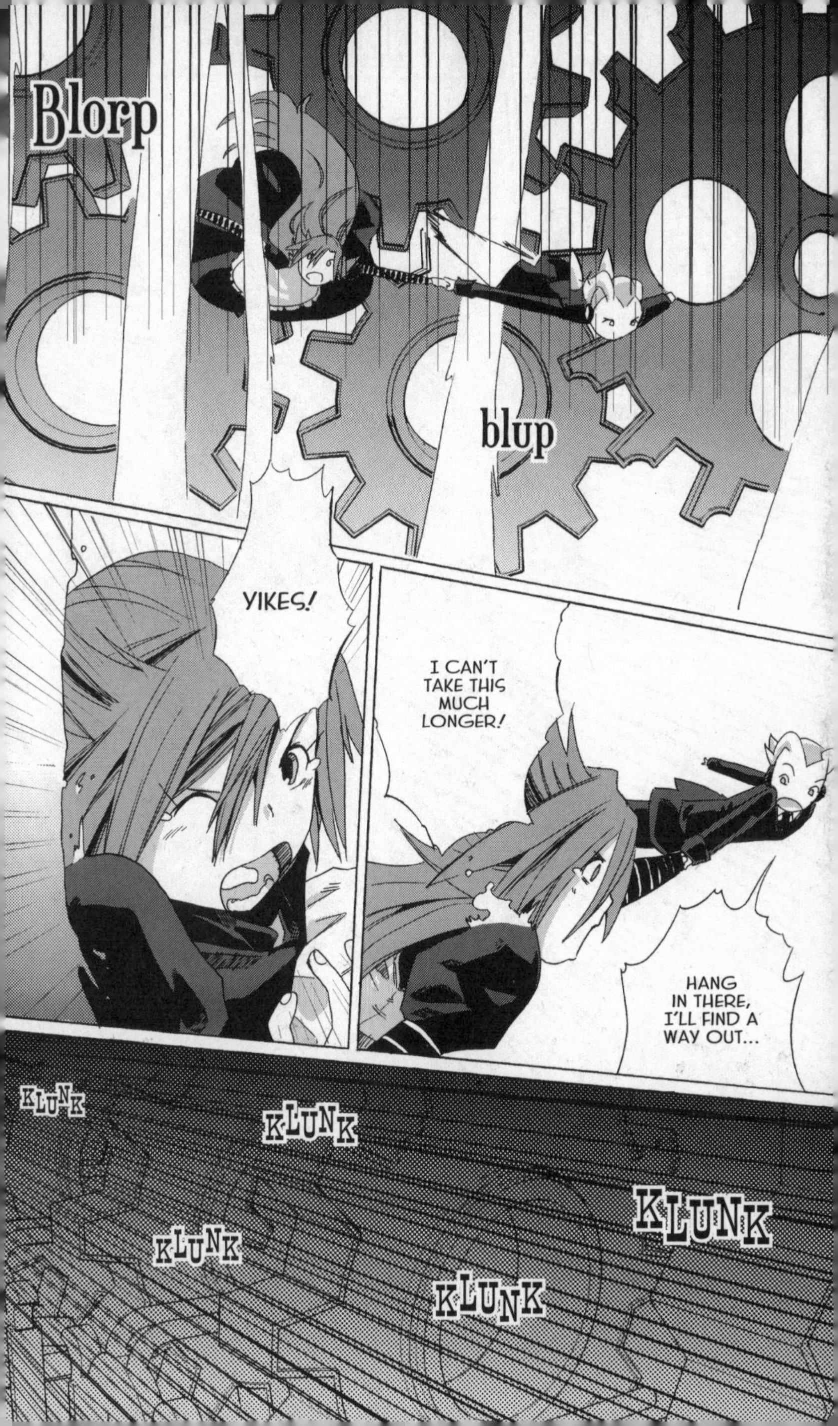
Blorp
blup
YIKES!
I CAN'T TAKE THIS MUCH LONGER!
HANG IN THERE, I'LL FIND A WAY OUT...
KLUNK
KLUNK
KLUNK
KLUNK
KLUNK

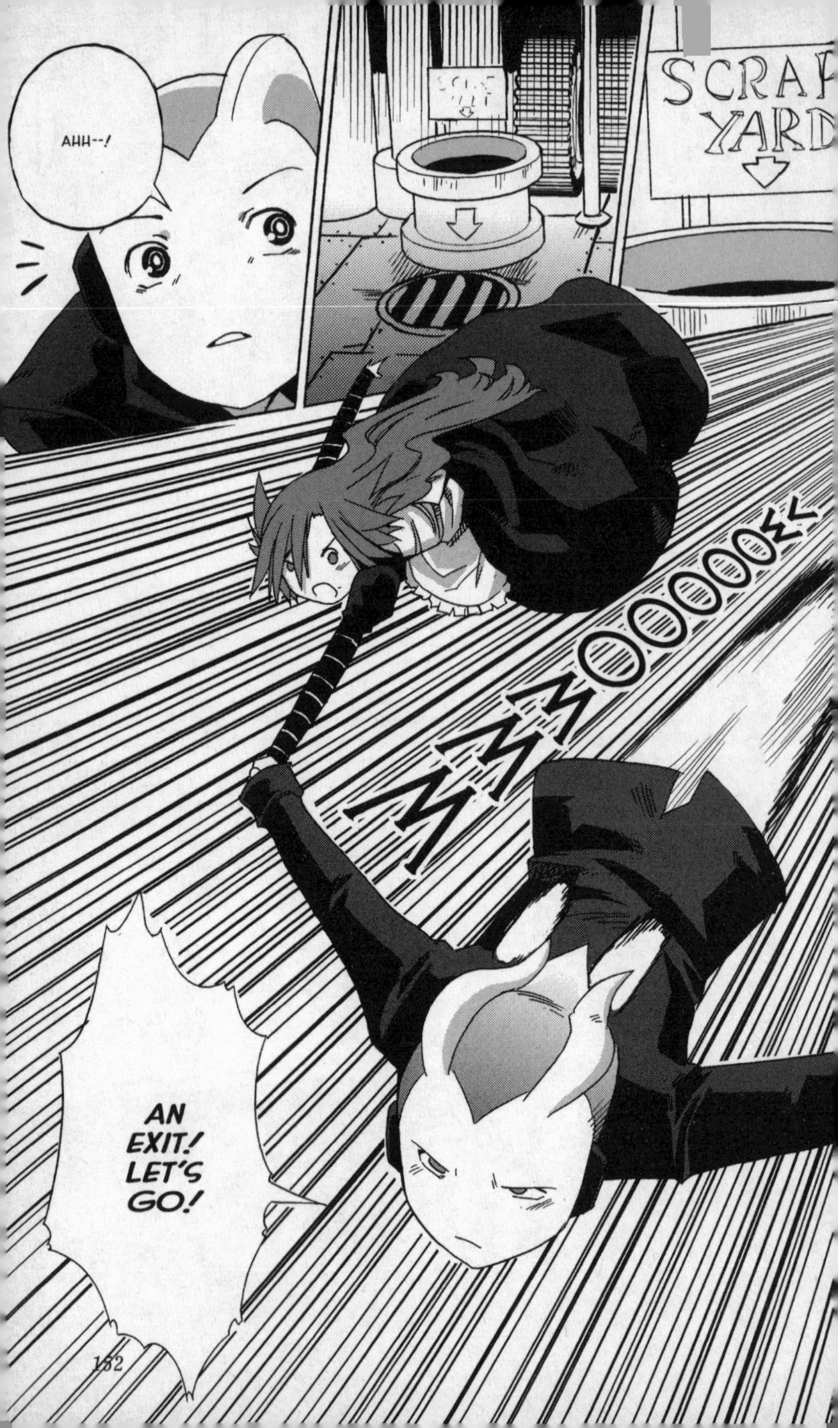
AHH--!
SCRAP YARD
AN EXIT! LET'S GO!

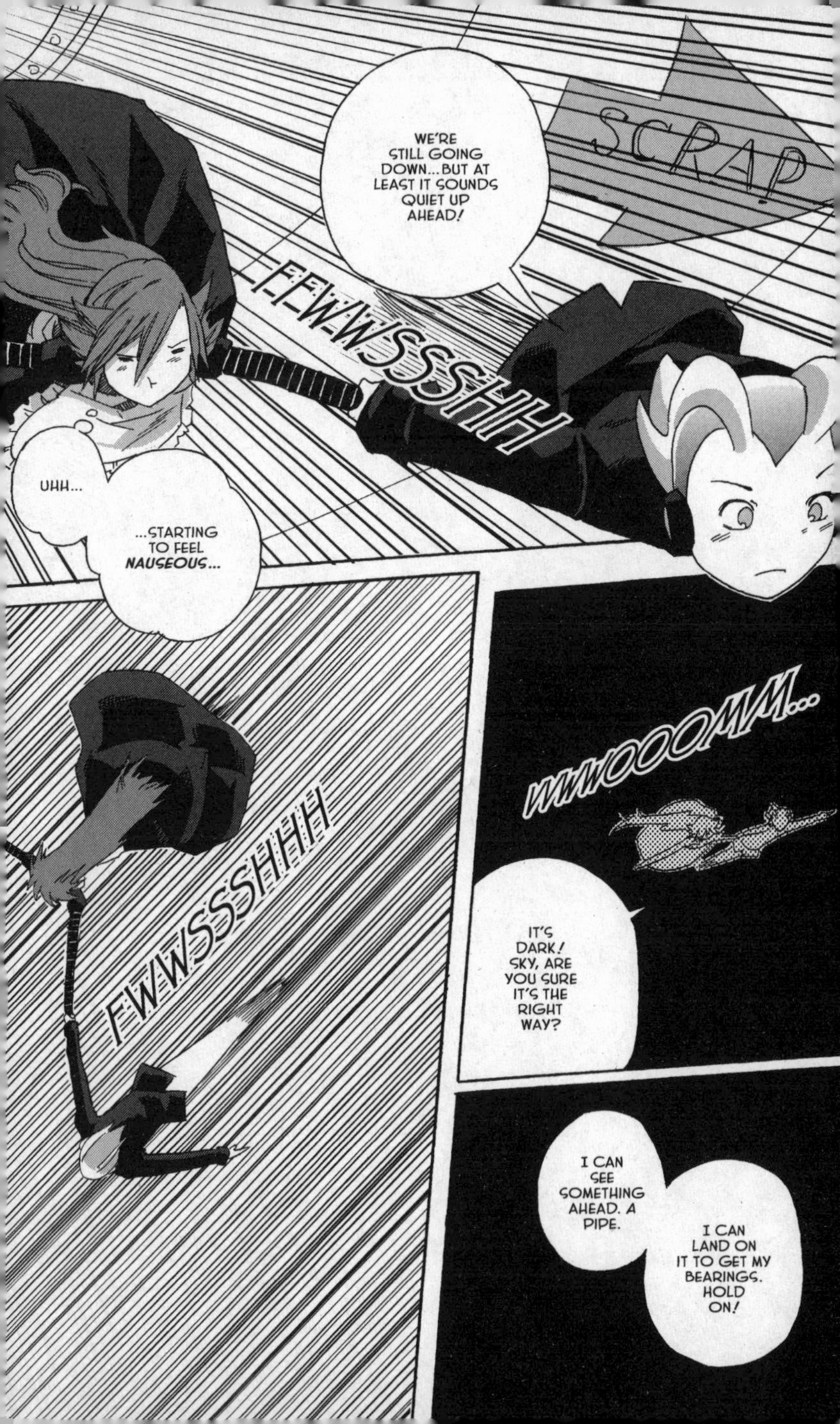
WE'RE STILL GOING DOWN... BUT AT LEAST IT SOUNDS QUIET UP AHEAD!
SCRAP
FFWWSSSHH
UHH...
...STARTING TO FEEL *NAUSEOUS*...
FWWSSSSHHH
WWWOOOMM...
IT'S DARK! SKY, ARE YOU SURE IT'S THE RIGHT WAY?
I CAN SEE SOMETHING AHEAD. A PIPE.
I CAN LAND ON IT TO GET MY BEARINGS. HOLD ON!

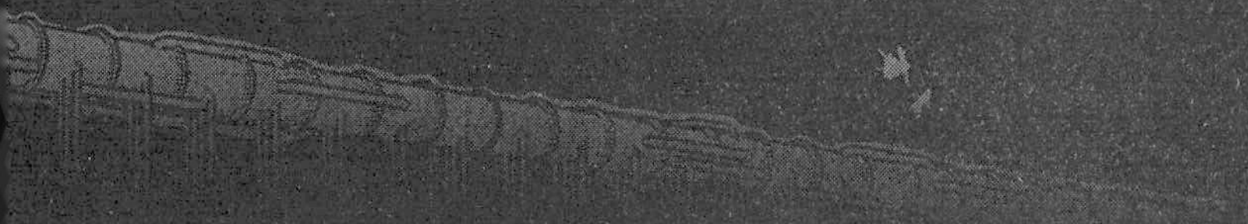

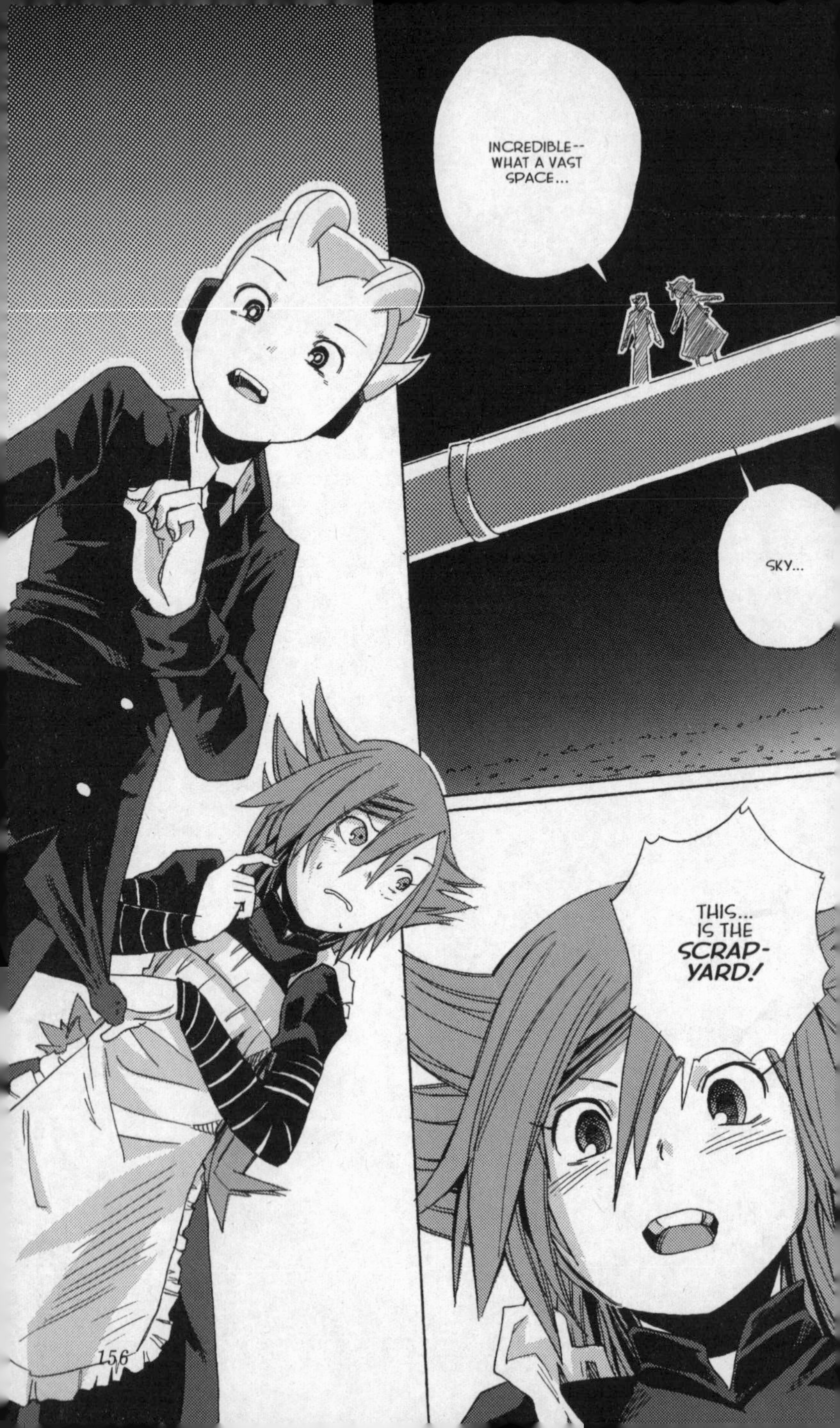
INCREDIBLE-- WHAT A VAST SPACE...
SKY...
THIS... IS THE SCRAP-YARD!

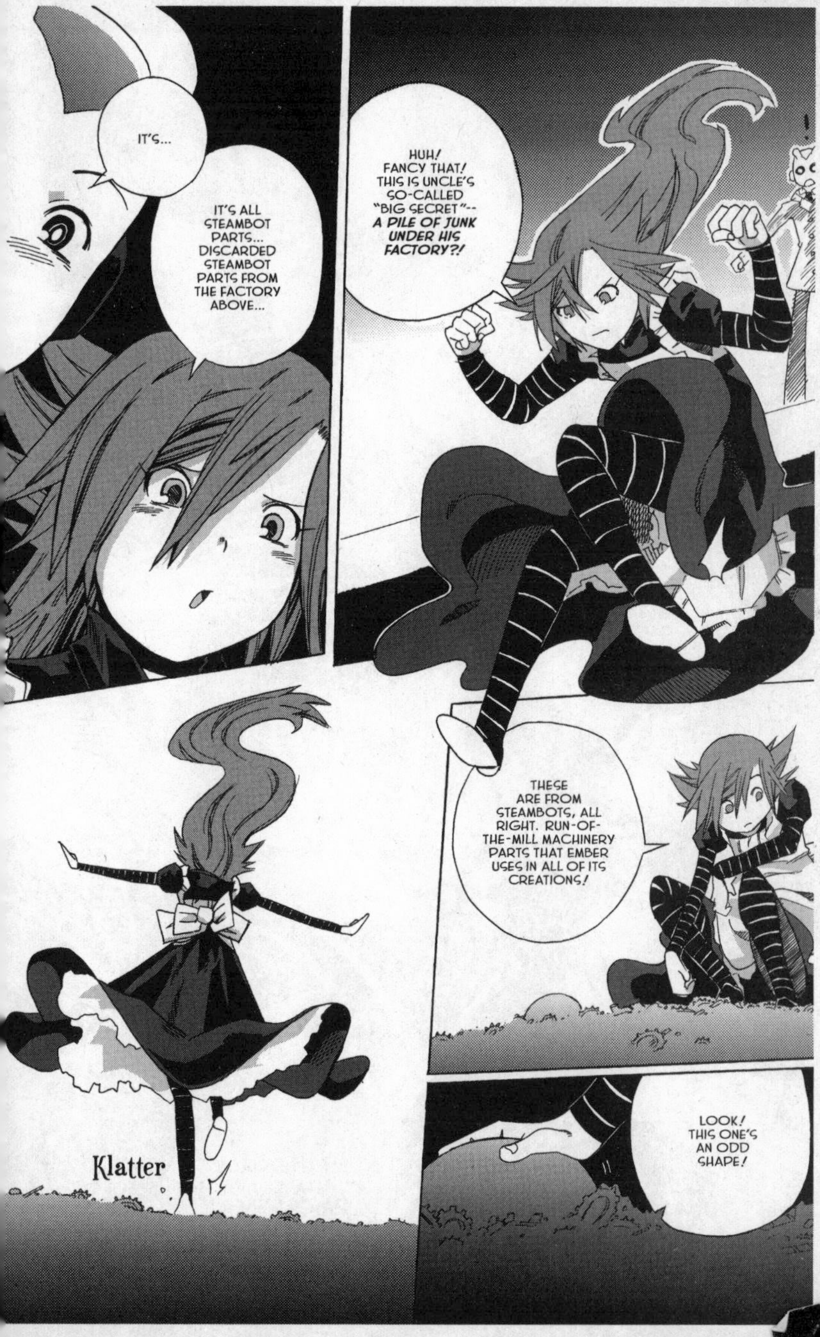
IT'S...
IT'S ALL STEAMBOT PARTS... DISCARDED STEAMBOT PARTS FROM THE FACTORY ABOVE...
HUH! FANCY THAT! THIS IS UNCLE'S SO-CALLED "BIG SECRET"-- A PILE OF JUNK UNDER HIS FACTORY?!
!
Klatter
THESE ARE FROM STEAMBOTS, ALL RIGHT. RUN-OF-THE-MILL MACHINERY PARTS THAT EMBER USES IN ALL OF ITS CREATIONS!
LOOK! THIS ONE'S AN ODD SHAPE!

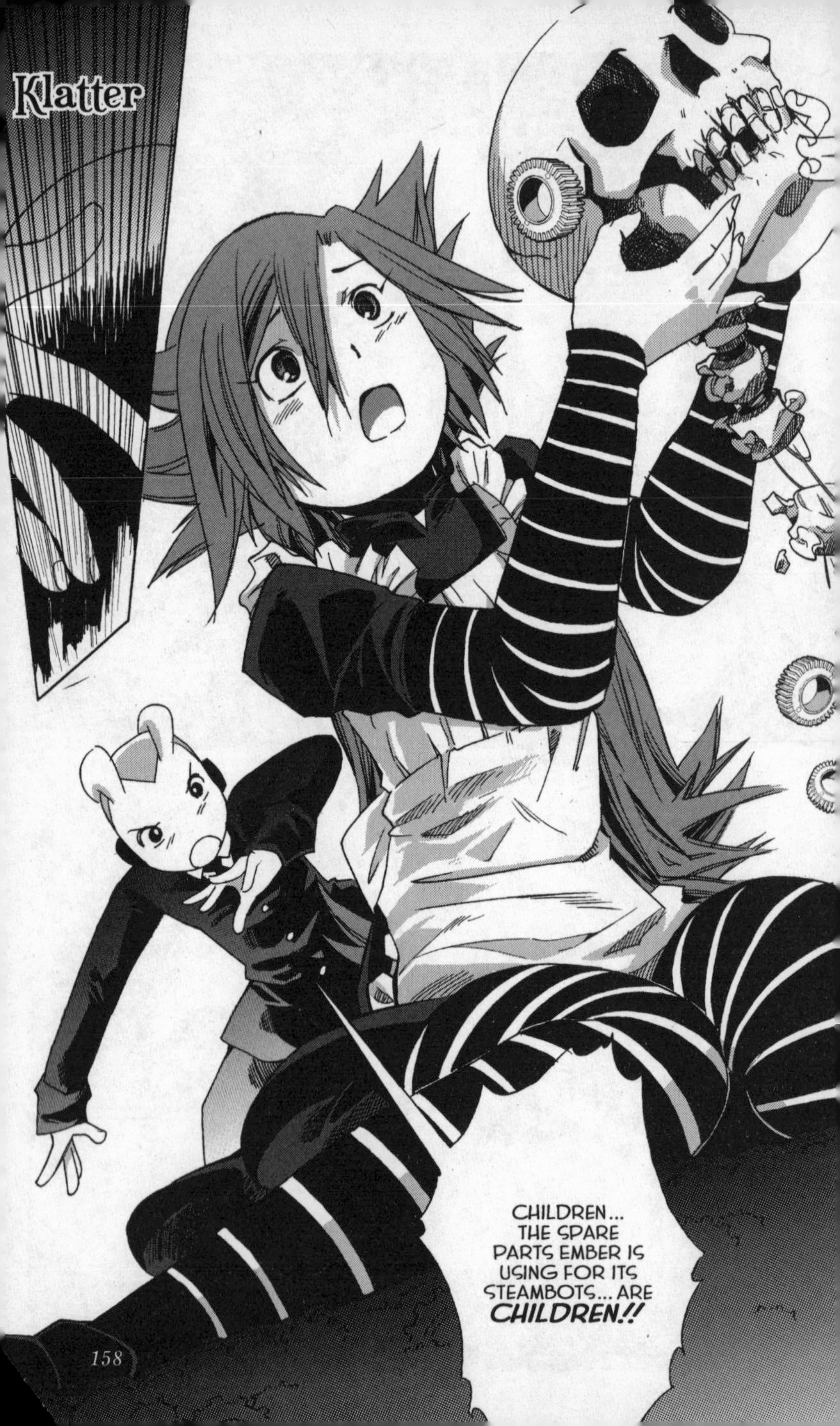
Klatter
CHILDREN... THE SPARE PARTS EMBER IS USING FOR ITS STEAMBOTS... ARE ***CHILDREN!!***

TO BE CONTINUED

ABOUT THE AUTHOR

Madeleine Rosca debuted as a manga creator in 2007 with her three-volume series Hollow Fields, which won an encouragement award from Japan's foreign ministry for best international manga and was nominated for best graphic novel in the Aurealis Awards for Australian science fiction and fantasy. Rosca was nominated for a best new talent award by Friends of Lulu. She lives and works in Hobart, Tasmania, with her husband and cat.

www.clockworkhands.com
Twitter: @MadeleineRosca